ONLY BY BLOOD

a novel by

RENATE KRAKAUER

INANNA PUBLICATIONS AND EDUCATION INC.
TORONTO, CANADA

We gratefully acknowledge the support of the Canada Council for the Arts and the Ontario Arts Council for our publishing program. We also acknowledge the financial support of the Department of Canadian Heritage through the Canada Book Fund.

Only By Blood is a work of fiction. All the characters and situations portrayed in this book are fictitious and any resemblance to persons living or dead is purely coincidental.

Cover design: Val Fullard

Library and Archives Canada Cataloguing in Publication

Krakauer, Renate, 1941–, author
Only by blood / Renate Krakauer.

(Inanna poetry and fiction series)
Issued in print and electronic formats.
ISBN 978-1-77133-209-5 (pbk.). — ISBN 978-1-77133-210-1 (epub). —
ISBN 978-1-77133-212-5 (pdf)

I. Title. II. Series: Inanna poetry and fiction series

PS8621.R34O55 2015 C813'.6 C2015-901835-8
C2015-901836-6

Printed and bound in Canada

Inanna Publications and Education Inc.
210 Founders College, York University
4700 Keele Street, Toronto, Ontario, Canada M3J 1P3
Telephone: (416) 736-5356 Fax: (416) 736-5765
Email: inanna.publications@inanna.ca Website: www.inanna.ca

MIX
Paper from responsible sources
FSC® C004071

In loving memory of my parents
Charlotte and William Tannenzapf

Chapter 1

Mania, Warsaw, November 2005

"I KNEW YOUR MOTHER'S FAMILY, you know," the old man says in his country accent.

Mania stops short, her stethoscope in her hand. She gazes at Janusz Bojarski's face and says, stupidly, "You know my mother?"

It is amazing what she learns from her patients, but this is completely unexpected coming from the man sitting on her examining table, his face a weathered map of wrinkles, his wiry body reflecting a lifetime of physical labour. How had he ended up in Warsaw? And what connection does he have to her mother? She applies the stethoscope to his back while trying to hear his words.

He says, "Our families were neighbours in the village. Actually, your mother was a little older than me. It was her sister, Irena, who was my *koleżanka*. Are they both in Warsaw now?"

Mania cannot imagine this wrinkled stranger and her mother and her mother's sister as children playing together in a faraway, poor village. As she winds the pressure cuff around his arm, she says, "My mother lives here but we don't know where Irena is. My mother lost touch with her after the war."

A feeling of sadness flows through her and she wonders, *Can you miss someone you've never met?* Perhaps this feeling is just a recurrence of the childhood loneliness she had experienced when she and her mother were each other's only family.

"I can understand how that happened," he says. "The Ukrainians burned our villages and expelled all us Polish people from our homes after the war. They thought that they'd have their own country, Ukraine. Ha! They came under the Soviet boot instead."

Mania has always felt outrage at her people's suffering. "What a terrible time that was!"

Her patient nods and his frail upper body sways as he gets off the examining table, his gnarled fingers fumbling with the buttons of his shirt.

"It was terrible. When we were expelled from our homes, families got broken up. You could say we were lucky to be resettled in other parts of Poland when so many were killed."

Mania has no answer to this. She is aware that she knows nothing about her family history. She hands *Pan* Bojarski a prescription and helps him to the door.

"Please get that filled at the pharmacy," she says, "and make an appointment to see me again in two weeks."

"Thank you. Say hello to your mother for me."

"I will."

Closing the door before the receptionist ushers in the next patient, Mania takes a few minutes to settle herself. Why hasn't her mother, Krystyna, ever told her what happened to her family? What about Irena? Where is she? Was she killed? Perhaps it has all been too painful for Krystyna to recall. There may have been a massacre. Or a rape. She cannot bear to think about that possibility. Tomorrow morning, when she goes to see her mother, she will use the visit of Janusz Bojarski as an opener to ask her for more information. Seeing that old man makes her realize how quickly Krystyna is aging. There is no time to lose if she wants the full story of Mama's family history.

On Saturday morning Mania stands on her balcony and fills her lungs with the crisp November air. It is not yet seven o'clock, but Mama will already be waiting. Her first words will be, "You're late." She sighs. She knows that she should appreciate every moment with her mother in her waning years, but it is hard to resist the urge to crawl back into bed beside her husband. Closing her eyes, she turns her face to the sun as it creeps over the tops of the buildings across the street. It feels like her mother's hand stroking her cheek. As the sun will inevitably set, so will her mother disappear from her life, but unlike the sun, when her mother goes, she will not be coming back. The sound of clicking footsteps breaks into Mania's thoughts and she opens her eyes. It is a young woman, her purse slung over her shoulder, striding purposefully up the sidewalk toward the next main intersection where she will likely catch the tram for an early shift at work. Mania turns back inside – filial duty calls.

She likes the peacefulness of the apartment in the early morning, her only companions the hum of the refrigerator and the ticking of the kitchen clock. On week-days before going to work, Mania and Witold exchange a few words, like many couples who have been married a long time do, about the weather, their plans for the day, when each expects to be home. But now that has changed. Now that she visits her mother before work, Mania hurries out the door just as Witold pours coffee for himself and starts reading the morning paper. She will have breakfast with her mother.

Today, Witold is still snoring in bed when she leaves her apartment. A quick glance down the hall confirms that her neighbour, *Pani* Glowacka, is keeping an eye on her as usual through a crack in the door. *That old snoop!*

When she arrives at her mother's apartment, Krystyna is already fully clothed in a long-sleeved, navy blue dress. Mania marvels that her mother's fingers can still manage to do up the small cloth-covered buttons from the waist to the neckline. Her snowy hair is loosely pulled back into a chignon – another feat of agility for a woman of her age. The pleasure of seeing her daughter blooms on her pale cheeks.

Once robust and vigorous, her mother's body has shrunk. Her proud, straight back is stooped; her fingers are arthritic and her gait is shuffling and unsteady. But Krystyna's face does not show the signs of physical deterioration as much as Janusz Bojarski's, even though he is a few years younger. Her cheeks are still smooth as porcelain. Her pale blue eyes shine with intelligence and her mind is as sharp as a scalpel. Mania has tried to persuade her mother to move in with her and Witold, but this suggestion is always dismissed with a wave of the hand.

Before Krystyna can say it, Mania smiles and says, "Yes, I know I'm late, Mama. Sorry!"

Krystyna turns back from the door and goes into the kitchen with Mania following close behind. She pours them both cups of strong, freshly brewed coffee. On the kitchen table, which overlooks a view of the street, she has laid out a basket of pumpernickel bread and a plate of cold cuts, cheeses, and sliced cucumbers and tomatoes. Mother and daughter sit opposite each other at the sturdy, old wooden table.

"Aren't you glad I persuaded you to take this table from the Glowackis when they upgraded?" Mania asks. "It's fine solid oak and still good as new."

"I didn't want the Glowackis' cast-offs," Krystyna says. "But I managed to put my pride in cold storage long ago."

"There was nothing wrong with *Pani* Glowacka's hand-me-down clothes."

"I could never afford the kind of clothes that woman discarded. I wanted pretty things for you and an occasional dressy outfit for myself."

"By the time you applied your sewing magic to the *grande dame's* wardrobe, it didn't resemble the original in any way."

Mania tries to steer the conversation to the past. Perhaps she can get Krystyna to tell her about the family Mania has never met. She mentions *Pan* Bojarski, the neighbour from Krystyna's village who came to see her at the clinic yesterday.

Krystyna says in a clipped voice, "Never heard of him."

"But Mama, he remembers you. He said that he was a friend of Irena's."

"He's a liar."

"Why would he lie?"

"I don't know. Why do people lie? Maybe he wants to get on the good side of his doctor."

"Oh, Mama, that's ridiculous! Why won't you ever talk to me about your family and your life in the village? My patients tell me all kinds of stories."

"I'm not interested in reliving the bad old days. Life is much better now, thank the Lord."

Mania finds her mother's attitude frustrating. Her elderly patients freely reminisce about the hardships they lived through on the farms when they were children and the upheavals and tragedies that brought them to Warsaw when the city was rebuilt following its complete destruction in 1944. They talk about their fear and repression under the Communists.

"I know you went through hell, Mama," she says.

"We were poor. What's so interesting about that? The Russians came and left, then the Nazis came, then the Russians came back and almost killed us. Why should I recall those terrible times?"

Mania can see that her mother is getting agitated. Her hand, holding the coffee cup, has started to tremble, and her voice has risen in pitch. She decides to return to the subject again when Krystyna calms down. Perhaps she needs to be less direct. So, she begins in a chatty voice to talk about *Pani* Glowacka again, who spied on her this morning. No matter how early Mania leaves home, her neighbour's door down the hall is always open a crack. She had stopped for a while after Mania caught her in the act a couple of years ago and called out a loud and cheery "Good morning!" But she is at it once more.

"She must be very lonely," Krystyna says, "if she has nothing better to do than to keep track of your comings and goings."

"I'm sure she is, poor woman," Mania says. "Since her husband died, her son never comes to visit her from England."

In an unusual show of emotion, Krystyna takes her daughter's hand and says, "She's not lucky like I am."

At one time, *Pani* Glowacka had been considered the lucky one. Under the Communists, her husband had been a high official and they could afford a housekeeper. That had been Krystyna's first job when they came to Warsaw.

"Did you see *Pani* Glowacka's hat at church last Sunday?" Mania says.

Krystyna chortles at the recollection. "You can dress up an old hen, but she still won't look like a spring chicken."

"Did you recognize that it was the same hat she wore to your wedding to Tadeusz and to Marysia's christening? That ridiculous feather is looking a little bedraggled."

They are both silent for a few moments, remembering Tadeusz, who died thirty-seven years ago. Mania cannot believe such a long time has already gone by. Krystyna, who tries hard to be stoic, is blinking her eyes.

"Sometimes it seems like only yesterday that he was sitting right where you are," Krystyna says.

"I miss him too, Mama."

It does not seem fair that Krystyna should have lost two husbands: the first one during the war and twenty some odd years later, Tadeusz. *It won't be long now and I'll have to deal with losing her,* Mania thinks with a shudder. How has she got herself brooding about her mother's death on such a lovely morning? She has to face it – her mother is ninety-six. How much longer can she have? It is too bad that we do not know when the end of life will come. If we did, we would not have to anticipate it needlessly. We could be prepared. Instead, since Krystyna had entered her nineties, Mania has had a sense of foreboding whenever the telephone rings, whenever she is out of town, whenever her mother has a sniffle or complains of the usual aches and pains of old age. So far, though, Krystyna has shown remarkable resilience and has bounced back from two bouts of the flu and a broken wrist.

As she butters another piece of bread, Mania asks casually, "Mama, how old were you when your parents died?"

Krystyna is not fooled and looks at her daughter as if to say, *You're just trying to trick me into talking, aren't you?* She says in a resigned voice, "I was just a child – about ten. They died within weeks of each other. It was a plague – the Spanish flu, they called it."

"So who looked after you?"

"I looked after myself and my younger sister. What do you think? In a village like ours, many people died. Nobody could take in other people's orphans. And I refused to allow them to send us away."

Mania stares at her mother. "But weren't you too young to live on your own?"

Krystyna shrugs. "Maybe in years. But I soon got old enough. Life has a way of teaching you how to cope."

"How did you manage?"

"A cousin in Wroclaw came and took my youngest sister, Antonia. Irena and I lived off the garden and the preserves and potatoes and apples my mother had stored in the cellar. I already knew how to bake and cook; I learned from my mother. When our supplies ran low, I went into town and got a job working for the Jewish family where my mother used to be the housekeeper. They were kind and often gave me clothes that their children outgrew. I was just a maid to start but my mistress realized I could cook, so I began to help in the kitchen. She taught me how to make some of their holiday dishes. She gave me leftover food to take home. She let me bring Irena to work. And when she died, I became the housekeeper. So now I've told you, are you satisfied?"

Mania's face flushes. "Yes, Mama. Thank you. But what happened to your sister in Wroclaw?"

"We stayed with her, don't you remember?"

"Oh, yes. She was married to Feliks, right? She wasn't very nice." Mania grimaces as she recalls how mean Antonia had been to her.

"She was a bitter harridan. Jealous because she had no children."

"Is that why we never saw her again?

Krystyna nods and picks at the food on her plate.

"But what about Irena? I don't remember ever meeting her. Did she die during the war?"

"No. The war tore families apart."

Mania recalls that this is what Janusz Bojarski had said.

"Have you ever tried to contact her?"

"No, I didn't know where she was. Anyway, it was such a long time ago. It was hard enough just to survive. Haven't you had enough dredging up ancient history?"

Krystyna gets up to clear the table. Mania is pleased with herself. She has managed to get her mother talking more than ever before. She takes over from Krystyna at the sink, washes the few dishes, and puts away the food. Then, she helps her mother with her coat and ties the kerchief under her chin. She is ready to go out on their weekly shopping trip. Mania could do the shopping herself in a fraction of the time that it takes her to pilot Krystyna down the aisles of the supermarket but that would deny her mother of one of her favourite pastimes. After the deprivation of the war years and the scarcities of the Communist era, Krystyna always marvels at the cornucopia spread before her in the bins – exotic fruits and vegetables like pineapples, avocados, eggplants, and mangos, all from foreign lands. She squeezes and inspects them for blemishes but to actually select and pay for one is another matter. Mania had bought Krystyna the first mango she had ever tasted, which she had pronounced delicious. When they get to the checkout, she counts out her money down to the last *grosik,* slapping Mania's hand away when she tries to pay, while people wait impatiently in line behind her.

Once back in the apartment, Krystyna puts the kettle on for tea. She collapses on the sofa, exhausted, while Mania puts everything away. Mania is satisfied to see all the food in her mother's refrigerator and pantry. So many of the old folks that come to the clinic never buy anything nutritious and subsist only on dry toast and tea. For Krystyna, a full pantry and fridge are her show of defiance against fate. She will never experience hunger again. When she is finished, Mania sees that Krystyna has fallen asleep. She takes the kettle off the stove, lifts her mother's legs onto the sofa, and covers her with an afghan.

She is about to leave for home when she notices her mother's shallow breathing. As she bends over to listen to her heart rate and take her pulse, Krystyna startles awake.

"I guess I fell asleep." She swings her feet to the floor and puts her hands up to her hair, adjusting some of the pins.

"Yes, you did. You were exhausted. I think we overdid it a little today. I'm not happy with your heart rate. Do you remember when you last had your blood pressure taken?"

When Krystyna cannot answer, Mania says, "I'll have to check your file back at the clinic. I might want to schedule you for some tests at the hospital."

"Absolutely not! What for? I'm ready to go any time the good Lord wants to take me. Everyone has to die some time and I've had a good, long life."

"You don't have to give Him a helping hand. All you may need is some blood pressure medication."

"I'm not taking any pills, so that's that. Now why don't you sit down and have a cup of tea with me."

"I'm sorry, I can't. I have work to do at home. We'll see you for dinner tomorrow."

She kisses her mother and leaves. She cannot wait to tell Witold how Krystyna opened up this morning about her family.

Sunday dinner with Krystyna after church is a ritual that Mania and Witold rarely miss. Since their daughter, Marysia, moved to Krakow with her husband, there are only three of them around the table. When Witold's parents were still alive, they used to visit them as well. And before Witold's brother emigrated to the United States, he would join them too. Krystyna used to enjoy making traditional Polish dishes, like *kartoflanik, pierogi, barszcz* with dill and sour cream, and a *piernik* to have with their tea – Mania's comfort foods – and still does when Marysia, Jerzy and their daughter, Anna, come back for Christmas and Easter.

When Mania was a child and Krystyna was working at the pharmaceutical factory, she could only prepare these traditional meals on special occasions; her daily shift would leave her so tired that she could barely stand when she came home. Every evening, Mania used to prepare a warm footbath with Epsom salts for her mother to step into the minute she got home.

Krystyna's cooking is now limited to a few special dishes since the poor circulation in her legs prevents her from standing for long periods of time. Mania hates to see her struggle at the stove with her swollen ankles bulging over the sides of her shoes. To spare her the effort, Mania now usually brings most of the dinner with her. This Sunday, Krystyna has insisted on cooking the stewing beef that she had bought the day before. Mania has brought a salad and baked an apple cake for dessert.

As Krystyna places the big bowl of stew on the table, the aroma of herbs and spices makes Mania's mouth water. To this day, she has trouble curbing her appetite. She has struggled with weight gain all her adult life. It is a carryover from the time when they were on the run from town to town, when there was a constant growling and clenching in her stomach, as if a large animal had taken up residence there, demanding to be fed. Her head had sometimes felt so light that it threatened to fly away. For a time, they had lived on bread, potatoes, cabbage and an occasional marrow bone for soup.

"Do you remember when I used to walk around holding my tummy and saying 'Mama, *brzushek boli*'?" Mania asks.

"And then you would disappear and come back with something to eat."

Krystyna nods. "In those days, I could usually scrounge up some half-rotten potatoes and wilted carrots or turnips from the greengrocer. My friend the baker would give me day-old bread. And the butcher was always good for soup bones or the occasional chicken backs. That's all I needed for a delicious soup that would feed us for a whole week."

As Mania watches her mother ladle out the stew, she says, "How I would have loved a meal like this!" She turns to Witold. "Did I ever tell you how I used to take the food right out of Mama's mouth? I was such a thoughtless brat."

Krystyna says, "No, you weren't. You were just a child answering the call of nature to feed a growing body."

"But I'm ashamed of it."

"No need to be. You would do the same for your child."

She's right, Mania thinks. There is nothing she would not have done for Marysia if it had been necessary.

Suddenly Mania asks, "Mama, do you remember carrying me on your back?"

Surprised by this question, Krystyna says, "Of course."

"How old was I then?"

"About six."

"Why didn't you let me walk?"

"You had no strength. You were just a bundle of sticks. Like a scarecrow. How could you run from the Nazis? Or the Russian soldiers? They robbed the local people of every scrap of food and used their furniture to stoke their fires. They raped the women. It was too dangerous to stay in one place. We had to run. Once in a while, we were lucky to get a lift on a peasant's wagon."

"Why did it take us so long to get to Warsaw?"

Krystyna makes an impatient gesture. "We had to wait until the war was over. And then we had no money for the train, so we walked from town to town and when I couldn't pay the rent, we left in the middle of the night. When I did find a place to settle, the people at work said I had to join the Communist Party. As if it wasn't bad enough that the Russians stole half of our country, I was supposed to join their movement?"

Krystyna turns away from Mania and asks Witold, who has been listening attentively while digging into his dinner, "How do you like my stew today?"

"Absolutely delicious," Witold says.

Krystyna chews on a slice of cucumber from the salad that Mania brought and says, "These cucumbers don't have the same flavour as the ones from our garden."

Mania asks, "The one you had when you were growing up?"

"That one and the one we had at the back of the house when you were little. Before we had to leave it all behind. See, now you've got me started about the old days and I can't stop."

"So don't! What else did you grow?"

"Beans and carrots and beets. And potatoes that lasted us for months. There were even a few apple trees. I've never tasted such delicious apples since. You used to pick the *agrest* and *porzeczki* from the berry bushes. I would take you into the woods behind the house for those wild berries and for mushrooms." Her voice drifts off.

Mania is stunned by this spontaneous recollection. Not that she is complaining; this is just the kind of storytelling she has yearned for. Krystyna shakes her head as if jerking herself back into the present. She has barely touched her food when she starts to lift herself from her chair to clear the table. Mania puts a restraining hand on her shoulder.

"I'll do that, Mama." She takes the dirty dishes into the kitchen and brings out the apple cake and tea. "I used your recipe to make this cake."

"It wasn't really my recipe. I learned it from my Jewish employer."

"No matter," Witold says, "I love it. I hope there's enough for me to have two pieces."

After dinner, Mania puts the leftovers in small plastic containers, which she hopes will provide her mother with at least a couple of meals during the week.

Sitting on the couch, visiting with her son-in-law and sipping a second cup of tea, Krystyna calls out, "You must take the stew home for Witold."

"We aren't eating at home this week," Mania lies. "I'd just have to throw it out. Please keep it."

"You must never throw out food," Krystyna says.

They compromise and Mania puts some leftovers in Krystyna's fridge and takes some home. By the time they leave her mother's apartment, the sun is sinking behind the apartment blocks. Witold and Mania walk home as the chill in the November air intensifies. Back in their own apartment, Witold puts the plastic container of stew in the refrigerator.

"You never throw anything out, just like your mother," he says. "There's always little bits of this or that in the refrigerator and sometimes they grow lovely moulds."

"No! I always eat leftovers! I was trained not to waste a morsel of food."

"That's the problem. You eat it and then you complain about your weight as you finish off something you can't bear to throw out. You don't have to be a human garbage can."

"Okay, stop it," she says. "I get the message. You don't know what it was like to be hungry."

Witold shrugs. He had grown up poor, but not like Mania. Perhaps it was because his father had not gone off to join the Polish army, leaving his wife to cope on her own.

They settle themselves comfortably in the deep armchairs in their living-room – both with their respective professional journals. But Mania can't concentrate. She looks around the room at the family photos on the sideboard, the Picasso and Modigliani reproductions on the wall next to several contemporary Polish artists, and feels the protective shelter of home.

Overall, this apartment has not changed since she and

Witold moved in thirty-six years ago. Mania resists change, even something as small as getting new coverings for the frayed armchairs and sofa. She recognizes in herself the need for stability after the constant moving around and upheaval in her early life. This is where Marysia was born and grew up. This is where she and Witold have lived the best part of their lives.

"Mama was more talkative in the last couple of days than usual," she says to Witold.

He lifts his head from his journal and says what she has been thinking. "Perhaps now that she's getting close to the end of her life, there are things that she wants to tell you but she's having difficulty overcoming a lifetime of self-censorship."

"Spoken like a true psychiatrist," she says. "You're probably right. Who knows how much longer she has? Yesterday, her pulse was weak and I didn't have my blood pressure cuff with me. I'll have to check her out on Monday. She won't let me take her to the hospital for a thorough workup."

"I can't blame her. I think I would feel the same. Why put herself through all these procedures at her age? For what? Another few months? Even another couple of years? Krystyna has lived a full life."

Intellectually, this makes sense to Mania, but the thought of letting go of her mother without making the greatest effort to keep her alive makes her stomach clench.

"I wish I could bring Mama and her sisters together while she's still with us. If they're alive. I can understand why she didn't keep in touch with Antonia. She was a witch. But I wonder what caused the rift with Irena?"

"It must have been something pretty serious to last this long," Witold says. "You never can tell what war does to relationships. Some people will hold a grudge for a lifetime over an imagined insult."

"Mama isn't like that," Mania said. "If anything, she's too forgiving. Look how friendly she's been with *Pani* Glowacka.

The old cow treated her like a servant when she worked for them, yet Mama is still her friend."

"Mania, your mother was a housekeeper for them. How did you expect *Pani* Glowacka to treat her? Like a guest in her home? But since she stopped working there, the old lady has been very nice to your mother. They're friends. Your mother doesn't have any other close friends. I think they're lucky to have each other."

"She has Sister Beatrice at the convent. They've been close ever since we came to Warsaw."

"That's true."

"But relationships with sisters should be different. Maybe it's because I'm an only child, but I can't imagine having no contact with a sister for years and years. And what about Irena's children? They'd be my cousins. I would have loved to have cousins as I was growing up." She sighs. "Maybe one day she'll tell me what happened between them."

"If she hasn't told you yet, I wouldn't count on her telling you any time soon," Witold says and goes back to his journal.

His skepticism puts a damper on Mania's hopes. *But I will find out one day*, she tells herself although she has no idea how or when. She picks up her journal but finds herself reading the same paragraph over and over without any comprehension. She puts it aside and speculates on what could possibly have caused the sisters not to speak to each other in sixty-one years.

Chapter 2

Róża, Galicia, December 1942

WHATEVER ELSE HAPPENED, Róża had to save the baby. Filled with fear at the enormity of what she was about to do, she turned to the infant lying next to her on the floor, her nerves thrumming like the overhead electrical wires that had been installed in town when she was a girl. Getting to her feet, she gently picked up the tiny bundle of rags, trying not to wake her. She stroked the fine brown curls and the silky cheek with a fingertip, nestled the baby's head under her chin, and stepped as lightly as a dancer around the sleeping bodies crammed into every square foot of the floor. After all this time together, the smell of their unwashed bodies still made her gag. Every snore and snuffle startled her. What if someone woke up and saw her? But all the lumpy shapes, wrapped in shabby blankets against the cold seeping in around the windows and doors, lay still. Only the moon, peeking in through the torn sheet covering the window, witnessed her departure.

From the door, Róża threw a soundless kiss to her husband, where he lay curled up in the corner; then, she bade a silent farewell to her brother and his wife, who was snuggling their little girl. An overwhelming sense of guilt filled her. She should be taking her sister-in-law and niece with her. But she wrenched herself away and turned the door handle. She had to be strong. Evading the Nazis and their collaborators would be hard enough with just her own baby. With another woman and child in tow, the risk of capture would be too great. The squeal of the rusty door hinges stopped her in her tracks for a few seconds. Would anyone wake up now? No one stirred, so she slipped away like a shadow.

She froze at the creak of her steps as she reached the stairs. When the silence resumed, she flew the rest of the way down until she was out the front door of the old stone building. Panting to catch her breath, she scanned the street with wary eyes. The baby was staring at her with an intensity that could only mean she understood the need to be quiet. At the age of eighteen months, Hanka had already learned how to survive in the ghetto. The number one rule for babies was not to cry in case it attracted the attention of police or Gestapo, who enjoyed nothing more than finding hidden Jews. Last week, terrified neighbours downstairs had piled pillows on top of a crying three-year-old, silencing him forever. A few days later Róża had pulled aside the sheet over the window just a fraction and stared in horror as a Gestapo officer on the street snatched a baby from a woman's arms, tickled it under the chin, and then flung it against a brick wall as if he were smashing a watermelon. She knew that she had to get her baby out of there.

She had already realized how vulnerable Hanka was when she left her with her sister-in-law, Rachel, every morning before she went to the slave labour camp. She had thought that Rachel would look after Hanka as if she was her own child. Not only were she and Rachel family, they were also friends. They had an agreement: one of them would go to work while the other one stayed behind to look after both children. Having worked in her father's store, Róża was used to buying, selling, and haggling. She would be better than Rachel at bargaining with the local population outside the ghetto gate, where a brisk trade took place. Whatever they had been allowed to take in their one valise per person when first herded into the ghetto was now used to barter for food. Róża would hide the steadily decreasing items of her trousseau – silk nighties, embroidered sheets, and pillowcases – under her coat and bring back bread, cereal, and milk.

All day Róża worried about Hanka while she worked at the recycling depot, sorting clothes that the Nazis stole from the Jews to send to Germany. Did Rachel give her enough to eat? Did she clean her diapers regularly? Did she take her out of the cot so she could crawl around on the floor? What would they do when all their possessions were gone and there would be nothing left to trade? Most importantly, she was terrified of what would happen if there was a raid by the Nazis. Would Rachel save Hanka?

A few days ago, when Róża had returned from work earlier than usual, she caught Rachel in the act of feeding her own little girl, Malka, the cereal that was meant for Hanka, who looked on with big eyes. She saw the hunger on the thin face of her child as she raised her skinny arms the minute she saw her mother. When Rachel had turned and seen Róża throwing an accusatory look at her, she had flushed.

"What?"

"You haven't fed Hanka, have you?" Róża had said, stifling the barrage of hateful words that were threatening to burst out of her mouth.

Rachel had stared back at her defiantly. "Malka is bigger than Hanka. She's hungry all the time."

"And Hanka isn't?"

"You can still nurse her."

"With what? You know my milk dried up weeks ago."

Rachel had said under her breath, "I forgot," but they both had known she was lying.

A worse betrayal had come yesterday. This time, when Róża had returned from work, the baby was fast asleep instead of clamouring to be picked up. Puzzled, she had asked Rachel why Hanka was sleeping when she would normally be anxiously waiting for her mama to feed her. Rachel had mumbled that perhaps she was more tired than usual.

Then it had dawned on Róża. "You didn't give her the Phenobarbital, did you?" This was a pill that Marek had managed to secure from his pharmacy. They were only to give the baby half a tablet in case of extreme danger to keep her quiet.

"So what if I did?" Rachel had said. "Two policemen came around today looking for Jews. You know that there's very little room to hide in the hole in the cupboard."

"She's just a baby! You could have squeezed her in! Instead, you drugged her and left her in the crib?"

Rachel had shrugged. "She looks like an angel. I didn't think they'd harm her. In fact, I saw through the peephole when one of them pointed a gun at her, the other one said, she's cute for a Jew kid. She's that Jew architect's niece, who's helping us with construction. We can get her after we have no more use for him."

Rachel had burst into tears and buried her face in her hands as Róża looked at her in horror. That was it. She had to save her baby. No more time to weigh the options. She would tell Marek that she was leaving in the morning. It would relieve pressure on him, too. He was finding it more difficult every day to bring back food. He had already been caught once on the street on his way home by two Gestapo officers, who forced him to stuff down half a loaf of bread and two potatoes he was bringing back, while they stood over him laughing. His shrunken stomach had rebelled, but he had pushed down the instinct to vomit. When he had finished, they had beaten him senseless, leaving him for dead. That night when he had staggered in, bruised and bleeding, Róża had greeted him as if he were a ghost. It had been well past curfew and she had been sitting filled with grief on her pallet, already mourning his death. She had stifled her tears, not daring to cry in case she would wake up those who were sleeping around her, but she had not been able to suppress a gasp when Marek had collapsed at her feet.

"We'll never get out of here," he had whispered.

She had held him in her arms. "Yes, we will. We have to. For the baby's sake," she whispered back, before someone shushed them.

Now she was going through their plan: getting Hanka out of this hellhole. To keep the baby quiet, Róża gave her a piece of rag soaked in sugar water to suck on. Tightly wrapping her comforter around herself and the baby, she stepped from the doorway, keeping close to the walls of the buildings. She walked quickly along the empty streets of the ghetto until she got near the main gate, where she pressed herself into a nearby doorway from which she could watch the labourers emerging from the streets and alleys. Just as the sky began to shimmer into a grey dawn, they gathered and formed two rows by the gate. Róża slipped in behind a heavy woman wrapped in a shawl and kerchief. She repeated a desperate plea to herself: *Please, please don't let the guard notice the bulge in my comforter; please, please, Hanka don't let out one peep.*

The guard on duty that day was the one they called "The Devil." He was a short, stocky Jew, who still maintained his bulk even though all around him people were starving and emaciated. Because he had had business dealings with the Germans before the war, he got certain privileges for himself and his family, one being his job at the gate. The Jews of the ghetto feared and hated him more than any other guard. Róża had seen the caricatures that were posted on the walls and fence of the ghetto, showing him with a forked tail, horns, and sharp pointy teeth. Whoever drew those was taking a foolish risk. You got killed for a lot less. But that morning he seemed to be in a good mood. He pulled aside a pretty young girl and focused his attention on her. The poor thing was shaking with terror. *This won't end well*, Róża thought. She took advantage of this diversion to slip behind his thick, broad back.

Once outside the gate, Róża separated from the line of workers and with trembling fingers ripped off her Star of David armband. She turned down the first lane without a soul in sight. She held the baby in her nest of feathers, uncovering only her face so that she could breathe easily. The exhilaration at her sudden freedom momentarily overcame her fear. Another quick glance assured her that she was not being followed. She began to run, aware that at any minute a bullet could pierce her in the back. Sudden death was preferable to ending up in a train to the death camp Belzec or in a pit in the woods. The Black Sunday Massacre that had taken place in October 1941, when 12,000 Jews were shot and buried in a mass grave, had left the remaining Jews in town with no illusions as to their eventual fate. A young man who had escaped from one of the trains spread the word about the ultimate destination.

A light drizzle began to fall as Róża slid, barefoot on the wet cobblestones. Scheindl, from down the hall, had stolen her shoes. The poor woman had gone over the edge after they had taken her son. Such a handsome five-year-old, and so smart. His mother had not been able to keep him cooped up in their room any longer. He had run down the stairs after a ball that rolled away and she had followed close behind, trying to catch him. Someone must have left the main door open as ball and boy emerged into the street. The shot rang out at that very instant. A man on the main floor managed to pull Scheindl back with his hand over her mouth. When he dragged her upstairs, she had kicked and flailed and screamed that she wanted to die, too. Others, afraid that all the commotion would draw attention to their building and the Nazis would start shooting inside, stuffed a pillow in her mouth. When they released Scheindl, she was subdued but completely mad. She tore her hair out in clumps and wandered in and out of rooms along the hallway, muttering unintelligibly. In Róża's room, she snatched up the shoes Róża had just taken off to massage her aching feet. Róża tried to wrestle them back but had not raised her voice for fear of attracting attention from outside. In a final burst of strength, the mad woman bit Róża on the forearm causing her to release the shoes with a cry of pain. She saw Scheindl wearing them when she ran out the door for the last time. She heard the single shot that had snuffed out her life. That bite still stung and now her feet hurt too. Róża tried to tread lightly, to skim the slippery cobble stones. Every step sent shooting pains into her soles and up her ankles and calves. As the lane opened into the market square, she was struck by the number of carriages, wagons, and people on the move. Everyone was preparing for the start of a business day: passengers were getting on and off a streetcar, going to work, and a few cars were making their way along the main street leading down one side of the square. Nobody was paying attention to her as she walked tentatively among them, gaining self-assurance, pretending it was just another ordinary day for her too. How strange it felt to pass familiar signposts that no longer belonged in her world: the café where she and her friends had lingered over coffee when they were students; the market stalls where she used to shop with her basket over one arm; her father's hardware store. As she approached it, she ducked her head and quickened her pace, hoping that no one would recognize her. The store was now under new ownership. From the corner of her eyes, she spied *Pan* Boyko perched on the stool behind the counter where *Tate* used to sit poring over his prayer book. The Nazi thieves had just given the business to *Pan* Boyko – a collaborator and perhaps even a murderer of Jews.

Turning onto a residential street, away from the *rynek* and its stalls, she passed the pink stucco house with white trim where Marek had lived with his sisters and parents. Criminals now enjoyed this beautiful home. Róża could not waste time on nostalgia or bitterness. She had to get off this street where, in her tattered dress, shoeless feet, and with wet strands of hair plastered to her face, she was now so out of place. Sooner or later she would draw someone's attention. Instead of her former self, the fashionable young daughter of the merchant, Bleiweis, people would see a beggar woman and would either shoo her away or a suspicious policeman would grab her. Not that she was afraid for herself. It was Hanka who had to be saved. Hitching up the comforter more securely around her shoulders, Róża shielded the baby's face from the drizzle and the prying eyes of Polish passersby and turned another corner.

At last she reached the outskirts of town where the houses petered out and the cobblestoned street was replaced by a rutted dirt road with small stones that bit into the soles of her feet and slowed her down with each step. Coming toward her were peasants trudging into town with their wares. The men wore their caps pulled low on their foreheads against the drizzle. Bent over from the weight of the heavy sacks they had tied onto their backs, they carried their produce to market. The women, in kerchiefs and shawls, juggled baskets of eggs and live chickens or geese. Róża crouched behind the bushes at the side of the road until they passed.

She never used to be afraid of the peasants. They had been regular customers in her father's store to buy farm implements. Her mother had helped them while her father sat behind the counter glued to his book until the money changed hands. Their Polish housekeeper had also helped out in the store when she did not have work to do in the kitchen. She had even brought her younger sister along to play with Róża and her cousin. But now Hanka's life depended on this housekeeper. She had to test the friendship of the sisters as she headed for their village to save her child.

The sisters were Polish and some Poles were willing to help Jews, not like the Ukrainians. One of their friends, a Polish doctor, was hiding a Jewish family in his cellar. But the Ukrainian caretaker of the building in which Róża and Marek had lived, and his greedy wife, were hateful people. They could not wait until Róża and Marek had vacated their apartment before they descended like vultures to appropriate their property on the day when all Jews had been forced to move into the ghetto.

The wife had said, "Isn't it a shame that you have to leave your lovely furniture behind."

Marek had pleaded with them to buy it at a fair price, but the caretaker had given them only a few *zloty*. They knew that they had to take what the Ukrainian offered; they had no other options. The couple got everything else for free – everything that could not be packed into the two suitcases Róża and Marek were allowed to take with them. These people were no better than thieves. They believed that all Jews were rich and had hidden vast quantities of jewellery and money in secret places that they would retrieve upon their return.

Róża was just as terrified of running into the Ukrainian militia as she was of the Gestapo. They had a reputation for cruelty and violence. The war had turned ordinary people into criminals and spies and betrayers of neighbours and friends. As Róża watched the peasants from her spot behind the bushes on the road, she knew that they would not hesitate to turn her and the baby in for a reward.

After the last peasant had trudged by and the final cart had rumbled past, Róża got up from her crouching position, chilled and soaked by the intermittent rain that fell like tears from a weeping sky. She touched her lips to the baby's cheek to check if she, too, was cold, but Hanka felt warm and dry. It was time to move on and stay safely off the road. The fields did not provide much protection, either, as vegetation was sparse, but she had no choice. She began to trek through the stubble toward a copse of trees at the far edge of a field. She reached it just in time. Soon, the ground shook with the rumble of wheels from approaching Nazi troop carriers, and Róża had to dive down among the tree trunks, almost smothering Hanka. When the trucks had passed, she struggled up and shook the dirt off herself and the crying child.

"Shh, shh, don't cry, sweetie. Mama's here," she cooed.

Rearranging the comforter around herself and Hanka, she headed for a larger grove of trees across a potato field. Her feet, lacerated with cuts and piercings from the gravelly road and stubbled field, welcomed the sponginess of the wet earth. Her toes groped for any potatoes that may have been overlooked by the peasants, but the field had been picked clean. What she wouldn't have given to eat one raw potato at that moment.

As she trudged across the open expanse, she felt as vulnerable as a red flag in the dreary landscape. Finally, she reached the willows lining the bank of the river. There, she and the baby could find some protection for a much needed rest. She peered under the willow fronds just as she had once done to find Marek when they used to meet here secretly before they were married. But there was no Marek here now, just a damp, dark hollow with branches dripping rain. To save Hanka, she had had to leave Marek behind.

Suddenly overcome with exhaustion, Róża collapsed on the wet earth of the riverbank. She rocked the baby, trying to keep her mind off her throbbing legs and feet. When Hanka opened her eyes and started to babble, Róża groped around under the comforter for a dried out heel of bread that she had stashed in her pocket. She eased herself and the baby down to the riverbank and dunked the bread in the water. Hanka stuffed it eagerly into her mouth. Róża returned to the protection of the willow branches where she deposited the baby on the comforter and returned to the river to gulp handfuls of icy water to still the grumbling in her stomach. She splashed water on her face and sloshed her damaged feet in it. Then she dried them with leaves and bound them with strips of cloth ripped from the slip under her dress.

Crawling in beside Hanka, she closed her eyes to try to recover some strength for the next part of the journey. She dozed off, then woke with a start to realize that Hanka was not beside her. She quelled her panic and was relieved to see that Hanka had managed to make her way to the edge of their protective cover and was holding out her little hands to catch the drops falling from the willow fronds. Now her own hands dripped as she licked the water off her fingers. Róża scooped her up, changed her wet diaper with a rag she had stuffed into the bag she had prepared for the trip and wrapped her in the comforter again. They had to get going. It was not safe to linger. Besides, she had no idea how much further it was to the village. She had only been there once before as a child and that had been by train. She refused to think about the possibility that she could get lost or that it was too far to get there on foot.

Now she just focused on putting one foot in front of the other, on pushing through the fatigue, on pushing through the pain, on pushing through her hunger. She moved through the woods where the ground was soft with sodden leaves, making it easier on her feet. Every step released a rotting smell combined with the odour of animals. Tree branches tore at her hair and face and scratched her arms and legs. She protected Hanka's delicate skin with the comforter and with her body. Eventually, she emerged from the forest onto a deserted dirt road.

Róża was frozen inside and out. She had lost all track of time. She did not know where she was or where the dirt road was leading her. The only relief came when she immersed her feet in puddles of rainwater. Nothing mattered except getting her baby to safety.

In her dazed state, she did not hear the crunching of wagon wheels until the cart was right beside her. Looking up, she saw an old man pulling a scrawny horse to a stop and staring at her from under bushy grey eyebrows. Around his shoulder peered a round-faced, wrinkled woman in a peasant kerchief. Róża stood motionless, clutching Hanka tightly to her breast and waiting for their judgment – life or death. They conferred in Ukrainian. Too frightened to run, she approached the wagon when the old man pointed with his thumb for her to get in. He even extended an arm to help her climb up. With Hanka snuggled beside her, Róża lay down on the straw and dozed off to the steady *clip-clop* of the horse's hooves.

She awoke when the cart came to an abrupt stop. The old man turned around and beckoned for her to get off at a fork in the road, in the middle of nowhere. The woman offered to hold the baby so Róża could climb down. Scrambling off the cart, Róża wondered if they were afraid to take her into a village where she would be identified as a fugitive. They had taken a risk in helping her.

"Thank you," she said as the woman passed Hanka down to her. "I'm sorry, I have nothing to give you."

"No need," the old man said gruffly, the woman nodded, and they rode on down the road.

Róża stood in the road, uncertain how to proceed. The sun broke through the clouds momentarily, low on the horizon. She began to walk toward the golden orb sinking into a blaze of red. After the spectacular descent, a violet haze lingered over the grey landscape. From her pocket Róża dug out a last piece of stale bread to give Hanka when she started to grizzle. As the last bit of colour drained from the evening sky, Róża saw what looked like smudges before her eyes. Disoriented and ready to drop from exhaustion, she wondered if her blurred vision was yet another obstacle she would have to breach in her effort to save Hanka. She blinked again and rubbed her eyes until she realized that what she was seeing was not a mirage but chimney smoke drifting in languid ribbons across the grey sky. The smoke ignited a spark of hope. *Where there's a chimney, there must be a fire and warmth*, she thought. *For the baby*. She trudged on, her feet like frozen tree stumps. By the time she reached the first door at the outskirts of a village, night had fallen. She no longer cared who answered; she could walk no further.

Her knock on the door was answered by a short, compact woman in an apron and kerchief, who was enveloped in the aroma of cooking potatoes and a halo of lamplight. Warm air radiated from the stove behind her. Wordlessly, Róża handed the baby to her. She was about to collapse on the doorstep, when the woman grabbed her with her free arm and dragged her inside. She sat Róża down at the wooden table in the middle of the room and stared at her.

Crossing herself, she said, "Oh, my Lord Jesus, Róża Bleiweis, what are you doing here?"

Róża managed to croak out: "I escaped. Thank God I found you, Irena."

When Hanka started to cry, Irena put the baby in her mother's lap and ladled some soup with big chunks of potatoes and carrots into a bowl. Picking up the baby, she offered her a small piece of potato. Hanka grabbed it in her fist and shoved it into her mouth. When Irena offered her spoonfuls of soup, the baby opened her mouth wide in anticipation for each mouthful. Finally satisfied, her eyelids began to droop. Irena wrapped her in a clean rag and laid her in a wooden box lined with a towel, and covered her with an old coat. She hung the comforter to dry near the stove.

Meanwhile, Róża soaked the last remains of soup from her bowl with a hunk of bread.

With a grateful look at her rescuer, she said, "Thank you, Irena. I don't know what I would have done if I hadn't found you."

"Shh!" Irena said, putting her finger to her lips and pointing to the sleeping baby. She brought a tin pail filled with warm water for Róża's feet as well as a pair of men's much darned socks and a pair of old boots.

"Where's Władek?" Róża asked in an anxious whisper. How would Irena's husband feel to see her and the baby in his home, Hanka covered in his old coat and she wearing his socks? Was he to be trusted? What about Irena? You could not take anything for granted in these days. If they wanted money to hide Hanka and they found out she had none, would they betray her for a reward? And who could blame them, they were so poor. She certainly did not expect Irena to hide her. Only the baby mattered.

"He's gone with the partisans," Irena said. "I'll keep the baby here and hide you in the cowshed."

Róża protested that she did not expect Irena to hide her. "Just keep the baby safe. That's all I ask. Will the boys accept her?" Irena's sons were only three and five years old and liable to blurt out Hanka's identity in the village.

"Don't worry. They're asleep behind the stove. Even the earth moving won't wake those rascals up. I'll tell them the baby is the daughter of my sister, Antonia from Wroclaw, and that her parents have to work all day so they sent her to stay with me to look after her. It's good that she's so cute. They'll like having a baby cousin. I think I'll call her Halinka – a good Polish name."

The hot soup had thawed out Róża's frozen emotions. She started to cry and said, "How can I pay you? I have no money."

"Never mind that now. Just dry your feet, put on those socks and boots and let's go the cowshed. I can't let you wander around the countryside in your condition. That's certain death."

In the shed, it was dry and warm. The cow was long gone, taken by the Nazis.

Before crawling up the ladder to a shelf above the stall, Róża said, "I can never thank you enough, Irena." She hugged the woman who would save Hanka's life and maybe even her own. "What happens if the boys come in here to play?" she asked.

"Cover yourself with straw and pull up the ladder. They won't be able to climb up. It will never occur to them that you're up there."

Before she fell asleep that night on the fragrant straw, Róża saw before her the accusing face of Rachel and the sad eyes of her little girl.

In this vision, Rachel said, "Why didn't you take us with you? I looked after your baby when you went to work. Don't you think you owe me anything? Have you no family loyalty?"

What must Max, her beloved brother, think of her now? Róża was filled with shame.

"I'm so sorry," she whispered. "I'm so sorry." She would probably never see them again. She wanted to explain that she had barely managed to save her own baby. She did not even know if she would see her husband again. How could she have taken on two more fugitives? She knew in her heart that she would carry around the burden of guilt for abandoning her loved ones for the rest of her life. But at least now her baby was safe.

Chapter 3

Mania, Warsaw, November 2005

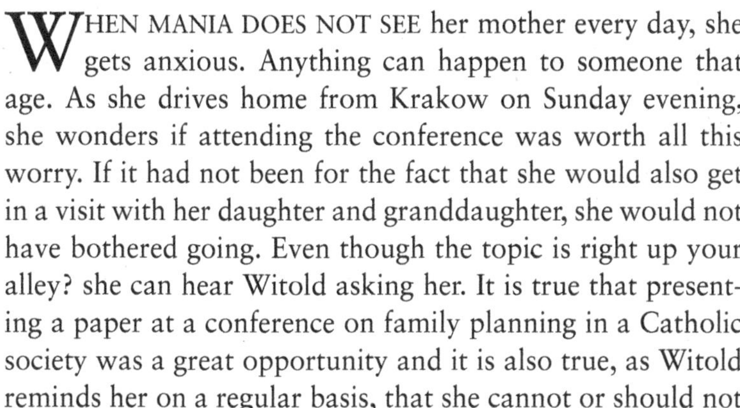

WHEN MANIA DOES NOT SEE her mother every day, she gets anxious. Anything can happen to someone that age. As she drives home from Krakow on Sunday evening, she wonders if attending the conference was worth all this worry. If it had not been for the fact that she would also get in a visit with her daughter and granddaughter, she would not have bothered going. Even though the topic is right up your alley? she can hear Witold asking her. It is true that presenting a paper at a conference on family planning in a Catholic society was a great opportunity and it is also true, as Witold reminds her on a regular basis, that she cannot or should not put her life on hold because of Mama. But still, all this inner conflict is wearing.

These thoughts occupy her mind as the traffic gets heavier the closer she gets to Warsaw. Her hands tighten spasmodically on the steering wheel and she fights the inclination to speed so she can get home more quickly. A smile comes to her lips as she recalls the time she spent with her granddaughter, Anna. Taking the child to church this morning was such a pleasure. Marysia and Jerzy never take her.

Mania still has not completely forgiven Witold for supporting their daughter at fifteen when she decided to give up her faith. She wishes that he had kept his atheism to himself. A part of her still blames him for depriving her of the shared experience of religion with Marysia but now she has Anna to go to church with whenever they are together. She loves telling Anna the old Bible stories she was raised on and involving her in the celebration of religious holidays. She believes that it is an important role she has as a *Babcia* to teach her grandchild the religion of her ancestors and the history of her country if the parents do not do it. Much of Poland's art and architecture are connected to the church. Mania recalls the look of wonder on Anna's face when, with the little girl's hand clasped in her larger one, she took her to the Bazylika Mariacka.

Even though it has been a couple of hours since she left, Mania can still feel the warmth of Anna's kisses on her cheeks and the hug around her neck. That will have to last her until she sees Marysia and the family in Warsaw at Christmas. She cannot wait to tell Krystyna that Marysia has agreed to send Anna to them for two weeks next summer. Krystyna will be thrilled – if she is still around. Mania crosses her fingers when this thought pops into her head.

When Anna was born, Krystyna said, "Never in my life did I imagine I would be a *Prababka*!" She still complains, "Why must they live so far away?"

"They have to make their own lives, Mama," Mania always says. She, too, misses having her daughter close by. Sometimes she wonders if the move was intentional so that Marysia could get away from the stifling love of her mother and grandmother.

She prefers Marysia's rational explanation: "Jerzy has a good position at the hospital and when I was offered the professorship at Jagiellonian University, I couldn't turn it down."

Mania arrives at home too late on Sunday evening to call her mother, but she asks Witold if he has looked in on Krystyna while she was away.

"Of course I did. You know I love the old lady almost as much as you do."

"I know you do," she says. "She loves you, too. But I get nervous when I don't see her daily. How was she?"

"Up to her old tricks. She refused to let me leave without

feeding me. In her opinion, a man on his own is incapable of boiling water. Without a good woman to cook for him, he'll starve." Witold smiles at his wife.

"I'm glad you kept her company for a while," she says.

On Monday morning, Mania stops at her mother's apartment before going to work at the clinic. She is so attuned to potential problems that she is on high alert when there is no answer after she rings the doorbell. *Perhaps she's in the bathroom and can't hear*, Mania thinks. Krystyna does not like anyone, including Mania, to walk in on her unannounced. Mania knocks hard on the door. This time when she gets no response, she fishes in her purse for the key she has for emergencies and unlocks the door.

"Mama, where are you?" she calls out.

"I'm in here," her mother's feeble voice responds.

Mania dashes into the bedroom, where she finds her mother lying on the floor in a pool of urine, her nightdress tangled around her. Her white hair is disheveled and her face is contorted in pain. Mania crouches down beside her.

"What happened, Mama?"

She grabs Krystyna's wrist to feel her pulse. It is weak and erratic.

"I fell," Krystyna whimpers. "I got up ... to go to ... the bathroom...." Her eyes close from the effort to speak.

Mania feels the familiar rush of adrenaline just as she does when faced with a work-related medical emergency. First she calls for an ambulance. Then, she tries to make Krystyna more comfortable by carefully changing her awkward position on the floor and laying a pillow under her head. Palpating her gently, she identifies the sources of her pain and covers her with a blanket. While waiting for the paramedics, she calls Witold to meet her at the hospital. She also calls her clinic to ask the nurse to reschedule her patients because she will not be coming in. When she cannot think of anything else to do, she crouches on the floor beside her mother, holding her hand and praying.

In the hospital, Krystyna is subjected to blood tests, X-rays and an electrocardiogram while Mania waits, feeling as if time has stopped. Finally, she has a private conference with the attending physician. He says that Krystyna has broken her hip but that this is not the major problem. She has suffered a heart attack and it is amazing that she is still alive because there is a lot of damage. He is waiting for the cardiologist, Dr. Radamski, to see her.

When all the tests have been done, Mania, not willing to acknowledge what she already knows, asks Dr. Radamski, "What do you think?"

"Hard to know for sure, but at her age, perhaps she has a few weeks to a couple of months."

Mania is shaken. This confirms what she knew but could not accept – that the end of her mother's life would be so sudden. She thought she would have time to get used to the idea while her mother faded away gently.

"There's no surgical option?"

"Do you really want to put your mother through that kind of trauma? We could put in a shunt but it's not guaranteed to help her."

"How about her hip?"

"I don't think putting her through hip surgery when she may not have much longer is advisable."

Mania understands all of this, but she felt compelled to ask the questions anyway. She nods and says, "In that case, when can I take her home?"

Dr. Radamski lays a sympathetic hand on her arm. "You can give her the medications to regularize the heart rate and to manage the pain. With your care, she can go home as soon as she's stabilized."

"Thank you, Dr. Radamski. I'll take a leave of absence from the clinic to look after her."

Dr. Radamski is a fine cardiologist and Mania is grateful for his understanding. Nevertheless, his words resound in her ears like a death sentence for Krystyna. Her mother will never come out of a wheelchair now; she will probably never even get out of bed. This radical change from the last time they spent together pierces Mania's insides. She is not prepared for Krystyna's passing. She is not ready to be an orphan, even at her age. She will be all alone, abandoned, the next in line to go. She feels foolish for entertaining these thoughts; after all, she has Witold, Marysia, and Anna.

She has had feelings of abandonment before that could not be argued away with logic. There were times in her youth when she had been almost paralyzed with anxiety and had had to push herself to go to school or to go to work. But it had always dissipated after a couple of days. She does not want to think about that now.

When Witold arrives, she tells him what Dr. Radamski said. "Look at her," she says. "She looks so fragile. It breaks my heart."

They stand by the bed, Witold's arm over Mania's shoulder, and gaze at Krystyna's inert form in the hospital bed. Her tiny and helpless body is hooked up to a heart monitor, an oxygen mask and various tubes administering medication by intravenous drip and removing waste by catheter.

Mania whispers in case Krystyna can hear, "She looks as if she could float away any time. It's all my fault. I should never have gone away."

"Nonsensc," Witold says. "You wouldn't have been with her the night it happened anyway."

"I should have made her move in with us long ago."

"You know you couldn't make your mother do anything she didn't want to do."

"That's true, but I still wish I could have prevented this. At least with us she might not have fallen going to the bathroom."

"Maybe," Witold says and squeezes her shoulder.

She is grateful that Witold does not contradict her with logic. It does not make her feel better. His solid, dependable presence is enough at the moment. Witold goes to call Marysia and tell her what happened. Several hours later, their daughter appears at the hospital room door and rushes in to hug Mania. Then she sits with her mother, keeping watch over Krystyna for two days before going back home.

After two weeks, Dr. Radamski says that Krystyna can be taken home. Mania prepares to take Krystyna to her and Witold's apartment, but Krystyna stubbornly refuses. She wants to be in her own bed. Not willing to fight with a weak old woman, Mania moves in with her mother and is relieved that Krystyna does not give her a hard time about that. She must realize how sick she is.

Krystyna sleeps fitfully during the next few nights and dozes most of the days. Her appetite is miniscule no matter what Mania makes to tempt her. One afternoon, Krystyna wakes up from a nap and calls Mania from the kitchen where she is making chicken soup in another effort to revive her mother's appetite.

"What is it, Mama? Does something hurt? Do you want a sip of water?"

Krystyna shakes her head weakly. "No. Please call Father Dominik. And Sister Beatrice. I feel ready to go."

Mania drops to the edge of the bed, grasping her mother's hands. "Oh, no, Mama! Not yet! I'm going to call an ambulance. I'll get you back into the hospital and Dr. Radamski can see you again."

Krystyna holds on to her hands with surprising strength.

"No hospital. I want to die at home. Please."

Mania checks Krystyna's pulse. It is very faint. She takes her blood pressure and it is high. Once again, she wants to call for an ambulance, but Krystyna says, "No!"

The realization that the time has come to let her mother go washes over Mania and tears run down her face.

"Don't be sad," Krystyna whispers. "I had a good life. I'm tired."

Her breathing is laboured and her eyelids drop like shades over her eyes. Mania stumbles off the bed and phones Witold, asking him to call the priest, the nun and Marysia. She returns to sit at the edge of her mother's bed, holding her hand and talking softly to her. She tells her how much she loves her and what a wonderful mother she has been. She says that without Krystyna's guidance and belief in her, she would never have succeeded in becoming a doctor. Krystyna's eyes remain closed but her face is peaceful and her brow is smooth.

"You have been my role model, Mama," Mania says, weeping softly.

Krystyna's lips barely move as she says, "Don't cry, *kochana*. I'm going to a better place."

This is how Witold finds them when he enters the bedroom. He is about to bring in a chair when the doorbell rings. It is Father Dominik with Sister Beatrice close behind.

Mania says, "Mama, Father Dominik and Sister Beatrice are here."

Krystyna opens her eyes and, looking directly at the priest, she says that she would like to speak to him alone. Mania and Witold retire to the living room where they sit down on the shabby sofa, while Sister Beatrice sits in an armchair. Mania can hear the steady murmuring of voices from Krystyna's room. "Why is it taking so long?" she asks.

Sister Beatrice says, "I suppose because it is the last opportunity for your mother to unburden herself."

"What could she possibly have to confess?"

"We do not know the inner workings of an individual soul. You may not think that she has committed any sins but she may see things differently."

"I'm certain my mother's soul is blameless."

Witold says, "Krystyna may have secrets you know nothing about."

"I can't believe that. She has never kept anything from me. Certainly nothing that would qualify as a sin," Mania insists.

"But you've complained about how evasive she was about the past."

"That's different. It was too painful to talk about."

Mania is sure that the only possible sins in Krystyna's life were committed on her daughter's behalf. During the war when they had nothing to eat and when they were on the run, her mother occasionally stole food when she found it and evaded rent collection when they simply had no way of paying. But she has more than made up for these transgressions during a lifetime as a devoted mother and wife and an upstanding member of her community. Besides providing a warm and loving home, Krystyna volunteered at the church and served as a lay assistant at the convent too.

Even when they had almost nothing, Krystyna managed to scrape together enough for parcels to the front lines for Mania's father: knitted sweaters, scarves, hats, and socks, all made from unravelled old items. She had also sent jars of jelly, pickled cabbage and cucumbers, dried apples that must have come from the garden of the house they had lived in before they had had to run away. Mania wishes she could picture her father wearing one of Mama's knitted creations.

After the Nazi defeat, Mania had accompanied her mother to the train station every day to search for her father among the half-dead refugees and ragged soldiers. How sad she had been to see Mama's disappointment every time they returned home alone. When Mama had been notified that her husband would not be coming back, she'd had a breakdown that she overcame only with the help of Sister Beatrice.

Mania's thoughts are interrupted by the priest emerging from Krystyna's bedroom. He approaches her and takes her hands in his. In a kind voice, he says, "Your mother wants to talk to you. She has very little breath left. You must let her speak uninterrupted."

Mania wonders why he would say such a strange thing. Why would she want to interrupt her mother? She is grateful that her mother is still able to speak. Witold guides her into the bedroom, while Sister Beatrice hovers like a benign presence behind them. Mania sits down on the bed as Krystyna starts to speak in a hoarse whisper through dry lips. Mania leans forward so as not to miss a single word.

"*Mója ... kȯchana ... ćorka.* I must set ... my life ... in order ... before meeting my Maker."

Something squeezes tight inside Mania's chest as she watches her mother struggle to speak. "Shh, Mama, don't exert yourself. You have atoned many times over for anything you're feeling guilty about."

"You must ... listen ... to me."

The priest's directive not to interrupt echoes in Mania's head. She does not say another word. Krystyna exhales and for a moment seems to stop breathing altogether. Then with a great effort, she says, "Find them ... make it right." Two more breaths and her hand in Mania's slackens and her face relaxes.

At first Mania is unaware that her mother has stopped breathing. She continues to gaze at the beloved face with its unmoving eyes, until Sister Beatrice comes over and gently lowers the lids.

When Mania realizes that her mother's body is lifeless, she lays her head on Krystyna's chest, sobbing, "Mama, please don't go yet! I love you!"

Beside her, Sister Beatrice says, "Say your final farewell to your Mama. She has gone to Heaven."

"She can't go yet. She has to explain...."

Behind her, Witold says, "Mania, she's gone."

Mania tenderly kisses her mother's cheeks and rests her face in the crook of her neck. "Leave me with her for a while," she whispers.

Sister Beatrice and Witold wait just outside the door.

When Mania comes out, she asks, "Did you hear what Mama said? What did she mean?"

"I didn't hear," Witold says. "I wasn't close enough. We can talk about it later."

Sister Beatrice says, "Now is not the time to worry yourself about that. You need to grieve first. Please talk to Father Dominik before he leaves. I will stay with your mother."

Mania turns to the priest. "Father, what did my mother tell you?"

"I cannot reveal what your mother said in her last confession. But I can tell you that something has weighed on her conscience for many years."

"Please tell me what it is. How can I make it right if I don't know what she was talking about."

"All I can say is that your mother seemed rather incoherent and assumed that I would understand her allusions to her family and her war experiences." The priest lifts his hands in a gesture of helplessness, his face reflecting compassion and sadness.

Mania persists. "Surely there couldn't have been anything so bad that it weighed on her conscience for years?"

Witlold tries to intervene. "Mania, leave it for now."

The priest says, "Who can tell? What may seem like a minor transgression to us can grow out of proportion in the mind of a good person who has kept it bottled up for a long time. You mustn't dwell on it now. You need to celebrate your mother's many wonderful qualities."

Finally, Mania nods and steps aside to allow the priest and Witold to take charge of funeral arrangements but Krystyna's last words reverberate in her head.

As he leaves, the priest makes a sign of the cross and says, "May the Lord comfort you in your bereavement."

"Thank you, Father Dominik," Mania says.

Sister Beatrice stays behind. "Why don't you go home and rest? I'll stay here until the people from the funeral home come."

Mania protests but Witold interrupts, taking his wife gently by the arm as he thanks Sister Beatrice for her kindness, and adds, "We will meet you at the funeral home tomorrow for the visitation. Let's go home, Mania."

Mania is so befuddled that she allows Witold to help her on with her coat and guide her to the elevator and the car. When they arrive home, she crumples into a chair at the kitchen table as he makes her a cup of tea.

She says, "Do you think Mama could have been delusional?"

"It's possible," he says.

Mania tells him what Krystyna said. "It just doesn't make sense to me."

"She was trying to tell you something with some urgency. It wasn't necessarily delusional. She just ran out of time. It's not uncommon for someone to try to get something off her chest at the very last minute."

"What could it be?"

"Maybe something to do with her sisters. She hasn't seen either of them for many years."

Just as Witold sets a sandwich before her and reminds her that her tea is getting cold, the door opens and Marysia rushes in. Seeing her daughter's red-rimmed eyes, Mania opens her arms to embrace her.

"Oh, Mama, I feel so bad," Marysia says. "I didn't get here in time to say goodbye to *Babcia*. I just got to her place and Sister Beatrice told me what happened. Was she lucid at the end?"

"She was very weak. She spoke to me but I'm not sure what she was trying to tell me."

Mania repeats Krystyna last words.

"Do you think *Babcia* was keeping a secret?"

Mania sighs. "I really don't know."

"Something was definitely troubling her," Witold says. "Now, both of you, drink your tea and I'll make some more sandwiches. I'm sure you didn't eat anything before you left Krakow, Marysia."

Witold lays more sandwiches on the table and says to Marysia, "The next few days will be very hectic. Can you stay for a couple of days after the funeral to help your mother go through your grandmother's things and clean out the apartment?"

Mania says, "Why don't you go home after the funeral and come back on the weekend when we can go over to Mama's apartment. I won't be ready to go there before that."

Marysia agrees and they sit eating their sandwiches and drinking their tea in silence, all wrapped in their own thoughts. To Mania the food tastes like sawdust. All she wants is to go to bed. Suddenly she looks up and says, "Maybe we should try to find Mama's sisters to invite them to the funeral."

"If you tell me their names, I'll look them up on the Internet," Witold says.

"I don't know Irena's last name or where she lives. Antonia used to live in Wroclaw. You can look her up under her husband's name, Feliks Barczak."

"All right. I'll do it tomorrow first thing. Now I think we both need to go to bed."

They say goodnight to Marysia, who is settling into her old room, and head for their bedroom. Mania is exhausted and drained of all emotion. She falls into a fitful sleep full of disconnected images and places that she does not recognize.

Since most of Mama's contemporaries have predeceased her, there are few visitors to the funeral home. Some of Mania's colleagues come to pay their respects. The funeral two days later is held in the chapel of the convent. It has played a large part in Mania and Krystyna's lives since they moved to Warsaw after the war. The nuns, especially Sister Beatrice, had welcomed them when they knew no one in the city and were destitute. They had taken Mania into the convent school as a day student until she graduated to the *Gymnasium*. Sister Beatrice had remained a close family friend over the years, in good times and in bad.

Father Dominik, the priest from her mother's church, gives the eulogy. He extols Krystyna's virtues: her strength and courage in overcoming the atrocities of war and the difficulties of life in post-war Poland; her devotion to her family and her faith; and her contributions to the convent and the church. The other mourners are few: the family, Sister Beatrice, *Pani* Glowacka, *Pan* Michowski, the butcher, *Pan* Rak, the baker, with his wife, and two elderly ladies from Krystyna's church. A few of Mania's friends and colleagues are also there. Witold had not been able to track down Antonia and Feliks in Wroclaw, nor had he any idea where to look for Irena.

Mania moves like a robot in a twilight zone. She has not cried since she the evening she sat at her mother's deathbed. She does not cry when she sees her mother's tiny body in the white satin-lined coffin surrounded by flowers. She does not cry when the coffin goes into the ground. Nothing feels real to her. At any moment, she expects her mother to stand beside her and make some comment under her breath about *Pani* Glowacka or to take her arm for balance and ask, "Who are they burying?"

Now back at home in the living room, she sits in the armchair by the window, the soft murmuring of voices eddying around her. She becomes aware of Anna climbing into her lap.

"I know why you're sad, *Babcia,*" Anna says, putting her arms around her grandmother's neck. "I'm sad, too, but I'd be sadder if it were my mother."

"You're a sweet child," Mania says. She kisses her granddaughter on each cheek and enjoys the feel of the warm little body next to hers.

In the kitchen, Witold makes tea to go with the sandwiches, cakes, and cookies he and Marysia had prepared earlier. Marysia carries in a tray laden with food. The mood in the room is somber. Even Jerzy, who is usually good-humoured, sits glumly on the sofa.

"Come, help yourselves," Marysia invites everyone to the dining room table.

Anna clambers off Mania's lap and examines the selection of cookies and cake.

"Eat a sandwich first, Anna," her mother says.

Reluctantly the little girl picks up an open-faced cheese sandwich on rye bread.

Jerzy asks, "How about a nip of vodka for everybody? I'm sure Krystyna wouldn't be happy to see us all looking so miserable."

"Good idea," Witold says and heads back into the kitchen for little glasses.

He brings back a bottle of vodka and also one of wine.

"Only a little bit of wine for me, please," Father Dominik says.

"I don't usually, but in honour of Krystyna, I, too, will have a very small amount of wine," Sister Beatrice says.

Witold pours wine for them and for *Pani* Glowacka and Marysia. When he comes to Mania, she nods at the vodka bottle. She watches the clear liquid flow into the glass.

Raising his glass, Witold says, "Let's drink to a wonderful mother, mother-in-law, grandmother, great-grandmother, and friend. We are full of sorrow that we have lost you. We'll never forget what we learned from you about courage and perseverance in the face of adversity. Father Dominik, Sister Beatrice, would you like to add anything?"

"Only that she was a woman of great faith. We will miss her at church," Father Dominik says.

Sister Beatrice adds, "And at the convent, too. She was a wonderful help at the school. The young girls loved her. And so did I." She dabs at her eyes and turns to Mania. "You and your Mama were my family."

"She loved you as a sister," Mania says. "I can't imagine what my life will be like without her. We were together so much that there will be such a big hole...." She shakes her head.

Anna stares big-eyed from one adult to another as they drink and wipe tears from their eyes. Mania lets the fiery liquid burn her throat. The alcohol lifts her slightly out of the pit of sorrow. She holds out her glass to Witold for a refill.

As the afternoon wears on, the priest and the nun make their departure, saying that they have to get back to their duties. Sister Beatrice squeezes Mania's hands and leans over her, whispering, "You know you can count on me for anything."

Pani Glowacka is the next to leave, shuffling to her home down the hall. Witold tells Marysia and Jerzy that they, too, should make an early start for Krakow so as not to arrive home too late. He will clean up after they leave. Marysia promises to come back on the weekend to help Mania clear out Krystina's apartment.

Marysia, Jerzy, and Anna hug and kiss Mania good-bye. After they have gone, there is an emptiness and silence in the apartment – a hole in the fabric of the family. Mania cannot seem to rise from her chair while Witold washes the dishes. She feels like an invalid – everyone had been so careful to tippy toe around her and to wait on her hand and foot. She picks up the vodka bottle and fills her glass once again. Tomorrow, perhaps, she will be stronger and not need this artificial relief from her grief. Tomorrow, perhaps, she will start digging through her mother's belongings. Tomorrow, perhaps, she will discover something that will help explain what exactly she is supposed to "make right."

With the numbness brought on by grief and vodka, Mania sleeps that night. Her dreams are visited by her mother's sisters: Antonia, grim-faced with lips pressed firmly together and eyes as hard as black marbles; and a short plump woman in a *babushka* wearing a large apron over an ankle-length dress. Her brown eyes are kind and sad. This must be Irena. Mania wants badly for her to speak but no matter how much she pleads, Irena remains silent until both sisters fade and she awakes in a tangle of sheets into an early dawn. As is her usual morning routine, she gets out of bed and prepares to visit her mother's apartment. Only now, Krystyna will not be there.

Chapter 4

Róża, Puźniki, February – August 1943

THE PROSPECT OF NEVER seeing him again gave her a piercing pain in her heart. But she and Marek did not matter anymore. How naïve they had been when they were first married! They'd had such hopes before the catastrophe of war destroyed everything. In this place, the only hope was the children. Hiding in Irena's shed, she was putting Hanka at risk. If any of Irena's neighbours caught sight of her, they would report Irena to the authorities. This knowledge kept Róża constantly on edge, afraid to breathe too loudly.

The night that Marek showed up in the cowshed, Róża clapped her hands over her mouth to suppress a shriek. She had just gone out to empty the pot she used to relieve herself into the privy as she did every night. Before climbing back up the ladder to her cramped hiding place, she stretched her stiff muscles and breathed in deeply of the sweet fragrant air. Suddenly, she sensed that something was wrong. With trembling fingers and unsteady feet, she scrambled up the rungs to the loft and covered herself with straw. She began to shake all over when she realized she had forgotten to bring up the ladder behind her. There was definitely a presence, a shadow, in the shed. She lay motionless, barely breathing. A man's footsteps approached.

A whispered voice asked, "Róża, are you here?"

Throwing off the straw, she flew down the ladder into his arms.

When they broke apart, the danger that his presence meant hit her and she pushed him away.

"Do you realize what you've done?" she hissed. "If anyone followed you, we're all finished!"

"No one followed me."

Róża was not reassured. "You can't know that for sure."

Marek tried to put his arms around her, but she shook him off. "I wouldn't do anything to put you in danger."

"You can't trust anyone. Irena's boys are already suspicious. They gave her a hard time about not being allowed to play in the shed anymore."

Marek's face contorted in alarm. "Maybe you should go somewhere else. We could hide in the woods together...."

"No, no, it's too cold. I think it's still safe. For a while, anyway. Irena told the boys that the shed is haunted by *Baba Jaga* who lives in the loft. If they tell anyone, she'll come after them. They're young enough to believe her. If they start poking around, I'll have to leave."

"All right, but let's not wait until it's too late."

Róża finally relaxed a little and scrutinized her husband's face and bedraggled body.

She said, "You look exhausted. You must be hungry."

She climbed back up the ladder and Marek followed her. She gave him a piece of bread that she had saved from the daily ration Irena brought her. When she saw how he wolfed it down, her heart was filled with pity. She said, "Irena can't look after both of us."

"Don't worry. I'm not staying. I'm going to the estate."

"But they've all gone to England. And their son is with the Polish army."

"They left Krystyna there to look after things."

"Oh, my God! Is it safe at Krystyna's? Won't you be putting Mirka in danger?"

"No, I think it's safe. It's a big place and I'll stay in the cellar. I made a delivery there once, so I know I'll be all right there.

It's only used for storage. The ceiling is low, so I'll probably develop a hunchback." He grinned at her.

Róża did not think this was funny. "What if the Nazis decide to put up their officers there?"

"They won't do that. It's too far from town."

"You seem very confident that Krystyna will take you in."

"She's a good woman. I'm sure she will. How's Hanka?"

"She's filling out a little even though there's never enough food. Irena can barely scrape together an extra potato and some bread for me. Since they took her cow and her chickens.... Well, it's not important. As long as she has enough for Halinka – we have to remember to call her that now – that's all that counts. Tell me what happened after I left."

Before launching into the account of his escape, Marek slid open his tattered overcoat with no buttons, unrolled the scarf from around his neck, took off his peasant's cap and let his body fall back in exhaustion. "You were right to leave when you did," he said. "The ghetto has been liquidated. There are signs posted on the fence that it's now *Judenrein.* All the Jews have been eliminated. It's deathly still. When I passed it, I couldn't breathe. The air seemed poisoned."

Róża rubbed at her eyes with the heels of her hands. "But you got away. How?"

"Believe it or not, I stole a horse."

She gasped. "How did you get away with it?"

He shook his head. She could see the amazement in his eyes by the moonlight flooding in through the open shed door.

"I don't know. I stayed hidden in the labour camp and didn't return to the Stanisławów ghetto with the rest of the group at the end of the day. That's how I missed the last transport to Belzec. I knew I had to get away before anyone realized I was missing. So when it got dark, I unhitched one of the horses. It knew me and didn't make a fuss. Nobody heard me."

"What about the horse? Is it outside?" This thought sent a shiver of fear through her.

"No, of course not. When I got off the road, I smacked it on the rump to send it back. I made my way here through the forest."

"What about our families? Is anyone left?"

"Everyone's gone, shot or deported."

"Oh, God!"

She crumpled sobbing into his arms. It was impossible to imagine. No more cousins? No more aunts and uncles? She had a big family. Surely she could not be the only one to survive? And what about Marek's family? He, too, had many relatives.

Clinging to his neck, she whispered, "Rachel and Malka? Max?"

"They, too."

He could not comfort her. It was her fault. She had left her brother and his family to their fate. She had expected it, but the finality of actually knowing it for a fact cut her like a knife. She felt the roughness of Marek's work-worn hands as he tried to dry her tears with them.

When it was Róża's turn to tell her husband about her escape, she described her journey and arrival, half-dead, at Irena's doorstep. She told him how sick the baby had been at first – probably from drinking the creek water; how she, Róża, had barely held herself back from running into the cottage to tend to her. She told him how Irena consulted with her every night during that time as to what she should do to bring the baby back to health. Thankfully, Halinka had recovered and was now rosy-cheeked and cheerful, but Róża was worried that the child was still not walking. Marek tried to reassure her that children developed at different rates. Besides, he thought that the baby's early deprivation in the ghetto had most likely contributed to her delayed physical development.

He said, "Once summer comes, she'll get fresh air and sunshine and she'll be running all over the place."

"But she's almost two years old! She should be walking already. She needs milk to build her bones but there isn't any now that the cow is gone. Potatoes, carrots, and onions aren't enough for a growing child."

Marek shrugged helplessly.

Róża said, "Actually, I have a plan and now that you're here, I can do it. I need money. I want to buy a goat."

Marek stiffened with alarm. He said it was a foolish idea and all she would accomplish was to get caught. He pleaded with her not to embark on such a dangerous scheme.

"I have to do it, Marek," she said. "I can't bear to see our child growing up underdeveloped and weak. Besides, with my blond hair and blue eyes, I can pass for Aryan. Please give me the money."

Finally, he gave in. "All right, if you're determined." He ripped open the cuff of his left pant leg and gave Róża their last gold coin. He had saved it for the past two years, knowing the time would come when it would be indispensable.

"Be careful. Come back safe."

"I will," she promised, trying to project confidence although she was quaking inside. Until that night, her plan had only been a concept; now Marek's sudden appearance had made it a possibility.

"I'd better go before it gets light," he said. "I'll try to come again."

They hugged and kissed and he slipped out of the shed. Watching him cross the field until he blended into the darkness, she wondered how long it would be before she would see him again.

The next day, as soon as there was a hint of grey in the sky, Róża got ready to go. She combed the straw out of her hair with her fingers and made two braids. After she tied a kerchief peasant-style under her chin, she straightened her dress and wrapped her shawl tightly across her shoulders. Carrying the boots Irena had given her the day she arrived, she climbed down from the shelf, stored the ladder behind her and slipped out of the shed. Outside in the misty gloom, the peasants were not up and about yet. She pulled on the boots and ran toward the creek bank where she collapsed against the trunk to catch her breath. Before continuing, she broke through the ice for some water to splash on her face and to drink, hoping it would not have the same effect on her as it had had on the baby. With quick glances in all directions, she assessed the chances of being spotted in the barren fields. She knew she had better stay close to the trees and bushes along the creek bank. Gradually, the grey of the dawn turned into a milky, overcast morning. The only sounds were her own footfalls on the soft ground and the occasional rustle of branches and dried leaves as small animals and birds foraged for food. At first these sounds startled her, but soon she accepted them as a source of comfort that the wildlife allowed her into their world.

At the outskirts of Pużniki, Róża had a moment of panic. She was about to venture out of this Polish village toward one of the many Ukrainian ones surrounding it. She knew of the historic enmity between the Ukrainians and the Poles. They were on opposite sides in the war. So not only was she afraid as a Jew, but also as a Pole.

The Petrenkos lived in Bortniki and had shopped in her father's store for farm implements. She had not been at their farm since her parents had brought her there as a child. How would she find it among the peaceful cottages with smoke curling from their chimneys without being detected? What about the people going about their daily chores tending to animals, getting water from the pump, and other outdoor activities? They would be sure to notice a stranger in their midst. It was too late to turn back. All she could do was hope that bundled up as she was, she looked just like any other Ukrainian peasant woman passing through. It helped that she spoke their language if anyone stopped her. But it would be better to avoid being discovered. To that end, she made her way from tree to tree, bush to bush, as cautiously as possible. Since asking for directions was out of the question, she searched for familiar signposts.

Finally, Róża thought she recognized the Petrenko's place at the end of a row of houses by the rooster weather vane perched on top of their roof. She walked up to the door and knocked. When *Pan* Petrenko opened it and saw her, he was speechless. He pulled her quickly into the house. His wife approached from behind him, wringing her hands.

"*Bozhe miy*! What has happened to you?"

"I'm fine," Róża said. "Just a little tired from my long walk. I need your help."

When the Petrenkos had shopped at her father's store, Róża's mother, who had often worked there helping her husband, would chat with the wife while the men conducted their business. The two women had liked each other and had exchanged bits of gossip, stories about their children, and recipes.

Once the door was safely shut, *Pan* Petrenko immediately asked after her father. He and his wife knew that her mother had died many years ago and had attended her funeral. When she told the couple that her father had become very sick in the ghetto and was taken away by the Nazis, *Pan* Petrenko shook his head and made tsk-tsking sounds. *Pani* Petrenko wiped tears from her eyes with her apron and folded Róża into her arms. Róża was close to tears herself, but she pulled away gently and focused on her purpose for being there. Without further preamble, she told them that she wanted to buy a goat. The Petrenkos exchanged nervous glances, but when Róża pulled out the gold coin from her pocket, *Pan* Petrenko nodded.

"Olga, why don't you give the young miss something to eat? I'll be back soon."

He took the coin and left while his wife seated Róża at the table. She ladled some soup from a big pot on the wood stove into a bowl and set it, with a chunk of bread, in front of Róża. Although her throat was so tight that she didn't think she could swallow a thing, Róża managed to eat it all, even wiping the bowl clean with the last crust of bread. *Pani* Petrenko sat on the edge of her chair and watched her, occasionally directing anxious glances toward the door and twisting her apron in her hands.

When *Pan* Petrenko came back, he was dragging a white nanny goat behind him by a length of fraying rope. Róża saw him through a small gap in the curtains that were drawn across the window. She had been standing there for what seemed like hours, picking at her nails, and getting more nervous by the minute. Seeing him tying the goat to a post in the yard, she was ready to fly out the door if it had not been for *Pani* Petrenko's restraining hand.

"Wait until it gets dark. It will be safer."

Róża was grateful for the woman's caution. Once inside, *Pan* Petrenko told them that he had bought the goat from someone he knew, no questions asked. Róża was so relieved that her mission was almost over that tears came to her eyes as she expressed her gratitude to him. Then she waited until nightfall, when the moon and stars would light her way back. For the trip back, the Petrenkos gave her some oats for the goat and half a loaf of bread for herself. They wished her well and she thanked them again for their help, but they minimized what they had done for her and gently but firmly directed her to the door.

Turning back to the creek to follow the path to Irena's, Róża pulled the goat behind her. She could still be caught, but having come this far, she was less afraid. Every few minutes she stopped to listen for footsteps and to look for lantern light. The woods were quieter than on her early morning way from Pużniki now that the animals and birds were sleeping, except for the occasional hooting of an owl or the scratching of a small night predator. Nothing bothered the goat. She just ambled along, stopping every now and then to eat the oats that Róża gave her or to drink from the hole Róża made in the ice on the creek. When she bleated, whether in appreciation or complaint, Róża froze. The sound echoed in the silence, but all remained calm. The animal would not be rushed no matter how hard

Róża tugged on her rope. When the stars began to fade in the sky, Irena's cottage finally came into view. Irena's grim face peering through the window greeted her upon her return.

"Where have you been?" Irena said, coming out into the yard.

"I bought a goat so Halinka could have milk." Róża handed the rope to Irena.

"You could have got us all killed!"

"I was careful. Besides, if they'd caught me, you'd probably be better off without me."

"If they'd tortured you, they could have dragged out of you where you've been hiding and we'd all have been shot."

"I'm sorry, but it's done now and I wasn't followed, so you don't have to worry."

Still in a bad humour, Irena led the goat to the shed and Róża followed, dragging herself up to the loft. She was tired, cold, and hungry. She ate the potatoes Irena had left for her, wrapped her shawl tightly around herself, covered herself with straw, and fell into a deep, dreamless sleep.

Later that day, Róża heard Irena milking the goat into Halinka's enamel cup. Through a crack in the platform, she watched the child put her hands around the cup and lift it to her mouth tentatively. As soon as she tasted the first mouthful, her face broke into a smile.

"Mmmm," she said, a white moustache forming on her upper lip. Then, she guzzled it all down. Róża hugged herself with pleasure.

Meantime, the boys stood by, curiously watching. They did not come into the shed very often any more. Now, Róża wondered if the presence of the goat would prove too tempting for the little boys and it would overcome their fear of *Baba Jaga*. Suddenly, her hidden existence became more precarious.

Róża heard Andrej ask his mother if he and his brother could have some milk too. She said that it was only for the baby. As soon she went inside with Halinka, the boys pulled at the poor animal's teats and squirted milk into each other's mouths, laughing and dribbling it down their jackets. What if they told the other children in the village about their new goat? The parents would be sure to ask questions. Who could afford a goat in these days of hardship? What in the world would induce Irena to suddenly buy a goat? And most of all, they would speculate on where and how she got the money. The boys were young. How could they be expected to keep such a secret?

Róża was somewhat reassured when Irena came out and caught the boys molesting the poor animal and warned them to stay out of the shed and not to mention the goat to anyone. If they disobeyed, not only would she beat them within an inch of their lives, but *Baba Jaga* would get them in their sleep. If they were good, she would make cheese from the goat milk for the whole family and she would even give them some milk too.

There was no denying that on a daily diet of goat's milk, Halinka got stronger. Soon, she was walking. Her first steps were tentative and shaky. As spring arrived and a green shimmer of buds curtained the creek, Halinka's toddling became sturdier. If she plopped to the ground in a sudden fall, she would no longer cry for help to be picked up but clambered up on her own. Her bottom was well-padded and tumbling down was not painful any more. Soon, she was running around the yard like a typical flat-footed toddler. Watching from her peephole in the shed, Róża felt a mixture of pride and envy. How she wished that she could swoop the child up in her arms and kiss her all over, like Irena did. But Halinka was not hers now. Not for the time being anyway. And who knew for how much longer? She sank back on her straw nest, her pleasure erased, and hopelessness overtaking her. She had not seen Marek since his first arrival. The days in hiding seemed endless. What would become of them?

Now that the weather was beginning to get warmer, Róża no longer shivered beneath her shawl. The painful chilblains on her feet gradually disappeared. She ventured out into the fresh air at night more regularly and cleared her lungs of straw dust and the smell of goat and human excrement. Then one day, Marek showed up again. She greeted him just outside the door of the shed with an embrace that took all her strength. All her fear, anxiety, and depression seeped out of her body as she collapsed against him like a rag doll.

"I've been so worried. I began to think I might never see you again," she said.

"Shh, it's all right. I'll try to come more often now that the weather is better."

They talked about their situation and Marek speculated on how much longer the war would last.

He said, "After the war...."

She interrupted. "If we survive."

He smiled. "It doesn't hurt to dream a little."

So they did, although Róża thought that their hopes for the future were more like fantasies than dreams. She wanted so badly to believe that some day they would have a home, a modest little house or apartment on a quiet tree-lined street with a park nearby for the children to play in. They would both have jobs they liked and that would provide them with enough to eat and pay the rent – nothing extravagant, nothing fancy, just a normal life. When she was with him, it was easier to believe. Alone, with nothing to occupy her mind, she was often filled with despair.

The warm, gentle breezes of spring and early summer did not last long. Soon the blazing heat of midsummer made the shed unbearably hot during the day. On some days, there was not even a whisper of air. Róża could see the heat shimmering above her as she lay listless on the straw, her body bathed in perspiration. Sometimes, she had difficulty restraining herself until it was completely dark before she climbed down from the shelf and went outside.

The next time Marek visited, she told him that she could no longer bear the itch and smell of her own body. It seemed as if they both got the idea at the same time – the creek. Róża scanned the surroundings, searching for possible danger in the shadows. She held her breath so that she could attune her ears to the slightest noise. Except for the chirping crickets, all was still. Even the moon seemed to smile down on them. Holding hands, they crept carefully past the cottage with its sleeping inhabitants, and made their way to the water, as if drawn by magnets.

With every step, Róża's bare feet barely touched the earth until they reached the rippling surface of the creek, which reflected the watery images of willow branches, stars, and moon. It was so clear that Róża could see pebbles glistening on the bottom. Toward the middle, the water swirled into a deep pool. She wanted to fling herself into the middle, but Marek held her back, putting his forefinger across his lips. Slipping out of their clothes, they slid in slowly and noiselessly. They washed each other's bodies until they glistened. Desperate to get rid of the itch in her head, Róża ducked under the surface and rubbed and scrubbed with her fingers until her scalp tingled. Coming up for breath, she shook out her hair like a wet dog. Marek did the same. She gazed at him as if she was seeing him for the first time. He was so thin, and his thick, shoulder-length hair lay plastered to his head. Beads of water clung to his eyelashes and beard. She was overcome with love for this man who was her partner in the greatest disaster that had ever befallen them just as he had been in the good times when they were first married. She wound her arms around his neck and they kissed, long and unhurried. They made love in the water, and it was as if the outside world of misery, fear, and danger was washed away by the creek current along with the dirt and grime from their bodies.

It was a short respite from reality, but a welcome one. Róża thought, *Now I can go on for another little while. Who knows how long?* They scrubbed their clothes, washing out the lice that had gathered in the seams before they put them on again.

The cool wetness of the cloth was refreshing next to her skin. Before turning back, they sat under the fronds of a willow tree for a while.

"This is like the tree where we used to meet under before we were married," she said.

"We were hiding then, too," he said.

"No comparison," Róża said. They had been so young and innocent then. It seemed like that had been someone else's life.

They had had to keep their meetings secret because his mother had not approved of her. Her family had not been prominent enough, nor rich enough for *Pani* Bromberg. They were from the merchant class, not scholars or intellectuals. It had made Róża bristle. Her mother-in-law was gone now, and all her pretensions and social climbing had come to nothing. The Nazis had taken her with the first transport to Belzec. Marek had been distraught, but there was nothing he could do. Nor could he have done anything to save his sisters. Róża had liked and admired her sisters-in-law. They had been kind to her, despite their mother's disapproval. Now, they, too, were gone.

As Róża lay back on the soft ground, such a luxury after endlessly enduring the prickly straw, she must have dozed off because the next thing she knew, Marek was nudging her shoulder.

"Hey, it's time to go back."

She scrambled to her feet.

"Do you want me to walk back with you?" he asked.

"No, it's all right. You need to get back to the big house."

Before they parted, they kissed and agreed to do this again. They went in opposite directions to their respective hiding places. Back on her shelf, Róża lay down on the straw and slept.

The summer was kind in other ways as well. Irena's garden was a gift. Róża welcomed the beans, peas, carrots, and cucumbers that began to supplement their staple of potatoes and bread. Irena even brought her an occasional egg from the ones she got in return for her produce at the market.

The only pleasure in Róża's constricted life was watching Halinka. She was talking all the time now – to the dog, to the goat, to the boys – as well as to herself. Róża worried when Halinka pestered the boys to play with her. She had no one else to play with because the cottage was set back at the outskirts of the village. Irena was too busy in the summer to keep the child occupied. Róża watched anxiously as the boys plotted different ways to tease the little girl. One day, they hid the faded piece of flannel that she clutched in her hand when she went to sleep. Irena must have had a sixth sense about what they were up to because she appeared out of nowhere with a willow switch.

"Hey, you, *paskudnici*! Give the baby back her *szmatka*! Aren't you ashamed, teasing a baby?"

Andrej returned the rag. "We're only playing," he said. He was getting tall and lanky.

"That's right, we're only playing." Staszek, still a chubby little guy, parroted his older brother.

Another day, the boys were sitting on the step in front of the cottage with nothing to do.

Seeing Halinka emerge, Andrej announced, "Look who's here!"

"Watch her," Irena told the boys.

"We're not bloody babysitters," Andrej muttered under his breath.

"Yeah, bloody babysitters," Staszek imitated him and tried to look mean.

"Mama loves her more than us," Andrej said, resting his head in his hands.

Róża could hardly hold herself back from running down and snatching her child into her arms. She watched as Halinka flopped down on the step between them. She idolized those two boys, bubbling over with excitement when they did not push her away.

Andrej jumped off the step and said, "Let's play *partyzanci*!"

They pretended that they were partisans, like their father, hunting Nazis. Andrej put his stick over his shoulder like a gun and swaggered around the yard, kicking his feet in the dirt, scattering the cigarette butts discarded by the German soldiers who periodically came through the village. He stopped, picked up a couple of butts and dug into his pocket for matches, which he must have stolen from the stovetop. He managed to light one butt for himself and one for Staszek.

No sooner were the two boys puffing away when Halinka clamoured, "Me too! Me, too!"

Róża sensed that this would not end well. She stuffed her fist into her mouth to keep from shouting a warning to her daughter.

"You're too little," Staszek said.

"No, I big!" Halinka pouted and stamped her foot.

"All right. You can try mine," Andrej said, winking at his brother. He held out the lit end of the cigarette butt to Halinka, who eagerly clamped her lips around it. For a breathtaking moment, Róża saw the excitement in her child's eyes change to puzzlement and then to pain, as they welled up with tears and she screamed, "Mama! Mama!" Róża bit down hard on her knuckles while the boys whooped with laughter.

Irena came running out of the house, picked up the little girl, hugging and kissing her. "*Sha, sha, dziewcyznka.* I'll put some fat on it and it'll be all better."

Róża's body ached with emptiness, as Halinka wrapped her chubby arms around Irena's neck and snuffled into her shoulder.

Irena turned to yell after the boys, "No supper for you tonight!" By that time, they were half-way across the field.

Halinka was such a cheerful baby that Róża could not understand why the boys did not love her. Even their vicious-looking black mongrel, Bobo, adored her. He would bare his teeth and growl in his throat at any stranger, but never with Halinka. He followed her around so slavishly that when she stopped suddenly and he bumped into her, he accepted her smack on his snout in meek submission. Not so the goat, who butted Halinka whenever she came into the shed and got too close. The child would let out a howl, and the dog would snarl and bark at the goat.

One day, Róża saw something that made her bowels churn – a Nazi officer approaching the cottage, while Halinka was playing by herself in the yard. *I knew this would happen! Someone reported us.* Was it the goat? Was it a suspicious neighbour? Or did the boys let something slip?

The dog, who had been lolling peacefully in the sun beside Halinka as she dug in the dirt with an old spoon, suddenly perked up his ears and began his low growl.

"*Sha*, bad doggie!" Halinka waved her hand.

The animal rose, arched his back and barked in such a frenzy at the German officer that Irena came running out to see what the fuss was about. The German officer did not budge from the moment the dog started barking. He looked at Irena.

"Is that your child?" he asked, pointing at Halinka.

"Yes, she is," Irena said, crossing her arms.

Róża wanted to close her eyes, not to see what would happen next to her child, but she could not and continued to stare in fascination and horror. Thank God that Irena did not say that Halinka was an orphan she had found in the woods. Thank God that the boys were not around.

The dog was gradually approaching the officer, alternating barks with growls, his eyes fiery with rage, his body prepared to spring. At that moment, Halinka dropped her spoon and ran to Irena, arms raised.

"Mama! Bobo not like man."

Irena lifted her up and they watched the standoff between the German officer and the dog. Suddenly, the German whipped out his gun and shot Bobo in the head. The dog staggered and fell lifeless to the ground in a pool of blood. Halinka shrieked and buried her face in Irena's neck, sobbing wildly. In her loft, Róża sat stunned, her eyes fixed on the German. Would he shoot again? But with slow, deliberate movements, he returned his gun to its holster and looked directly at Irena as if to say, one wrong move and you're next.

He said, "There are rumours that people are hiding Jews in this village. Are you one of those people?"

Irena held her ground. "Why would we hide Jews here? I'm a widow and I can barely feed my own family."

He glared at her and seemed to be assessing her truthfulness. Finally he said, "All right then. Keep your eyes open. If you suspect any of your neighbours, you had better let us know. Good day to you, *Pani*." With that he turned on his heel and marched off.

Hearing the Jeep pull away, Róża watched as Irena took the crying child into the cottage, while the body of the dog lay splayed out in the yard. Soon, the boys came out with shovels to remove him. She could see tears running down the face of the little one, who kept wiping his eyes and nose on his sleeve. The older boy kept his emotions under control with a grim face.

By nightfall, Róża was in a state of panic. She was sure the German would be back, probably with reinforcements. What could she do? Where could she go? What about Halinka? When Irena came with her food that night, she burst out with her string of questions.

Irena held up her hand. "You don't have to worry about the child. I'm taking her and the boys to my sister in Wroclaw on the morning train."

"Is it safe?"

"It's better than staying here and waiting until he comes back to shoot us all."

"You're right. But what should I do?"

"The best thing for you would be to hide in the forest. There are other Jews there. Also partisans. There's no hope for you here."

"You're right. I'll wait until you leave."

That night Róża did not sleep at all. When she did doze near morning, she awoke in a sweat with the vision of standing before a Nazi firing squad. Positioning herself at her peephole an hour or so later, she watched as Irena walked to the train station, carrying Halinka, with the boys trailing behind her like ducklings. Each of them held a bundle with a few possessions for the trip. After they had gone, she fell back on the straw overwhelmed with the sudden knowledge that she was now totally alone. With all her loved ones gone, was there any reason to keep up the struggle to stay alive? Was there any purpose to running into the forest? It was already well into August. Soon it would be winter again, and she did not think she could survive the cold in the forest. She might as well die right here, right now.

Chapter 5

Mania, Warsaw, November 2005

MANIA LEAVES A NOTE for Witold, who is still sleeping, and heads out for her mother's apartment. She is about to ring the bell, knowing how her mother likes to answer the door herself, when she remembers that Krystyna is gone forever. She fumbles with the key in the lock but cannot bear to step into the oppressive silence. Somewhere, amidst the dust motes shimmering in the morning sunlight, an invisible presence hovers.

"Mama?" Mania says.

Her mother's imprint is everywhere: her favourite armchair with its permanent depression in the seat cushion, the ivory-coloured doilies crocheted by Mama's flying fingers, and the faint scent of her favourite lily-of-the-valley perfume. Tears fill Mania's eyes as she takes off her coat and scans the living room furniture.

Drying her eyes, Mania folds the doilies gently into a plastic bag to take home. Nobody will want the table and chairs from *Pani* Glowacka and the credenza she and Mama had bought in a second-hand shop. Not even a charity. Yet Krystyna had treasured each piece. She had come to Warsaw with nothing. Their first home had been one room in *Pani* Cybulska's flat. From there, they had moved to their own two-room apartment, which they had furnished with cast-offs. And, after a few years on a waiting list, Krystyna had finally got a government apartment in which Mania could have her own bedroom. What a luxury that had been! Mania loved the iron bedstead that must have been salvaged from some hospital. She had repainted it white and Krystyna had made a cover for her duvet that looked like a spring meadow.

When Krystyna had moved into this seniors' apartment ten years ago, she had brought everything with her except what used to be in Mania's room. What her mother had cherished most was her collection of framed family photographs that she displayed on the credenza and on the walls. Every year, more had been added. Mania selects two: one of Krystyna and Tadeusz on their wedding day, and one of Krystyna holding Marysia at her christening. Marysia may want the rest. They are mostly duplicates that Mania had made for Krystyna and a whole gallery of school pictures of Marysia and Anna at every age.

The invisible gap in the photo gallery is the collection of sepia-toned pictures of grandparents, stern and upright, like those in other people's homes. There are also none of large family gatherings for celebrations of holidays, christenings, and name days because there was no extended family. This is a reflection of the big hole in Mania's life, which Marysia and her family have partially filled. With Krystyna gone, the longing for family returns: not for grandparents – she is too old for that – but for aunts, uncles, and cousins, with whom to share her grief and joy. As a child, she had watched enviously as her classmates went to spend Christmas and Easter holidays with their families. She had imagined their crowded family feasts while she and Krystyna ate alone at a table for two. All of her mother's cooking and baking and even the invitations of friends and neighbours like the Glowackis had not made up for the lack of relatives. Had her mother known how she felt? They had never talked about it.

Mania tries to shake off her sadness to tackle what lies ahead. She is already feeling overwhelmed and she has not even started yet. She knows it is a delaying tactic, but decides to make a pot of coffee. While it percolates, she takes out bread and cheese from the refrigerator and sets a place for one at the table where she used to sit across from her mother. Breathing in the aroma of fresh coffee, she wonders if she is wrong not to wait for Marysia, who might have helped to keep her from becoming immobilized by memories or sidetracked by emotion. After eating a sandwich, she rinses the dishes, refills her coffee cup, and goes firmly into the bedroom.

At the door, she is struck by the scene of bed covers thrown back, untouched since Krystyna's body was taken to the mortuary. She puts down her coffee cup on the dresser, once more succumbing to tears. Then, she rips off the sheets, duvet and pillow, and piles them near the front door. The linens are worn so threadbare that she can see through them. She bundles them up for the garbage. The rest will be cleaned and donated to charity.

Things do not look as bad now that the bed is stripped. In the closet, she finds dresses and suits neatly hung up, shoes lined up on the floor in pairs, and purses and hats in boxes on the shelf above. Every item recalls a time from the past. The dresses and suits speak to Krystyna's simple but elegant taste and her skill as a dressmaker. Throwing or giving these things away will be like giving up a piece of her mother. She fingers the floral summer dresses next to the sober brown, navy, and black ones. These were the housedresses Krystyna wore every day, the kind that a whole generation of women donned for shopping and housework – no pants or jeans, no track suits, no running shoes. There are also the two good suits Krystyna wore for funerals and special church services. She unzips a plastic garment bag in one corner and buries her face in the royal blue, silk suit her mother wore for her wedding to Tadeusz. She takes the suit out and sits down on the bed with it. Krystyna had copied it from one she had seen in the window of one of the most elegant stores in Warsaw. Examining the fine finishing of the seams and darts and the delicate embroidery,

Mania is filled with admiration for her mother's deft touch with the needle.

Mania thinks back to when Krystyna first started dropping Tadeusz's name in conversation. She began to be suspicious and one day she asked her mother, "Is Tadeusz your boyfriend?"

Krystyna had blushed and said, "Tadeusz and I would like to get married."

Mania had been stunned. At fifteen, she thought that her mother was too old for boyfriends. It was disgusting. Besides, what would happen to her? Would Mama send her to the convent school as a resident so that she could live here with Tadeusz? She brooded about this for days until the day Krystyna invited Tadeusz to tea. She insisted that Mania had to meet him.

At the table, Mania gave Tadeusz quick sideways glances. Just as she had thought. He was old, at least forty-five. His hair was grey at the temples and curled all over his head. He asked her all the stupid questions adults usually ask: "What's your favourite subject at school?" "Do you play any sports?" "Do you do any other after school activities?" She answered briefly and, with her mother's piercing eyes on her, was borderline polite. She noticed that Mama was using a china teapot and cups and saucers, as well as an embroidered tablecloth reserved for special occasions. Taking advantage of the visitor, Mania managed to put away three butter cookies and a piece of coffee cake before she excused herself by saying that she had to finish her homework.

The Sunday visits continued. Once, Tadeusz brought a bottle of cherry brandy and Mama got out crystal glasses that Mania had never seen her use before. They even gave her half a glass. When Tadeusz began to go to church with them, he came home for midday dinner afterwards. Her mother made special dishes and laid out the table beautifully. Tadeusz continued to try to get Mania to like him but she resisted. She wished they would finally get it over with – the wedding – so she could find out what was going to happen to her.

Late one Sunday afternoon after Tadeusz had left, Krystyna knocked on Mania's door. "May I come in? We need to talk."

"What about?"

"Tadeusz and I want to get married, but I won't do it if it makes you unhappy."

The sadness in her mother's face filled Mania with guilt. "Mama, if you want to marry him, it's okay with me. I can go live at the convent."

"Absolutely not! This is your home."

"But you love him, I can tell." Mania turned her head away so her mother would not see her tears.

"Yes, I do love him, but I also love you. Tadeusz will never take away what we have between us, my darling."

"Are you sure?" Mania whispered.

"I promise." Krystyna got up and crouched beside her daughter. They embraced for a long time.

The next time Tadeusz came over, Krystyna stopped Mania from going off to her room after dinner. The three of them talked about what it would be like when Tadeusz moved in and how they could rearrange their routine so everyone could manage to get out on time, like using the bathroom in the morning, wearing robes over pyjamas on Saturday mornings, taking turns doing dishes and helping Mama, and so on.

In spite of herself, she began to appreciate Tadeusz more. He did not try to pressure her or bribe her with gifts or flattery. He was patient and kind. One day she realized that he was becoming a part of their family.

It was a small wedding, neither of them having any relatives. A few people from their work came and the Glowackis were there, too. Sister Beatrice beamed throughout the whole ceremony, which was conducted by Father Dominik in the convent chapel. Mania stood up for her mother in a shimmering pink dress made from one of *Pani* Glowacka's cast-offs, which her mother had decorated with embroidered flowers around the bodice. Tadeusz had not been married before and had no children. One of his co-workers acted as his groomsman. Both men were dressed in their best suits, worn only to church and on special occasions.

Mania was surprised how transformed her mother looked. Her blonde hair lay softly on her shoulders rather than severely pulled back as on every other day. She even put on a little lipstick and eyebrow pencil for the occasion. Standing in the rich blue silk suit and matching cloche with a tiny veil, she looked softer and smaller than usual beside Tadeusz. For the first time, Mania saw Krystyna as an attractive and desirable woman, and not just as her mother

After the ceremony, the few guests were invited back to the apartment. Mania and Krystyna had prepared open-faced sandwiches, wine, vodka, tea, and sweets that they had baked. Their first Christmas together was filled with warmth, music, wonderful cooking aromas, and visits from their friends. Tadeusz replaced the father that she had never known. When the warm weather came, he took her on hikes and exploratory bicycle excursions to neighbouring towns and villages. She finally had a complete family.

Tearing herself away from the blue wedding suit, Mania hangs it back in its plastic bag. She cannot bear to part with it; she will keep it. She turns to her mother's dresser and starts opening drawers. There are piles of socks, stockings, and underwear, repeatedly washed, mended, and carefully stored. Removing one rolled-up pair of socks, Mania sees clear evidence of neat rows of darning. Krystyna had taught Mania how to darn socks, but did Marysia even know what a darning egg was? Darning was a lost art. Krystyna's sewing kit is in the sock drawer and in it is a darning egg. She cups it in her hand and slips it into her pocket. The sewing basket also contains bits of elastic and garters along with a selection of scissors, spools of thread and needles. Should she keep any of it? She rarely sews or mends anything. Krystyna always did it for her. She will probably have to find a seamstress now. Frozen with indecision for a moment, she suddenly pulls out the socks and underwear drawers and dumps everything on the bed, including the sewing kit. When Krystyna's church stockings unfurl like black ribbons, Mania sees not only the evidence of darning but how her mother used nail polish to stop runs from going below the hemline. She almost says out loud what she is thinking: *Mama, why didn't you buy new stockings, for heaven's sake? You weren't that poor anymore!* She stuffs them with everything else on the bed into a large plastic garbage bag.

As she opens other drawers, she hopes that perhaps a sweater or a scarf will call out to her, "Save me! Your mother loved me!" She sets aside two silk scarves that catch her eye – a cerulean one for herself and a pale peach one for Marysia. Next, she examines her mother's sweaters. Like the doilies from the living room, they are examples of Krystyna's fine handiwork. Her fingers, once nimble and slim, continued to slip the needles in and out even when they had become bent with age and arthritis. She sets them aside for Marysia to check out.

After some time of steady sorting, Mania stands back with a sense of accomplishment: the dresser drawers are now all empty and except for Mama's wedding suit, and the two silk scarves, everything in the closet will go to charity.

Suddenly, there is a knock at the door.

"Mama, are you in there?" Marysia calls out.

Mania lets her daughter in and says, "I thought you were coming on the weekend."

"I was going to, but I suspected you'd start without me, so I took a couple of days off work. I wish you'd waited."

Avoiding Marysia's eyes, Mania says, "I wanted to be alone with Mama. For the last time."

Marysia sighs and walks into the bedroom past the bags filled with bedding and the one for the garbage.

"Is there anything worth keeping here?"

Mania shows her the sweaters and doilies.

"The sweaters are old and worn and I have no use for doilies," Marysia says.

"That's got nothing to do with it! When I touch these things, it's as if I'm touching *Babcia's* fingers," Mania says.

"Okay, Mama, you can clutter up your life if you want. Just let me know what I can put into garbage bags."

"I've done a lot already, so don't rush me! I may want to keep one or two of the sweaters. I think one or two may still be good for wearing around the house. The rest can be set aside for charity."

"Is there anything else you want to keep?" Marysia persists.

Mania opens the plastic bag with Krystyna's silk suit. "*Babcia* wore this at her wedding."

"You're not going to keep it, are you? What will you do with it?"

Mania shrugs. "Maybe I'll look at it once in a while when I want to think of her. When I want to feel her presence." She feels embarrassed; Marysia is so sensible, so practical. To divert her, Mania picks up a bundle of lace-edged hankies.

"How about these? Wouldn't you like one as a keepsake? Maybe one for Anna? They don't take up much room."

"Nobody uses hankies anymore. Did people actually blow their noses into these things?"

"More like delicately dabbed their noses. *Babcia* did all the lace work."

"If she'd been born fifty years later, *Babcia* could have been a brain surgeon."

Marysia sorts through the hankies and selects one for herself and one for Anna. Mania sets the rest aside with the doilies and sweaters that she will take home.

"How about this scarf?" Mania asks, draping the pale peach silk scarf that she picked out for Marysia around her neck. "It looks lovely on you. Sets off your hair."

Marysia nods and says, "Okay. Now let's sort out the storage closet."

"That should be easy," Mania says.

They open the closet in the hallway and begin to fill boxes with extra blankets and winter clothes for donation. Periodically Marysia takes a plastic bag to the incinerator. As the late afternoon sun is coming in through the window, they realize that they forgot about lunch. They go into the kitchen and pull out crackers and a tin of sardines. Marysia puts water on the stove for tea. Meanwhile, Mania opens a small velvet box that she has found on a shelf in the closet they were emptying. In it, she finds the various pieces of jewellery that she has seen her mother wear over the years. The find rekindles her grief. Gently caressing a string of pearls she had given her mother as a birthday present, she hands it to Marysia.

She says, "They say that pearls pick up a person's skin tones so they look different on each wearer. I hope you'll feel closer to *Babcia* wearing these."

The usually unsentimental Marysia smiles and asks her mother to fasten the necklace for her.

Mania slips an amber broach, which Tadeusz had given to Krystyna on their fifteenth wedding anniversary, into her pocket. The rest of the beads and bracelets – costume jewellery – she gives to Marysia for Anna to play with for dress-up.

As they eat their snack and drink their tea, Mania suddenly feels overcome with fatigue. "I think we've done enough for one day. We can come back tomorrow to finish up. There's still the kitchen, living room and dining room. I don't think that will be as hard. Mama didn't have anything valuable; at least nothing of sentimental value."

"What about her hand-embroidered tablecloths?" Marysia knows her mother's weaknesses.

"Well, maybe I'll keep just one of them."

"With the matching napkins?" Marysia teases.

"With the matching napkins," Mania agrees, with a smile.

Marysia says, "I'd like to leave early tomorrow."

"I think we may be finished by noon. Your father and I can

pick everything up for the charity box on the weekend."

They tidy up in the kitchen. Mania gives the bedroom and the storage closet one last look when something stuffed into the corner of the top shelf catches her eye.

"I forgot about that afghan," she says to Marysia, pointing it out.

She pulls it down and admires the fine knitting and intricate pattern that Krystyna designed with shades of pink, rose and purple yarn. She has to keep that.

Marysia says, "What's in that box up there?"

"I didn't see that. It's a shoe-box but *Babcia* kept her shoes on the bottom." Mania reaches up and takes down the box. It is light and doesn't rattle. She sits on the bed with the box on her lap, Marysia peering over her shoulder. When she lifts off the cover, she sees that it is stuffed with papers.

"It looks like *Babcia's* filing system," she says, as she takes out old bills. She is aware of her disappointment that this is all there is. At some level she expected more, perhaps letters from her father at the front or from Mama's sisters. It would have been so exciting to find a diary or a journal. Mama never talked to anyone, so it is possible she might have committed secrets to paper. Under the bills, Mania finds the marriage certificate of Krystyna and Tadeusz. Her eyes well up.

Marysia puts an arm around her shoulder. "You'll want to keep that," she says.

Mania sets the document aside. She is near the bottom of the box. There are permits, licenses, and work records from years ago. So much paper work and bureaucracy was associated with the Communist era in Poland. At the bottom of the box, the faded lining is coming away from the edges. Just as she is about to put all the useless papers back in and take the box out to the garbage, she spots a piece of paper that seems to have either slipped or been shoved underneath the bottom lining. She pulls it out and discovers a yellowed envelope without any writing on it. *This is more like it,* Mania thinks, her heart beating a little faster. She opens the flap and finds a couple of black-and-white photos with crimped edges.

"Yes!" she says. "This is what I was hoping for."

The first picture is that of a young man in uniform wearing an officer's cap. His face is very serious as he stands at attention and stares directly out of the photograph. On the back it says:

Dearest Krystyna,
I think of you all the time.
Please wait for me.
My love forever,
Krzysztof
June 1940

Mania says, "Oh, my God! This is a picture of my father, your grandfather. I've never seen one before. I asked Mama if she had a picture of him but she said everything was lost in a fire. Why did she hide this from me?"

Mania is shaken by the thought that her mother had lied to her. Why? She had so wanted a picture of her father, something to hang on to, to keep his memory alive for her during those years when she felt so alone. Her eyes are glued to her father's face as if he can say something to her. His eyes are so direct, so piercing. How proudly he wore his country's uniform! How he must have longed to come back to his wife and child.

Marysia's voice breaks into her thoughts. "Is this you and *Babcia*?"

She is holding up the second photograph, in which two women stand with two children on a country bridge. One woman has her hands on the shoulders of a girl of about three years of age. The other one holds a younger child in her arms.

Mania turns her attention to the people in the picture. "You're right! That's me with *Babcia*!"

"Wow!" Marysia exclaims, peering closely at the picture. "You were so cute, so pretty with your blonde braids. And

Babcia was beautiful. Do you remember this picture being taken? Do you know where it is?"

"No," Mania replies. Despite concentrating as hard as she can, she cannot recall anything about the scene.

She gazes at the young Krystyna, the skin smooth over her high cheek-bones, strands of her fair hair falling out of the bun at the at the nape of her neck. Her face is serious and her posture in her summer dress is ramrod straight.

"I've told you Mama was a beauty," Mania says, awash with sadness as the image of her mother in old age flashes before her.

"To me she just always seemed old," Marysia says. "But in this picture, she's young. And elegant. I didn't know *Babcia* was such a fine dresser."

"What are you talking about! She was an accomplished seamstress. When she had the money, she dressed like a model in the latest fashions that she copied."

Mania stares at the other woman and child. This is a woman of peasant stock, shorter and dark-haired, in a full ankle-length skirt and long-sleeved blouse. Curls peek out from under a kerchief tied behind her neck. It is not clear if the baby she is holding is a girl or boy, but it has a head of dark curls and a chubby face with a turned down mouth ready to wail. Marysia asks, "Who's that, Mama?"

Mania turns the picture over but there is nothing written on the back. "It could be *Babcia's* sister, Irena, with her child, my cousin."

"It's too bad that *Babcia* never let us meet them. It would have been nice to have some relatives."

In her daughter's voice Mania hears echoes of her own regrets. "It sure would. I was so lonely as a child. One day I'm going to find out the whole story."

"I say leave it alone. If *Babcia* didn't want you to know, she must have had a good reason. What do you want to go raking up the past for?"

Mania is annoyed. "Because with her last words, she wanted

me to find somebody and I'm going to do it!"

"Don't get excited, Mama. I won't stop you. Now let's go. I think we've done enough for one day."

Mania puts the pictures back in the envelope and the envelope in her purse. She has discovered two priceless treasures and picked up a couple of loose threads in the garment of her mother's life. It remains for her to unravel the rest until she is satisfied that she has fulfilled her mother's last wish.

Chapter 6

Róża, Pużniki, September 1943 – June 1944

SHE WAS NOT SUPPOSED TO BE in the vacant cottage. Irena had told her to hide in the forest after she left with the children. Róża had considered it but it did not make sense. What if Marek came back? If he saw that she was gone, he would think she had been shot or taken away. Besides, she was not sure she could make it on her own in the woods. So she settled into the cottage come what may. It was certainly more comfortable than that filthy shed, which was fit only for farm animals.

In her haste to get away, Irena had left some food on the table. Róża rationed out the partial loaf of stale bread over a few days for herself and scraped clean a pot of leftover cereal. When that was gone, she survived on the flour and grain still in the pantry, which she baked and cooked up at night so that no one would see the smoke from the chimney. She supplemented this with potatoes, carrots, onions, and berries, which she gathered from the garden at night. In this way, she kept her body alive. Mentally, though, she was going steadily downhill. When day after endless day Marek did not come, she began to accept that he was dead and she would see him on the other side. There was nothing and nobody left to live for. Death would be a welcome visitor. The prospect of torture was her greatest fear. She did not know if she had the strength to keep her mouth shut if subjected to extreme pain. The Nazis were beastly clever. They could force her to reveal the hiding place of her loved ones. This prospect was so horrible that she stopped eating in an effort to starve herself to death in advance of possible discovery. At first, her stomach cramped; then, her throat and mouth screamed for water. Finally she sank into a torpor.

One afternoon, Róża thought she was seeing things through the cottage window. A woman was dragging a child by one hand and holding a large bundle in the other. Trailing behind her, kicking up small puffs of dust with their feet, were two boys. It could only be Irena and the children. Róża panicked. She had to get out of the cottage; they must not find her here. She slipped out through a back window, falling into the berry bushes and from there ran into the shed. Breathless and exhausted, she pulled down the ladder, hauled herself up onto the platform, dragging the ladder behind her and collapsed on the straw. When she got over the haste and alarm of her escape, all she could think of was Irena's return with the children. Why were they back? It did not make sense.

That evening Irena came into the shed and gasped when she saw Róża. "I was afraid you'd still be in here! Why aren't you in the woods?"

Róża barely had the energy to sit up. "I couldn't go. Why did you come back? It's dangerous."

"It's dangerous everywhere," she said tersely.

"How long were you gone?" The days had become a jumble in Róża's head. It could have been a week; it could have been a month.

"Eight days."

"I thought you were going to stay with Antonia in Wroclaw."

"We did. But it didn't take long for my dear sister to turf us out. The children were too noisy, she said. And they ate too much. She doesn't exist for me anymore."

"There was nowhere else for you to go?"

"Where was I supposed to go? You think that there are people lining up to take in a woman with three children?" As Irena turned away, she said, "I'm going to bring you something to eat. You look like a ghost." She left and returned with some cold potatoes and a cup of water.

After a few bites, Róża could not eat any more. Gradually, over the next few hours, she forced herself to finish the food and drink the water. How could she explain to Irena her refusal of food? The fog in her brain began to clear with the intake of nourishment. In her present situation, nothing had changed, she concluded. The Germans or Ukrainians were bound to find her sooner or later. There were no signs that the war was ending. Again, by her very presence in the shed, she was putting Halinka and the whole family at risk. She arrived at the only logical conclusion. If she intended to live, she would have to leave this place. If not, she had to devise an exit strategy that did not include wandering in the forest by herself.

The autumn days were still warm but the nights were becoming inceasingly cold while Róża vacillated. What to do? Her continued existence in the shed endangered her daughter, Irena and the boys. But going into the woods alone terrified her. Perhaps she could gradually starve herself and then, before losing consciousness, she could drag herself into the woods, where her corpse could be found, without implicating anyone. She began by eating a smaller portion of what Irena brought her every day to shrink her stomach. The rest she threw in the bushes behind the shed. Every day, she assessed her strength to see if it was the right time to leave but every day it seemed that she was not weak enough yet. She did not want to linger in the woods. She wanted her death to come quickly once she fled the shed.

As November approached, the cold wind seeping in through the slats made her teeth chatter. That was an encouraging development. Irena told her about a frozen body found in the field. No one knew who it was but it must have been a runaway Jew. Róża thought that maybe she could freeze to death right here instead of in the woods. If the Nazis found her, Irena could say that she was also an unknown runaway who had crawled into the shed to die. Róża consoled herself with these thoughts as she curled up like a snail and closed her eyes. Her days took on a dreamlike haze; she was no longer hungry, but the terrible dryness in her throat and the cracking of her lips forced her to drink.

Images of her family began to appear before her. They were so real, she could almost touch them if only she could stretch out her tired arms. Sometimes, she was in the kitchen helping her mother; sometimes, in the store with her father. One happy time, she found herself with her brothers and her parents at the Sabbath table, which was covered with a snowy cloth. The candles in her mother's silver candelabra flickered hypnotically. Chicken, potato *kugel*, and honeyed carrots emitted delectable aromas. Her father was wearing his *yarmulke* and stroking his long white beard, a bottle of sweet red wine in front of him. His gentle presence presided at the head of the table as he led off the singing of the familiar Sabbath songs in a rich baritone underlying the younger, lighter tenors of her brothers and her mother's alto. The sound of their melodious voices was so beautiful that it made her weep. Raising her hand to her face, she felt her icy fingers on her cheekbones. Bits of straw stuck to her face. Tufts of her hair lay on the straw. Her body was numb with cold when she heard her mother's voice, hissing with fury.

"What do you think you're doing, Reizele?"

Her mother's Yiddish nickname for her flooded her with guilt at how she had insisted, when she turned thirteen, that her parents call her Róża, a respectable Polish name.

"*Nu*, answer me!" her mother demanded. "What are you trying to do?"

Straining, Róża lifted herself up on her elbow and licked her flaky lips. She had stopped speaking to Irena some time ago and her voice emerged as creaky as a rusty hinge. "I'm leaving here. I'm coming to be with you."

"Why?"

"It's too dangerous. For everyone. If the murderers find me...."

"So you want to sacrifice yourself? You stupid, stupid girl. You need to live! So many of us are dead and you have the *chutzpah* to help the Nazi beast kill you?"

"But Mama, I'm so tired and cold."

"Stop feeling sorry for yourself. You can't afford to be tired. And if you're so cold, ask that so-called Polish friend of yours to let you move into her attic."

"But Mama...."

"Don't give me any more buts! God gave you life; make the most of it. Don't you dare come here before your time!"

Her mother's furious face faded away before Róża could explain how she could not possibly move into Irena's attic and how the life God had given her was worthless and she did not want it any more. She waited for her mother to come back so she could tell her all these things but her mother did not return; nor did any of her other family members.

Lying on the straw, Róża was so confused that she forgot where she was and in an effort to stand up, she hit her head on the roof of the shed. Falling on all fours, she clutched the shawl around her shoulders, spit out bits of straw from her mouth, and lay down again, too exhausted even to weep. She fell into a fitful sleep until dawn when she tried to make sense of her mother's words. What did Mama know? She had never been in this kind of situation. She had no right to order her around. She had never seen her mother so angry before. If Mama would not speak to her when she got to the other side, all the pain and suffering would be for nothing. Maybe it was worth another try.

One bitter cold night when Irena's head showed up above the ledge where she lay, Róża pushed herself up to sitting and wrapped her arms around her shivering body.

"Irena, I have to ask you something," she whispered.

Róża saw the shock on Irena's face. Was she coming up to

see if Róża was dead yet? How long had she been lying mute and immobile anyway? Her head felt like it would float away, her body was quivering and insubstantial. Yet a spark of life remained, she was sure of it. So she repeated her question with all the puny strength she could muster.

All Irena could say was, "What is it?"

Róża tumbled the words out before she lost her nerve. "Winter is coming. I can't stay here. I'll die from the cold. You must let me stay in your attic."

Irena's face blanched. "Are you crazy? What if the children hear you? Or Germans come to the house for food and find you?"

Once she got started, Róża felt as if she had been injected with some kind of drug that made her blood course more rapidly through her body and sent energy to her spirit.

"Don't worry about the children. I'll be quiet. They haven't discovered me in here yet. And if we spot Germans coming, I'll run into the woods."

Irena lowered her eyes and bit her lip. Seeing Irena's fear, Róża was tempted to retract her request, but there was a pressure in the small of her back as if someone were pushing her. She could not turn around but she was sure it was Mama and so she straightened her shoulders.

Finally Irena said, "All right. On Sunday when we're in church, you can move into the attic. But if there's even a hint of trouble, you're out."

She was about to leave when Róża said, "Do you think you could leave a blanket for me?"

Putting her hands on her hips, Irena spat out, "What do you think this is, a hotel? Me and the children, we have one blanket and the comforter you brought with you for Halinka. Where do you think I'll get another blanket?"

With that she was down the ladder and out of the shed in a flash. Róża wondered if she had pushed Irena too far. She had to be so careful. If the woman reached her breaking point, she could turn her in for a nice reward. Everyone knew that there were Jews hiding in the area. Sometimes, children would find them in the woods in caves and told the authorities so they could get a reward. Until the Sunday of her proposed move into the attic, Róża lived in dread. She prayed for her mother to come back again, to give her another injection of courage. Her mother did not come and she remained alone except for her daily visits from Irena with food. Every day she now whispered, "*Dziękuję,*" to show her gratitude.

While the family was in church on Sunday morning, Róża ran into the cabin and up to the attic, pulling the ladder up behind her and shutting the trap door. Her heart was beating fast, and she was shaking like a leaf. Crouching down near the stovepipe that led from the wood stove below, she was finally able to warm herself. Never had she appreciated such warmth before. Even at night when the fire went out and it got cooler, there was still some residual warmth around the pipe. The first thing Irena did at dawn when it was cold enough to make your teeth chatter was to light the fire. Although she had not supplied Róża with a blanket, Irena had given her a couple of flour sacks to use as covers. The extra room in the attic gave Róża a chance to stand up in the middle where the steep, thatched roof came to a point. She could work out the cramps in her legs and the stiffness in her back. Irena visited her every night when the children were asleep, exchanging the slop pail for a pot of food. To Róża the new living arrangement was a vast improvement and gave her a new lease on life.

One Sunday morning, Róża pushed aside the board covering the gap in the side of the roof that served as a window. As she breathed in the cold fresh air, she suddenly froze. Someone was sneaking from one snow covered bush to another across the barren field. She rubbed her eyes to make sure they were not playing tricks on her. The figure was real and it was Marek. Her heart leapt into her throat.

She had believed for so long that he was dead; she had not even allowed herself to grieve for him for fear that once the tears started, they would never stop. Now here he was, coming closer and closer. She had to intercept him before he headed for the shed. She clambered down and ran to the door, gesturing wildly at him. He ran to her and they embraced. Finally, she dragged him inside and up to the attic.

Marek's surprise at her new living arrangements was only surpassed by Róża's joy at finding him alive. They fell into each other's arms, mouths and fingers hungrily clutching at each other's bodies. The whole village was in church, but they felt like they were the ones performing a sacrament. It had been so long since love had overcome fear. Róża clung to Marek like a drowning woman as he lowered her gently to the floor. When he lifted her dress, she opened herself as a parched plant gratefully drinks in the rain. Afterwards, they collapsed, spent, in each other's arms, lying quietly for a few minutes until they began to talk in rushed whispers. So much to say and so little time to say it in before Irena and the children returned from church. Róża told Marek about Irena's aborted attempt to run away with the children after the visit of the Nazi officer, who shot the dog, and how she had been moved to ask for a bed in the attic. Marek explained to Róża that he had been confined to his cellar hiding place because Krystyna had been forced to provide lodging for some Nazi officers for several weeks. Róża gasped. What if one of them was the one she had seen?

"Don't worry," Marek said. "I overheard them saying they had orders to go east."

"But what about Mirka?" she asked with a tremor in her voice.

"I think she kept her in a back room somewhere. You know how big the manor house is."

"Thank God!" she said, feeling a huge burden lift from her shoulders.

There was so much more to talk about, but it was time for

him to go; the church bells were ringing and Irena and the children would be back soon.

"Stay strong," Marek said as he hugged and kissed her goodbye. "I'll be back next Sunday when they're all in church." Then he was down the ladder and away as she watched him until he became a distant speck over the fields.

Even in her improved hiding place, Róża began to chafe at her captivity in the attic. She had to be perfectly still when the children were in the house. She could not go outside when they were outside. She felt as if she were in a prison. Once, when she was desperate for a breath of fresh air, she ventured out when the boys were at the priest's school and Irena was at market with Halinka. She felt so exposed in broad daylight that she did not try it again.

Marek's weekly visits helped to stave off Róża's loneliness and isolation. Watching Halinka was her daily joy. The cracks in the attic floor allowed her a good view of life centred around the big wood stove and the wooden table in the middle of the room. The bed where they all slept was a large frame with a straw-filled bag that served as a mattress. It lay next to the stove, so that even as it cooled overnight, Halinka could huddle beside Irena on one side and Staszek on the other for warmth.

The close bond that Halinka had developed with Irena was like a splinter in Róża's heart. Some day, she vowed to herself, she would be the mother to her own child. The thought that by war's end Halinka would likely not remember her plunged her into despair, especially if the child were to see her mother looking like a human scarecrow. The Germans believed that the Jews were subhumans. In her lowest moments, Róża felt like one. She would let her hands travel over her body, fingers counting her protruding ribs, her hands cupping her deflated breasts. Her arms and legs were like sticks. She kept tightening the rope that tied her dress around her waist so that it did not hang like a sack over her wasted frame and roll up to her armpits during the night. Being stripped of her physical self was only part of what they had taken away from her that made her human. They had also taken her family, friends, books, music and useful work. This was not a life; it was existence at the most basic level. In her own mind, she was little more than an animal now, responding only to the instincts of hunger, thirst, and fear.

One day, before she had a chance to run into the woods as she had planned with Irena, two German soldiers and an officer suddenly appeared, banging on the door. Róża froze when she recognized the officer. He demanded food and a place for him and his men to sleep for the night. She heard their raucous laughter, their drinking – they seemed to have an endless supply of vodka – and their dirty talk about women and Jews. When they fell asleep, their snores and snorts, their every movement increased her terror. Irena and the children had decamped to the shed to sleep, and the thought that only a thin wooden partition separated her from these brutes made her shake uncontrollably.

The next morning, they left, taking every last morsel of food with them, except the bag of coarse flour Irena had hidden under the floorboards and the potatoes outside in the cold cellar. In the early days, there had still been eggs until a couple of passing Germans had demanded chicken for dinner. The goat, too, was gone now. Róża assumed that Irena had sold her for the travel expenses when she and the children had gone to Wroclaw. There must be a little money left because Irena occasionally still went to market for a couple of eggs and a piece of cheese for the children.

The "visits" of German soldiers were a terrifying experience not only for Irena and Róża but for all the village women, too. If the soldiers did not drink themselves into a stupor, they grabbed any girl or woman they could find for their sexual pleasure. If there were officers along, they would demand that their subordinates bring them girls. When she was in the shed, Róża had been able to hear them carousing on a couple of occasions and had tried to block her ears to the shrieks of the poor women. This time, there had been no women. This commanding officer seemed to be rather puritanical. He forbade his men to touch Irena, a mother of three children. Róża wept with relief when they left and Irena and the children could return to their home.

As the weather grew milder and winter began to turn to spring, no more Nazis showed up and Róża relaxed a little. The ice on the creek melted, and Irena began to take the laundry down to wash it in the swiftly churning current. Róża watched as the children went along: Halinka carrying a large bar of yellow soap, Staszek clutching the washboard, and Andrej lugging a bundle of dirty clothes. At the edge of the creek, Irena organized an assembly line. She scrubbed each item with the soap and handed it to the boys to rinse free of suds in the swirling water. Halinka made a nuisance of herself, nagging them to let her "play." Finally Irena gave her a chip of soap, a sock to wash and sat her in front of a rock on which she could scrub. The child rubbed the sock diligently for a few minutes and then handed it to Staszek, who took it from her, leaned over and splashed it in the water.

Halinka cried out, "Let me do it!"

"You're too little," Staszek said.

"I'm big!" As if to prove it, she slid off the rock, puffed out her chest and stood on her tip toes.

Before she could determine what had happened, Róża heard a big splash, Halinka's screams, and Irena's shouts as she waded into the water. Distraught, Róża searched the landscape with wild eyes until she caught sight of her baby being carried downstream, her arms and legs thrashing and kicking wildly. She turned away to climb down to rescue her, ignoring the danger, when the screams stopped. Going back to her hole, she saw Irena holding Halinka, gasping, crying and dripping wet. Keening and rocking on her heels, Róża watched Irena wrap the child in her shawl and carry her home.

Irena said, "*Dzięki Bogu! Dzięki Bogu,*" at the same time as Róża whispered "Thank God!"

"I'm taking Halinka inside," Irena shouted to the boys. "You better finish the laundry. If I find out that either one of you had anything to do with her almost drowning, you'll regret the day you were born!"

"It's not our fault she slipped!" Andrej said.

"It's really shallow, anyway," Staszek said, his voice shaky. "I can almost stand even in the middle."

"I don't want to hear another word out of either of you! I'll deal with you later!"

In the cottage, Irena ripped off Halinka's soaked clothing, wrapped her in towels, and sat her close to the stove while she heated up some milk. Róża watched through a crack in the floorboard and even as she felt relief flooding her, she wondered where Irena had got the milk. Perhaps she was hiding the goat with Krystyna.

How easily children forget, Róża marvelled. In no time, Halinka was babbling about her adventure and wanted to go out again. Irena would not let her and put her down for a nap instead. She was still sleeping when the boys came in later with the washing. Before letting them eat, Irena pulled them aside and, without a word, showed them the willow switch that she used to instil discipline. Two chastened boys sat down at the table to their meal.

After this incident the behaviour of the boys toward Halinka changed. Perhaps they had come too close to losing the girl whom they had begun to love as their baby sister. Whatever the reason, they now became Halinka's protectors. On Sunday mornings, when they walked to church, dressed in their best clothes – frayed and shabby, but clean and mended – each one held tightly to one of Halinka's hands. They no longer ran ahead to meet up with friends, leaving Irena behind with the little girl. When it came to mealtime, they devised a rule – the first and the last of the potatoes or *pierogi* or hard-boiled eggs in the bowl were reserved for their *sioszycka*.

Still, there was no end to the war. One mild sunny Sunday morning when Marek was visiting, two Ukrainian militia men barged into the hut rummaging for food. Róża, barely breathing, dug her fingers into Marek's arms. When a military cap poked through the trap door of the attic, her eyes locked with those of a young man standing on a chair.

"Hey, Luka, come see what I found!" the soldier cried out. He indicated with his rifle for Róża and Marek to come down.

Legs trembling, Róża dropped into the man's powerful arms, forgetting about the ladder. Marek followed. Huddled in the middle of the room, they faced the ruddy-cheeked young soldier, smirking with pride at his discovery. The other one, Luka, looked older. He had several days' growth of beard on his gaunt, hungry face. He demanded to know who they were and why they were up in the attic. They pretended that they did not understand Ukrainian, even though Róża understood quite well what he said to Bogdan, the boy who had found them: "These two are Jews for sure." He ordered Bogdan to take them out and shoot them. Bogdan obeyed with obvious pleasure, prodding them in the back until they reached the wagon they had parked in front of the cottage. When Róża was about to collapse from shock, he grabbed her under the arm and forced her to stand upright beside Marek.

"Back up against the wagon and put your hands up!" Bogdan shouted, motioning with his hands what he wanted them to do. Then he shouldered his rifle, trigger finger at the ready.

So this is how it ends, Róża thought, staring at the youth, *not at the hands of a Nazi butcher, but by a pudgy-faced boy still in his teens.*

Suddenly, Luka called out, "Stop! Don't shoot them! They may be spies. We should get the commander. He'll interrogate them. Then we can shoot them."

Bogdan lowered his rifle in obvious disappointment and indicated for Róża and Marek to drop their arms.

"Should I go get him?" Bogdan asked Luka.

"No, you stay here and guard them. I'll get him."

Luka trudged off while Bogdan pushed them back into the cottage with the butt of his rifle, giving a few extra digs into the small of Róża's back to make up for having lost the opportunity to kill. He slammed the door, leaving Róża and Marek staring at each other, barely comprehending what had just occurred. Marek went over to the window.

"He's tending to the horse," he said.

"What are we going to do? How can we warn Irena?"

"There's nothing we can do. I'm sure that Irena is smart enough not to come back if she sees a strange wagon in her yard."

"I wish he'd shot us. This waiting is like slow torture. If we have to watch him shoot Halinka, I won't be able to bear it." She began to cry.

"Where there's life there's hope. Look, he's unhitching the horse and taking him down to the creek for a drink. I knew he was an idiot! Let's go." Marek grabbed Róża's hand.

"What if he sees us from the creek and shoots us?"

"What makes you think he's a good shot? These Ukrainian boys aren't well trained. I doubt they can shoot anyone except at close range. It's our only chance."

Marek pushed the door open just wide enough for them to slip through. Róża kept her eyes focused on her husband's back. If she got shot, she did not want to see it coming. Hand in hand they ran until they reached the woods.

"Oh, my God!" Róża said, out of breath. "I forgot to close the door. When he comes back, he'll know we're gone."

"I'll do it," Marek said. He dropped her hand and she watched him from behind a tree trunk, her heart pounding. His run there and back seemed endless but Bogdan did not return from the creek.

When he got back, Marek grabbed Róża by the arm and said, "We have no time to lose. Let's go!"

They ran until Róża could run no more. By then, they were deep in dense vegetation. Marek created a hiding place for them in a cluster of trees, piling bare branches and sodden leaves over their bodies. The ground on which they lay was still soggy and muddy from melted snow. Under such conditions, it was impossible to stay for more than one day. For the next two days they wandered, only resting when Róża, her legs swollen and covered with insect bites, could go no further.

She sat with her back against a tree trunk and said she was ready to die. "Let's go back. Maybe it's safe again."

Reluctantly Marek agreed and they emerged from the forest after nightfall. There was no sign of the Ukrainians or of any Germans near Irena's cottage. The smell of cooking potatoes lingered in the air. A sharp pain went through Róża's stomach. They peeked in through the window and saw Irena sitting with her needle and thread by the light of a candle while the children slept.

"Do you think that Irena and Krystyna will continue to hide us now that we have no more money?" Róża whispered.

Marek shrugged. "We have to hope. You and Irena were friends as children. Krystyna worked for your parents. Maybe that still counts for something."

"How much longer can this last?" Róża felt so weighed down it was as if leg irons were attached to her feet.

"The German officers I saw at Krystyna's still had shiny boots and pressed uniforms. They didn't look like losers." He paused and looked at her questioningly. "Should we?"

With a sigh of resignation, she nodded and tapped lightly on the door. When Irena appeared, her face turned grim on seeing them.

"You can't stay here," she said.

Marek said, "Only her. Not me."

Róża asked, "Did they come back?"

Closing the door behind her so as not to awaken the children, Irena beckoned to them to follow her into the shed.

Once inside, she said, "I saw the wagon when we were returning from church. I made the children wait in the shed while I crept up to hear what the soldiers were saying. The commander wasn't too pleased with the two young ones for letting you escape and he screamed at them for being idiots. But he had orders to move east, so they didn't have time to search for the escaped Jews. You're lucky."

"Does that mean I can stay here for a while? It's unbearable in the woods."

Irena didn't reply.

"Oh, please, Irena. I beg you. Marek says it can't last much longer."

Marek nodded vigorously and finally Irena relented. "All right. But you must stay in the shed. No more attic. And if anyone finds you, I'll say I never laid eyes you before in my life and you just sneaked in without my knowledge."

"What about food?"

"I'll only bring you things that don't need dishes so there won't be a trace of me helping you."

Róża nodded abjectly. After the hardship of the forest, she was grateful for this bare existence. She kissed Marek goodbye and he disappeared into the darkness. Irena returned to the cottage without uttering another word. That night, Róża, up on her shelf and covered with straw, curled into a foetal position, and fell into an exhausted sleep.

Only a couple of weeks passed before disaster struck again. One night, Róża awoke to the smell of something burning. She crawled over to her little window and saw wisps of smoke curling over the treetops that had just begun to bloom. *Oh, my God, there's a fire in Pużniki!* Tongues of red and orange flames were licking their way across the rooftops down the road from Irena's cottage. Was this a sign of the end? Were the Nazis setting fire to the whole area as they retreated? Soon enough, she heard movement downstairs. Irena had woken up and was hurrying to dress Halinka and rushing the boys out the door. As she continued to stare out of her hole in the shed, frozen with indecision, Róża spied a shadow heading toward her. It was Marek. Just as he opened the door, Róża came down the ladder. Without a word, he took her hand and they took a quick look at the crowd mesmerized by the flames before they ran behind the shed and into the woods.

Róża pulled at Marek's hand to stop and take one last backward glance. The flames were hungrily devouring the thatched roofs of the poor villagers' simple homes. Women were wailing and children, after getting over their first fright, were dancing around as if it were a party. Meanwhile the men began to organize a chain of water carriers from the creek to try to douse the flames.

"Is the manor house on fire, too?" Róża asked Marek, with a note of panic in her voice.

"Of course," he said. "It's the bloody Ukrainians. Who do you think they hate most of all the Poles – the nobles whose heels they've felt on their necks for years."

Róża thought of the Petrenkos and their kindness to her. She could not imagine them condoning anything like this. If it was the Ukrainians, then they must have been the young, hot-blooded nationalists who wanted to get rid of all Poles and Jews from their "homeland."

"What about Krystyna and Mirka?"

"I don't know."

"Oh, my God!"

"I didn't say they were dead. I think I saw them leave. They had enough time to run away. But we have to get out of here before someone spots us."

With one final look, Róża noticed that Irena's cottage still stood untouched by fire. She tugged at Marek's hand and whispered, "A miracle!"

Then they ran into the woods. The night was black with no moon and only pinpricks of stars, which were soon obliterated by clouds and smoke.

"What is the use of going back into the woods?" Róża asked, when they stopped.

"Róża, we can't give up. There's nowhere else to go. It'll be better this time. It's warmer now than last time. And maybe we can find the partisans. Anyway, staying here is suicide. They'll blame us for starting the fire."

"We'll starve to death," she said.

"No we won't. Look," Marek put her hand into his pockets. She felt onions, carrots, and potatoes. In a rag he showed her bread that he had wrapped up before running out of the flames.

Marek prodded her. "Let's go."

They ran until they had to stop to catch their breaths, but not for long. Marek insisted that they get as far away as possible to avoid detection.

Eventually, they found a cave in a rocky hill behind some raspberry bushes. Marek pushed Róża in and piled up pine branches blocking the entrance after he crawled in behind her. With her husband's warm body next to her, and the clean scent of pine filling the air, Róża felt a small stirring of hope. Maybe all was not lost. They had had so many close calls, so many miraculous escapes. But realistically, how many more chances could they expect? How much longer could she hold out? She was not strong like Marek, either physically or emotionally. She thought of her mother. Had she not said that it was Róża's duty to survive? She had to cling to that memory. She had to cling to her love for the remaining fragments of her family. She had to cling to even the slimmest chance to grab at life. Maybe, just maybe, she and Marek could survive after all.

Chapter 7

Mania, Warsaw, November 2005

MANIA IS SITTING UP in bed, propped up by pillows, trying to read. She glances over at Witold who is surrounded by his medical journals. She turns her attention back to her book but it is no use. She cannot concentrate on the printed page while thoughts of what had happened earlier in the day buzz in her head.

Closing the book, she picks up the picture of her father that she found in Mama's apartment. She peers into his eyes, trying to detect in them any hint of a connection to him or a corresponding resonance in herself. There is nothing. She admires the jaunty tilt of his cap and his proud posture. Her thoughts wander to other items she handled among Mama's things and their associated memories. Throughout her childhood, the longing for her father and the loneliness of being an only child with one parent had always been there.

Next door, Marysia lies in her old room. She will be eager to go to Krystyna's apartment in the morning so she can start for home in the afternoon. Mania would rather give it a pass for a day or two. She needs time to deal with her jumbled feelings and to sort out her confusion over her and her mother's past. She needs order, not this patchwork quilt of memory. Even things that were important to her – like Tadeusz's funeral – have become blanks. In going back to that time, it occurs to her that she was not in the country when her stepfather died. What a relief! No wonder she has no memory of it.

"Witold," she says, "how well do you remember your parents?"

Witold puts down his journal and says, "What do you mean? I remember them very well."

"How old is your mother when you think of her? Do you remember your father from various times in his life or mostly from when you were a boy? Or from pictures?"

He thinks about it for a while. "We remember people from the time we were involved with them, so of course I remember my parents mostly from my childhood and then in old age. I didn't see them as much in their middle years after I left for university and after we got married."

"And your earliest memory?"

"I don't know – when I was about three or four years old, I guess."

Mania shows him the picture of her father.

"I don't remember my father at all. I found this picture in a box with some of Mama's bills and old papers. He doesn't even look vaguely familiar."

"How old were you when he left for the war?"

"According to the date on the back, he was already serving in the army when I was two years old."

"So how can you expect to recognize him in the photograph?"

"Mama could have shown me this one or other family photos. She talked about him until she got the notice that he had been killed at the front. Then, nothing. She hid this picture from me. She said all of the family photos were destroyed in a fire. Why would she lie?"

Witold shakes his head. "Who knows why people tell lies?" He studies the photograph and glances at Mania. "He was a fine-looking young man. You look more like your mother than him."

Mania says, "He was too young to die. I wish I had known him. I wish she had at least framed this picture and put it on the dresser in her room or on the credenza with others of our family."

"Maybe she put it away when she married Tadeusz."

"No, it's never been out."

"Maybe it was too painful for her to see it every day."

"She could have given it to me! I'm angry that she deprived me of even this tiny connection to my father."

"I can understand, but think about it from her point of view. She was a young widow who had gone through a lot, caring for a child alone in the chaos of war, finding out that her husband had been killed. She dealt with it in the best way she knew how."

"Right. By suppressing it."

When they had first come to Warsaw, Mama used to drag Mania to the train station every day to survey the crowd on the platform in search of her husband, Mania's father. Although Mania was only seven years old, she knew in the pit of her stomach that her father would not show up. If he did come back and she did not recognize him, she would feel terrible. She could imagine him trying to kiss her and her pushing him away. She had hated those trips to the railway station – people elbowing and shoving and calling out names. Sprinkled among the civilians had been soldiers straggling back from the front, bandaged, missing limbs, thin as rails. She had gripped her mother's hand, afraid that if she got lost in that mass of humanity, she would never find Mama again.

One day it stopped. There was an official-looking letter for Mama on the hall table where their landlady, *Pani* Cybulska had laid it. Mama held it in her hand and stared at it for a long time before ripping it open and scanning the message. With a cry of pain that cut right into Mania, she ran into the room they rented and dropped onto the bed, sobbing into the pillow. Mania did not know what to do except to lie down beside her, pat her back and say, "What is it, Mama? What's wrong?"

Mama said in a strangled voice, "It's your *Tato*. He's not coming back."

Mania felt guilty at the sudden relief that swept over her. No more worry about sharing Mama with a stranger who was supposed to be her father. No more visits to the train station. Soon guilt came back and overcame relief as she became aware of her mother's pain.

"What happened to *Tato*, Mama?" she asked.

"He was killed."

Mania wanted to know how he was killed and who did it, but she was afraid to ask. Her mother often said that she asked too many questions.

As she lay beside Mama with her cheek against her back, Mama said, "I'm going to stay in bed, sweetheart. Can you get yourself something to eat?"

"What about you, Mama? Don't you want any supper?"

"Not right now."

Reluctantly, Mania left their room and went into the kitchen they shared with the Cybulskis. *Pani* Cybulska invited her to join her three children around the table and eat with them. When they were finished, *Pani* Cybulska gave Mania a bowl of soup to take in for her mother. But Mama told her she was not hungry and Mania took the soup back to the kitchen.

That night, Mania fell asleep curled up beside her mother. The next morning, Mania was awakened by the landlady's knock on the door. Krystyna lay in a fetal position with the covers pulled up to her chin. She opened her eyes only long enough to ask *Pani* Cybulska if she would send Mania off to school. Her mother's face was bloated and ravaged from crying.

Pani Cybulska brushed Mania's hair, straightened out her clothes, and told her to wash her face before sitting down to breakfast with her children. For the next few days, Mania dragged her feet to and from school. Mama did not go to work. She stayed in bed, her eyes became dull, her skin took on a sallow tint, and their bedroom smelled stale and stuffy.

Finally, Sister Beatrice took things in hand.

She said to Mania at school one day, "You poor thing. I know all about your Mama not being well on account of losing your *Tato*. *Pani* Cybulska has been to see me. We have to do something for your Mama."

Sister Beatrice went home with her. First, she opened the window, allowing in the crisp autumn air. Then, she sat down on the bed beside Mama and talked to her quietly. While Mania sat clutching her hands in her lap, the nun helped Mama get washed and dressed.

"I'm taking your mother to the convent guest house until she feels better. You can stay in the residence."

"I want to stay with my Mama." Mania worried about what would happen to her if her mother died.

"You can't stay with her, but don't worry. We'll look after her well and soon she'll take you home again. You'll like it in the residence. Some of the girls from your class are there."

The nun packed a few things for them and they set out for the convent. A senior girl was charged with taking Mania to the dormitory while Sister Beatrice took Krystyna to the guest house. Mania clung to her mother until the last minute when Krystyna kissed her and gently pushed her away. She promised that they would see each other soon.

The stay in the residence was one of the most painful events in Mania's life. Not only was she separated from her mother from whom she had never been apart, but she could not sleep in the room full of girls who snuffled, wheezed, snored, and called out in their sleep. The girls from her class were not welcoming, either. They had already formed friendships to which she was an outsider. After an initial show of curiosity as to the reason she was there, the girls lost interest and ignored her. She withdrew more and more into herself.

The three weeks until Krystyna was considered well enough to go home seemed never-ending. Finally, when she came to pick her up, Mama's eyes were clear and her posture was proudly upright as it had always been although she was thinner and paler. Mania was overjoyed when she saw her appear at the door of the dormitory, running to her and flinging her arms around her while the girls stared. When they resumed their life in their room in *Pani* Cybulska's apartment, there were no more trips to the train station, no more references to her father, and no more talk of his heroism and his expected return home.

Mama went back to working for the Glowackis. *Pani* Cybulska recommended Mama to them to take over her job as housekeeper when she had found a better job on the assembly line in the pharmaceutical factory. The Glowackis were good to Krystyna. *Pani* Glowacka, who liked to dress well as befitted her station as the wife of a man with an important job in the government, let her take home leftover food and hand-me-downs. Mama's skilled hands turned *Pani* Glowacka's discards into lovely clothes for herself and Mania.

After two years of working for the Glowackis, Krystyna found out from *Pani* Cybulska that there were openings in the factory. She applied and was hired immediately. *Pani* Glowacka grumbled at losing her, but she stayed in touch. Being out from under that woman's watchful eyes made Krystyna more relaxed. She had often complained to Mania that her former employer was too keen to stick her nose into her business. After thanking *Pani* Cybulska for all her kindness in providing them accommodation on their first arrival in Warsaw and on guiding her to steady employment, they moved to a two-bedroom apartment. Mama could now afford the rent for a more spacious place, which included a regular kitchen and a bedroom for herself and for Mania. No more cooking on a hot plate in their room! No more sleeping together in one bed! Oh, what sweet luxury!

Mania was now old enough to take on some chores when she got home from school. She had to get the fire going in the wood stove, so that it was cozy and warm by the time her mother got home. She studied at the kitchen table until it was time to start dinner. Then, she peeled potatoes, put them in a pot of water on the stove, cut up vegetables for soup, or heated up leftovers from the day before. What she liked best was preparing a foot-bath for her mother. Mama's feet hurt after a whole day standing on the assembly line. She collapsed on the sofa as soon as soon as she entered the door and took off her coat, hat, and gloves. Mania pulled off her mother's shoes and stockings and gently put her feet in the basin filled with warm water and Epsom salts. She massaged each foot until Mama sighed with pleasure.

When Mama said, "You're the best daughter in the world," Mania glowed with pride.

Sister Beatrice had been a great help to them in settling down in Warsaw. She had smoothed the way for Mania in the convent school from the beginning. For Mania, being in a classroom had been a new experience. She had never attended school before. Mama had taught her how to read and write and to do simple arithmetic. She had been shy and timid with other children. But after a quick assessment of her skills, Sister Beatrice took her to a classroom with girls her own age. There, she introduced her to a friendly young nun, who took Mania under her wing. Sister Beatrice brought Mania into her office for regular chats to find out how she was doing, and she encouraged Mania to participate in a girls' after school club, where she soon began to make friends.

Mania was aware that her relationship with her mother was much closer than that of her friends with theirs. Krystyna was not a member of any women's groups. She did not join in the gossip with other mothers at family events at the convent school. Mother and daughter were each other's confidante: at night, over dinner, they talked like equals, Mania recounting the events of her day at school and Mama about her day at work. They were each other's best friends.

So many years later, Mania recognizes that her relationship with her mother had one big gap – there was never any talk about family or about the past. She will talk to Sister Beatrice and *Pani* Glowacka to try to get a fuller picture of her mother's early life. Surely, Major Glowacki wouldn't have allowed his wife to hire a housekeeper without knowing anything about her. Maybe the old lady still has some documentation that hasn't been thrown out. Mania feels incredibly stupid that she doesn't even know her mother's birthplace. All these years she's only thought of it as "the village." But what village? Where? She only knows it was the same place as her patient, *Pan* Bojarski, is from and that it was in that part of Poland which is now Ukraine. Perhaps it's on his file at the clinic. She will check it at work. "I need to talk to Sister Beatrice and *Pani* Glowacka," she says to Witold.

He looks up from his journal and says, "What about?"

"I want to ask them if they know anything about Mama's family."

"Do you think she confided in them?"

"No, she didn't confide in anyone, but *Pani* Glowacka was her first employer in Warsaw and she was, still is, a big snoop. And Sister Beatrice was a friend from the moment we came here. She helped Mama through her first depression when my father died. She was there for her when Tadeusz died. She may know more about Mama than she's telling me."

Krystyna's second "nervous collapse" had happened when Mania and Witold were in Algiers. One day, Mania received a letter from Sister Beatrice informing her that Tadeusz had died suddenly and that her mother was in the convent guest house again. He and Krystyna had been together for fifteen years.

Witold came into the apartment to find her weeping. She passed the nun's letter to him wordlessly. Witold made all the arrangements: releasing Mania from the rest of her teaching contract at the university, booking her return flight to Warsaw, and taking her to the airport. At the Warsaw airport, Mania rented a car and drove to the convent, where she went directly to find Sister Beatrice in her office.

"How is my mother, Sister?" Mania asked.

"She has taken your stepfather's passing very hard. He was a very sick man."

"What was wrong with him?"

"Pancreatic cancer. He was in terrible pain, and she nursed him every moment. With the Lord's mercy, it didn't last too long – not even three months."

"He was sick for three months?" Mania was incredulous. "Why didn't anyone contact me? I would have come right home. And I could have been here for the funeral."

"Your mother didn't want to interrupt your year abroad. When Tadeusz died, I took matters into my own hands. I brought her to the guest house and decided to write to you. Your mother was in a terrible state at home, just like after your father died."

When Mania saw Krystyna, she was shocked at her gaunt features, with her cheekbones like points threatening to poke through her translucent skin. Her dress, which had always fitted nicely over her breasts and hips, now hung in loose folds.

"Hello, Mama," Mania said, bending over to kiss her where she sat by the window in her tiny room.

"What are you doing here?" Krystyna asked in a listless voice. "I told Sister Beatrice not to tell you."

"I'm glad she did. You need me."

"Pshaw! I'm all right."

"Mama, I want to take you home," Mania said.

Krystyna did not put up any resistance when Mania threw her few belongings into her old suitcase. She dressed her mother in her winter coat as if she were a child, and with a hand under her arm, she walked her out of the convent and into her rental car. Sister Beatrice followed close behind.

"If you need my help for anything, just call me. I will pray for her."

"Thank you, Sister. It's good to know that I have someone to turn to, especially with Witold still in Algiers."

Once they arrived in Krystyna's apartment, Mania settled her mother on the sofa and unpacked her bag. She checked the refrigerator and made a list of groceries that she would have to go out to buy. Krystyna followed her activities with dull eyes.

"When are you going home?" she asked.

"I was hoping I could stay here with you until Witold gets back."

"What about your own apartment?"

"When we left for Algiers, we gave up our apartment."

"So you'll stay only until you find a place?"

"When Witold comes back in four months, we'll start to look."

"You're always welcome in my home."

It was only when Mania told Krystyna that she was pregnant that her mother's spirit began to revive. But just as she had never spoken about Mania's father after he was killed on the front, she rarely referred to Tadeusz.

Now Mania asks Witold, "Do you remember our time in Algiers?"

Looking up, he scans the African masks on their walls and the wooden carvings on the bookcase, and says, "That was quite an adventure."

Rather than Witold's masks and carvings, Mania's favourite mementos of that time are the dresses and skirts that Krystyna made for her from the bolts of cloth she brought back. They looked so colourful and exotic back home. She still has them somewhere in the back of her closet although she thinks she's too old to wear such bright clothes now. How hurt she was when Mama wouldn't sew anything for herself from the fabric. Now that she's an older woman herself, she understands why.

"Maybe for you it was exciting. For me it was more harrowing, having to come home to look after Mama. I never really wanted to go."

Witold turns to her in surprise. "I didn't know that. We didn't have to go."

"I know. I didn't want to stand in your way. So I thought it was the right thing to do. Get us out of the country for a while. You know, after you had that fight with your father."

"You're probably right. Those were the peak days of paranoia in this country."

"I always suspected Mama was in on the plan too. Just another secret she kept from me."

Mama never did admit that Witold's father had called her about getting the young couple to Algiers. It was 1968, and Mania was working in pediatrics and Witold was finishing his psychiatry residency. Witold's father, *Pan* Wiśniewski, wanted to sponsor him to join the Party. He thought that through membership his son would have greater opportunities for career advancement. But Witold refused. Mania worried that there might be negative repercussions. But Witold was firm. It was not because he was rebellious. They had heard about student unrest in Europe and America, but it did not really touch them. Nothing like that could ever happen in Poland under the Communists. They didn't like the Communists, but they were not suffering. Life was good if you worked hard and did not get into political discussions with people. Witold did not share his father's ideology; all he cared about was medicine and more specifically, psychiatry. Until that Sunday dinner with his parents.

"There's a neurologist working at the hospital who is consistently by-passed for promotion," Witold said. "I can't understand it. Others who aren't half as bright as he is keep getting appointed over his head."

"What's his name?" Witold's father asked.

"Jakub Bergman. He's a couple of years older than me."

"Well, there you have it. He's a Jew. He won't get far."

"Why not?"

"Don't be naïve, son. It's the way of the world."

"That's ridiculous!" Witold was about to say something else when Mania put a restraining hand on his arm.

She said under her breath, "Getting into a fight with your father won't help Jakub."

Witold calmed down, and they did not talk about Jakub again.

When they got home, he said, "How could you sit quietly and listen to that prejudice? Jakub's our friend."

That was true. So was his wife, Shancia, who also worked at the hospital as a pharmacist. Their families had been murdered by the Nazis. But Jakub and Shancia had reconstructed their lives with two young children and a close circle of friends.

"I'm sorry if you feel I let you down. I just find your father so intimidating. What's the point in arguing with him?"

"That's the problem. He never listens. I thought I'd managed to come to terms with his autocratic behaviour, but I guess he can still get a rise out of me."

"He knows what buttons to push. He just has to mention any kind of injustice and you go charging off on your horse with your sword drawn."

"I just can't accept his blatant anti-Semitism after what happened to the Jews in Poland. There's hardly any of them left here."

"It's Party policy."

He shook his head in disgust, and Mania thought that was the end of it.

A few weeks later, the Bergmans made a surprise visit to Mania and Witold. Over coffee, they explained that they had come to say goodbye. Witold was shocked that their friends had decided to leave Poland. He said that their lives were rooted in this country; what had driven them to such a drastic decision? Mania could understand wanting to leave a place where you were not welcome, but she did not say anything. This turned out to be the case. The Bergmans could no longer overlook the anti-Semitism that had increased dramatically since the Six-Day War in Israel in 1967. Like all Polish Jews, they had to prove their loyalty to the state or they would be accused of being Zionist spies.

"That's ridiculous," Witold said. "You're no more spies than we are."

"It doesn't matter. The government is putting the loyalty of all Jews under suspicion even though there's no substance to it. It's the same old hatred rearing its ugly head again."

"But you're doing important work."

"I know, but we can't live here under these circumstances."

Witold tried to get them to stay by starting a petition at the hospital supporting the Bergmans. Mania was torn. She wanted to help her friends but she was frightened for Witold. They had never done anything this public before. She was not political. Who knew what ramifications there might be if you drew attention to yourself? As it turned out, hardly anyone at the hospital signed. They must have been frightened too, or maybe they just did not care. Unfortunately, Witold's father heard about the petition and he was furious.

When he telephoned, Mania could hear him shouting at Witold from the earpiece. "Are you trying to ruin your career?"

Witold shouted back at the unfairness of it. He pointed out to his father that the departure of a gifted neurologist like Jakub Bergman would be a huge loss to the hospital and to medicine in Poland. His father just hung up on him.

Shortly after this incident, Witold asked Mania, "How would you like to go to Algiers to teach at the medical faculty there?"

She was surprised and puzzled.

"What's this about?" she asked.

"There's an opportunity for me to go, and I asked if you could come too. They agreed."

"Who asked you?"

"The director of the hospital."

Mania's heart leapt into her throat. Immediately she had her suspicions about this sudden "opportunity." Even if she wanted to go, it would be hard to leave her mother, although Mama did have Tadeusz now. She would also hate to leave her placement in pediatrics, which she loved. Before considering it, she needed to know first if this transfer had actually been ordered.

"What if I don't want to go?" she asked.

"Then we won't go," he said.

That calmed her down a bit. She loved her husband and she did not want to stand in his way, if this was something that he wanted. Still, it was sudden and unexpected. Witold had not applied for an overseas assignment. They were few and far between. It seemed strange to Mania that he was asked over others who were keen to go. She told Witold that she suspected his father was behind the offer.

"But why would he get involved?" Witold asked.

"Because he wants to get you out of the country. You've criticized the state. And that's never a good idea."

Witold considered this but wanted to go anyway. It was a chance to see a part of the world they would never get to see otherwise. They could save some money and even have a baby when they came back. That last argument was persuasive, though Mania still had reservations. She was in no hurry to overthrow a life she was happy with to go adventuring in a place she knew little about. When she discussed it with her mother, she was surprised at how eagerly Krystyna and Tadeusz supported the idea. She had expected that her mother would be reluctant to let her only daughter go so far away, especially to Africa. She asked Krystyna if Witold's father had talked to her or Tadeusz, but could not get a straight answer. Instead Krystyna and Tadeusz extolled the benefits of travel and experience abroad. Mania got the impression that they weren't being truthful. Apparently Krystyna had come to the same conclusion as Witold's father, whether under his direct influence or not, Mania would never know. When she and Witold discussed this opportunity again, Mania agreed to go to Algiers even if there was an undercurrent of coerciveness in it.

Witold has fallen asleep over his reading. She removes the

journal from his hands, lays it on the night table and turns out both lights. *Tomorrow is another day,* she thinks, smiling at Krystyna's nightly mantra.

Maybe it will not be so bad. The things she still has to do in Krystyna's apartment are not fraught with as much emotional baggage as what she did today. When she is finished, she will have to start her search. First, she will check *Pan* Bojarski's file when she goes back to work to see if the village of his birth is listed. Then she will arrange a visit with *Pani* Glowacka followed by one with Sister Beatrice. Tracking down Aunt Irena will be the biggest challenge but she is ready for it.

Chapter 8

Róża, Pużniki and Stanisławów, June – August 1944

SOON, RÓŻA'S RELIEF that they had found a dry protected place – the cave in the hill at the edge of the forest – began to fade and the darkness of depression gradually replaced it. There was nothing to eat and whenever Marek ventured out to steal food from the surrounding villages and farms, she was convinced that he would not return. One day melted into another. Nothing mattered anymore. Her old life was gone. Her family was gone. There was no future. The sooner this interminable hiding ended, the better.

Lying on the dirt floor of the cave, she thought that it might be pleasant to die here. Her body could return to the earth from where it came. She imagined the cool earth covering every inch of skin, which now itched unbearably from the bites of lice, mosquitoes, and other unknown insects.

When Marek was not coming or going on his expeditions, he talked and talked in a low urgent voice. He was bound to find hidden Jews or partisans. It was only a matter of time. All they had to do was hang on a little longer. She knew he was trying to arouse her interest, but mostly she just listened to the tone and timbre of his voice, not the words. It was so soothing. She was tired of hanging on. Her body was beyond pain and her hunger was an omnipresent sensation of emptiness and cramping. She began to feel so light that she was sure she was floating near the top of the cave. From above, she looked down on her swollen legs and belly. It was strange to be so fat in those parts and yet have your ribs stick out on your chest, your arms like twigs, your skin hanging off the bones like empty sleeves.

When Marek brought her some berries from the forest, she could not swallow at first, even though Marek fed them one by one into her mouth. Eventually, they went down and coursed through her digestive system with gurgles and grunts until her insides exploded into diarrhoea. She had to drag herself out on all fours from the cave to relieve herself so frequently that it left her completely exhausted. When Marek came back with some bread and eggs, she was thankful that she had managed to keep them down and got some of her strength back.

One afternoon, they heard the voices of children approaching. Marek pushed Róża deeper into the cave and pulled the pine boughs over the opening. The children came closer as they spied the raspberry bushes right outside their hiding place. Their sweet young voices spoke Ukrainian, the language of those cruel soldiers who had almost killed them, and a chill crept up Róża's spine. She recognized her old friend, fear. Suddenly, their hiding place was flooded with sunlight as one of the children pulled away the pine branches, curious to see what was behind them. Over Marek's shoulder, Róża saw a pretty little girl of about ten with chestnut braids wound around her head. Her mouth opened in a perfect rosy circle.

"Look what I found!" she shouted. "There are Jews hiding here."

Róża's gaze locked onto a pair of shiny black eyes.

"Let's go tell!" the other girl said, coming up beside her.

As the two of them ran off, the child's breath and the heat of her young body lingered in the air. Róża pushed herself up against Marek and slid her arms around his waist, resting her face against his back. They would die together. That was a good way to go.

Marek peeled her fingers off and said, "We have to get out of here."

He climbed out of the cave and pulled her behind him, scrambling through the undergrowth of the woods. Scratched and bleeding, they fell, worn out, at the edge of the river. Marek looked around.

"I'm not sure where exactly we've ended up," he said, "but we can't hang around here. The Ukrainians are sure to find us. The children will bring them."

Marek trudged through the woods, pushing aside branches and undergrowth to make it easier for Róża to follow. Soon they arrived at a creek, perhaps even the same one that ran between the manor house and Irena's cottage and they stopped to drink and splash themselves with the cool, clean water. When Marek tried to drag Róża back up, she turned beseeching eyes to him and shook her head.

"I can't go on," she said in a feeble voice. "You go."

He was about to give her an argument, but recognizing that she was at the end of her endurance, he left her under the protection of a willow tree. Róża leaned back with a sigh. It would not be so bad to die here, either, listening to the ripple of the current, the twitter of the birds, and the rustle of the leaves in the breeze.

"Wake up, Róża." Marek was rubbing her hands. "Come on, we have to go."

"I thought I was dead," she said with disappointment. "I don't want to go anywhere."

"Stop it! I found my way back to Irena's place. I managed to persuade her to hide us for just a couple more days until you get your strength back and then we'll leave. Let's go."

Supporting her under the arm, he helped her crawl along the creek back toward the wooden planks that served as a bridge across the creek near Irena's cottage. They made many stops to allow Róża to rest. In the final leg of their journey, they crawled through the bushes into the garden around the back to Irena's yard, constantly on the lookout for anyone who could spot them. When Róża heard the children's voices coming from the shed, she knew that was not where Irena intended to hide them. Marek tapped on the back window and Irena came around to lead them to the tall grasses behind the outhouse and from there to a pile of straw, which she shoved aside, revealing the cold cellar underneath. It was just a simple excavation where she stored potatoes, and that was where she wanted them to hide.

"Fast! Fast!" she said, casting nervous glances around.

Marek backed in first with Róża on top of him. The space was too small for them to lie down side by side. For a second, it reminded her of one of their lovemaking positions in the early years of their marriage and a weak tremor went through the lower part of her belly and thighs. It amazed her that in her emaciated condition she could still feel aroused.

She lay her head in the crook of Marek's neck and whispered, "Am I too heavy for you?"

He tightened his arms around her and kissed her. "No."

In the meantime, Irena covered them over with the straw that stank of urine. They could hear her calling the children as she walked away.

That night they heard a group of German soldiers pounding on Irena's door. They commandeered a meal but did not stay the night. Ignorant of what lay beneath the pile of straw in the yard, they emptied their bladders over the heads of the fugitives. Róża began to gag at the stench and thought she would throw up, but burying her face deep into Marek's neck, she managed to stifle the urge by breathing in his yeasty, sweet odour mixed with the loamy smell of potatoes and earth.

Long before dawn, Irena came back, uncovered them and said, "You can't stay here. The Germans are coming through all the time now. I think they're in retreat. I've brought you some food to take with you back into the forest."

"We can't go back into the forest," Marek said. "If they're in retreat, they'll be coming through there, too. So will the Ukrainians on their way home. We'll get shot for sure."

She said, "But you can't stay here. You put us all in danger."

Róża could see how fear struggled with compassion in Irena's face as they sagged before her, barefoot, ragged, and shrunken.

Finally Irena said with a sigh, "All right. Go there, to the burnt-out manor house."

The sun had yet to come up and Róża could not even see the shadow of the manor house.

In a frightened whisper, she asked, "What happened to Krystyna and Mirka?"

Irena shook her head. "I don't know. They disappeared. I'm afraid they probably died in the fire."

Róża's hands flew to her mouth and she cried out, "Oh, no! Marek, I thought you said that you saw them run away. That they were safe."

Marek turned white. "I thought I did. I guess what I saw was just shadows." He enfolded her in his arms and the two of them held each other.

After a few minutes, Irena said, "There's no time to waste. You must go. Here, take the food." She handed them a cloth-wrapped bundle of bread and potatoes and left.

Marek took Róża's hand and coaxed her to follow him stealthily through the tall stalks of gain in the field to the creek. There they drank some water and rested for a while. Suddenly Róża felt a tremendous commotion in her insides and before she could stop herself, everything poured out of her. Marek was soon afflicted in the same way. They lay exhausted in their stench for some time.

"We didn't even eat any berries," she whispered through dry lips to Marek.

"It's from drinking the water from the creek where the German horses shit. Let's get out of here before it gets full light," Marek said.

The sun was beginning to rise above the horizon as Marek hoisted himself up and, pulling Róża's flaccid body up with him. He dragged her to the creek, where he first washed himself and then gently helped her to wash. The water was icy cold but it seemed to revive her. After splashing her face, she cupped her hands and was about to drink, when he slapped her hands away.

"No, you can't do that! Remember what just happened!"

"I don't care. I'm so thirsty," she said. "I want to die anyway."

"Do you want to die in pain? With cramps and diarrhoea?" Marek pinned her arms to her sides. "Let's try to reach the pump at the manor house."

She let him lead her across the plank bridge to the other side and up the hill to the pump. When Marek pushed down on the handle, brown rusty water gushed out of the spout.

"Wait," he said.

Soon pure, sparkling water followed and Róża held out her hands to catch some and bring it to her flaking lips. They both drank their fill before they realized that without any trees or bushes around it, the pump, like the manor house, sitting on a hill, was completely exposed now that it was full morning. The blackened remains of the house and barn were a few metres away and could provide shelter. Róża wondered how Irena's cottage had escaped the flames while the impressive manor house, home of the Stefanski family that Krystyna was supposed to be looking after while they were in England, had burned almost to the ground. God must have marked Irena's house for rescue. Her father used to say, "God's ways are not for man to understand." She certainly could not understand Him and His ways, but at least Halinka had been spared.

Marek said, "Come on, let's go. We have to hide before someone finds us."

Róża clung to him as they stumbled, like two crippled old people, around the back of the ruins to the garden where the berry bushes were thick and close to the garden wall. Beside the bushes was a large willow tree. Marek pushed through the waist-high grass and weeds and bushes and the tree's hair-like fronds to a natural shelter of tamped, bare earth.

"There are still lots of vegetables in the garden so we don't have to rely on the berries," Marek said.

Róża was too tired to care. Food was the last thing on her mind. Pain and fatigue overwhelmed her. She crumpled to the ground and cradling her head against Marek's shoulder, fell into a deep sleep. When she awoke, pale strings of light shone into their sanctuary. It was early dawn. She must have slept for a long time. Marek was gone. When she parted the bushes, she saw him in the garden. He came back with his pockets full of carrots, potatoes, onions, beans, and an old tin can of fresh water. At his urging, she took a few bites of the raw vegetables, but she found that her teeth had become too loose because of her poor diet, and so it was too difficult to chew the produce. That evening, Irena came with bread and cooked potatoes, which she was able to eat.

They continued in this fashion with only the weather changing every few days from sunshine to rain, when one clear, starry night Marek said, "I think the Germans are losing the war. We've been here about four weeks at least. The peasants are gathering the harvest. I predict that the Germans won't last the summer. The Russians are on the way!" Here Marek grabbed Róża and would have lifted her off her feet in exultation if she hadn't put a restraining arm on his shoulder.

"How can you tell?" Róża asked. "Maybe it's another false alarm like a couple of years ago."

Marek waved his hand dismissively. "The situation was completely different when the Germans attacked Stalingrad two years ago. I think they have been tremendously weakened since then. They wouldn't be trudging in retreat through the forest as Irena told us if they were still behaving like winners. Besides, I recognize the sounds of the airplanes overhead. And the gunfire. Those are Russian rockets that are lighting up the sky."

"How can you be sure?"

As planes rumbled overhead, he said, "I've made a study

of the different sounds of the German and Russian firepower. Those are Russian bombers, I can tell."

As the next few days and nights wore on, Marek listened to the gunfire and gently urged Róża back to life. He stroked her like a baby back into sleep if she awoke with a nightmare. In the daytime, he cajoled her into eating and drinking just a little bit more every day. He pointed out that they had not heard German soldiers stomping by in some time. He even crooned songs to her that they used to love dancing to.

"Remember how I used to step on your feet?" he asked. "You were such a wonderful dancer. I felt so bad that I was grateful to my friends who were eager to dance with you. I let them have the tangos and the foxtrots and the waltzes, but the slow dances, they were all for me and you. Your body against mine. You were so light on your feet that you barely touched the ground."

In this way, Marek managed to reach her, a tiny step at a time, until she even gave him a half smile.

One night, his arms tightened around her and she felt his breath in her ear. "Listen, Róża!"

There was the thudding of soldiers' boots. Her body went rigid. But when they heard the voices, Marek said, "It's the Russians! They've come!"

Róża lifted her head. She heard the musical quality of the Russian language and allowed it to warm her a little. Neither of them slept for the rest of the night as they listened to the planes overhead and bombs falling. Finally at dawn, they heard Irena's voice before they even saw her.

"Come out! Come out!" she called.

When they emerged from their hiding place, they saw her running toward the ruins of the manor, waving her arms, a big smile on her face.

"You're free!"

At first, not believing that she had heard right, Róża stared at Irena in silence. When Irena clapped her hands and said,

"It's true, you're free," Róża finally took in the full meaning of those words and her knees buckled. She fell to the earth with a cry of pent-up pain that echoed in the still morning air, even silencing the birds. For a while, the words spoken to her by Marek and Irena were an incomprehensible din of sound.

"Come on, darling." Marek was trying to pull her up. "Irena has brought us some food. Let's eat and get out of here. Irena thinks it's still dangerous for us to stay. Some of her neighbours may be angry if they find out she has been hiding Jews during the war."

Róża stumbled to her feet, her face devastated and bathed with tears. Her eyes imploring, she said, "I want to see my baby."

Irena gazed at Róża with pity and nodded. "I'll bring her here. I don't want the boys to see you. I don't know what they would say in the village if they did. They think of Halinka as ours, a part of our family. I don't know how they would react to seeing you embrace her."

She started to walk away and turned back for a moment. "Please don't be upset if she doesn't recognize you."

Later that day, while Róża paced impatiently and Marek tried to keep her calm, Irena returned with Halinka in tow. The child was chattering away until she saw Róża and Marek. Róża knelt on the ground holding out her arms to her. When she saw Halinka's eyes cloud over, she tried to imagine the picture she presented to the little girl: a ravaged face, an emaciated body clad in rags, a wild woman's eyes.

She dropped her arms, but called out softly, "Come to Mama, sweetheart."

Clinging to Irena's leg and pointing, Halinka said, "Mama? Who's that?"

"Go to the nice lady," Irena said and gently guided the child to Róża, who wrapped her arms around the rigid little body, covering her face in kisses and nuzzling her soft neck. Halinka turned her head to Irena and with a push, freed herself from Róża's grasp. She ran back to Irena.

"Mama! That lady scares me."

Irena picked her up. She looked apologetically at Róża. "I'm sorry. I told you she wouldn't recognize you. Two and a half years is a long time."

Róża got up from the ground, wiped her eyes on her arm and nodded. "I know. But it hurts just the same."

At this point Marek, who had been standing in the background, approached Halinka and smiled. The child's eyes widened with horror and she emitted a shriek. "Mama, *kto ten dziad?*"

Irena said, "It's not an old beggar, *kochana;* it's a man who knows you and loves you."

As Marek reached out a hand to pat the child, Halinka began to shake her head and whimper, "*Nie! Nie! Nie!*"

Róża looked from her husband to Irena, wringing her hands. What was this freedom to her if she could not get her child back?

Marek stepped back. He said, "I can understand the poor child's afraid of me. I look a fright. Why don't you look after her for another little while, Irena? We'll go back to the city, get cleaned up, get settled, and we'll come get her in a couple of weeks."

Róża could not tear her eyes from Halinka. She watched Irena walk away with her and would not budge until she discerned that the door of Irena's cottage had been closed. Then she let Marek lead her to the creek where they washed up. They ate the food Irena had left for them and departed the village, skirting the main road. Once they were well away, they began their trek to Stanisławów. The pebbles dug into Róża's feet, and they had to stop frequently as she became easily tired. She wished that she had those old boots of Vładek's that Irena had given her on her first night, but when they ran into the forest the night of the fire, she had left them behind. Irena had made no mention of the boots when they came back. She had probably kept them for her older boy, who was growing like a weed. Marek, too, was barefoot. He was gaunt, with a thick bushy beard that had a grey streak right down the middle. His hair was long and also streaked with grey. No wonder Halinka was frightened of him. Washing in the creek had not done much to improve his appearance. He had picked up a thick stick along the way and used it as a cane. As he limped along, he looked like a prophet from the Bible, who might, at any moment, wave his staff and predict, with a booming voice, that the world was coming to an end. *Maybe it is,* Róża thought grimly. It certainly did not look promising to her.

Considering all she had lost, she did not know how she could ever live a normal life again among Ukrainians and Poles after what they had done to help the Nazi murderers. As they trudged along, her thoughts floated free, settling in a dark place within her. This was not the kind of person she used to be. Everyone used to say how Róża was a party girl, always fun to be with, cheerful, optimistic, and enthusiastic. She had organized the best scouting events. But that girl was gone forever. Even the young mother with the modern attitude to child-rearing was gone; the teacher whom the students loved because she could make math fun and understandable was gone. And who was this in her place? A bereft madwoman, a stranger. She let Marek drag her along as she put one foot in front of the other, with no awareness of where they were going or what they were passing.

They began to meet other survivors on the road trickling out of the woods. One bedraggled group of four told them that they had tried to join the Polish partisans but the partisans would not have them. They were also from Stanisławów and had been led by a formidable Jewish woman, a chemist from the leather factory. She had been shot by Nazis combing through the forest, as had most of their compatriots. When Róża heard where they were from, she came to life momentarily and asked about any news they may have had of her family. Marek asked too. Only one name was familiar to them – a distant cousin of Róża's, a member of their group who had been one of those killed.

With all her family gone, Róża could not imagine what festivals and holidays would be like. As for imagining thousands murdered and buried in the Jewish cemetery and thousands more taken to the death camp of Belzec, these numbers were too staggering for comprehension. Only the stragglers they met, the remnants who had survived in the forest in hiding, or on Aryan papers, were real.

Further along the road two more shadows emerged from the woods. One was a man from a neighbouring town. He had no idea how far away he had wandered. When he and his family were transported to Belzec, he and another man had managed to detach two boards from the cattle car, providing them with a narrow opening through which they could squeeze and jump. He had urged his wife and children to follow him and had gone first to show them how. A few others had gone after him, but the members of his family must have lost their nerve because he never saw them again. When the train had disappeared around a bend, he had crawled and limped through the bushes in the same direction, looking for them without success.

The other person was a young woman who had lived on a prosperous farm with her parents and eight brothers and sisters. She had not been there when the Nazis came to their farm. Once she returned and saw the dead bodies of her family, she ran for protection to the local priest, who took pity on her and hid her in his cellar. Eventually, she was discovered and raped repeatedly by German soldiers. They had left her for dead and killed the priest. After she had come to, she continued to live in the priest's house, surviving on the bit of food remaining there. But someone must have seen her because she heard a search party coming the night that she ran away into the woods.

These horrible stories dragged Róża further down as they wandered through an eternal night, regardless of the golden sun above and the greenery of the fields and trees on either side of the road. When they reached the town of Monasteszyska, they found that a Jewish committee had already been created to help survivors. They listed their names and those whom they were looking for, without any hope of finding anyone. The committee had set up a soup kitchen where Róża and Marek had their first real meal in years. They were unable to eat their fill as their stomachs had shrunk. Marek vomited up most of what he had eaten while Róża's throat closed up and her stomach cramped after only a few spoonfuls of soup and a piece of bread. The committee had also opened a clothing depot, with articles that must have been left behind by the Nazis in their haste to evacuate. The survivors were able to cover their nearly naked bodies with whatever they needed. Róża and Marek found shoes. It would be a relief not to feel the piercing stones on the road any more. He also got a suit, which hung shapelessly on his emaciated body, while she got a sweater and a dress, also much too big for her. A belt to cinch around her waist with an extra hole pierced beyond the smallest one completed her outfit.

Without any mirrors, Róża and Marek examined each other and pronounced that they looked presentable enough to head off to Stanisławów to see what remained of their home. The group who had trudged down the road together separated, going in different directions. Even the only other person from their town did not accompany them.

"I have nothing and no one there anymore," he said, "except nightmarish memories. I'm heading for Wroclaw and when the war ends soon in the rest of Europe, I will be on the first boat from Hamburg to America. I have a brother there, in New York. Maybe I can put all of this behind me."

Marek and Róża wished him well and envied the possibility of a new start. They got a lift part of the way in a farmer's cart and then a Russian transport truck full of soldiers picked them up and took them right into the market square in Stanisławów.

When the driver of the lorry let them off, the soldiers shouted, "Good luck" to them.

Róża gazed around the square in amazement. It was like a time warp. Stores and apartment buildings stood as before, including her father's hardware store on the corner. People went about their business, women with shopping baskets, men in suits and hats. They seemed untouched by the war. She began to doubt her own senses. Perhaps it had all been a terrible nightmare, or, perhaps this was a mirage. But no, Marek's arm was real when he nudged her to walk toward their street, as were the cobblestones beneath her worn feet. Every few steps she stopped to blink and gawk like tourist.

It became obvious that people were not used to seeing bedraggled people like her and Marek on the street by how they stared and then turned away with distaste as if it offended them to see such depravity. They were no longer the respected citizens they had once been. On their own street, a neighbour, carrying her shopping bag came toward them, took a look at them, and quickly crossed to the other side, eyes lowered.

"*Pani* Majewska," Róża called out. "Don't you recognize me? It's Róża Bromberg."

The woman stopped and examined them for what seemed like a long time before she said, "*Pani* Bromberg? *Pan* Bromberg? What are you doing back? We thought you were all dead."

"Well, as you can see, we aren't," Róża said.

"Sorry to disappoint you," Marek muttered.

"You'll find that your apartment is occupied," *Pani* Majewska said. "Good day. I wish you well," she mumbled and scurried into her front door.

Sure enough, when they reached their apartment and knocked on the door, *Pan* Romanyuk, the caretaker of the building, came to open it and stood gaping at them.

"We're back," Marek said.

"Fanka, come quick," the caretaker called in a panic to his wife, who came forward wiping her hands on her apron.

"*Bozhe miy!*" she said. "We thought you were dead."

"As you can see, we're not," Marek said again. Róża wondered how many times they would have to repeat this over the next few days. So far, she had detected no welcoming warmth for their return. She suspected that this would be the prevailing tone of all their former so-called friends and neighbours. After all, they had all disappeared or made a hasty retreat or stood watching as they had been herded into the ghetto.

Pan Romanyuk and his wife turned their backs to confer in rapid whispers, leaving Róża and Marek standing in the hallway. When they turned around, *Pani* Romanyuk said, "I'm very sorry to tell you that when you didn't return, the Soviet authorities gave us this apartment. We have a certificate. It's all official."

Marek said, "I think it was the Germans who allowed you to take over our home and the Soviets let you stay because you lied and said that you've always lived here."

The colour rose in *Pan* Romanyuk's face. "Now see here! We didn't know you were coming back! We are the official tenants and if you want to do something about it, you'll have to deal with the authorities. We don't intend to move."

Pani Romanyuk stepped in front of her husband and said in a conciliatory tone, "Why don't you come in and I can make you something to eat."

Peering over her shoulder, Róża could see her mother-in-law's mahogany dining room table, chairs, and china cabinet. She said, "And will you serve us on our own dining-room table?"

Pani Romanyuk got flustered and twisted her hands around her apron. "We paid you for that. You sold it to us, in case you've forgotten."

Marek said, "No, I haven't forgotten. Nor have I forgotten the price – a fraction of its true worth."

Pan Romanyuk shoved aside his wife and stepped closer to face Marek. "We did good by you, as the Lord is my witness. We didn't have any more money. And we didn't give you up to the Gestapo like a lot of other people who gave up the Jews."

"That's true," Marek said, putting an arm around his wife's shoulders and turning away. "Thank you for the offer of food. We won't be troubling you anymore."

Without Marek's prodding, Róża would have remained rooted to the spot. They went down the stairs in silence. Although she knew Marek was right to back off, that there was nothing they could do, she seethed at the injustice.

Back out on the main street, they saw *Pan* Barylski in front of his shop, Barylski's Menswear.

"Do you see?" Marek asked Róża. "He's wearing my suit and hat!"

Peering closely at the man, Róża recognized the suit, unless it was an excellent copy. Marek had had it tailored in the latest fashion from Paris for *Rosh Hashana*, the Jewish New Year. He had sold it back to the tailor at a fraction of its value. There were not many double-breasted, dark grey cashmere suits among the shopkeepers in town, Róża was sure. *Pan* Barylski squinted at them for a moment in disbelief. Then, he quickly tipped his hat and scurried inside.

"A little warm for a cashmere suit, wouldn't you say?" Marek said to Róża.

They walked on until they came to a small house on a modest lane, leading off from the market square. Marek knocked on the door. A short, plump woman with a neat bun of salt-and-pepper grey hair answered. Her face was unlined and her cheeks were pink. She wore orthopaedic shoes and a navy blue, long-sleeved dress. For almost a minute all she could do was stare at them open-mouthed.

Finally, she said, "The young Master? I cannot believe it."

"Yes, Ewa. It's really me."

The woman clasped him in her arms. It struck Róża that now Ewa could encircle his frame easily, whereas in the past she could not have done so. Her joy at seeing them was a balm to Róża's tortured soul. At least one person was happy to see them back alive. Ewa had had a long history with Marek's family. She had been Marek's *mamka*, or wet nurse, and the bond established so long ago had endured. Well-to-do women like Róża's mother-in-law had employed wet nurses for all of their babies. Now, Ewa lived alone as all her children were grown and living elsewhere. Before the war, Marek had visited her regularly, bringing her a trinket or a treat like a box of chocolates or a small bottle of *eau de cologne*. They had not gone to her for help in the early days of the war because her home was close to the police station.

Ewa and Marek held each other for a long time. Then, wiping tears from her eyes with a hankie that she fished out of a pocket in her dress, she released him and held him at arm's length, subjecting him to close scrutiny.

Ewa said, "What have those devils done to you, my dears? Come, I must feed you."

While she prepared scrambled eggs, Ewa brought them up-to-date on what had happened to other family members. She had heard that one young cousin of Róża's had escaped from the ghetto and was making his way to Australia or America. No one else had been heard from, and, her voice breaking, she suspected that they were all dead. Putting the eggs on the table with fresh bread and butter, she began making a pot of coffee.

Róża was numb at the extent of their losses, but soon hunger overcame sorrow. She said, "Thank you, Ewa. This is delicious."

Marek asked, "Where do you get this good food? Aren't there food shortages?"

"Ah, you didn't see the bare shelves in the stores, and the line-ups for milk, butter, and eggs are long. As for meat, people are lucky if they find one scrap a week. But I am only a single person and my needs are few."

"What about war damage? Everything looks like it did before."

"We were not bombed. Only the Jewish quarter, where the ghetto was located, is in ruins."

They stayed with Ewa for a week while they looked for work. This was not difficult for Marek. The Soviet regime needed pharmacists and he found employment immediately. First he had to shave off his beard and get his hair cut, which exposed the pallor of his sunken cheeks and exaggerated the prominence of his dark eyes and aquiline nose. As luck would have it, the pharmacy had a room beside it, which they could equip with some cheap furniture and make a little home for themselves.

The only thing that kept Róża going was the thought of getting Halinka back. It was on her mind day and night. As soon as they settled into their room, she wrote to Irena to say that they were coming on an early morning train to the village several days later. As they walked down the road to Irena's house, Róża could feel curious eyes on her, adding to the nervous churning in her stomach and the speculation spinning around in her head: *What if Halinka won't come with us? What if Irena won't let her go? What if Irena demands more money than we have? What if the boys are hostile?*

Once they arrived at Irena's cottage, they found her welcoming them with a smile, and the boys and Halinka were dressed in their Sunday clothes. Their cheeks looked as if they had been polished. Halinka's curls glinted in the sunlight.

Róża and Marek brought in bags of provisions for Irena and presents for her and the children. Although every cell in Róża's body ached to envelop Halinka in her arms, she held back to let the child get used to her. Halinka stayed close to Irena's legs, hiding her face shyly whenever Róża smiled at her. While Marek told Irena how they had got themselves settled back in town and were looking forward to taking their daughter home with them, Róża pulled out cake and cookies from her bags. The boys looked on with greedy eyes. They had grown and an air of menace, real or imagined, seemed to emanate from them.

The first sign of trouble came when Irena said, "I don't

know if Halinka will go with you. She is very attached to me. To the boys, too."

With an edge in her voice, Róża said, "She has to come home with us." She wanted to add, *You selfish woman! You have two sons! She's the only one I have left.* Irena could not understand her losses in a million years.

She finished taking out food that she had brought: meat, cheese, bags of barley and oats and other staples that she knew Irena could use. Then, she turned to another large bag and pulled out presents: a new shawl for Irena, shoes for the boys, and a big doll for Halinka.

Róża held the doll out to her daughter. "See her eyes? They open and close. She has rosy cheeks like you. Her hair is brown and curly like yours. Do you like her pretty red dress with the white apron?"

The child looked on with fascination.

"Go, take it, Halinka," Irena said. "The dolly is for you."

Halinka approached Róża and reached out for the doll. She was completely mesmerized. She had never seen anything like this before. Watching her, Róża was on the verge of tears. It was amazing to see how an inanimate object could mean so much to a child.

"Would you like to give your dolly a name?" Róża asked.

Halinka nodded and thought for a moment. Then she said, "Zosia."

"That's a lovely name," Róża said.

While the boys were trying on their shoes and Halinka played with her doll, Róża helped Irena prepare lunch. It was like the occasional festive meal she remembered inhaling jealously up in the attic – thick pea soup, potatoes, farmer's cheese and fresh bread. They sat around the table to eat: Róża and Marek on the only two chairs at each end, the boys on the bench on one side, and Halinka and Irena on the bench on the opposite side. When they finished, Róża slipped Irena some money and thanked her for her help, knowing it was not much, but it was all they had. She asked if she and Marek could take Halinka for a walk to get acquainted. It chafed that she had to ask permission to take her own child, but she did not want to create a scene. It was better to have Irena's co-operation. The little girl took Zosia and the three of them walked into the village. They saw the train tracks in the distance and Róża's eyes lit up. She let go of Halinka's hand and let her skip ahead of them.

"Marek," she whispered, "I can't take much more of this. I want to go home."

Marek sighed and nodded. "All right. If we hurry and take the child back to Irena, we may be able to catch an earlier train than we planned."

"No, I want to take her with us now."

Marek stopped in the road. "What are you saying? We can't do that. She'll cry and scream."

"She'll do that whenever we take her. Might as well be now. Just leave it to me."

"But she'll want to say good-bye to Irena and the boys. How can we repay that good woman by snatching the child?"

Róża grabbed her husband's arm and pulled him along. "We paid her with all we had. We can send her more money. The child is ours. We have every right to take her. Our timing is perfect. I can hear the train, can't you?"

Seeing indecision in Marek's face, she said, "If you try to stop me, I'll throw myself under the train."

They hurried forward and caught up with Halinka. Róża took her hand. "Let's go see the train."

"I like trains." Halinka trotted beside her.

At the station, Marek bought their tickets, while Róża sat on the bench on the platform and chatted with the little girl. There were no other people boarding at this stop.

"Do you think Zosia likes trains, too?" Róża asked.

Halinka put her head close to the doll's and replied, "She says, 'Yes'."

"Good. Then maybe we can go inside and go for a ride. Wouldn't that be fun?"

Halinka's eyes opened wide at the prospect of this adventure. She nodded.

"Can Mama and Andrej and Staszek come, too?"

"No, they're too late. See? The train is here already. Just think of what you can tell them afterwards."

This satisfied the little girl and she allowed Marek to lift her aboard and to settle her by the window, where she could watch the countryside fly by in utter amazement until she fell asleep.

"I think there'll be hell to pay when we get her home," Marek said.

Róża could not stop smiling. "I'll deal with it, don't worry. I'll write to Irena right away and send her more money to thank her for everything she's done for us. I haven't got a job yet, so I'll devote myself to making Hanka happy."

Already, Halinka had become her Hanka again. Already, Róża was planning the next step: to leave Poland far behind and to make a new home somewhere else.

Chapter 9

Mania, Warsaw, December 2005

MANIA WOULD LIKE TO cancel Christmas this year. With her mother gone, it will be a sad occasion. Mostly, though, she has to do it for Anna. She cannot disappoint the child. So, she sits in the kitchen with a pad of paper and a pen, and makes lists of the things she has to do. On the counter, she has laid out pans, rolling pin, cookie cutters, and other baking tools that she has brought back from Krystyna's kitchen. Just looking at it all and the blank page before her makes her tired. What an effort it takes to push back the grief every time she thinks of the hours she and her mother spent together in the kitchen. And the hole in the circle around the dinner table will be unbearable.

In recent years, Mania would start arguing with her mother weeks before Christmas over how much work Krystyna would do in advance. Mania had wanted to take over the cooking to spare her mother, but Krystyna would not hear of it. Every year she had only had to bake cookies and make a salad or two. Krystyna had done the rest. Mania had tried to help in other, less obvious ways, like peeling potatoes, chopping vegetables, and shopping for ingredients. In short, she had been present in Krystyna's kitchen as much as possible during the preparation period and acted as general helper and *sous-chef*.

Now she will have to do the *Wigilia,* the special twelve-course dinner on Christmas Eve, on her own. It is high time that Marysia started to take on more of the responsibility. But, since she does not live nearby, she cannot even be here as a helper. Anyway, her daughter's strengths do not lie in the kitchen. If asked, she will bring things she can buy and not prepare anything herself. *And what's wrong with that?* a voice says in Mania's head, to which she replies, *It's just not the same.* Store-bought food never tastes as good as homemade. The idea that you can get ready for Christmas Eve without effort borders on sacrilege, never mind the associated guilt. *The chain of tradition will be broken soon enough*, Mania thinks wryly, *when I'm dead and gone. I've become part of the generation standing next in line for death.* She is also a member of the last generation of Poles who grew up before commercialization and materialism crept in around religious holidays and so she feels a responsibility to stay true to the old ways.

Picking up her pen, Mania makes lists: one for cleaning, washing, and polishing; one for shopping; and, one for the menu for the traditional meatless *Wigilia* meal. All of this has to fit around her work duties at the clinic. How had Mama got everything done without ever making a single list, even when she was still employed at the factory? Mania considers hiring someone for the cleaning. It is not the same as not doing the baking and cooking yourself. She decides against it. If Mama could do it, she can too. Besides, she needs to keep busy, to keep her mind occupied, rather than dwelling on Krystyna's last words. She has to banish the image of Krystyna's face as she lay on her deathbed. Whenever the sight of her mother's lifeless face, the blue eyes forever dulled, pops up before her unexpectedly, she is frozen in time. It takes effort to shake herself free of the image and to get back on track with what she is doing.

It has always been important to her to make Christmas a joyous time for Marysia and now also for Anna because it was not much fun for Mania when she was a child. The only enjoyable part was baking with Mama. She had particularly loved the process of kneading *chałka,* letting it rise, and then braiding it. Mama had always let her have her own small piece of dough to shape as a miniature replica of the larger loaf. Now, she would continue this tradition with Anna. With limited resources, Mama had not been able to afford the traditional twelve-course meal, but even a piece of chocolate, a costly treat in those days, had symbolically served as one course.

The Christmas she and Mama spent with Aunt Antonia and Uncle Feliks in Wroclaw in 1943, before they came to Warsaw, was the worst ever. Aunt Antonia and Uncle Feliks were childless and their home was not a welcoming place for Mania. Every surface was either covered with a doily, a china figurine, a crystal dish, or some other fragile knick-knack. Aunt Antonia watched Mania's every move.

Uncle Feliks was a mouse of a man, permanently hunched over. Though he did not have the courage to stand up to his wife on most things, he regarded Mania with kind brown eyes and a warm smile, much to Antonia's displeasure. He worked in an office at the city hall and took his lunch with him. This was grudgingly prepared by Antonia and wrapped in a clean white cloth. Her aunt scrubbed and polished floors and furniture all day even though she had already scrubbed and polished them the day before.

During the Christmas preparations, Uncle Feliks made himself scarce in the evenings by staying late at the office and on Saturdays by going to the library. Mania went with him as often as she could get out of helping around the house. These were the only pleasant times during that visit: sitting beside her uncle at a long wooden table, each of them immersed in a book.

Because the apartment had only two rooms and a kitchen, Mania and her mother had to sleep together on the couch in the front room. There was nowhere to go to avoid her aunt or to be by herself. Antonia complained at every opportunity, even when Mania was on her best behaviour.

One day Antonia burst out, "Can't you keep that child quiet?"

"But she is being quiet," Krystyna said. Mania was sitting at the kitchen table, drawing a picture on a piece of brown paper.

"Tell her to stop that infernal humming."

Mania did not understand what she had done to cause her aunt's face to twist with rage. She was not aware that she had been humming.

Antonia said under her breath, "She behaves just like a Jew brat."

Mama's face turned red. She raised her hand as if to strike Aunt Antonia, but she stopped it in mid-air. "You're a spiteful and jealous woman," Mama said, tightlipped.

The tension between her mother and her aunt was as taut as a wire about to snap, until Antonia dropped her eyes, turned on her heel, and stomped off into her bedroom, slamming the door behind her. Mania was shaking. It was her fault. Mama had fought with her sister because of her. She gathered up her paper and pencil and curled up in the corner of the sofa, trying to make herself invisible. She heard her mother hiss at Antonia's back, but she could not make out the words. Antonia did not speak directly to Mania for the rest of their stay.

That night Mania asked her mother as she snuggled up next to her, "What is a Jew, Mama?"

"That's a person who isn't Christian. They don't go to church like we do. They don't believe in our Lord Jesus Christ."

Mania gasped. "Ooh, then they're bad, aren't they, Mama? Will they burn in Hell?"

"No, they're not bad, sweetheart. They just … well, they've just taken the wrong path. Our Lord is merciful to those who know not what they do."

"Do you know any Jew people, Mama?"

"I used to work for a Jewish family. They were very good to me."

"Why did Aunt Antonia call me one?"

"Because it's the worst insult she could think of. She's jealous that she doesn't have a beautiful daughter like I do. Now go to sleep."

Mania still did not understand why her aunt was so angry with her but when Mama kissed her and wrapped her arms around her, she felt safe and fell asleep. After that incident, she kept out of her aunt's way. When helping Mama bake, she was careful not to spill a single speck of flour on the floor. She polished every pot, pan, and bowl that Mama washed until they shone and put them away exactly where they belonged. But nothing she did softened Aunt Antonia's scowl.

Now the ringing of the timer on the oven reminds Mania to take out a pan of cookies. She calls Witold and asks if he is ready for tea and a snack. When he agrees, she carries a tray with two mugs and a small plate of warm cookies into the living room. Witold comes out of his study to join her.

"A preview of the goodies for Christmas," she says, laying the tray on the coffee table.

"Mmmmm, I love the aroma of baking almost as much as I love eating the result," Witold says. They sit down, each with a mug of steaming brew and bite into the crunchy sweets.

"Did I tell you about the miserable Christmas Mama and I spent with Aunt Antonia and Unlce Feliks?" Mania asks. The empty, achy feeling of that time comes back to her now and she stuffs another cookie in her mouth. *That memory is not good for my diet*, Mania thinks.

Witold nods and says, "She was never softened by the Christmas spirit, was she?"

"No. Can you imagine being hungry when you're supposed to be having a twelve-course meal? There was food; I was just afraid to eat it. Antonia eyed every morsel I put in my mouth. The only thing I enjoyed was going to church and spending Saturday afternoons at the library with my uncle."

"Maybe they couldn't afford to have two extra people living with them."

"What do you mean? Mama paid for our keep! She turned over almost her whole paycheque from the coat factory to Antonia."

"She sounds like a bitter woman. I wonder if she was traumatized in childhood. You don't know much about your mother and her sisters when they were little, do you?"

"No, I don't," Mania says. "But I can understand why Mama never wanted to have anything to do with her."

Mania shakes off the memory of Antonia's harsh face, and remembers those Christmases past when they would get invited to friends. At a table with a full set of parents, children, and grandparents who had no relationship to her, Mania had felt like a misfit. Even the Glowackis had invited them when Mama worked for them. Their son, Benedykt, was close to Mania's age. She had hoped to experience a real *Wigilia* at their home, but she was disappointed. She and Mama had been the only guests and Major Glowacki presided at the head of a formal and subdued dinner. The only fun had been when Benedykt stole sideways glances at her and made faces. When she could not suppress a giggle, the Major had asked if she could share with the rest of them what was so funny. Her face had flamed but she could not tattle on Benedykt, who sat solemnly beside her eating his dinner.

Mama could not have enjoyed those dinners too much either, since *Pani* Glowacka had still expected her to act as a housekeeper, not a full guest, and to do all of the serving and cleaning up. Though they had been invited to the Glowackis even after Mama no longer worked there, by then they had started to have their own *Wigilia* with their own traditions and customs and with their own guests. Sister Beatrice, who was far from her family, and an orphan girl who boarded at the convent school, had joined them. Then, when Major Glowacki died, his widow had come to them, too, because Benedykt had moved to England and did not return for Christmas.

Since their family has grown, Christmas has become filled with the traditions that Mania and her mother developed over the years. On the day before Christmas, Marysia, Jerzy, and Anna arrive at noon, announcing that they want to help to prepare the food and the decorations. Mania has been working frantically to finish her preparations in time. She wants to say that if they really had wanted to help, they should have come a day or two earlier, but she holds her tongue in respect for family harmony. Witold and Jerzy carry their bags into the bedroom in which Marysia grew up, while Mania hugs and kisses Anna and helps her off with her winter clothes.

Heading into the kitchen, Marysia says, "Is there anything to eat? We've had a long drive and we're hungry."

Witold says, "When have you ever had to ask if there's anything to eat in your mother's house?"

He leads them to the table and Mania brings out hard boiled eggs, cheese, bread, tomatoes and cucumbers. Witold makes coffee and gives a glass of milk to Anna. They finish their lunch with a *babka* full of raisins that Mania baked the day before.

"Now that you've fed us, Mama, we're ready to work," Marysia says.

"Why don't you clean up the lunch dishes and Anna and I will make the *chałka*? I've been saving it until you came, Anna."

Mania wraps her granddaughter in one of her aprons for their special task together. On the little girl, the apron reaches down to the floor. She lets Anna measure the flour and the water and break eggs into a bowl. When the dough is mixed, Anna helps with the kneading and then they set the dough aside to rise.

Anna skips off to help Witold and Jerzy decorate the tree with apples, oranges, candies, and nuts wrapped in colourful paper and aluminum foil, just as they have done every year. Anna adds some of her own creations – chains made from coloured paper and a string of cut-out felt reindeer. Jerzy hangs some hand-blown glass ornaments on high branches and the two of them drape thin strips of clear paper – "angel's hair,"

Anna proclaims – over everything. Witold gets a stepladder to secure the silver angel on the top of the tree. Mania takes a break from the kitchen to admire their handiwork and is full of love and contentment watching her little family.

When it is time to finish the *chałka*, Mania pulls off a piece of dough for Anna and shows her how to braid it. She coats the large and small breads with beaten egg yolk and puts them into the oven. While the bread bakes, Mania takes out a serving platter, covers it with a white cotton napkin, and lays some straw (a reminder of the stable of Christ's birth), evergreen sprigs, and *oplatki* on it. Marysia then covers the table with a cloth that Krystyna had embroidered with a delicate pattern of tiny flowers. Together, they lay out the best china, cutlery, and crystal.

That evening, decked out in their holiday clothes, everyone sits in the living room with glasses of wine, cognac, and *krupnik*, except Anna, who has a glass of raspberry-flavoured soda water. Mania feels the warmth of the honeyed vodka as it goes down, which helps to keep her sadness at bay at Krystyna's absence. She asks Witold for a refill. The windows, the decorations on the tree, and the candles on the table seem to have an extra sparkle this year, as if they are in a conspiracy to cheer her up. Carols from the CD player fill the apartment with a holiday atmosphere, while tantalizing aromas waft in from the kitchen. The first knock on the door is from *Pani* Glowacka.

"Happy Christmas!" the old lady says, handing Mania a plate of strudel, the filling of apples and raisins oozing out of its paper-thin crust. This has been her annual contribution to the Christmas Eve dinner.

Sister Beatrice arrives shortly afterwards, bundled up in overcoat and woollen hat and scarf. Her cheeks are rosy from the cold since she has walked from the convent. Unless she is in an emergency situation, it is unthinkable for the nun to take a taxi, and she had vehemently refused Witold's offer to pick her up even though she is now close to ninety. She hands a bag of tangerines to Mania.

After their guests have had a chance to nibble at some nuts and crackers with olive tapinade – Marysia's recent innovation to their *Wigilia* celebrations – Mania invites everyone to sit down at the table. For several moments they stand undecided as to what they should do with Krystyna's chair at the head of the table. Mania had set a place for her and refuses to move the chair away. Conscious of the absence in their midst, they join hands and say "Grace" before starting their festive meal.

As she clears dishes between courses and brings in more food, refusing offers of help, Mania secretly refills her glass with *krupnik*. Gradually, her face takes on a pink glow and she is able to relax. Over dessert and drinks, they sing Christmas carols but, by then, she is too tired and fuzzy-headed to sing along. When it is time to dress and go to church for midnight mass, Mania can barely raise herself out of her chair, but once out on the street, the crisp night air revives her. She is happy to have Witold's arm for support as they join the stream of other families heading in the same direction. Christmas Eve and Good Friday are the only times that he accompanies her to church.

The next morning, Mania wakes with a headache and sits with a cup of coffee as she watches her family members open their presents. Anna is thrilled with her new bicycle and a doll with a full wardrobe. The adults have given each other books, scarves, and sweaters. Mania smiles with pleasure at the beautiful emerald pendant Witold gives her and fastens it around her neck. Then Mania takes Anna to church again. She is secretly happy that nobody else wants to go to the service with her. She can have Anna all to herself. Sitting next to her granddaughter in the pew, she immerses herself in the service.

Back at home, Mania tells her daughter about her plans to seek out Krystyna's sisters, especially Irena.

"How will you find them?" Marysia asks.

"I'll talk to Sister Beatrice and *Pani* Glowacka. One of my patients told me he was from the same village as Krystyna and Irena. The name of the village is Puźniki but I can't find it on the map. It was probably wiped out by the Ukrainians. I'll try to search the Internet for information about the displaced Poles from Ukraine "

"It seems like a time-consuming project without much hope of pay off."

Mania is surprised at her daughter's lack of enthusiasm for her plans. "Aren't you interested in your roots?"

"Not particularly. It's like a fad now. Everybody's into genealogy. What's the point? I'm more interested in the life around me today."

Mania shakes her head. "You sound like *Babcia*."

"She was a smart woman. I don't think she'd approve of your obsession with what happened to her sisters. If she'd wanted to keep in touch with them, she would have done it long ago."

Mania's holiday contentment evaporates. She is annoyed that Marysia has the gall to present herself as the interpreter of Krystyna's wishes.

"You don't know what you're talking about. Mama told me she wanted me to find them and I will."

They finish lunch in an uncomfortable silence until Witold says, "Let's clean up and go out for a walk. I challenge Anna to a game of dominoes when we come back!"

Marysia and her family stay for a few more days after Christmas before leaving for Krakow. At first, the apartment seems empty but soon Mania enjoys the resumption of her quiet life. One late afternoon when it is Witold's night to work at the hospital, Mania invites *Pani* Glowacka over for a cup of tea. The old lady is delighted to accept. Mania puts the kettle on and lays out two cups and leftover cookies from Christmas.

"You are looking well, my dear," the old lady says, helping herself to three cookies. "I've been worried about you, going back to work so soon after you put so much effort into preparing for Christmas. Without your mother here, the whole burden was on your shoulders. It cannot have been easy. So much to do!"

"I welcomed it. I forget to miss my mother when I'm busy."

"She was a wonderful woman. And you were a wonderful daughter. You were her whole world, you know."

"We were very close." Mania tries to control the tremor in her voice.

"You're lucky to have a husband to lean on. Your mother was like me – a widow. Children can never make up for the companionship of a husband."

Mania feels guilty that she has not been more generous with her time to her lonely neighbour. Even now, she has only invited her because she wants information about her mother.

"That's true. Witold has been a great help. You must have missed the Major a lot when he died," she says.

"I still do. When he left me, I didn't think I would ever get over it. But life goes on."

"It must be hard with your son and his family in England. You don't have any family here, do you?" It seems to Mania that Krystyna had been *Pani* Glowacka's only friend.

"I had an older brother, but when he died, his wife never contacted me and my nieces and nephews are no better than strangers," she says.

"I'm so sorry. Not having any relatives when I grew up, I find it hard to understand when family members become estranged." After a pause, she asks, "Did Mama ever talk to you about her sisters?"

"Your mother was a very private person, but I do know that she had two sisters."

"Do you know anything about her childhood home and family?"

Pani Glowacka stares for a moment into her tea as if the answer lies in its amber depths. "I believe she came from a village that is now in the Ukraine."

"Yes, I know. A patient of mine told me that he knew her and her sister there. Mama never spoke of it."

"How strange that your mother didn't share stories about her childhood with you. One of the regrets of my life is that I never had a daughter. I love my son dearly, but I wish I'd had a daughter to share confidences with."

"It is special to have a daughter," Mania agrees, feeling some resentment that Mama had not taken more advantage of the opportunity for sharing. "Did Mama tell you anything at all about her family?"

"I'll tell you what I can, but at my age my memory is not so good any more, especially when it comes to names."

Mania sits forward in her chair. "I'll appreciate anything you can tell me."

Pani Glowacka settles back in her chair and seems to weigh her words carefully as she says, "As you know, my husband had an important position in the previous regime. In those days, because your mother worked for us, she had to have a security clearance. The Major had access to sources not available to most people. He found out that your mother came from a respectable farming family. I believe that both her parents died during the Spanish flu epidemic of 1918. Your father served in the Polish army during the Second World War and was killed on the Russian front with other Polish patriots. Your Aunt Irena's husband joined the partisans and was killed by the Germans." She folds her hands in her lap with a satisfied smile as if she has accomplished a major task.

Mania feels a flutter of excitement. "Do you know my mother's maiden name? And her sister Irena's married name?"

Pani Glowacka says, "No, my dear, I don't remember that. It was all so long ago. Did your patient not have that information?"

"No, he didn't remember it. He only saw my mother in church in recent years. "

Mania is disappointed. Her neighbour's account had started

so well. *Pani* Glowacka must see that Mania's face has fallen because she says, "Now wait a minute. I may be able to help. We did have some papers clearing your mother to work for us. I may still have them. I haven't touched the Major's files, you know. I could look through them."

Mania's hopes are raised again. "Could you, please?" She is about to confide Mama's last words to the old lady, but thinks better of it. Mama would not approve. This is family business, not something she wants to talk to *Pani* Glowacka about. But the old woman does not seem to feel any urgency to start looking through her husband's files just yet. After a bit more chit-chat, Mania is increasingly impatient and distracted. She knows it is rude, but she begins to clear away the dishes.

"I'm sorry, *Pani* Glowacka, but Witold will be home soon and I have an early clinic tomorrow morning."

"Of course, I understand." The neighbour gets up and dusts off her skirt.

"When do you think you might have some more information for me?"

"Why don't you knock on my door after work tomorrow?"

"Thank you so much. That would be wonderful."

The next day, Mania cannot wait to visit *Pani* Glowacka. She throws her coat and purse on a chair when she gets home and heads for her neighbour's apartment. The old lady answers on the first knock as if she has been waiting. Mania sees that the coffee table is laid with sweets and cups and saucers, so she knows that she will have to be patient during the visit. Over a cup of tea, *Pani* Glowacka tells Mania how she has virtually turned her husband's study upside down. It has not been touched since his death except for regular dusting.

"It was no easy matter, my dear, going through the Major's old files. It took me the better part of the day."

"I do appreciate your effort. Did you find anything?"

Pani Glowacka seems reluctant to speak. "I didn't find anything important, just a reference letter from Krystyna's brother-in-law in Wroclaw, Feliks Barczak. I don't know if I should say any more if your mother didn't see fit to tell you...."

"What is it, *Pani?* Please tell me."

"Well, what was missing from your mother's file was a marriage certificate and a birth certificate." Her neighbour avoids Mania's eyes and instead concentrates on drinking her tea and munching on a cookie.

"So that means that you don't know my mother's maiden name?"

"That is correct."

"But you said that the Major would have made a thorough check of her background And that he knew Mama's parents had died in the Spanish flu epidemic."

"Yes, that is correct too. I can only assume that he got that information from your uncle, *Pan* Barczak. The Major would not have hired her without clearing her background. "

"Why do you think there are no documents?"

Pani Glowacka shrugs. "It was a common occurrence in the post-war chaos and confusion that people arrived in Warsaw daily who had lost everything. Sometimes documents got misplaced or lost in later years, too. We didn't keep the Major's study locked."

"You're surely not suggesting that my mother would have stolen them from the file?"

"No, no, of course not, my dear! I'm just saying —"

"Without papers, how will I ever find my mother's family?"

"It's too bad your mother was so secretive."

"She didn't like to talk about her past, but I wouldn't necessarily call that secretive." Mania bristles at this suggestion.

Pani Glowacka clears her throat. "All right, I will tell you my suspicions. When I couldn't sleep last night, I turned this problem around and around in my head. I think your parents were not married."

Mania gasps. "Why would you say that?"

"Because there was no record of a marriage in the Polish

archives. I do know that your father's family, the Stefanskis, were landowners in that part of Poland. If there had been a marriage, it would have been recorded. But there is no marriage certificate."

Mania is struck speechless by this bit of information. How could her very proper mother, who watched Mania's skirt lengths as a teenager with an eagle eye and gave every boy who took her out the third degree, be an unwed mother? It would have brought terrible shame to the family. Mania imagines Krystyna, all alone and pregnant, not knowing where to turn for help. Now that she sees so many girls in this position in her clinic, her heart goes out to that long-ago Krystyna who had to struggle on her own at a time when the church and society had such rigid sanctions against any evidence of unsanctioned sexuality.

Mania muses out loud. "I wonder if my father's family helped her at all?"

"I don't believe they did, my dear. Your father probably didn't tell them. They were gentry. They left for England before the Soviet army came in."

Mania wonders if the gentry's son, her own father, led her mother astray, maybe even raped her. But no! She's sure her father must have known about the pregnancy and they probably planned to marry when he returned. Surely he could not have just been stringing her along so he could get letters and parcels from a pretty girl while in the midst of the horrors of combat. Every soldier needs a girlfriend back home to keep his spirits up at the front. But Mania can't beleive that the love her father professed on the back of that picture she had found in Mama's apartment was not sincere.

"Do you know if the Stefanskis ever came back from England?"

Pani Glowacka shakes her head. "No, I don't, but I doubt it. They would have taken whatever they could out of the country before the Soviet Union confiscated their property."

No point in looking for them, Mania thinks. They probably did not even know she existed. She doubts that Krystyna would have wanted her to contact them after all these years.

"Perhaps your Uncle Feliks or your Aunt Antonia, if they're still alive, can help you."

"I guess I'll have to try to find them."

Seeing her disappointment, the old lady says, "Now, now, my dear, no need to be upset. It was all a very long time ago. Just remember that you come from a respectable Polish family. Not rich, but not peasants. No Jews or spies in the family, either."

Mania finds this very small consolation. She gets up to leave.

Pani Glowacka says, "But you haven't tried my sponge cake. I baked it just for you."

"I'm sure it's delicious but I'm sorry, I can't right now." Mania's stomach is in a tight knot. She is certain that if she puts even a morsel in her mouth, she will throw up.

"In that case, I will wrap some up for you to take home to your husband."

"Thank you," Mania says. As the old lady cuts the cake and wraps it in a napkin, she asks, "Do you happen to know the address of the Barczaks?"

"No, I'm sorry. The Major contacted your uncle at the municipal office."

"Thank you, *Pani* Glowacka. You have been a great help."

"I'm glad. But be careful, my dear. When you start digging, you may find what you were not looking for and some of it may not be pleasant."

These words ring in Mania's ears as she heads back to her own apartment. *Pani* Glowacka had been a trustworthy friend to her mother. A woman of her generation and age, she must have been shocked to realize that Mania's parents were likely not married, but it is not that important to Mania. She does want to find out her mother's maiden name, though.

A few days later, Mania goes to see Sister Beatrice.

"That was a lovely *Wigilia* at your home, Mania," Sister

Beatrice says. "Your mother would have been proud."

"Thank you, Sister. I learned everything from her."

"How are you feeling, my dear? It has only been two months since she was taken from us."

"I still have times when I get depressed, when I realize Mama isn't here anymore. I still talk to her in my head. Her favourite sayings and opinions pop up daily."

"I miss her, too," Sister Beatrice says.

Mania has not shared the information about her illegitimacy with anyone but Witold.

"Sister, you know what Mama's last words were. Now that Christmas is over, I'm trying to devote more time to finding out more about her family. Did she ever talk to you about her childhood?"

"A little bit, when she was here in the guest house. Not much that will help you, though. You probably already know that she had two sisters and that she didn't get along with one of them."

"Yes, I do. Did she tell you where Irena lived after the war and what her married name was?"

"She may have, but I'm sorry, my dear, I can't remember those kinds of details anymore."

"I understand. But I wish I knew more of my history. It would help me to know whom she wanted me to find and what she wanted me to make right."

"Yes, that must be frustrating. There is no shame in giving up a search when there isn't enough information to go on."

"You mean Mama won't be stuck in limbo if I don't make amends for something she did?"

"Of course not! Father Dominik heard her last confession and gave her the last rites. Her soul is blameless."

"What about me? Don't I have some responsibility for correcting some possible wrongdoing that she may have done?"

"No, my dear. You need not feel it on your conscience, especially since you do not know what 'it' is. You are a good person. Please learn to forgive yourself."

"Thank you, Sister. That's a big relief. I will continue to look for Mama's sisters because I'd like to heal any possible rift in the family. But it may be too hard. We couldn't even find my mother's sister or her husband in Wroclaw for the funeral."

"I think you're on the right track. If you can find out about Krystyna's estrangement from her sisters, you may get to the heart of the matter. I wish I could help you, my dear."

"You have, Sister. Thank you."

Although the nun has not given her any information or revealed any of her mother's secrets, Mania is grateful to her as she leaves the convent. Krystyna's last words have rung in her head like a command, something she was obliged to do or suffer the consequences, like the sins of the father that are visited upon the son. Sister Beatrice has lifted that obligation from her and now she can pursue the search with a lighter heart.

Chapter 10

Róża/Rose, Toronto, July 1966

MR. BENEDETTI MIXED VEGETABLES and flowers in his front garden, not like the "*mangia*cakes," as he called mainstream Canadians, with their neat lawns and floral borders. Soon the tomatoes would ripen beside the wrought iron fence separating his property from the Brombergs. Unlike Rose Bromberg, who tried to cast a small shadow, Mr. Benedetti was as flamboyant as the profusion of red roses climbing up his verandah railing. Whatever poverty and deprivation he and his family had suffered in Italy, they had chosen freely to immigrate to a land of opportunity. They had not been persecuted for who they were; they had not had their families wiped off the face of the earth; they had not fled after the carnage to the first place that would accept them.

Mr. Benedetti was not afraid to be himself in his adopted country. Rose envied his self-confidence. She and her husband, Mark, worked hard to blend in. Soon after their arrival in Canada they had anglicized their first names. In Helen, they had succeeded in raising a real Canadian child. She had no accent; she dressed and looked like a Canadian-born girl; and, she had married a Canadian boy. When Helen was growing up, Rose sometimes marvelled at this child who seemed like a stranger in her home. She felt like the bird who sits on the egg dropped in its nest by the cuckoo.

Although they did have some common ground with the Benedettis because they, too, were immigrants, Rose and Mark kept a friendly distance from them. They gladly accepted Mr. Benedetti's annual offering of tomatoes, cucumbers, and beans; they chatted about the weather; they shared information about their children's latest accomplishments at school; but, they had never seen the inside of each other's homes.

Rose and Mark kept their European past under wraps when they talked to their neighbours. People did not need to know that they were Holocaust survivors. Sometimes Rose's evasive answers to Mr. or Mrs. Benedetti's questions about her hometown and her origins bordered on rudeness, but she did not care. No, she was not Polish, but she was born in Poland. No, they did not have any family left "over there" – except under the ground or in the very air hanging over the land, she wanted to say, but never dared. A tight-lipped smile was usually enough to end the conversation and she would go back into her house. Sometimes, she had to lean against the inside of the door for a few seconds afterwards and breathe deeply to slow down her heart and wipe her mind clear of the turmoil that threatened to erupt through her calm exterior, an exterior that took some effort to maintain. "It is easier to not get too close to people," she told Mark.

They did not befriend other survivors, either. What would be the point in sitting around retelling stories of their suffering? "Who needs it?" she would ask Mark. It would not change anything and would just make her feel worse, bring on her nightmares. The threat of those nightmares was enough to suppress Mark's natural inclination to be open and friendly.

Walking up the steps to her front door, Rose glanced at their garden to see if the grass needed cutting yet. Mark managed to do it most of the time except when he was working evenings at the pharmacy. Then she would do it, but it was not a task she enjoyed, like he did. He kept the grass looking smooth, almost like artificial turf. He had planted a border of alternating pink and white petunias across the front of the house just under the porch. In Rose's opinion, if he had

had the time, Mark would probably have created a miniature botanical garden.

Once inside the front door, Rose picked up the mail from the floor, dropped her shoulder purse and her canvas bag filled with books and student papers at the foot of the stairs and slipped out of her shoes. Although she loved teaching, she would have enjoyed the summer off just to read and relax, even to rent a cottage on a lake if she could persuade Mark to take a week or two off work. But she and Mark had agreed that they should increase their savings first. To that end, she taught summer school. Another couple of years and maybe they would be more financially secure.

When they had first arrived in this strange country after the war in the winter of 1949, they were penniless refugees. Toronto was a much bigger city than they had expected. Rose had felt intimidated by the people milling around on the streets and in the stores, jabbering away in English that did not sound like anything she had learned at school. There were too many automobiles and streetcars and too many tall office buildings. Where were the vast tracts of ice and snow that they had expected to see everywhere in Canada? In preparation for the cold, Rose had arranged with a tailor to make them all heavy winter coats, and leggings for Helen, before leaving the displaced persons camp. She had spent hours knitting hats, mitts, and sweaters. Boots had been ordered from the shoemaker. How strange their little family must have looked to the locals, especially poor Helen. When Rose had taken her to register in school, they saw that the girls wore pretty dresses and Mary Jane shoes with white ankle socks, not hand-knitted sweaters, heavy woollen pants, and leather boots. The ribbons in their hair had tied back curls rather than the ends of braids. The children had stared at the new girl in her strange outfit. How should Rose have known that in this country children may have gone to school dressed for winter, but once inside an overheated school, they discarded their outerwear in a locker room and pranced around in dirndl skirts and lightweight machine-made clothing? Helen had blamed her mother for making her stand out even when Rose tried her best to help her child assimilate by getting her new clothes. But making them herself – and she was not an accomplished seamstress -- or buying things at the second-hand shop had hardly helped her daughter to fit in.

While Mark had looked for work, Rose had been lucky to find two rooms with the help of the Jewish Immigrant Aid Services as soon as they arrived. It had been on the second floor of the very same street that they lived on now. Rose had been terrified that they would end up sleeping on the park benches or wandering the streets. Their landlady had been Mrs. Goldbloom, a woman who needed the rent money but could not reconcile herself to the idea that she had to share her home with strangers. They had to tiptoe upstairs to their own quarters past her living room, but they could never evade her. It was as if she lay in wait for them just to cast a baleful eye their way no matter what hour of day or night. Rose had been convinced the old lady went through their things when they were out. She had not known what to do when Mrs. Goldbloom complained that Helen made too much noise. At eight Helen had been a quiet child, who spent many hours reading, but Mrs. Goldbloom heard her every step overhead as if she were a thundering elephant. Rose had suggested that perhaps a cheap rug would muffle the noise, which only outraged the old woman.

"What do you think, I'm made of money? My poor husband, may he rest in peace, left me a very small insurance policy so I wouldn't be turned out on the street. But carpeting yet? That he didn't provide for."

It had all came to a head when Helen brought home a friend. Rose was thrilled that finally her daughter was fitting in at school. Mrs. Goldbloom had other ideas.

"*Es toig nish,*" she had said in Yiddish. "It won't do. It's too noisy."

"Mrs. Goldbloom, they're children."

"My son never made such a racket."

Rose had wanted to say, *That's why your son now lives in California and never visits you*, but she refrained. Since she had no intention of barring her home to Helen's friends, she knew they would have to move. A "For Rent" sign down the street provided the perfect solution. She and Mark arranged immediately to move into the upstairs of the Benedettis' house.

Mrs. Goldbloom was surprised that they were leaving after only six months, especially to move into a *goyish* home. After all she had done for them – taken them in off the street – and this was how they repaid her? When they had ended up buying the semi-detached house next door from Mr. Benedetti a few years later, Mrs. Goldbloom was convinced that they must have come into money from *Wiedergutmachung*, the fund for reparations for Holocaust survivors, just like all the *greenes*. Meeting Rose on the street, she did not hesitate to tell her this and turned a deaf ear when Rose had denied it. In the end, Rose had walked away from her and, after that, she crossed the street whenever she saw her old landlady.

Unlike Mark, who loved owning his own home, Rose was ambivalent about being a property owner. She would have preferred to continue renting. Putting down roots even in a safe place like Canada was not a good idea. She had pointed out to Mark how complacency had worked against the Jews of Europe, who could not pick up and run when they needed to, but he told her she was paranoid. What was wrong with a bit of paranoia when it was based on facts, she wanted to know, but he would not listen. She had dealt with it by not accumulating possessions. The Nazis and their local collaborators had stolen everything she cared about from their home: the furnishings they had lovingly selected when they were first married, her grandmother's silver Sabbath candlesticks; the silver cutlery and fine china that had been their wedding presents. Such things could never be replaced. Best not to even try. In her new home, she bought only the cheapest dishes, cutlery, and pots.

Rose's attitude had always been to make the best of a bad situation. Mark believed in starting over. To her, this was utmost foolishness. What hopes did they have of ever recreating the life they had had before the war? When Mark gazed at their paltry little lawn outside the window, she could not understand how he could be satisfied after the large country home his family had owned just outside of town. In their orchard had grown apple, pear, and cherry trees. The gardens surrounding the house had bloomed with white and purple lilac bushes, masses of peonies, and roses of every hue. As a boy, Mark had picked fruit from every tree and gathered bouquets of lilacs for his mother. Rose had wished that he could have a greater opportunity to get his hands into the soil than just planting petunias, but that was a luxury that they could not afford here.

For Rose, hard work had served as an anaesthetic for pain and suffering. It kept her from thinking and remembering. She did not want to be like the people she read about – people who had breakdowns, even committed suicide; who were obsessed about the past, or who joined groups where they talked incessantly about their experiences. No, that was not for her and Mark. The only people she wanted to emulate, for Helen's sake, were the genuine Canadians, who had not suffered, whose lives had not been uprooted, who marched forward without a backward glance.

When Helen had married Joe, a lawyer from a prominent and well-to-do Jewish family in the city, Rose had felt a sense of relief and accomplishment. She had thought that she deserved a large measure of the credit for her daughter's happiness. When Mark had demurred, saying that Helen was making her own future, Rose reminded him that it was their efforts that helped create the image of a family that Helen would not be ashamed of. She had reminded him of how they had sacrificed to buy Helen nice clothes so that she could mingle with the right class of people, and how they had sent her to university to meet educated young men suitable for marriage. She was hurt that this was not self-evident to Mark because it was so obvious to her that her single-mindedness continued to pay off in how carefree Helen became when she went to university. Soon after she and Joe married, they had bought a roomy, split-level home in North Toronto and soon they would have children to fill up those empty bedrooms. That was also due, Rose believed, to the fact that she and Mark had never burdened her with the stories of the past.

Thinking of Helen's new home, Rose headed downstairs to the basement. It was time to bring up the boxes that Helen had stored there for many years and ask her to take them to her new home. Rose thought that she should not have to deal with her daughter's inability to throw anything out. Helen had not learned from her that possessions just weighed you down. Rose began to carry boxes of books, photo albums, notes, and exams upstairs.

When the last box was in the kitchen, Rose made herself a cup of tea and collapsed into a chair. Idly, she opened the flap of the box nearest to the table. Pulling out a handful of photographs, she was struck with how happy Helen looked, her arms around friends who were complete strangers to her mother. With a pang, Rose realized that she had not often seen her daughter with such a happy face at home. She and Mark had often discussed how moody their daughter had always seemed, something they had attributed to the common angst of the teenage years.

Rose pulled out a thick wad of foolscap pages held together by a dried out elastic band that crumbled in her fingers. The first page was titled: *My Journal by Helen Bromberg*. Intrigued, Rose began to read.

January 1, 1954

My New Year's resolution is to keep a journal. I'm starting it today and I'm going to write in it every day.

I want to be a writer! I don't have money to buy a hard cover notebook. Next year when I'm old enough to start baby-sitting, I'll save up my money to buy one. Maybe I can work out a secret code so if anyone finds this journal, they won't be able to read it. Mom is such a snoop! I have to find a good hiding place. I'm going to tell the whole truth about everything in here!

Rose was aghast. *I was a snoop?* It was a mother's duty to know what was going on with her child. Helen should not have wanted to keep secrets from her mother. She had provided the child with food on the table, a roof over her head – she wanted for nothing, for God's sake! Her life was free from suffering. She hesitated about delving further into Helen's scribbling, the childish nonsense of a daughter who defamed her mother, who had done everything for her. But she could not stop herself and picked through the pages at random.

March 12, 1954

I'm officially a teenager today! Mom and Dad don't make a big deal about birthdays, but Mom actually bought me a present – a nylon blouse with a Peter Pan collar and a black velvet ribbon at the neck. Of course she sewed the skirt to go with it – a full circle ballerina skirt. All the girls have them. Mine is not as nice as the bought ones. Oh, well!

After school I went to Shirley's house. Shirley gave me an autograph book for my birthday. It has different coloured pages in it and I'm going to get every one to sign it before we graduate from this school. When her mother gave us some mandelbroit and milk, I noticed the blue numbers on her arm. It was creepy, like a brand on an animal. I got goose bumps. Later I asked Shirley what they were for. She said her mother got those in Auschwitz during the war. The Nazis did it. When I got home, I told Mom about the numbers and asked if she and Dad were in Auschwitz. She said no, they were in a ghetto. I wanted to know what a ghetto was and was it very bad and she started to freak out. What did I want to know that stuff for? I didn't need to go poking into what wasn't my business. It was better for me not to know, etc. etc. etc. She really scared me.

Rose stopped reading. Her hand was shaking. She had no recollection of this incident. *I was right*, she thinks. There was no need to rehash that monstrous time with a child. For whose benefit? Shirley's mother was a stupid woman. She should have worn long sleeves.

Dad heard her screaming at me and came into the kitchen, still holding his newspaper. He put his arm around Mom like I wasn't even there. I don't even know what I did wrong. I just asked a simple question! Dad always takes Mom's side. I stormed off into my room. Now I'm writing it all down for posterity. I hate Mom! I live in a crazy family!

Rose doubled over in pain and the pages fluttered to the floor. To be hated by your own child, the child you had rescued from certain death; that was the height of cruelty. She held her hands over her face and felt tears running down her cheeks. *If she only knew,* Rose thought. A small voice in her head said, *It's your own fault that she doesn't know.* Slowly, she got herself under control. She was very good at that. She had had lots of practice. Picking up the pages at her feet, she continued to read.

May 15, 1954

Friday is the best day of the week. I rush home from school and Mom lets me help her make challah for Shabbes. She always gives me a piece to make my own little challah. I like being with Mom in the kitchen. It's the only time I feel like maybe she loves me a little bit. She asked me about school and I told her about Shmuel, the new boy. The kids say he just got off the boat. I think he's nice and cute. So what if he talks with an accent? He has thick dark hair that falls over his forehead and his eyes are the nicest deep blue, almost purple. He walks me home from school and we talk about our favourite books, what kind of music we like, the other kids in the class and the teachers.

Mom told me that when she was a girl, she used to help her mother bake for Shabbes, too. My grandmother's name was Golde. I asked her to tell me about my grandparents. I wish they were still alive. A lot of the kids at school have Bubbies and Zaydes. They go visit them on the weekends. Mom said that she had wonderful parents, but she had a special bond with her father, my grandfather, Nathan. Sometimes I feel that way about Dad, too. Anyway, she told me about the time when she was a little girl and ran away from home. Her father got a search party organized and when they found her in the meadow picking flowers, he lifted her up high in his arms and hugged her. He had a thick beard that tickled. But when her mother saw her, she yelled at her for causing them all that worry. My grandmother sounds a lot like Mom.

When Mom got older, she said that her father put her to work in the store after school. She'd dust the things on the shelves, make neat rows, unpack boxes and help customers find what they were looking for. When she talked about that, her eyes got all blurry and teary, and I thought, Oh, no, she's going to cry. So I took her hand. She just wiped her face with the dishtowel and said let's get back to work.

Rose had loved making *challah* with her mother the same way that she had done it with Helen. It was like a chain that connected the generations. They must have stopped baking together soon after Helen got to high school and felt too grown up for such things.

June 4, 1954

Today while we were kneading the challah dough I asked Mom if they had parties when she was my age. One of the girls in the class is planning a graduation party with boys! Next year we'll all be in high school. I hope Mom will let me go. So I wanted to know what it was like when she was my age. Guess what? She went to her first dance when she was 13! I'm 13 already and the graduation dance will be my first one, too! Her dance was from her scouting organization. I was jealous when she told me how popular she was. I don't even know if anyone will ask me to dance. I hope Shmuel is going. Maybe he'll ask me. I can picture Mom at the dance twirling around to those old-fashioned tangos and waltzes with different boys. She still loves to dance and drags Dad to any party where there's music. I'm proud to have a mother like her. I can imagine them dancing when they were young. I can't imagine Shirley's mother or Stella's mother dancing. My mother is still beautiful. She doesn't even look old. Mrs. Friedman is short and dumpy but I have to admit, I like her a lot. Mrs. Goldberg is just wrinkled and boring. She always asks me and Stella, "So are you good girls?" What does she think we're going to say? "No, we're very bad. We kissed all the boys in Mr. Brown's class in the lane behind the school!"

Mom was also athletic when she was a teenager, not like me. That's another way that we're different. I'm such a klotz.

I asked Mom about Dad. She said he was from a rich family who owned a farm outside of town where they had big orchards. He had three sisters, each one prettier than the one before, she said. He was very handsome. He still is! Lots of girls were in love with him, but he chose her. She had a big smile on her face when she said this. She hardly ever smiles.

That hurt Rose, but it was true. She did not have much to smile about. All her happy times were in the past, like the visits to Mark's family farm when they picked cherries, and sneaked a kiss when they thought no one was looking. She had loved his sisters and not one of them had survived. They were such fine women, much worthier than she was. She shook her head in perplexity and sadness at the unfairness of it all and went back to reading.

June 20, 1954

School will soon be over for the year. Yay! I'm going to camp for the first time this summer. I can't wait. I'm a little bit nervous, though, because I'm going with Shirley and she's so pretty that none of the boys will look at me when she's around. I wish I had straight blonde hair and blue eyes just like Mom but I'm stuck with brown curls and brown eyes like Dad. I'd look much better as a boy!

Shirley's mother just had a baby and she's so old – at least 40!!! The baby's name is Basia after some aunt or cousin who was killed by the Nazis. She has a little prune face. Shirley's mother was telling us stories about when Shirley was a baby. So when I got home I asked Mom what I was like as a baby. Was I cute? She said what a stupid question. Of course you were cute. All babies are cute. That's not true! Basia is a baby and she's not cute. I asked when did I start walking. She said she didn't know. I asked how come. Because I was with some Polish woman when I was little. Why? Because it was too dangerous for them to keep me. When I asked why it was dangerous, she said to stop with all the questions already and she'd tell me when I got older. I don't see what getting older has to do with it. I bet she'll never tell me because she didn't love me as a baby and doesn't remember.

Doesn't remember? Rose repeated this to herself in a shocked whisper. Oh, my God, how could she think that? *My darling girl,* she wanted to say, *it hurt me too much to tell you that you couldn't walk until you were almost two years old, until I gave Pan Petrenko money for the goat so you could have milk. It broke my heart to see your spindly legs and tiny ribs sticking out.* No amount of trying had allowed her to forget that her own child had called another woman "Mama."

September 28, 1954

Today, we went to synagogue for Rosh Hashana. I was excited to see Shmuel in shul. I got butterflies in my stomach thinking about him. Shirley says I have a crush on him. I found him sitting three rows behind Dad. I sat beside Mom. She looked so elegant in her navy blue hat and grey suit. She kept poking me to show me the page so I would follow in the prayer book and not daydream. I wish Shirley was here, but her family is not religious. I heard Mom say to Dad that they're Communists. I don't know exactly what that is, but they don't go to shul and her mother doesn't light candles on Friday night. I wonder if that's why I'm not allowed to stay at her house overnight.

I wish Mom had bought me a new dress for Rosh Hashana instead of making me a dress out of one of her old ones. She says I'm too hard to shop for because

I've grown so much that there's nothing in the children's wear department to fit me. I know Mom thinks I'm fat. So why does she keep shtupping food at me? She says I don't appreciate what it's like to be starving hungry. When was she starving? Once I asked her and I got a smack across the face. I wonder if Shmuel thinks I'm fat. I'm going on a diet and I don't care what she says! I wish I was adopted. Or born to another family. I hate my family. I can't wait to escape.

Rose felt another stab in her heart. She could not bear to read on but she must. This was her punishment for being a bad mother.

December 15, 1954

I came in from skating with Shirley this afternoon and I thought nobody was home. It was so quiet. I was going to my room when I heard their voices from the bedroom. My ears perked up and I decided to spy on them. Their faces looked so different. It made me think that they're wearing masks every day when I'm around.

Dad said, "God has been good to us. We survived and we have a normal life."

Mom said, "No, we can never have a normal life. Never for me. Not without Mirka."

Tears were running down her cheeks. Dad put his arms around her, but Mom spotted me over his shoulder in the crack in the door. She got flustered. I could tell. She wiped her face with a sleeve and came out. She asked me if I had a good time and if I wanted some hot chocolate.

I asked her who was Mirka and she said, "Nobody you know."

She started fussing at the stove and Dad went

into the living room with his book. Do they think I'm stupid? I can tell when people are telling secrets and they don't want me to hear. I went into my room and started writing in here. I don't know why they treat me like a little kid. I'm old enough now to know how to keep family things private.

December 16, 1954

Last night when I went to bed, I couldn't fall asleep. I tried thinking about the things I did that day, like Mom told me to once before when I couldn't fall asleep, but it didn't work. All I could think about was who was Mirka. Mom never cries in front of me, but she was so sad when she mentioned Mirka, that I figure it was someone very special in her life. Maybe a sister? That would have made her my aunt. I wish I had a sister. Even an aunt would be nice. I'll have to pick a time when she's in a good mood to ask her about Mirka.

Rose took in big gulps of air. No, she would not go down that road. Some things did not bear thinking about. She forced herself to read on.

February 10, 1955

This was the worst day of my life! Now I know for sure Mom hates me. Every day, she yanks a brush through my hair and makes me braids. Nobody else at school has braids. I decided that there's no way that I'm going to the Spring Fling with braids tied with ribbons like a little kid. I'm going to be 14 soon for heaven's sakes! So last night when Mom and Dad were asleep, I hacked off my braids with Mom's sewing scissors. I fluffed out my hair and looked in the bathroom mirror and I liked it. I used to wish I had straight blonde hair like Mom. I hated my curly hair. But when it's short, it looks kind of cute. It makes me look older – hooray! No more heavy weight down my back, either. I shoved the braids into the bottom drawer of my desk under a pile of notebooks and went back to bed. I knew there'd be trouble in the morning, but in the meantime, I was happy.

When I came into the kitchen for breakfast, my heart was pounding so hard I thought I'd have a heart attack. Mom looked at me like I was a little green man from Mars. She said, "How could you do such a thing?" I told her I hated those braids. I skipped breakfast, grabbed my books and jacket and escaped out of the house to school. When I came home, Mom refused to speak to me. Dad stared at me and shook his head. He asked me why I did it. I said, "I'm sick and tired of being called a 'greenie'." He asked me what that means and I told him it's for people who just came off the boat. He asked who called me that and I said some of the kids at school.

He said, "You have beautiful hair. It is the colour of chestnuts. You should not have cut it because of some stupid comments from your classmates." That made me feel bad. I hate making Dad sad. Mom just sat there. Her face was like stone. All of a sudden, she got up and stomped out of the kitchen. Dad went after her, leaving me all alone feeling like a criminal. I heard Mom banging around in my room. When I ran in, she was sitting on my bed, with all my stuff all over the floor – my books, my underwear, socks, everything from my desk drawers, too. She had the braids in her lap. Dad was sitting beside her with his arm around her. I couldn't believe it. It was like they both ganged up on me. I yelled at her.

"You went through all my private things! You messed up my books!"

Dad held up the braids and said how much I had hurt Mom. She was crying. She said, "The Nazi butcher dragged my cousin, Etka, across the square by her braids. She was my best friend. The beast was on his white horse. After her body stopped twitching, he took out his knife and cut off her hair. They were just like these."

I just wanted crawl under a rock. Dad said I had to apologize, so I did. But you know what, deep down inside, I didn't feel sorry one bit. I was glad I did it. Sure, I felt bad for hurting Mom, but it was my hair and I should be allowed to do with it what I want. So there!

So this is why she hated me, Rose thought. *Maybe I should have told her.* After the war, she was hurting so much that it had not occurred to her that maybe Helen was affected, too.

Rose heard the front door open and close. Mark was home from work.

He came into the kitchen and asked, "What's wrong? You've been crying."

Numb, she held out the sheaf of foolscap to him. He glanced through the pages.

"Did you know she hated me?" Rose asked.

"What makes you think she hated you?"

"She says so – in her own words. Read it. Everything was all my fault. If only I'd told her the truth."

"It wasn't just your fault. I withheld the truth from her too. We wanted her to have a normal childhood."

"How could we ever have imagined that after what we went through we could give our daughter a normal childhood? Do you think she still hates me?"

"Don't be ridiculous."

Mark began to read Helen's journal, turning one page after another, a deep frown on his face.

"What do you think we should have done differently?" Rose asked.

"I'm no child psychologist, but maybe we could have got some help at the time. Maybe we could have explained things to her at a child's level."

She nodded. "I was selfish. I was only thinking of myself and my own pain."

"We were traumatized. Is there anything we can do now? Maybe you can talk to her when you give her back the journal."

"It's too late. She's happy now. Why open it all up again? I'm just going to put it back in the box and we can take it over on the weekend with all the other boxes."

"Rose, I think we have to talk to her."

"Maybe some day when she finds it and asks questions."

Rose knew Mark was right. But she had been quiet for so long, she could not break her silence now. The pattern of silence was etched deeply into her relationship with Helen. Besides, she believed it was in Helen's interests not to raise the specter of the past. Who knows what consequences would follow? Best to leave well enough alone.

Chapter 11

Mania, Warsaw, May 2006

AT THE FIRST SIGN of buds on the trees, Mania has a resurgence of hope about finding her mother's family. It is a nice time for a road trip. So what if they do not find anyone? At least she and Witold will get out of the city for a while, have a brief vacation and spend some time together. She is sitting at the kitchen table mulling over how and where to start, while Witold is rummaging around in his study getting ready to go to the office. Now that Mama is gone, she no longer has to rush off in the morning before him. Even her visits to church before work have stopped.

When he joins her for breakfast, she says, "When we get home tonight, let's plan a trip to Wroclaw. I want to look for Antonia."

Witold says, "But I thought you didn't like her. And your mother didn't get along with her either. Why bother?"

"Because she's my only hope for finding Aunt Irena."

"She may no longer be alive."

"True, but both sisters were younger than my mother and Antonia was the youngest. On the off chance that they're still in the telephone directory, I've searched phone numbers in Wroclaw for Feliks and Antonia Barczak and they're not listed. I called the city administrative offices for contact information about Feliks, but they said if there's anything, it'll be in the archives. So I really want to visit the municipal offices in person. Besides my uncle's employment records, they should have residential records too."

"All right, I'll arrange to take a few days off work."

"Yes, me, too. It'll be a nice trip if the weather holds. We can stop off on the way back for a visit with Marysia and make it a week's vacation."

"Good idea. I'll see you tonight."

That evening, after a full and busy day, Mania and Witold confirm the dates for their travel. In preparation, Mania looks up old folks' homes and nursing homes in Wroclaw on the Internet in case her aunt or uncle or both may be in one of these facilities. Over the next few days, she makes phone calls of enquiry to these places, but they bear no fruit. No one has heard of Aunt Antonia or Uncle Feliks.

Mania is undeterred and they set off in early May. In the Wroclaw municipal offices, they receive some incredulous looks from the staff when they enquire about how to find the address of people who lived in the city over sixty years ago. One clerk takes pity on them and leads them to the city archives. Mania manages to find the last known address of the Barczaks. She will not have to go to the employment office to ask them to look for someone who probably has not worked there for at least the last twenty years. That night when they check into a hotel, Mania goes to sleep satisfied at the progress she has made so far and excited about the next day's prospects.

After breakfast, they arrive at the address where the Barczaks used to live. Mania stands outside for several minutes to try to dredge up a memory of the place but the vague image she recalls of an imposing grey stone building bears little resemblance to the rundown four-storey apartment block before her. It is a building in the old style with tall narrow windows and an entrance paved with cracked asphalt that leads into a courtyard overgrown with weeds. In 1944, when it was still relatively new, it probably had been truly impressive to a six-year-old who had never been to a city. Now the peeling paint on the window frames, the rust on the wrought-iron balconies, and the crumbling cornices signal that the people who live here must be poor.

Mania and Witold walk in through the entrance off the courtyard and encounter the cooking smells of cabbage and potatoes in the corridor. At the caretaker's door, they knock and wait. A man with unkempt grey hair, who is wearing an undershirt and suspenders dangling from his waist, opens the door.

Mania says, "Hello. We hope you can help us. We're trying to find tenants who used to live in Apartment 31 – Antonia and Feliks Barczak?"

He shakes his head. "No one by that name here."

"I know they're not here now, but they were here some time ago."

"When?"

Mania is embarrassed when she says, "After the war, when my mother and I visited. They were my aunt and uncle."

"Ha! Ha! You expect to find some people here from that long ago? You must be joking."

"Please, is there anyone who might still remember them?"

The man scratches his unshaven face. He regards Mania as if he cannot believe someone could ask such a stupid question, but finally he shrugs and replies, "I've only been the caretaker here for the last six years. There's one old crone down the hall you could talk to. She's still here because her daughter can't make her move to the old folks' home. It's Apartment 12 on your right. Her name is *Pani* Jakubowska."

"Thank you," Mania says and they head to a dingy grey door marked with a large black 12. They knock several times very loudly before they hear the shuffling of feet and a hoarse old voice calling out, "I'm coming! I'm coming!"

A woman wrapped in a shawl with wisps of white hair showing lots of pink scalp appears at the door. She is thin, bent, and bony and has beady, suspicious black eyes.

"What do you want?" she barks.

"*Pani* Jakubowska, I am Doctor Mania Wiśniewska and this is my husband, Doctor Witold Wiśniewski. We were wondering if you could tell us anything about Antonia and Feliks Barczak, who used to live here. They were my aunt and uncle. The caretaker said that you are the most knowledgeable person in this building."

Mania can see the old lady's hostility fading as soon as she hears the word "doctor." Her compliment about the woman's superior knowledge has also helped. She invites them into her parlour to sit down on a faded floral sofa covered with lace doilies and bustles into the kitchen to get refreshments.

Soon, she returns with a plate of stale biscuits, a teapot, and three cups on a tray.

"I'm sorry, this is all I have," she apologizes. "I don't often have company."

"This is just fine," Mania says.

She knows how lonely old women like this one and *Pani* Glowacka welcome the opportunity to play hostess. They are like the women who come regularly to her clinic with complaints, some genuine, some imagined. What they truly yearn for is human contact.

Pani Jakubowska sits down opposite them in an armchair and asks, "So what is it that you want to know?"

Mania explains that the sudden death of her mother left her unable to contact her mother's sister, Antonia, to attend the funeral, since they had lost touch with her and her husband. She would like to know the whereabouts of the couple. Since they were younger than her mother, she hopes that they are still alive.

"They used to live in this building," she tells the old lady. "Do you remember them?"

"I do. Your Aunt Antonia was a most unpleasant woman, with a mouth that permanently sucked lemons. I can understand why your mother lost touch with her. What did she have to complain about, pray tell? Her husband, Feliks, was a sweet-natured man. Too good for her, if you ask me. She treated him like a dishrag."

"I don't suppose you'd remember when my mother and I came to stay here for a few weeks in 1944?"

"Oh, my, that was a long time ago. Just when I had my baby. She's all grown up and living in Warsaw now, my Tinka. She has given me two wonderful grandchildren...."

Mania interrupts to get the woman back on track. She does not have the patience to sit through a long discourse on the Jakubowski family. She does a lot of listening in her clinic but she is not on duty now.

"But do you remember when my mother and I were here, *Pani*?"

Derailed from her own narrative, *Pani* Jacubowska seems confused and irritated as if she does not know who these people are and why they are in her living room.

"My mother and I came just before Christmas..." Mania prompts.

After what seems like an interminable silence while the old lady sifts through her memories, she says, "You must have been the girl who came to me after school. You took the baby for a walk in her pram while I made supper for my husband. She was a very colicky baby and I couldn't get anything done. All day she'd cry and cry, except when she was wheeled along in that pram. I tried everything. Gripe water, chamomile tea...."

"I don't remember taking a baby for a walk."

Pani Jakubowska asks, "Did you have blonde braids?"

"Yes."

"Did you have a key to the house when you came home from school?"

Mania had not thought of this. "No, I didn't. My aunt wouldn't allow my mother to give me hers."

"Aha! I knew it. That sounds just like your auntie, the old bat. You're the one, no question about it. She didn't like you coming to my place, you know. What would the neighbours think? That you were helping me out with the baby like a maid? Oh, no, that would never do. So she must have given you a key after that."

"Do you know what happened to my aunt and uncle?"

"What do you think happens to old people? She died, like everyone else who stayed in this building except me. I come from a long line of people who have lived to a ripe old age. I will celebrate my ninetieth birthday in two years and my daughter had better make me a big party. It's the least she can do for me."

"When did she die, *Pani*?" Witold asks in a calm voice before Mania can prod the old woman again.

"Let me see ... it was before the new caretaker came ... and after Tinka moved to Warsaw.... Maybe ten years ago?"

"And *Pan* Barczak?"

"You'd think the old fellow would have come to life after the witch died. But he became a hermit. Never went out except to buy a few groceries. Didn't have any visitors. Eventually, when we hadn't seen him go out for some time, one of the neighbours contacted the Social Services to check on him and they arranged his transfer to an old folks' home."

"Which one is he in?" Mania asks. "I called all the ones I could find on the Internet but no one had heard of him."

Pani Jakubowska looks puzzled.

Witold explains. "My wife means that she researched old-age homes here on the computer."

"Oh, well. That place wouldn't have a computer! It was supposed to be closed years ago. I know all about these places. They're like prisons for old folks, but that one is like a prison from the Middle Ages. My daughter, God bless her, has been trying to put me into such a place for the past few years. I love her as only a mother can, but why can't she just take me into her home in Warsaw? It's big enough. She says her house has stairs and she's busy with work and couldn't look after me.

Who looks after me here? No one, that's who. She gives me money and I have two wonderful grandchildren. Let me see, Janina is the oldest...."

"*Pani,* excuse me," Witold says as Mania fidgets, "can you please give us the name and address of the old folks' home where Feliks Barczak may still be living?"

If Mania does not stifle her natural inclination to feel sorry for the woman whose wrinkles are etched in sorrow and grievance against her only daughter who has deserted her, they will never get back to their search. The old lady pours more tea. She will make them wait and answer them in her own good time.

"Let me see.... Hmmm.... I think it is the *Dom Spokojnej Starosci....*"

"Can you give us the address?" Mania has pen and paper in hand to write it down.

"That may not be the right name. And the address, well, I don't know that. It's not far from here. You go left down this street from the entrance until you hit the main street and turn right. Then it's on the right-hand side down a small side street – I can't remember the name – about three or four blocks after you make the turn."

Mania realizes that this is as much as they are likely to get out of her and quickly gets up.

"Thank you so much for your hospitality, *Pani* Jakubowska. And for supplying us with such useful information."

She shakes the woman's hand and heads to the door. Witold is right behind her.

"Goodbye! The cookies were delicious," he says as they leave.

"I can give you some to take with you..." she calls after them but they make their escape down the corridor without turning back.

Once outside the building, Mania takes a deep breath to clear her lungs of cooking smells, old age, and poverty. "I hated to do that to her. She's so lonely and needs someone to talk to, but we just don't have the time."

"You're right, of course. Let's go and see if we can find this nameless old folks' home with no fixed address."

It is a lot easier than they expect. Tucked away down a side street they find a tired old three-storey red brick building with a tarnished nameplate beside the door. When they go inside, they have to pass a lineup of old people in wheelchairs to get to the reception desk. Some of them are dozing, bent over with their heads almost in their laps. Others are leaning back against headrests, their mouths open and eyes closed. One resident with a long white pigtail down her back follows their progress with lively interest in her pale blue eyes as they walk by.

The young woman behind the counter is reading a paperback book and does not look up when they approach.

After waiting to get her attention for a couple of minutes, Mania says, "Can you tell us, please, if Feliks Barczak still lives here?"

She gives them a bored look and says, "Room 39 on the third floor. He never has visitors."

There are no elevators. They walk up the dingy stairs flanked by walls with peeling paint of indeterminate colour. When they reach the third-floor corridor, the gloom is intensified by the faded, dark grey carpeting. There is only one ceiling light that casts shadows on the dirty walls. The combined reek of urine and disinfectant hangs in the air. Peering into the open doors of the rooms, Mania sees four to six beds in each. Old people are slumped in armchairs or lying on their beds. Several radios are on, competing for airtime, and one television set shows the smiling face of a game-show host. Through the door to Room 39 Mania sees only two beds. Perhaps Feliks was given this superior accommodation in recognition of his years of loyal service to the local government. Mania knocks before entering. With Witold following her, she steps in and sees a fragile old man dwarfed by a stuffed armchair. He has a newspaper in his lap and a pair of spectacles rest on his nose. His eyes are closed. There are a few wisps of hair over his bony scalp. He is dressed in a faded blue, long-sleeved shirt and baggy pants, both much too big for him. Probably his younger self once filled out this outfit. On his feet is a pair of well-worn felt slippers. There is no one else in the room. Mania approaches the old man and puts her hand on his arm.

"Uncle Feliks?"

He opens his milky blue eyes and looks blankly at her and Witold.

"Uncle Feliks," she says again, "do you remember me? I'm Mania, the daughter of Krystyna, Aunt Antonia's sister."

The old man stares at her, uncomprehending. "Who are you?" he asks in a voice dry and raspy from lack of use.

"I'm Krystyna's daughter. Your sister-in-law, Krystyna. We visited you when I was a little girl."

Mania pulls up a chair to sit in front of Uncle Feliks. He squints, peering at her, and finally his eyes clear as understanding gradually penetrates his consciousness. He says, "I remember your mama. A lovely woman and she had a child with her."

"That was me, Mania."

"Ah, yes. You and your mother disappeared one day without bidding us goodbye. My wife never forgave her sister."

Mania shifts uncomfortably in her chair, while Witold takes advantage of the awkward moment to come forward and introduce himself. After shaking Feliks's arthritic hand, he sits down on the edge of his bed.

Mania says, "Uncle Feliks, I'm so pleased that you haven't forgetten us."

Witold pours him a glass of water from the nightstand and the old man drinks before replying, "Oh, I remember the past very well. It's the present that eludes me. Every day seems exactly like the day before. It becomes a complete muddle in my head."

"I'm sorry you lost your wife." Mania makes the standard condolence comment without much conviction.

Feliks waves his hand dismissively. "Our life together was not a happy one. When I met Antonia, she was a secretary in the municipal office where I worked. She was a lovely, unpretentious young woman. When we married, we were happy together for the first few years. She continued to work. Then things changed."

"Can you tell me why, Uncle Feliks?"

"I think it was because we could not have children. She quit her job to wait until she got pregnant. When it didn't happen, she became bitter. Eventually we gave up hoping and she went back to work."

"Did she ever tell you where she came from?"

"Oh, yes. From a village in what is now Ukraine. She was sent as a child to live with her aunt and uncle in Wroclaw.

"How did she get along with her sisters?"

"Not good right from the start. She was bitter that Krystyna sent her away to Wroclaw after their parents died. I couldn't see how Krystyna could have done anything else, she was just a child herself, but Antonia always thought that Irena should have been sent away instead of her."

"Did you and Aunt Antonia ever go back to the village?"

"Yes, we went to Irena's wedding. It was a typical village affair with everyone piled into the church. There was lots of delicious food prepared by the women. And lots of vodka, too." He smiles at the recollection. "Irena married a local boy. He was killed fighting with the partisans. She was left with two sons, poor girl."

"I don't suppose you remember anything about the wedding of my mother?" Mania knows there never was such a wedding but a shred of hope still lingers in her mind.

"I'm sorry, that I cannot remember." He thinks for a while. "I think that's another thing Antonia held against Krystyna. She wasn't invited to your mother's wedding, or to your christening. It didn't matter that your mother explained that they were married quickly by the priest because her husband was going off to war. It really galled her that Krystyna married into gentry and she didn't get to meet her in-laws."

Mania thinks, *How outraged Antonia would have been had she known that there never was a wedding!* She decides not to say anything about that.

Feliks sighs. "But that is all ancient history now. How is your dear mother?"

"My mother died a few months ago. I didn't know how to contact her sisters to tell them." Mania briefly describes to Feliks how her mother died, what she said, and how she and Witold have found him.

He listens attentively. "Your mother was a good woman, despite what Antonia thought."

"Uncle Feliks, I'd like to get in touch with Aunt Irena. Do you know if she's still living in the village?"

"That is not a happy story either."

"What happened?"

"After the war, the Ukrainians burned down many Polish villages to chase out the people living there."

"Is that when Mama and I ran away and came here?"

Feliks pauses to think before he replies, "No, I think you and your mother came before the war ended. At the end a part of Poland was given to the Soviet Union, which made it into a Ukrainian state."

"Do you know what happened to Aunt Irena and her children?"

"They were left homeless and had to be relocated."

"Did you and Aunt Antonia help her?"

Feliks shakes his head sadly and says, "I'm ashamed to say that we didn't. Irena tried to get us to help her once before. She was afraid that the Nazis were after her. Antonia sent her packing."

"And yet she let me and my mother stay, at least for a short time."

"Yes, but Irena had a Jewish child with her besides the two

boys. Even Antonia couldn't refuse Krystyna with only one child."

"I'm surprised that Irena came back again."

"Poor woman. She had nowhere else to turn to. With the Nazis gone, she didn't have that Jewish child with her anymore, so she probably thought Antonia would be kinder to her. But she wasn't. She said that it was bad enough when Krystyna was here with only one child and then ran off without even a thank you. She wasn't about to open our home to two wild boys. I was at work when they arrived, but the neighbours told me that she wouldn't even let her sister and the boys inside. She just handed them some food and told them to leave. It broke my heart. We didn't have any children of our own and it would have given us a family."

"Do you know where they relocated?"

"We never heard from Irena again. A lot of people from that area were sent to Opole."

What a heartless creature that Antonia was, Mania thinks and then muses out loud, "I wonder if Irena is even still alive."

Feliks shrugs. "Who knows? I seem to have outlived everybody – the few friends we had, my colleagues from work, our neighbours. I have not been able to figure out why. What earthly purpose has the good Lord destined for me to fulfill by leaving me on this earth for such an extended period of time?"

Mania strokes the old man's hand. "Perhaps you can help shed some light on my mother's early life."

"How can I help?"

"Mama hardly talked about her family. Did Aunt Antonia ever tell you about what it was like growing up with her sisters?"

"Not really. She was so full of resentment that she never spoke of happy times in her childhood. I learned to tune her out. I was not such a good husband. I did not know how to make my wife happy."

He looks so sad that Witold quickly reassures him that as a psychiatrist, he can say from his experience that no one can make another person happy. That has to come from a person's own inner resources. Feliks gives him a wan smile, without any indication as to whether he believes this or not.

Mania is still focused on her mother. She asks, "Do you have any idea why my mother would cut all contact with Irena?"

"I'm afraid I can't explain that to you, my dear. But it may not have been a deliberate act. When your mother left us, she left no forwarding address. In the upheaval of population transfers from Ukraine to Poland after the war, it was difficult to find people."

"Especially if they didn't want to be found," Mania says, realizing suddenly that her mother's move to Warsaw put her further away and in the largest population centre of Poland – a perfect place in which to get lost if that was her intention. She studies her hands before she says, choosing her words carefully, "I have reason to believe that perhaps my mother and father weren't married when I was born. Did Aunt Antonia ever say anything about this to you?"

Felix purses his lips. "It was all so long ago that I can't honestly remember if she did. But if she knew, I'm sure she would have been outraged at such immoral behaviour."

"Did the two of you ever speculate why Mama made such a sudden departure from your home without even saying good-bye?"

He rubs his temples as if this will make his memory clearer. It is also a sign that he is getting tired.

"Antonia was such a mean-spirited hostess to you and your mother that quite frankly, I wasn't surprised when you left. Although I must admit that I thought it was out of character for your mother not to even leave a thank-you note. It just fueled my wife's anger. She said Krystyna was ungrateful, had no moral character and was a Jew lover too. You know she worked for Jews, don't you?"

"Yes, I do."

"They corrupted her, Antonia said. But then, they were the

ones who helped her look after Irena as a child, so it's understandable that Antonia hated them, isn't it?"

His gaze at Mania seeks confirmation that this explanation for his wife's behaviour does make some sense.

Mania pities him and says, "Of course, Uncle Feliks, it's understandable. Do you remember Aunt Irena's married name?"

The old man makes a peak of the fingers of both hands under his chin as he concentrates.

Finally he says, "It's ... it's ... it has something to do with the first man, Adam. I remember that. It could be Adamek, Adamski or Adamowicz. Something like that. Her sons' names were Andrej and Staszek."

He looks so pleased with himself that he could retrieve those two names that he smiles with pleasure for the first time during their visit. His smile warms Mania so much that she leans over and kisses his paper thin cheek.

"Thank you, that's very helpful. Now I think we had better leave. We have tired you out enough for one day."

"Oh, no, I have enjoyed your visit, and I'm glad it has been helpful to you."

"I hope we can come again with the results of my search."

"Any time, my dear, but make sure it's before my overdue release from this life."

"Is there anything we can bring you? Some special food or treat? Magazines or books?"

"Thank you, but I want for nothing. You see, I have the newspaper here and I don't even have the energy to read it. I get enough to eat for my small appetite. No, my wants are few."

He leans into Mania's hug. She feels like he might break with too much pressure. Witold clasps both his fragile hands in his.

On their way out, Mania says, "What a lovely man. That bitch, Antonia, didn't appreciate him."

"Don't be so quick to judge. You don't know what brings people together. He did say she was a lovely young woman when he first met her."

"That's true. We should have brought him a box of chocolates or something and not gone in empty handed."

"Yes, but we were in a hurry and didn't even know if we'd find him there."

They walk along the main street until they come to a variety store where they buy a box of chocolates. Then they make their way back to the old folks' home. Feliks is once again sleeping in his armchair but this time, they do not wake him up. Tearing a piece of paper from her notebook, Mania writes him a note of thanks and leaves it and the box of chocolates on the bed before tiptoeing out of the room.

She hopes that she has not come to a dead-end in her search. It may not be easy to find someone in a city like Opole with a last name that starts with "Adam".

"On to Opole, then?" Witold asks.

"Not yet. I think I need to do some more research on the Internet. If I find either of Irena's sons, I should call in advance to prepare them for our visit. In the meantime, let's go to Krakow and visit Marysia as we promised."

They spend the night in Wroclaw and leave for Krakow in the morning. Mania looks forward to sharing the progress she has made with Marysia, even though the last time they talked, her daughter showed little interest in her search. Regardless, she will enjoy her visit, especially spending time with Anna.

Chapter 12

Rose, Toronto, 1980 – 1996

When Mark had suggested a vacation trip to Europe in 1980, Rose balked. To her, Europe meant the loss of the ones she had loved and nightmares in which Krystyna and Irena and her murdered family appeared. She had no desire to go back there.

"Rose," Mark had spoken patiently to her, "when I talk about Europe, I don't mean Poland or Ukraine. I don't want to go to those places either. Or to Germany, for that matter. There are many other beautiful and interesting places in Europe: Italy, France, Spain, to name a few. Wouldn't you like to see the world-famous works of art in great museums and historical sites we've read about? Canada is a young country. Here we make a big deal out of a building that's only one hundred years old."

Mark had sold the pharmacy and Rose had retired from teaching – although she was still substituting – and he wanted to enjoy some of the fruits of their hard work. Now was the time to travel, Mark had said, before they were too old and decrepit. He had been excited by the idea of seeing famous places and experiencing different cultures while Rose was not. She did not care much for traipsing all over the place and living out of a suitcase. She liked stability and routine. Going to foreign countries, you did not know what to expect. If you could not speak the language, you would not know what they were saying about you.

"What if we run into anti-Semitism?" she had asked.

"The world has changed, Rose," he had said. "You have to stop being so paranoid."

Mark would not be put off. He had showed her travel brochures for the centres of European art, music, and culture, and tried to persuade her that once in a lifetime, you had to visit Paris, the City of Light.

With a great deal of trepidation and a promise from Mark that if things did not work out she would not have to go on any more trips, Rose landed in Paris and fell in love with it. She could not get enough of the art in the Louvre, the Musée d'Orsay, and the Musée Rodin. She had become, on this trip, a tireless walker, busy exploring the streets that rang in her ears with the sounds of the French Revolution that she had studied in school. When her feet could not carry her another step, she and Mark stopped to eat at the cafés where she imagined famous writers drinking espressos and writing in their notebooks. Sometimes, they just bought a baguette, cheese, and a bottle of wine and sat in the Tuileries Gardens enjoying a picnic lunch and the life around them.

After that trip, Rose was an enthusiastic participant with Mark in planning their trips to Rome, Florence, Venice, Amsterdam, Madrid, Lisbon, and Barcelona. Once again, she could feast her eyes on the works of the Great Masters. In these cities, too, they had wandered the streets, exploring shops, restaurants, and parks, and always brought home mementos of their travels, such as a painting or a ceramic vase. Finally, their home had begun to acquire some of the accessories that Rose had always rejected as possessions that tied you down.

Israel had become a favourite destination. There, they discovered distant relatives and school friends with whom they could reminisce about the old days without subterfuge. These people had known her from before. Although they had not gone through what Rose and Mark had because they had left Poland before the war, they listened in fascination and horror to the accounts of what had happened in their hometown. It had been hard on Rose to return to experiences that she had suppressed for so long. Even the nightmares had come back. But it had also been a huge relief to unburden herself to people who understood her. She had come to look forward to a visit to Israel every two to three years.

Their travels, which had lasted for fifteen years, were thoroughly documented by Mark with his trusty Leica, the one extravagance he had allowed himself before they left the DP camp in Germany. That was another chapter in her life that Rose preferred to forget.

In 1946 they had left their hometown, Stanisławów, by stealth of night. Life under Communism had not been to their liking. Always there had been shortages. Once again, anti-Semitism had reared its ugly head. When Róża had finally found a teaching job, a huge portrait of Josef Stalin had hung in her classroom, his beady eyes following her every move. As for the pharmacy where Marek had been the manager, it had seemed that the surveillance by the NKVD, the Soviet secret police, had been a daily event.

Their secret departure required them to leave everything behind. There followed wanderings through several displaced persons camps until they had finally landed in one near Munich, where they had cooled their heels for two years, waiting for their applications to various countries to be accepted. The United States and Canada did not allow in any Jewish refugees and Britain had put a strict quota on numbers permitted into Israel.

Those two years in the DP camp had been hell for Róża. While she had languished in their one-room apartment with the bathroom down the hall, Hanka had been in school and Marek had been employed as a science teacher at the technical school. Marek had reminded her that at least they had not been required to live in the dormitories like the other refugees, thanks to his job. This had been little consolation to Róża, as her physical and emotional health had declined. First she had

had to be hospitalized for pneumonia. Then she had lost most of her teeth due to the dietary deprivation during the war years. When she had fallen into a deep depression and had a nervous breakdown, they realized that they must leave Europe behind.

Finally in 1948, a distant cousin of Marek's in Canada had thrown them a lifeline. He, too, was a pharmacist and had been able to offer a job to Marek, and thus, a sponsorship for the family to Toronto, where they would be able to start a new life. Marek's Leica camera and Hanka's featherbed had been the only personal belongings that had made the ocean voyage with them.

It was the Leica that Mark had used to document their new life in the new country. Each photograph had been labelled in white pencil on the black page of the album with the date, location and the names of the people in it. When Mark had discovered colour slides, he labelled and sorted them just as meticulously as he had done his photographs. After dinner with the family on Friday nights, he often darkened a room and presented a travelogue on the screen, the albums with the black and white photos of their early years in Toronto, safely stowed in a cabinet, largely neglected. Helen and Joe had generally been an attentive audience while the grandchildren, Jessie and Richard, when they were young, would watch impatiently for a few minutes and then dash upstairs to play or watch television.

Rose did not share her husband's obsession for recording their lives. She relied on her memory, not pictures, to do that for her. Photographs, like life, were ephemeral. They could easily go up in smoke as had all those of her loved ones. Besides, even if she'd had albums full of images of her family it would not bring anyone back. Every time she looked at them would be a reminder anew of all she had lost. To her, it would be like repeatedly picking at a scab that was trying to grow over a wound. As for leaving the albums full of memories after she and Mark were gone, she thought it was all foolishness. She had no desire to memorialize her life. Helen and the grandchildren certainly would not be interested in a pictorial record of their travels or likely even their early years in Canada. And further into the future, no one would care about anything they left behind. Within a generation or two, no one would remember them at all.

In the spring of 1995, after Rose and Mark returned from one of their Israeli trips, Helen noticed that her father had a persistent cough.

"You should see a doctor about that, Dad," she said.

"I feel fine," he said. "It's just a postnasal drip. I always get it after I've had a cold."

"You may be right, but it wouldn't hurt to consult the doctor anyway."

Over Mark's objections, Rose made the appointment and began to worry, worst-case scenarios playing out in her mind as usual. She told herself that she would kill herself if anything happened to Mark. They were so closely bound together that she was sure one could not survive without the other. As she hovered over him, she chastised herself: *I should have noticed that cough. How come Helen did and I didn't?*

By the time they saw their long-time family physician, Dr. Simon, Rose was wringing her hands in a state of near panic. After listening to Mark's lungs with his stethoscope, Dr. Simon sent him for a chest X-ray, explaining to the distraught Rose that it was standard procedure when a patient had a persistent cough but nothing that she had to worry about.

A week later, the doctor's office called for Mark to come in for an appointment. Rose clutched her purse with white knuckles while they sat in the waiting room. Mark was unconcerned and told Rose to stop overreacting. After what they had been through, they should be able to handle any normal illness. But she could not heed his advice. To her, after what they had been through, any further troubles, no matter how they palled in comparison, might be just enough to push her over the edge. It would be a tipping point. She prayed, *No more suffering, dear God, please, no more suffering.*

God must not have been listening because when Rose heard the doctor say the phrase "shadow on the lung," she knew that her worst fears were being realized. So as not to infect Mark with her own panic, she managed to freeze a neutral expression on her face until she got home and called Helen.

"Helen, you have to talk to the doctor," she said. "I think there's something seriously wrong with your father."

Mark was on the extension. "Dr. Simon says that it's probably nothing."

"I didn't hear him say that. I heard him say 'shadow on the lung'."

"That's the only thing you heard him say. What you didn't hear was that he can't give a diagnosis until I have more tests and for us not to worry."

"He probably says that to everyone. Helen, please call Dr. Simon. Get him to tell you the truth."

Helen agreed, and the next day she reported back to Rose. Her voice sounded nervous and hesitant.

"Mom, you were right about the shadow on Dad's left lung. But an X-ray doesn't tell you what that shadow is. For example, it could be pneumonia or some other infection. Dad's never been a smoker, so it's probably nothing serious. Dr. Simon wants him to go for a biopsy to check it out. There's no point in you worrying about it now."

Her daughter's words fell like stones into Rose's heart. How could she not worry? If she prepared herself for the worst, anything less than that would be a reprieve. On the other hand, this could be the doom that she had been expecting all her life. They had been living on borrowed time. They had become too comfortable and let down their guard, forgetting that disaster lurked around every corner.

She said to Helen, "If the doctor didn't suspect anything, he wouldn't need to check it out."

"Mom, you can't be such a pessimist. Dad needs you to be strong."

"I have to be realistic." She started to sob. "I don't want him to die! I couldn't bear it."

"Mom, is Dad there? Get a hold of yourself. If he sees you like this...."

"No, he's gone out for a walk." Rose gulped down her tears and blew her nose. She knew that Mark had gone out because he could not stand her moping around.

"That's better. Now remember, Dad's just going for tests. He's not dying any time soon."

"Please come with me," Rose begged.

Helen took the day off work when it was time for Mark's tests and drove them to the hospital. Besides the biopsy, Mark had a CAT scan and his blood was taken for testing. When she dropped them off at home, Mark was ashen from fatigue, and Rose from anxiety.

"Call me as soon as you hear anything," she told her mother.

Rose went through the next few days in a trance, jumping every time the telephone rang. Although she knew that she was making Mark nervous, she could not control her emotions. That week was the longest one in her life. Finally, the call from the doctor's office came. Once again, she was asked to bring Mark in for an appointment. Over Rose's insistence that she bring him in immediately, the receptionist said that the first opening she had was in two days. She also refused to put the doctor on the phone because he was with a patient. Rose spent two days in an agony of worry. During the nights, she could not sleep.

Finally, Mark confronted her. "Rose, you have to stop this. I can't live with you hovering over me. If I'm sick, I'm sure that the doctor will do what he can to treat me. In the meantime, I feel fine."

Rose made a supreme effort to mask her feelings. After all, she had been doing it for years for the outside world and for her daughter. But never before for her husband. They had always been honest with each other, even during their darkest days.

Helen came with them to see Dr. Simon. He told them that the tests revealed lung cancer, but that with radiation and chemotherapy, it could be stopped. He assured them that Mark would get the best of care from the well-known oncologist, Dr. Edward Hamilton. Helen nodded as if she had already known about the specialist's reputation, but Rose had barely heard him. To her, the doctor's words were equal to a death sentence. She had never heard of the specialist and did not trust doctors anyway.

Before they left Dr. Simon's office, Rose asked what Mark's chances of recovery were. The doctor said that they were very good; however, he wasn't able to predict the future. In other words, Rose thought, he knew nothing for certain. On their way out, the receptionist was instructed to book Mark's appointment with Dr. Hamilton and his first radiation treatment.

Mark asked, "Can you please make sure it's after Passover?"

Rose grabbed his arm. "Mark, how can you think of Passover at a time like this? You should start treatment right away."

Helen said, "Mom's right, Dad."

Mark was adamant. "Who knows, it may be my last *Seder*. I don't want to let it go by without celebrating with my family."

As they left the doctor's office building, it started to rain and Rose was sure that this was a sign, a black omen of worse to come.

Mark conducted the first *Seder* with his usual aplomb. He led the singing of the traditional songs, told the story about the Exodus from Egypt, and explained the symbols associated with the holiday as he had done every year: *Pesach* – the Paschal lamb, whose blood was used to mark the doors of the Israelites so that the Angel of Death would bypass them; *Matza* – the unleavened bread because the Israelites did not have enough time to let their bread rise when they left Pharaoh's Egypt; *Maror* – bitter herbs to symbolize the bitterness of their lives in slavery in Egypt. Although Rose had seen Mark performing the ritual year after year, now she absorbed every word as if this was the last time she would hear his voice read the familiar passages. She pasted a smile on her face and pretended to join in the festive spirit.

Sitting around the table were the people Rose loved most in the world – her husband, her daughter and her grandchildren. Unlike in previous years, she had not extended an invitation to any of Helen's or the grandchildren's friends, except for the steady girlfriend of her grandson. Rose did not think she could handle the pretence of being a gracious hostess for anyone but her family. In the middle of the table flickered the candles, reflected in the bottle of sweet red wine. Mark's cough had become worse in the last couple of weeks. As the evening progressed, it broke into the rhythm of his chanting. Every time it hacked through his body, Rose felt a simultaneous squeeze in her heart. Mark seemed unbothered and with the occasional sip of water, he sailed right on telling the story of how Moses parted the Red Sea so that the Israelites could cross.

Just before everyone arrived that evening, Mark had said to her, "You have to stop looking at me like that, Rose. The kids will think I'm dying. And why would it be so terrible if I do? I keep telling you, the last fifty years have been a gift. I'm a lucky man."

Rose tried her best for the kids. To her the fifty-year gift was not that great. There had always been periods of depression and nightmares. And although the last fifteen years of travel and retirement had been a joy, she now believed that a time of reckoning had arrived. They would have to pay for that luxury.

She came to with a start when she noticed that the chanting had stopped. Helen was casting an anxious eye in her direction and Mark, too, was looking at her and grinning.

"Rose, we're hungry. That's against the law in this house."

It was time for the festive meal. Rose flushed and hurried into the kitchen, with Helen following close behind. They brought out platters of traditional food: first, the *gefilte* fish, then chicken soup with *matza* balls, brisket with *kugel*, and sweet carrot *tsimmis*, sponge cake and tea. Between courses, she and Helen cleared the dishes and carried them into the kitchen. At the table, Rose perched on the edge of her chair and picked at her food. She had spent hours in preparation but she could not eat. Anxiety and dread lay heavy in her guts.

At one point, alone with Helen in the kitchen, she said, "What are we going to do about Dad?"

Helen laid down the platter with the cake that she was taking into the dining room and put her arms around her mother. Rose burst into tears, something she had never before done in front of her daughter. They had never had a relationship of close physical contact before.

"Mom, as soon as Passover is over, Dad will start his radiation therapy at Princess Margaret Hospital. It's the best place for cancer treatment. Dr. Hamilton is an excellent oncologist. Dad will get the best of care. We have to keep his spirits up. It won't help for him to see you break down."

"I know," Rose said, extricating herself from Helen's arms and wiping her face with a dishtowel. She gazed into her daughter's eyes and saw there a poorly disguised concern. "You're worried, too, I can tell. We can speak the truth to each other."

Helen shook her head. "The truth is, we don't know anything at this point. It's far too early to talk gloom and doom. Dad has a good chance to go into remission. He's lived a healthy life and we have to keep a positive attitude. That counts a lot in cancer treatment."

Helen picked up the cake again and turned to take it into the dining room. Rose breathed deeply a few times to compose herself. She was lucky to have Helen to share this ordeal with her. Now, as a middle-aged woman, Helen was a lot easier to get along with than in her youth. But Rose wished that they could be closer. There was just too much history between them and too many secrets that stood in the way. Too bad that it was taking a misfortune to strengthen their bond.

Back at the table, she smiled for the benefit of the grandchildren so as not to communicate her fear on this special night. They were sensitive young people. Both Jessie and Richard kept looking her way with creased brows and questioning eyes. As the evening wore on, Mark's voice became hoarse, and his hand trembled as he poured the wine. Rose could tell he was getting tired. She clenched her hands in her lap, digging her nails into her palms to prevent herself from doing anything dramatic, like clapping her hands and cutting the *Seder* short and sending them all home. She wanted to put her husband to bed.

Finally, the last glass of wine was drunk and the last piece of *afikomen* was eaten. Helen offered to help clean up, but Rose just wanted everyone to leave. She told Helen she would do it all in the morning. Rose and Mark stood at the door and gave goodbye kisses all around. As Helen hugged Rose, she whispered in her ear, "Be strong, Mom."

Quiet descended on the apartment. Rose insisted that Mark go to bed and not, as was his usual custom, help her with the clean up. For once, he did not object. Dismissing what she had told Helen, Rose attacked the dishes in the sink, a task she always found therapeutic. With her hands in hot soapy dishwater, she could let her thoughts roam and her tears flow.

The next day, Mark looked so worn out that Rose called Helen to ask if Joe could please take over conducting the second *Seder*. That night a pall hung over them all. Rose did not even try to hide her anxiety. The *Seder* was dispatched quickly and even the requisite four glasses of wine did not dispel the sombre mood.

Helen must have told the kids, Rose thought. *Well, why not. They're young adults now.* No *need to protect them. From now on they have to be prepared for anything life throws at them. Mark and I were about the same age when the world we knew ended.*

Mark's treatment included radiation therapy followed by a course of chemotherapy. It began right after the last day of Passover. Rose developed a routine, taking Mark down to the hospital and back home. He lost his hair, suffered from nausea and rested a lot, but his spirits were good and she allowed herself to hope. After a few weeks, the tests showed that the treatment had minimal effect on Mark's cancer. Instead, the cancer began to metastasize and seven months after being diagnosed, Mark had to be hospitalized.

Rose watched helplessly as his muscles wasted away and his face became gaunt. He tried valiantly to shield her from seeing his pain, but she felt it as if it were wracking her own body. Terror consumed her as it had on her worst days hiding in the woods. She could not sleep or eat, had nightmares, and went through her days in a state of perpetual bewilderment. She spent every hour from early morning until late evening at Mark's bedside, trying to will him back to health, but saw him slip away from her regardless.

She let Helen deal with the physicians, especially the oncologist, who intimidated her to speechlessness. When Joe and the grandchildren visited Mark, she was barely aware of them. Only Helen's presence beside her anchored her and temporarily chased away the Angel of Death suspended over Mark's bed. Helen took a leave of absence from work to come every day and help her mother.

Although Rose could not imagine life without Mark, she no longer prayed for him to return to her. She just wanted him to be free from pain, to go peacefully. What remained of the robust man she had spent her life with was an unbearable sight – a mere shell of the man. She watched as he faded in and out of consciousness. On the verge of total exhaustion herself, she refused to leave him except when Helen insisted and Joe physically accompanied her to the car and drove her home, promising to pick her up early the next day. She was determined to be at Mark's bedside until the very end. Nothing else existed for her. She wore the same dress every day. She did not wash her hair or hide the dark circles under her eyes with makeup.

One afternoon when Helen was keeping vigil with her mother in the hospital room, Mark whispered to his daughter, "Come closer."

Helen moved to the bed and took Mark's hand.

Rose shivered when she heard him say, "I want you to promise to look after your mother."

"I'll do my best, Dad. If she'll let me."

"She will need you when I'm gone. Try to understand her. She has suffered more than you can imagine … so much tragedy … such loss."

Rose covered her face with her hands. *Why now? Why must he tell her now?*

Mark continued, "She loves you more than her life. She may not always show it."

He ran out of breath and Rose raised her hand. "Enough!"

With one final effort, Mark said, "A hard lesson she learned from the war … too much love attracts the Angel of Death."

With these last words, he relaxed his bare and vulnerable head on the pillow, and the wrinkles on his white, translucent skin smoothed out. He closed his eyes and his breathing seemed less strained.

Shaken and puzzled by her father's words, Helen sat holding his hand as he slept. After a time, she laid his hand down gently and got up with a sigh.

Helen said, "Mom, I'm going home now to have dinner with Joe. Why don't you join us? Dad is resting. You'll collapse if you keep on like this."

"No, you go. I'll go home for a few hours later tonight. I promise. I'll get a cab."

"Okay, I'll be back in the morning. Call me if anything happens. And don't stay too long. You need some sleep."

She kissed her mother and left her sitting by her father's bedside. Rose must have drifted off because suddenly she was aware that darkness had fallen outside the window and the room was completely silent. Maybe she could leave for a couple of hours. Mark looked so serene. When she moved to kiss him good-bye, she saw that he was no longer breathing; his heart had stopped. She fell on his neck, kissing him and weeping uncontrollably.

It had taken from April when Mark had been diagnosed with cancer until the end of November for it to kill him. It had taken cancer to change Rose from a strong independent woman to a shaky, broken shell of her old self. She could not remember much about the next few weeks. Joe made all the funeral arrangements, while she and Helen huddled in her apartment, letting the activity whirl around them during the seven days of *shiva*. Family and friends came and shared stories about Mark and passed around pictures of him at various stages of life. Even former customers from the pharmacy visited and recounted anecdotes of his kindness and helpfulness in their times of need.

After the *shiva*, normal life should have resumed, but it did not. For days Rose sat by the window gazing out at the grey skies and the bare black branches of the trees of a typical early December in Toronto. She could not have borne it if nature had flaunted the colours of the other seasons in her mourning. Helen asked her if she wanted to stay with her and Joe for a while. But Rose only wanted to be alone in her apartment. She spent long hours thinking of the past and remembering her life with Mark, back to when she was still Róża and he was Marek in Poland. She pored over the old photo albums. Now she wished that there were pictures of their families from before the war. Without any visual images except those in her mind, there was not anyone else in the world with whom she could share family memories. In the privacy of her own home she wailed out her grief without restraint. There was nothing she could do to fill the space he had left, the hollowness inside of her.

Helen came regularly to visit. On Friday nights she would pick Rose up for dinner with the family. They failed to raise Rose's spirits without Mark there. She would turn to comment to him on something someone had said or to check if he had enough food on his plate, and he was not there. She would end up looking blankly into the face of one of her grandchildren instead.

Helen visited her at home, as did Jessie and Richard. They did not understand that she did not mind being alone. It was becoming too much effort just to talk to others. As for appointments with the doctor or the dentist, she would have ignored them if Helen had not made them and driven her there. Helen even insisted on taking her to the hairdresser every few weeks. Why bother, she wanted to ask, but it was too much trouble to argue so she went along with whatever her daughter wanted from her.

Every few days, she went to the little plaza next to her apartment building to shop for food – bread, a pint of milk, a packet of cheese, a box of cereal. That was all she could carry. Besides her family, this was her only contact with people. Her preference was to stay in her apartment or, when weather permitted, to sit all day on the balcony overlooking the city, forgetting the time, dreaming about her life with Mark.

When the memories became too dark and painful, she would rise and immerse herself in household tasks. There was nothing like the humming of the vacuum cleaner to push out dark thoughts. More and more of the time, she just sat and let her mind wander. She had no patience for books or even the television.

Helen tried to get her to join a seniors' club, to learn to play bridge, to go to the local community centre. They had all kinds of great activities there, Helen told her, like exercise classes, water aerobics, a book club. Rose dismissed these suggestions out of hand. She preferred her own company. Rose was well on the way to becoming a recluse.

Chapter 13

Mania, Warsaw, May – June, 2006

BACK IN WARSAW, Mania goes over the information she has gathered so far. She knows that Antonia is dead and Feliks is in an old folks' home, and that Irena and her family had to leave the village. If she is still alive, Irena probably lives in Opole. Mania now suspects that her mother had no way of knowing where Irena had moved. This did not explain why she did not try to find her sister. Mania wonders if it may have had something to do with her own illegitimacy. If her father had survived the war and her parents had married, she thinks the sisters would have reunited, although she has a nagging sense that there is more to the family estrangement than that. She will have to find Irena to get to the bottom of it.

Mania searches the online telephone directories and, after several mistakes, eventually finds one name that looks promising: "Stanisław Adamowicz." She calls and waits anxiously until a man with a deep, rumbling voice answers.

"Good morning," she says. "My name is Mania Wiśniewska and I'm looking for Irena Adamowicz. Are you her son?"

"Why do you want to know?"

"I'm the daughter of Krystyna, Irena's older sister."

There is a long silence on the other end of the line.

Finally, he says, "That's not possible. My Aunt Krystyna died a long time ago. You must have the wrong family."

Mania draws in a breath of relief. "You're mistaken about my mother. She died only a few months ago. I wanted to let your mother know before the funeral, but I didn't know how to get in touch with her. Are you Staszek or Andrej?"

"I'm Staszek. My brother died five years ago."

"I'm so sorry. Can you please tell me how I can get in touch with your mother?"

Another silence. Then, "Why should I upset my mother when I still don't know if you're telling the truth?"

"I tracked down Irena and Krystyna's sister, Antonia, in Wroclaw. Though she has passed on, I found her husband, Feliks. He helped me to find you. Would I do that if I were lying?"

"I don't know. But tell me this: All these years we've heard nothing from Krystyna and believed she was dead and suddenly you show up and say she wasn't. Why would I want to disturb my mother on such a flimsy excuse? "

"Please let me talk with her. I can explain everything."

After another long silence, Staszek says, "My mother lives with me and my wife. She's old and feeble. I don't want to upset her. What do you want from her?"

"On her deathbed, my mother asked me to make things right. I think she felt bad about breaking relations with her family. I want to talk to your mother about patching things up."

"It's a little late for that, don't you think?"

"Yes, it is very late, but not too late for me to fulfill my mother's last request. Don't you think your mother might welcome an opportunity to resolve any unfinished business between the two of them?"

"I can't speak for my mother. Where are you calling from?"

"Warsaw."

"Give me your telephone number and I'll call you after I speak to my mother."

He calls back within half an hour and asks if they can come that weekend. Mania quickly agrees.

Staszek gives her directions to their home and says, "I'll have to prepare my mother for seeing you. I hope it won't be too much for her. She's not so strong any more. My wife, Jadwiga, would like you to come for dinner at one o'clock."

Mania can hardly contain her excitement. "Yes! Thank you. I hope you don't mind if my husband comes, too."

On Saturday, she and Witold get an early start for Opole. After leaving Warsaw's city limits, they gradually find themselves on a highway with fields of wild flowers on one side and seedlings of corn on the other, basking in the glorious golden sunlight. It lifts Mania's spirits. She is excited about meeting Staszek. Finally, she has a cousin. Other people take cousins for granted, often not paying any more attention to them than as casual friends. For her, this trip is like going on a treasure hunt with the promise of finding something very valuable. The fact that Staszek was not as excited as she is about meeting a long-lost cousin does not trouble her. When he is reassured about her identity, she fully expects a warm reception. It is Aunt Irena whom she is truly eager to meet. That connection to her mother calls to her with a physical urgency.

She says to Witold, "I think Staszek is still suspicious of me. Why didn't Antonia tell Irena that we were alive?"

"You heard what Feliks said. She refused to communicate with Irena. Besides, she was jealous of the relationship between her two sisters. Holding back information was another way to get back at them, to put a wall between them. Soon, you'll hear Irena's version of what happened. Just don't get your hopes up too high. She's an old woman and her memory may be muddled."

They drive on in silence until Witold puts on a CD of Vivaldi's *The Four Seasons*. She knows he is trying to soothe her, but her nerves stay taut. There are too many unanswered questions. When they approach the city, the traffic picks up. There are tall apartment blocks on both sides of the highway. They make the turn down a broad, tree-lined avenue into the centre of the city. Mania asks Witold to stop so that she can buy flowers to take for Staszek's wife and a box of chocolates for Irena. Then, following Staszek's instructions, they continue until they reach a narrow, cobblestoned street, lined with old two- and three-storey buildings. Witold parks the car in front of a Soviet-style grey block stone building with three floors and a heavy metal door. The brightly painted window frames and wrought-iron balcony railings spilling over with flowers call to mind an old grandmother trying to hang on to a semblance of youth.

They walk through the main entrance, past a small lobby with a double row of mailboxes to another door, then up well-worn cement steps to the third floor. Behind closed doors they hear the high-pitched voices of children, the blaring of televisions and radios, and the muffled sounds of adults talking, arguing, and laughing. Cooking smells assail their nostrils – cabbage, onions, and roasting meat. When they reach Staszek's apartment, Mania suddenly loses her nerve and asks Witold to knock. A tall man with stooped shoulders opens it almost instantly. He has a shock of thick brown hair generously streaked with grey and he wears a striped, short-sleeved shirt. Mania steps forward and says, "You must be Staszek."

"Yes, I am."

Mania introduces herself and Witold and there is an awkward moment as they all shake hands and Staszek invites them in.

A short, round woman about their age dressed in what looks like her Sunday best, complete with apron, hovers behind Staszek. He introduces her as his wife, Jadwiga. She beams and welcomes them. Her homey presence makes Mania more comfortable.

"These are for you," she says, handing the flowers to Jadwiga. "And these are for Aunt Irena." She gives the box of chocolates to Staszek.

Flushing with pleasure, Jadwiga bustles away to find a vase for the flowers. Mania recognizes the familiar aroma of roasting goose coming from the kitchen, although the weather is too warm for using the oven and the apartment is stifling. It must be because they are being treated as special guests.

Straight ahead is the living room, where Mania's eyes are immediately drawn to a tiny old woman perched on the edge of a dark red sofa. A cushion bolsters her back and a step stool supports her feet. Bright hazel eyes peer out of a face wrinkled as a dried apple. With a pang of recognition, Mania notices that the afghan covering Irena's legs is knitted in the same pattern that her mother had once used.

Staszek bends over his mother and says gently, "This lady says she is Aunt Krystyna's daughter. She has brought you some sweets."

Irena brightens at the sight of the chocolates as Staszek opens the box.

Mania approaches her. "Aunt Irena, I am so happy to see you," she says, with a catch in her throat.

Irena beckons her to come closer. "I don't hear so well anymore," she says, taking Mania's hands in her bird-like ones. "Who did you say you are, my dear?"

Mania repeats in a louder voice: "I'm Mania, Krystyna's daughter."

The old lady looks puzzled. "Which Krystyna?"

A nervous tremor goes through Mania. After all the trouble she has gone to finding her, will Irena turn out to have dementia? She says, "Your sister, Krystyna."

Staszek says, "Remember, Mama, I told you that this lady called from Warsaw. She said that she was Aunt Krystyna's daughter and that she wanted to meet you."

Irena says, "Oh, yes, my sister, Krystyna. She died many years ago, poor thing."

Mania says, "No, she didn't. She died a few months ago."

Irena turns a bewildered face to her son. "Staszek, what is she saying?"

"Mama, she says that Aunt Krystyna didn't die when you thought she did."

Irena turns to Mania. "How can that be? I saw the fire with my own eyes. No one was left alive in that house."

More interested in the chocolate box that Staszek has put on the coffee table than in Mania, Irena reaches to make her selection. She pops it into her mouth and sucks on it greedily as she picks out another one.

"Aunt Irena..." Mania starts, trying to get her attention.

Irena turns to her as if she has forgotten that she has a visitor. "Come sit beside me, my dear, and you can tell me what you want."

Mania sits at the edge of the sofa and searches her aunt's face, eager to find some resemblance to her mother, but there is none. Her mother had blue eyes in an oval face with high cheekbones, a refined nose, and a bow mouth. Irena's eyes are brown and her face is round like a cherub surrounded by a white froth of curls. Krystyna's hair was straight and smooth as the breast of a dove. Perhaps Marysia's curly hair has come from Aunt Irena.

After popping the second chocolate into her mouth, Irena directs a curious gaze at Mania and Witold, who takes this as his cue to step forward and introduce himself.

"He is a handsome man," she says to Mania. "I hope that he is good to you."

Mania flushes in embarrassment but nods and asks if they can talk about her mother.

Irena directs a shrewd gaze at Mania and says, "I didn't know your mother. I thought you wanted to talk about my sister, Krystyna, who died in a fire."

"I am here to tell you that your sister survived that fire and that I am her daughter. She died only a few months ago."

Irena puts her hand to her heart. "Please do not tell me such a lie or surely you'll give me a heart attack."

"But it's the truth. I'm Krystyna's daughter."

"I don't remember that Krystyna had a daughter. If she ran away, why didn't she tell me that she was alive?" There was a plaintive tone of complaint in the old voice.

Mania is disappointed that Irena's memory is so weak that she cannot even remember that her sister had a daughter when they all lived in the village. She is becoming increasingly more discouraged.

"I don't know why Mama didn't try harder to find you. Uncle Feliks says that there was so much moving around after the war that people lost each other."

"Who is Uncle Feliks?" Irena seems to be getting more confused by the minute.

"Your sister Antonia's husband."

Irena looks relieved to finally catch on to something familiar. "Oh, him. He was married to that witch. Has she driven him to an early grave yet?"

"No, she died a few years ago and he's in an old folks home. He said you two didn't keep in touch."

"Why would we? When we were afraid that the Nazi would come back to shoot us like he did our poor dog. Remember Bobo, Staszek?"

"Yes, Mama," Staszek says. When Irena seems to have lost her train of thought, he prompts, "What happened after the Nazi shot Bobo, Mama?"

Irena perked up. "Why, I took you children away! I wasn't going to sit around waiting for him to come back."

Mania asks, "Is that when you went to Aunt Antoina's in Wroclaw?"

"Where else could I go? I didn't have anyone else." She shakes her head indignantly. "That witch. We stayed for a few days and then she turned us out. The children were too noisy!

Staszek nods vehemently. "That was the first time we went to her, Mama. The second time, after the fire, she wouldn't even let us in. She was a terrible woman. No family feeling at all."

In the meantime, Irena is mulling something over, her lips moving as if she is talking to herself. Mania watches in fascination, not knowing if she should interject, until finally, Irena says, "If you are who you say you are, how come you could find me and Krystyna couldn't?"

"We had lots of help from the Internet," Mania says, but sees a lack of comprehension on Irena's face. "We used a computer. Mama didn't have one. It helped us to track down Uncle Feliks. He told us that you might be living in Opole."

"How did he know that?"

"Because he knew about how the Ukrainians burned down Polish villages after the war and how people were deported from their homes."

Irena is suddenly transported into a vision only she can see. She wraps her arms around herself and shakes back and forth.

"Oh, the fires. There were flames everywhere. We were so frightened. We were left with nothing."

Staszek steps over to pat her gently on the shoulder. "Mama, that was a long time ago. You're safe now in my home. I'll always protect you." He gives Mania a warning look.

Mania says, "I didn't mean to upset you, Aunt Irena."

Irena slowly turns a sad face to her niece and says, "Are you still here?"

Almost ready to give up, Mania says, "Yes, I am, Aunt Irena. Do you feel up to telling me what you remember about your sister, Krystyna?"

Irena says, as if dredging up a long-lost account of the past, "Krystyna died in the fire that burned down the big house. My house didn't burn in that fire." Irena stops to blow her nose into a hankie she takes out of a pocket.

Gently, Mania says, "What I am telling you is that she didn't die. She ran away to Wroclaw to stay with Aunt Antonia."

Irena's eyes widen in wonder. "Antonia took her in? And she refused me?"

"Yes, I'm afraid so. Uncle Feliks thinks it's because of the children. She said three children would be too much for her."

Staszek says, "There was only me and Andrej by then."

"Even that was too much for her, the old cow," Irena says bitterly.

Mania tries to divert her back to talking about Krystyna.

The old lady shakes her head to reorient herself. She says, "Krystyna was like a mother to me when I was a child. You can't imagine how I mourned for her when I thought she was dead. Now you say she wasn't dead all those years. I don't know what to think."

Staszek says, "So where was she that whole time?"

Mania says, "It was an awful time. We couldn't stay with Antonia, she was so mean to us. We ran from one place to another, first from the Nazis and then from the Russians. Mama was busy trying to put a roof over our heads and some food in our bellies. Then when we finally arrived in Warsaw and life settled down a bit, she wanted to put the past behind her."

Irena cannot keep up with everything Mania is saying. Mania hopes that Staszek will repeat it for her at some later time.

Now she says, "Is there anything else you can tell me about Krystyna?"

Irena says, "She changed when she got older. Maybe she was a little like Antonia – trying to reach beyond her station in life. She liked to dress up. She liked when the boys looked at her even though she thought that they were all beneath her. Except that son of the Count, who started coming around to the hardware store. I bet he didn't marry her after the war like she thought he would, did he?

Mania dropped her eyes to her hands in her lap. "I'm not sure if they married. She waited for him to come home from the war, but he was killed and never returned. So many years later, she married a wonderful man named Tadeusz. The marriage lasted fifteen years and then he died too. Mama died a couple of months ago. I didn't know how to find you to invite you to the funeral."

Recounting these events renews Mania's grief. She feels inadequate in summarizing a full life in just a few sentences. What were marriage and death except a couple of road markers along the way? She would need a lot more time to tell Irena about Krystyna's hard life, about her two breakdowns; about the joys of family life that Krystyna finally achieved with Tadeusz, her granddaughter and great-granddaughter.

Irena is bewildered by this new information and turns to Staszek. "Did she say that the Count's son died in the war?" Staszek nods. "But that one was not Krystyna's husband," she says.

"That's right," Mania says. "Someone told me that they never married."

"He was her undoing, my poor sister. That fancy son of the gentry turned her head. I told her he would never marry her."

Mania realizes that sometimes Irena's memory is quite good. "His family never helped her. We were very poor."

"The war did terrible things to everyone," Irena says and reaches for another chocolate.

"What about when you and your sisters were children? Those must have been happy times."

As if the chocolate is fuel for her memory, Irena begins to talk in a dreamy way.

"When we were little, my sisters and I lived on a farm. Krystyna and I used to help our father as soon as we could walk and carry. Antonia was still a baby. Mama worked for the Blciweis family as a housekeeper. They were Jews who owned a hardware store in town. Father used to buy his farm equipment there. Then the plague came and took our parents. It was terrible. Krystyna looked after us, but she was just a child herself. The priest wrote to some people in Wroclaw. They took the baby, Antonia. *Pani* Bleiweis took on Krystyna as a kitchen maid. I went along. I used to play with their daughter, Róża, who was my age. When Róża got older, she went to the *Gymnasium*. We didn't play together any more. She had to study, and I started working in the store."

When Irena's voice fades, Staszek says, "Mama, maybe that's enough for now."

"Maybe a little water," she whispers. Jadwiga brings in a glass of water and Irena sips. It is as if she has stored up this narrative for such a long time that once started, it continues to spill out.

"One day, Władek came in to buy some nails. He was from our village. We started to go out for walks together. When he asked me to marry him, I said yes. I wanted a home of my own. We didn't have much money, but we were happy. And then we had our two boys."

She stops again. There is a faraway look in her eyes and a smile on her lips. Mania sees that Staszek is leaning forward, watching his mother for signs of fatigue.

Mania asks, "When did he join the partisans?"

"As soon as the Germans came and destroyed our happy life. Władek was a patriot. But he was killed early in the war and left me a widow with the boys." She dabs at her eyes. "I didn't know from one day to the next what food I could put on the table. One day, Róża fell through my door. She brought me Halinka, her daughter."

Irena breaks off to blow her nose and wipe her eyes. Staszek is standing by, very tense, ready to whisk his mother away at the first indication that she has had enough.

But Irena soldiers on. "Róża gave me some money for taking her child. I needed it, but I would have taken her anyway. I loved that little girl. She loved me too. She called me Mama. At the end of the war, Róża and Marek came and took her away from me. They didn't even let me say goodbye."

Staszek says, "It was awful what they did. After what Mama did for them. It was unforgivable."

The old lady says, "They loved her too, and they wanted her back. But why couldn't they let me say goodbye? Why couldn't they let me visit her once in a while?"

Staszek is getting agitated at his mother's obvious distress.

He says, "Come, Mama, let's have dinner now. We can talk some more later."

Irena gets up with the help of his arm and shuffles to the head of the table where she is seated on a chair with a cushion like a child so that she can reach the top. Mania is moved by Irena's story. She is impressed with Staszek's kindness to his mother. She and Witold sit down on the opposite side of the table from Staszek and his wife, although Jadwiga is mostly in and out of the kitchen during the course of the next hour and a half and barely sits for a minute. She brings in one dish after another – potato soup, roast goose, dumplings, cabbage, potatoes, beets, applesauce, and two kinds of cake with tea for dessert.

Throughout the meal, Mania tries to relax and push down the questions that are bubbling up inside her. Staszek is watching over his mother protectively. It is Witold who does most of the talking, telling them about their life in Warsaw, while Jadwiga keeps piling second helpings on their plates and will not take "no" for an answer. Seeing how Irena eats slowly and chews every mouthful carefully reminds Mania of her mother: Irena enjoying the soup – creamy and smooth and easy to eat; Staszek cutting up her meat in small pieces; Irena picking at it like a bird but concentrating more on the potatoes and vegetables; and Irena enjoying the sweet cake to the last crumb. When they return to the living room, Jadwiga brings out tea and more sweets – poppy seed cookies.

With some prompting, Irena resumes her story.

"I loved that little Halinka like my own baby. The boys loved her like a sister, didn't you, Staszek?"

Staszek nods.

Witold, who was quiet before dinner, now asks, "Did the boys know that she was a Jewish child?"

"Oh, no. That was too dangerous. I told them she was my sister Antonia's child, their cousin from Wroclaw. I said she was with us because both parents had to work. Ha! Ha! What a joke! My sister Antonia who couldn't have any children! She didn't know I gave her one! A Jewish child yet. She hated Jews."

Mania asks, "But didn't you have to tell her the truth when you ran away from the Nazis? When you went to her for help that first time?"

"I didn't tell her anything. She guessed. I had to deny it because of the boys. I'm sure that was the reason she was so mean."

"But why did she turn you away the second time, after the war, when you no longer had the child?"

"It didn't matter. People were mad at those of us who hid Jews during the war. Antonia was no different. She wouldn't have anything to do with me."

Staszek says, "Lots of people were like that. In a neighbouring village they killed a priest who hid a Jewish woman during the war."

Mania is shocked and also impressed that Irena took such risks for a Jewish child. But she is anxious to get off this topic and to hone in on her own history.

"Aunt Irena, what happened to my mother before the war, when you married Władek and lived in the village? Did she stay with the Bleiweises?"

Staszek can see his mother's eyelids drooping, so he resumes the narrative. "She did. That's where she met the Count's son, when she was working in the store. One day he came in and they started going out together. When the Russians came, everything changed. *Pani* Bleiweis died and her husband went to live with one of his sons. The communists nationalized all businesses, but they let the son continue to run the hardware store for the state. When the Count and Countess escaped to England, they asked Krystyna to look after the manor house. The Russian army took it over to house some officers and they kept her on."

"When did the Nazis invade?" Mania asks.

Staszek says, "That was at the end of the summer of 1941. They took away all Jewish property. They gave the Bleiweis store to a Ukrainian. The Jews were evicted from their homes and closed up in a ghetto in the Jewish quarter. The Nazis weren't interested in the manor house. The Russians had done a lot of damage to it and it was too far from town anyway. So Krystyna stayed on there."

Irena soaks a cookie in her tea and sucks on it while her son talks.

Staszek continues. "Nobody wanted to hide Jews. If any of Mama's neighbours had betrayed her that she had a Jewish child, the Gestapo could have shot all of us on the spot. Even though Andrej and I didn't know it at the time, Mama also hid Róża in our shed and later, even in our attic. Can you imagine the risks she took? Those people hardly showed their gratitude afterwards." A note of bitterness creeps into his voice as he concludes his story.

"Was Krystyna also hiding Jews?" Mania asks.

By this time, Irena's head is drooping on her chest. Staszek gets out of his chair and bends over her.

"I'm sorry," he says, "but I think my mother has had enough for one day. Perhaps you can come back again?"

Before waiting for a response, he practically carries Irena down the hall, presumably to her bedroom, for a nap. Her eyes remain closed.

Mania understands how easily an old person can get worn out but it does not keep her from being disappointed. She had hoped that she would hear about her childhood in the manor house during the war. She exchanges glances with Witold and waits until Staszek returns. They can hear Jadwiga washing up in the kitchen.

Staszek says, "I'm sorry. Mama gets tired very quickly. She's not used to company. This is such an emotional issue for her. Perhaps you can come back tomorrow."

Before they left Warsaw, Mania and Witold had talked about the possibility of staying away for a few extra days, and now they both nod and get up to go.

Mania says, "Can we come in the morning, about ten o'clock?"

Staszek agrees as he walks them to the door. In the car on the way to the hotel, Mania says, "It's too bad that Irena didn't tell me more about Mama and me."

Witold says, "What we heard was very interesting anyway. We didn't know about Halinka or what happened to the Jews."

"That's true. I guess I'm selfish. I'm more interested in my story than in Halinka's."

"I told you not to expect too much. She's an old person and even if she does give you more information tomorrow, it won't necessarily be accurate. At best, it will be her version of events, which might be very different from your mother's."

"But I don't have Mama's version! I don't have anything to compare it to."

As Mania sinks into her corner of the car seat, exhausted, she has some sympathy for Irena who is so much older and has less energy. Tomorrow she will ask if Staszek remembers her. He was there during the war, although he was very young. He may want to hear about what happened between his mother and his Aunt Krystyna as much as she does.

Chapter 14

Rose, Toronto, May – September 2000

ROSE SHOULD NEVER have given her daughter a key to her apartment. She had asked, "Why do you need a key? I'm always here when you come."

"What if you're in trouble, Mom, and you can't get to the door?"

"What kind of trouble?"

"You could have a fall or a heart attack, God forbid, or a stroke."

Reluctantly, Rose had agreed for Helen to make a copy of her key, but now she regretted it. With free access to her home, Helen came and went as she pleased. She often caught Rose unawares and stuck her nose into things that were not her business.

Rose felt that she had lost her privacy. The next time she heard the key in the door, she decided to ask Helen to phone before visiting in future. As Helen entered the apartment, Rose pushed herself out of her favourite armchair, using her hands on the arms as leverage. It was strange how difficult it was becoming to move herself even though she was now much thinner than she had been a few years ago. Increasingly unsteady on her feet, she planted one foot in front of the other carefully as she walked into the kitchen to put the kettle on for tea.

"Hi, Mom," Helen said, giving her mother a peck on the cheek. "What's new?"

"What should be new? Every day is the same as every other day," she said, carrying the teapot to the table.

Helen brought out two cups while Rose added a tin of cookies.

"Your days would have a lot more variety at Willow Gardens," Helen said as they sat down. "You could go to exercise classes, concerts, art classes, sing-alongs, discussion groups. You'd make new friends and never be bored."

"Who says I'm bored? I'm not moving. I like it here, and I'm staying. You'll have to carry me out in a coffin."

"Stop being morbid, Mom." Helen poured them each some tea and nibbled on a Digestive cookie. "Mom, are you eating properly?"

Rose immediately got suspicious. She stared at her daughter. "Why do you ask me such a question?"

"Because you look as if you've lost weight."

Rose waved off this observation with a flick of the wrist. "I eat enough. Once upon a time I would have been happy with a fraction of what I eat now."

"When was that?"

Rose was annoyed at herself for allowing this slip of the tongue. She had not talked about the war before, and she did not intend to start now.

"Don't be stupid," she snapped. "You know that we had nothing to eat in the ghetto."

"How would I know? You never talked about it. How did you survive without food?"

Now trapped in a conversation she had accidentally started, Rose wanted to get out of it as fast as possible, but she did not know how. That was dangerous territory.

Reluctantly, she answered: "We traded our few belongings outside the ghetto for a piece of bread, some potatoes – anything that we could get." She adds under her breath, "Until we had nothing left to trade."

Helen's eyes widened. "What did you do then?"

"When we hid in the woods, we survived on berries. Sometimes mushrooms. We had to be careful not to eat the poisonous ones. And Dad stole stuff from the farmers."

"Dad had to steal food?"

Rose got some satisfaction seeing the incredulous look on Helen's face. It was high time for her daughter to see that Mark had not been a saint. Not that Rose wanted to tarnish her husband's memory, God forbid. She missed him every day of her life. But he was only human and when pushed to the limit, he had done what he had to do. Just like she had done. They had been a team. What did the young people today know about suffering? They were soft. And that was a good thing. Never in a million years would she wish for her daughter to have to live through the hell that she and Mark had survived.

"Mom? Tell me more."

Rose shook herself out of her thoughts and looked around the room at the familiar surroundings to anchor herself back in the present – the teapot on the table, the toaster and cookie jar on the counter, the calendar from the hardware store on the wall. She picked up her mug of tea and took a deep swallow.

"I don't feel like talking about it."

"But why? I want to know. I've always wanted to know. Whenever I asked questions, you and Dad would clam up. Or you'd start to cry. Maybe it's time to tell me."

Rose set her mouth in a firm line. "I can't. It's too painful. Why should I put myself through it?"

"It's not just for me. Your grandchildren should know their family history."

Rose thought about this argument for a moment, then made up her mind. "No, Dad and I decided that we would leave the past behind. I'm not going to start reliving it now."

Helen gave an exasperated sigh and got up from the table. Rose watched as her daughter went to the refrigerator.

"What are you looking for?" she asked.

"I just want to see if you need anything that I can pick up for you when I go shopping."

"You don't have to do that. I go down to the store every couple of days."

"I know, but I'm not impressed with what you buy." Then Helen began peering into the pantry.

Rose said, "Stop that! I told you I don't need anything."

"So tell me why there is hardly anything in your fridge and why your pantry is as bare as Old Mother Hubbard's cupboard?"

"Maybe because I'm old and I have a small appetite." Rose could see by how Helen was standing there with her arms akimbo that this answer did not satisfy her. She tried again. "I haven't gone shopping this week yet."

"I give up!" Helen sighed and went to the door. Rose followed. She wished her daughter would stay a little longer, that they could have a regular conversation or even just sit quietly together, but they had never had that kind of relationship. Helen had always been Mark's daughter. Those two could communicate without talking. With her, Helen was more defensive. She would get prickly over the littlest things, taking offense if Rose suggested a better way to organize her kitchen cupboards or things she should cook for the children when they were young instead of buying prepared food like those cereals in a box instead of making porridge or Cream of Wheat. Or walking away in a huff because Rose did not want to discuss the war years.

Helen was standing at the door looking at her. She must have just said something while Rose's mind had drifted away. She would have to concentrate better when her daughter talked. Next thing, Helen would be using this as an excuse to put her in the old folks' home.

"So when will I see you again?" Rose asked.

"I'll come on Wednesday. I'll bring some groceries."

"Okay, dear, you can buy me some of that dark chocolate I like or those fruit-flavoured yoghurts," Rose said, trying to be conciliatory. They said goodbye and Rose returned to the kitchen where she poured herself another cup of lukewarm tea and sat brooding.

Wednesday afternoon, true to her word, Helen returned with groceries.

As she put away each item in the pantry, she called out, "Three jars of soup. Don't forget to refrigerate them after you open them. Two cans of tuna and two of salmon. When you've eaten some, put the rest in a plastic container and put it in the fridge. Don't leave it for more than a few days."

Helen closed the pantry door and said, "I'll leave this rye bread on the counter for now. You should put it in the fridge after you use it today so it won't get mouldy...."

"Stop, already! I'm not an idiot," Rose said. Actually, she did not mind Helen buying stuff for her as it saved her the trouble of going down to the corner store and back up the eleven floors in the elevator. But did her daughter have to talk to her as if she had completely lost her memory? It is true that she had once got off on the wrong floor and tried to insert her key into the lock of a door three floors below her own apartment until someone had pointed it out to her. And sometimes her food did go bad or mouldy because she forgot about it. But these things happened only occasionally and Helen should not make such a big fuss about it.

Unpacking the last grocery bag, Helen pulled out two bars of chocolate and put them on the table. Rose broke off a square right away, put it in her mouth, and let the bittersweet taste melt on her tongue. It had been so long since she'd had a piece of chocolate. It took her back to her childhood when her father always kept a bar under the cash register just for the two of them to share.

Helen was putting milk, butter, cheese, and eggs into the fridge, when she crinkled up her nose and said, "There's a bad smell in your refrigerator, Mom."

"There is? I don't believe it." Rose was proud of her acute sense of smell. It had been a problem when she and Mark had

had to hide in Irena's cold cellar, that hole the German soldiers used as a latrine. She had had to bury her face in Mark's neck to stifle her gagging.

"Believe it!" Helen said, holding her nose with one hand and pulling something out of the vegetable crisper with the other. "Do you know you have a bag of rotten onions in here?"

At arm's length, she held out a net bag of onions that had turned black and furry. Rose did not remember buying onions. She could not remember when she had last used an onion. She watched as Helen wrapped the item in a plastic bag and headed for the door.

"Wait a minute! Where are you going?" Rose asked.

"To the incinerator."

A sharp hunger pain struck Rose in the pit of her stomach. Like in the old days.

"You can't throw away food, Hanka," she said.

Helen stopped in her tracks. "What did you just call me, Mom?"

All Rose could think of was the pain in her stomach. "Give that to me!"

"It's just a bag of rotten onions."

"I can cut away the bad parts. I'm hungry." Suddenly, Rose's mouth started to salivate at the thought of the sharp taste of a piece of onion.

Helen came back into the kitchen, dropping the bag on the table. While Rose fumbled with it, her fingers clumsy in her hurry to get it undone, Helen buttered a piece of rye bread and handed it to Rose.

"Here, eat this."

"But I want some onion!"

"The onions are rotten. You can't eat them. I'll buy you some fresh ones."

Helen was bending down and speaking right into her mother's face. Why was she doing that? It was most annoying.

"All right! All right! Don't make a big issue out of it." Rose took a bite of the bread. The smooth feel of sweet butter on fresh rye bread tasted so good.

"What are you looking at me like that for?" she asked Helen. "You can have some, too."

"It's just that you're eating the bread as if you haven't eaten in a month. It proves my point. You don't eat enough."

"I'm not hungry most of the time. Right now I am. So what?" Rose took another big bite of bread. Already she was becoming full. "My appetite is small, that's all."

Helen picked up the plastic bag of rotten onions again.

"Where are you going?" Rose asked.

"I told you. I'm taking this to the incinerator."

This time Rose didn't object as Helen left the apartment.

When she came back and opened the fridge again, Rose asked, "What are you doing in my fridge?" Rose suddenly could not figure out why Helen was moving around in her kitchen as if she was in charge.

"I want to finish putting away the stuff I bought for you. I'm going to do that from now on so that you can have some healthy food to eat. And you'd better eat it! I don't want to end up throwing it out."

"Oh, no, you mustn't do that."

"Well, then, you'll have to eat it. What do you usually have for supper?"

Rose was about to protest to her daughter that it was none of her business but the words just came out of her mouth. "Toast and tea. Sometimes cheese. An egg."

"I'm going to make you something to eat." Helen started rattling around in the pots and pans drawer.

"But I just had—"

"One slice of rye bread. I know. I'll butter another one for you, and I'll heat up some of the soup I brought."

When the soup was ready, Helen poured it into a bowl and sat across the table from Rose, watching her eat. *It's as if I'm the child and she's the mother,* Rose thought, spooning soup into her mouth and biting into the bread. She had to admit that the beef and barley soup was almost as good as she used to make.

Helen said, "How about I get you a homemaker for a couple of hours a day, Mom? Or maybe Meals on Wheels?"

The good feeling that had suffused Rose as she basked in her daughter's attention immediately dissipated. She stopped eating and sat up stiff in her chair, hurt and insulted.

"What, do you think I'm a sick old invalid? I can take care of myself!"

"At least let me get you a cleaning lady. This place could use a good cleaning." Helen looked around her, grimacing.

"Who do you think you are, the Inspector General? I've looked after this apartment for years without any help. I don't want a stranger in my home."

When Helen left that day, Rose felt sad and lonely, as usual, but also relieved to be free of the criticism. These days, she was beginning to feel that she had to be constantly on her guard with her daughter. She used to be able to talk to Mark, but now she had no one except Helen and she was no substitute. She could not be open with her daughter, never had been. Keeping everything inside was getting harder. Sometimes, when memories came to haunt her, tears were dangerously close to the surface. Helen must not see her breaking down. As for having a stranger in her home, that was impossible. She would never have any privacy. What if this person caught her talking to Mark, as she sometimes did, and reported it to Helen? Her daughter would cart her off to the old folks' home for sure.

Rose had to prove to Helen that she could look after herself. She would have to be careful to throw out any unused food so that Helen would not find it on her visits, even though she considered throwing out food a major sin. One day, before Helen's next visit, as she went to the incinerator to throw out a perfectly good half loaf of bread, she ran into Mrs. Mandel from the apartment down the hall. Rose offered the bread to her neighbour, who was happy to take it. What a relief. Now Helen would not have anything to chastise her about. Another time, she gave most of a quart of milk to Frank, the nice caretaker, so he could take it down to the basement to use for his coffee. The problem was that sometimes she forgot and the vegetables rotted and the milk got sour and Helen found them. Then she had to put up with Helen's ranting again.

Helen had also started to dust and vacuum the apartment. Rose stood wringing her hands and telling her not to bother. She could do it herself. Rose thought Helen was only doing it to make her feel bad because nothing looked dirty to her. How much dirt could one person make anyway? One day everything came to a head.

Helen said, "Mom, I can't do this anymore."

"What are you talking about? Do what?"

"Your grocery shopping, your cleaning, your laundry."

"Who asked you?"

"If I didn't do it, you'd be sitting here in a pigsty starving from hunger."

"That's enough! Since your father died, you've shown me no respect. Now get out!"

Rose practically pushed Helen out the door.

"I'll be back when you calm down," Helen said as Rose slammed the door in her face.

"Who does she think she is?" Rose paced around the apartment, fuming. "She's just looking for an excuse to send me off to the old folks' home. You have to do something, Mark."

The silence in the apartment was not broken. Mark did not come to her and that made her even angrier. Just when she needed him, he disappeared.

Muttering to herself, Rose pulled out the vacuum cleaner, plugged it in and started cleaning the apartment. The vacuum cleaner had wheels. It was not that hard to move around. She took out the pail with rags and cleaning products from the storage closet. At first, she could not figure out how to fill the pail with water, but eventually it came to her that she must take it into the bathroom and fill it in the tub where she could put it right under the spout and add a squirt of liquid soap. There. She watched the water rise and foam up with a feeling of satisfaction. She could still manage some things on her own. She had never had a cleaning lady in her life. When the pail was almost full of water, she tried to lift it out of the tub, but it would not budge. She began pouring out water until she was able to get it out, with much sloshing and spilling. Gazing at the small amount of soapy water left, Rose wondered if it would be enough to wash the bathroom and kitchen floors. As she wiped the perspiration off her face with her sleeve, she decided that it would have to do and got down on her knees, dipping a rag into the water and bringing it out, dripping onto the floor. No squeegee mop for her. The only way to get the floor properly clean was on your hands and knees. After a few swipes around the bathroom floor, Rose was suddenly overcome with fatigue. She sat back against the wall and blew a breath up at her face to cool off. Maybe it was time for a break. Labouriously, she got back up to her knees and pushed herself up by using the edge of the tub for leverage. She stood up on shaking legs and shuffled into the kitchen to plug in the kettle for tea.

As she drank her tea, Rose noticed the pigeons on the balcony. Phooey, how she hated those dirty birds. She got up from the table, grabbed a dishtowel, and lumbered to the balcony door. Opening it, she waved the towel at the birds and yelled at them to get away. After she closed the balcony door, she dropped onto the sofa and closed her eyes to catch her breath. The next time she opened them, she glanced at the dishtowel in her hand, and wondered what she was doing in the living room. She must have dozed off. Pushing herself off the sofa, she noticed the dust on the coffee table and ran the dishtowel over the surface, moving a crystal vase in the process. Rose watched as it seemed to wobble in slow motion, fall over, and break into a thousand pieces. With a sigh, she gathered up some of the larger shards. Tears sprang to her eyes when a piece of glass cut her finger. She sat back heavily on the sofa and she sucked on her finger. Then she wrapped it in the dishtowel.

"Mark, where are you when I need you?" she moaned.

She could not see him but she heard him say, "Maybe you should call Helen."

She dried her tears. No, she would not do that. She had to try harder to be independent or Helen would put her into that old folks' home. Cleaning was not that important anyway. She did not care about it, so why should Helen? After all, she was the one who had to live here. It was not true that it was a pigsty. In a spirit of compromise, perhaps she would agree to Helen sending someone in to clean once in a while.

Over the next couple of days, when Helen still did not call or visit, Rose made a special effort to eat properly. She shopped in the corner store. She ate some fruit and vegetables, only nothing that had to be cooked. Everything worked out fine except when she tried to make hard-boiled eggs. Somehow, she lost track of time and the water boiled dry in the pot and the eggs exploded. What a mess! With a sloppy bandage still on her cut finger, she was not very good at cleaning it up.

When it came to the laundry, Rose was mystified that it had become such a complicated business. She used to do it all the time. Now, suddenly, she could not figure out the knobs and settings.

Finally Helen arrived. Rose awoke from a nap to find her sitting in the armchair, looking at her.

"How've you been, Mom?"

"Fine, my dear, just fine."

Still groggy from her nap, Rose went into the kitchen to make tea.

When they sat down over steaming mugs of brew, Helen said, "Mom, I don't think you've been so fine. There's hardly any food in your fridge and pantry. There's a pail of dirty water in the bathroom. Your hand is all bandaged up. What happened?"

"I had a little accident."

"That's why there's glass in the living room?"

"I thought I got it all cleaned up. I guess my sight is not what it used to be."

"And the pail?"

"I washed the floor. I was going to empty it...."

"But you forgot."

Rose shrugged and stared into her mug of tea. "What do you want from me?"

"You can't live on your own any longer, you know."

"This is my home."

"I know and I'm sorry, but I told you last time, I can't come here and do everything for you anymore. I have my job. I have my own home to look after. You can't manage on your own. You don't want a stranger around. What am I supposed to do?"

Rose's face brightened as an idea came into her head. "Why can't I live with you?"

For a moment, Helen was at a loss for words. Then she said, "I have stairs in my house. You can't climb stairs anymore."

Rose's face fell. Helen could have said she would fix up something on the first floor for her. Was that too much to ask? Rose was not going to beg.

She couldn't keep the bitterness out of her voice when she said, "If it's too much trouble for you to take care of me in my old age, you can send your cleaning lady here one day a week, okay? She can even do my laundry. Then all you'd have to do is pick up a few things for me when you do your own grocery shopping." Surely this compromise should satisfy Helen.

Helen sighed. "Okay, Mom. We'll try."

Things settled down for a while after that. Helen brought groceries. Maria, the cleaning lady, came on Mondays, and Rose stayed out of her way.

Then one night when Rose could not sleep, her mother floated into her bedroom.

"Mama, what are you doing here?" she asked.

"I wanted to see how you are."

"Oh, Mama, now that I see you, I'm fine."

She told her mother everything that had happened, and her mother nodded wisely and said Rose had done the right thing to let Helen send the cleaning lady. Mark, who had been a regular visitor, also agreed that she had to do whatever she could to keep Helen mollified. One night, her cousin, Shaindel, also came to her wearing a pinafore, while Mama hovered in the background in her ankle-length black dress. How mysterious and wonderful that they had not changed on the other side. Now she knew that there was nothing to be afraid of. She would join them one day soon, she hoped. As her mother had said to her once, loneliness was a curse. Rose took to spending more time in bed, looking forward to her visitors. Sometimes her brothers came, sometimes her father. But so far, only Mark and her mother talked to her. There was such sadness in her mother's eyes when she said, "*Meine teire tochter, die bist allein vi a shtein.*"

"Oh, Mama, now that you're here, I'm not so alone," Rosa sighed.

The next day, Helen found Rose lying in bed, half dozing under the covers.

"Are you sick, Mom?" she asked, a note of alarm in her voice.

"No, I just haven't got up yet. What time is it?"

"It's after four in the afternoon. Why haven't you been out of bed?"

Rose was disoriented. How did it get to be this late? What had happened to the day?

"I don't know." There was no way she was going to tell her daughter about her nightly visitors.

Helen sat down on the bed beside her mother.

"Mom, I think you need to go into a special residence. You can't live like this."

"What's wrong with how I live? It suits me just fine."

Helen threw up her hands. "You don't eat, you stay in bed all day! This is not fine. You need to live in a place where your meals will be prepared and someone can keep an eye on you. I've contacted Willow Gardens and they can have a place for you very soon."

"I don't want to go anywhere. I'm staying right here, thank you very much."

"You'll like it there. You'll have company. There are lots of other people your age at Willow Gardens."

Helen's campaign began in earnest. She dragged Rose to Dr. Simon and then to a specialist. It was decided that the move would be in Rose's best interests. Helen explained this to her in such logical terms that all of Rose's arguments flew out the window. Helen expressed concern for her safety. She told Rose she loved her and wanted what was best for her. She would feel so much better knowing that Rose was in a good place with good people taking care of her. *Blah, blah, blah,* Rose thought.

"What about how I feel? Doesn't that count for anything? I don't want to move. I'm comfortable here."

It was like talking to the wall. No one listened to her. Not even that nice son-in-law what's-his-name. Helen brought over boxes and began to pack Rose's stuff into them. Rose watched in stony silence. She refused to co-operate, even so much as to say what she wanted to take with her and what she would leave behind.

One day Helen showed up and said, "Tomorrow is moving day, remember?"

In truth, Rose did not remember. Sitting in her favourite chair, Rose began trembling. So this was it. She had gone through the last few weeks in a daze. She had done some silly exercises in Dr. Simon's office that Helen now called an "assessment". She vaguely remembered a discussion about selling the apartment, about Helen doing her banking for her. But had she signed anything? She did not remember.

After a sleepless night without a single visitor from the past to keep her company, Rose woke up with a sense of impending doom. The specific nature of it escaped her until she got out of bed and wandered into her living room. Everything was gone except her favourite chair. Cardboard boxes were piled up near the front door. As Rose looked around, confused and frightened, Helen's voice echoed in the empty apartment: "Moving day." She sat down heavily in the chair, gazed out at her balcony and hoped that she would not live much longer. Helen's conspiracy to rob her of the peace and quiet she deserved in her old age had succeeded. After all she had gone through, it wasn't fair. Maybe she should have expected this. Maybe she should have been prepared for the revenge Helen would take on her for all the imagined hurts and problems of her youth. In a sudden flash of clarity, Rose saw an image of Helen's journal, that teenage expression of hatefulness at her mother. This was to be her punishment for not being a perfect mother.

Things would have been different if Mark were still alive. Resentment sprouted in her like a weed. How could he have gone before her? It was not supposed to be that way. Together they had withstood the worst disaster of the modern age; they could have fought back against their daughter's evil plan to deprive them of their freedom. But on her own, Rose was not strong enough to stand up for herself, to fight for what she wanted. As she surveyed the skyline from the east-facing window of her eleventh-floor apartment, the golden canopy of the morning sun spread across the sky and lit up the lush greenery of the park nearby and the roofs of the residential area. How lucky those people were as they woke up to a morning of work, routine, and family life on such a beautiful day. She and Mark had been part of that community of early risers. They used to take their morning coffee out on the tiny balcony in good weather and watch the sunrise as if it were a performance mounted just for them. They would see the traffic down below and appreciate that they no longer had to join in its flow.

With a sad sigh, Rose stroked the arms of her favourite chair. At least Helen was letting her take this with her. She did not know what else Helen had packed in those boxes to move to the old folks' home or what she had done with the rest of the furniture. She had probably taken it to her own home or sold it and pocketed the money.

Getting out of the chair, Rose walked around the indentations in the carpet where the sofa and tables had stood. The dress and shoes she was supposed to wear were hanging, lonely in the empty closet in the bedroom. Rose dressed and went back to sit in the armchair to wait for her daughter to arrive. Soon there was a knocking at the door.

"Come in," Rose called out in a monotone.

The key turned in the lock and her son-in-law, Joe, and grandson, Richard, appeared. They leaned over to kiss her cheek.

"How ya doin', Grandma?" Richard asked.

"How do you think I'm doing? I'm being forced out of my own home into an institution. It's a black day in my life – what's left of it."

Richard shifted from one foot to the other and exchanged glances with his father. *He is a good boy,* she thought. The move was not his fault.

Joe said, "Come on, Richard, let's take these boxes downstairs. We can leave the chair for last."

When Helen arrived, Joe and Richard had just come back up for the armchair.

"Leave it for now," she said. "I've brought lunch. Mom," she said, opening a paper bag. "You can have the first choice of sandwiches. There's egg salad on whole wheat, salmon on rye and lox and cream cheese on a bagel."

"I'm not hungry," Rose said.

"Suit yourself. Do you want a coffee? I got one for you with cream and sugar, the way you like it."

"I don't want sugar." As Helen took it away, Rose relented. "All right, I'll drink it."

Richard and Joe leaned up against the window ledge with their backs to the balcony as they ate their sandwiches and drank their coffee.

When they were finished, Helen said, "Mom, please get out of the chair now. Joe and Richard have to take it downstairs."

Rose got up and faced her daughter. "How can you do this to me? After everything I've done for you. You were my miracle baby ... the only one to survive. And this is how you repay me."

"Don't start. We've been over and over this. You need someone to take care of you."

"Dad can take care of me."

As soon as the words came out of her mouth and she saw the look of horror on Helen's face, Rose realized that she had made a mistake.

"Dad's gone. He died five years ago." Helen took her by the arm and led her out of the apartment.

After that, Rose stopped speaking to Helen. She would not allow her tongue to betray her again. They went down in the elevator, and she cocooned herself in the front seat of the car. When they arrived at Willow Gardens, Rose clutched her worn black purse and refused to get out of the car. She knew it was hopeless to protest, but she was not going to make it easy for Helen.

"Come on, Mom. Please get out of the car," Helen said.

Rose didn't reply.

"I'll tell you what. If you really hate it, you can move back home in one month."

At that, Rose reluctantly swung her legs out and allowed Helen to put her hand under her elbow to stand up. They walked to the entrance together, arm in arm. Helen took her to the elevator and they went up to the fifth floor. When they got to the room that she had been assigned, the first thing she saw was a large window overlooking the garden. Joe and Richard had already placed the armchair in the corner near it so that she could have a good view.

Helen started unpacking the boxes and arranging clothes into the built-in closet and drawers. On the bed, which was against the wall, she spread out an afghan in cheerful colours of red, white, and blue that Rose had crocheted many years ago. A television sat on a stand opposite the armchair and a night table stood next to the bed. Rose saw that at least she would have her own large bathroom. She had to admit that it was certainly better than a hospital room. Joe and Richard put up her pictures on the walls. On the night table, Helen placed a framed picture of Rose and Mark from one of their holidays in Israel, with the panorama of Jerusalem in the background.

Seeing that picture of herself with Mark made Rose go weak in the legs. She stumbled into the armchair, still holding her purse in her lap. She watched the activity around her as shadows formed on the floor and walls from the setting sun. A young woman in a flowered smock and dark blue pants came in to draw the blinds and turn on the lights.

"Hi! You must be our new resident, Rose. I'm Michelle. I'm one of the staff on this floor."

Rose nodded, not smiling, not wanting to encourage her to believe that she was here to stay.

"Dinner is at five-thirty. The dining room is at the end of the corridor. I've put you at a table with some very nice people. I think you'll like them."

Helen said, "I thought we could take my mother out for dinner tonight. How about that, Mom?"

"No. I'm tired. I'm not hungry. I just want to lie down."

Rose could see that Helen was about to say something, but Michelle put a restraining hand on her arm.

"That's okay, Mrs. Teplitzky. If your mother is tired, she should rest. Many new residents feel the same way when they first move in."

"All right, then," Helen said. "We'll be going now." She kissed Rose on the cheek. Rose did not reciprocate.

"Don't forget your promise," she said. "If I don't like it in one month, I can leave."

Helen looked flustered and again seemed about to say something, but Michelle spoke up first. "That's fair, Rose."

Rose could have kissed her. She was going to like this Michelle. She allowed herself to smile directly at the young woman without including anyone else. After kissing her goodbye, Richard and Joe trooped out behind Helen. Michelle led Rose to the bed, taking off her shoes and covering her with the afghan.

"I'll come back later to help you get ready for bed," she said. "Perhaps you'll be hungry enough for a snack by then." Then she left, too.

Rose glanced at the photograph on the night table again and whispered to Mark, "See how low I've fallen?"

Her eyes drifted to her black purse beside the picture. She slipped it into the night table drawer. It was a tight squeeze but she did not want it sitting out in plain sight. You never knew who could wander into this room. The door was not locked. Rose closed her eyes and summoned her loved ones to commiserate with her.

Chapter 15

Mania, Opole, May 2006

WHEN MANIA AND WITOLD arrive at the Adamowicz apartment the following morning, Jadwiga has already put coffee and cake on the small table in front of the sofa.

After greeting everyone, Mania approaches Irena and says, "How are you feeling this morning, Aunt Irena?"

Irena looks at her without recognition and says to Staszek, "Who is this lovely lady?"

Staszek says to Mania, "Remember, she's hard of hearing." Then he bends to Irena and says, "She's Krystyna's daughter."

"How wonderful! Please come and sit beside me."

Mania's hopes for the morning plummet at this sign of Irena's failing memory. But the elderly have better long-term memory, so she will not give up yet. Maybe a photograph will help transport Irena into the past. She pulls out the one she found in the envelope hidden in the box her mother had used for filing her papers.

She points to it and says, "There you are with Mama and with your two little girls."

Irena says, "Is that my Halinka? Staszek, bring my glasses."

When Staszek brings them, she puts them on the end of her nose and examines the picture closely.

"Yes, it's Halinka. She was still a baby. It was taken just before the Germans invaded. We were already suffering under the Russians. Krystyna came with me when I went to Róża and Marek to see if they could give us anything – food or clothes for me and the boys. And they did help. Krystyna was looking after the big house. The Count and Countess had left some provisions when they escaped to England. She helped me out, of course. It was such a tragedy when she died."

"No, Aunt Irena," Mania says gently. "She didn't die." She realizes that Irena has forgotten their conversation from yesterday. "She took me and ran away from the fire."

"You were there?" Irena asks.

"Yes, look," Mania points to the child in the picture in front of Krystyna.

"That's Mirka. She died in the fire too," Irena says.

"That's me and I'm here to tell you that we both survived that fire."

Irena is perplexed as she looks at her and then at the picture. "Are you sure you are this same girl? That is Mirka who lived with Krystyna during the war."

"Yes, that's me."

Irena shakes her head and asks Staszek to bring her the photo album. With it laid out carefully on her lap, Irena turns the pages. They are frayed at the edges and the holes through which the rings go are mostly torn. She comes to a page with only one photograph on it.

Sadly, she says, "This is the only picture I have of them."

She points to a man, a woman, and two children in the black-and-white print. The woman has shoulder-length blonde hair, swept up at the sides with combs and hanging at the back in a pageboy. She has a sharp short nose, an unsmiling cupid's bow mouth, and pale eyes that look right into the camera as she holds a baby in a lacy shawl. Mania feels a strange connection to this woman and even the man – there is something vaguely familiar about him. He stands with his hand on the shoulder of the little girl with braids holding a doll. He wears a suit and he has a shock of dark curls flying off to one side. Unlike his wife, he has a wide grin and twinkling eyes. The children are the same ones as in Mania's photograph from her mother's apartment.

What am I doing in this picture? Mania wonders. She notices the doll in her hand and suddenly feels its weight in her arms. Rutka, that was her doll's name.

She asks, "Are these the people Mama worked for?"

She realizes that Irena has not heard her because she is off on a tangent again about Halinka and how her mother had brought her to Irena for safekeeping in the middle of the war.

She asks again, "Are these the Jews Krystyna worked for?"

Irena nods. "They were very good to us until they lost everything. After the war, they took back Halinka."

"Why am I in the picture with them?"

Irena is confused. She shakes her head. "That is Mirka."

"It's me as a child."

"It cannot be you," Irena says. "You have said that you are Krystyna's daughter. This is Mirka, the daughter of Marek and Róża. This picture is from *before* the war."

Irena is looking at Mania as if she does not understand and Mania wonders what she has missed in this conversation. She feels as if she has wandered into something like the hall of mirrors at the carnival where everything is distorted. She catches sight of Staszek and Witold who also look perplexed.

Mania says, "Of course, it's me. I look the same in this picture as in the one I showed you before with Mama and you." She pulls her photo out of her purse and passes it to Staszek, who peers at it and the one in the album.

Witold examines both photos, too. "It's the same child in both pictures. And the one with the braids certainly looks like you."

Staszek says, "Yes, that could certainly be you but if it is, then you cannot be the daughter of my Aunt Krystyna."

"But I told you, I am," Mania says, a tone of outrage creeping into her voice.

Witold sits down on the sofa next to her and puts his hand on her shoulder. "There may be some mistake here somewhere," he says quietly.

Irena examines Mania's photo and then her face closely. "I am very confused. If Krystyna had a child and you are that child, it was later. At this time," here she points to the two photographs, "Krystyna didn't have any children. Both girls belong to Róża and Marek."

Mania's heart is hammering and she finds it hard to keep her voice steady. "Maybe that's who these children are and there just isn't any picture of me ... except ... except ... Mama told me I was born in 1938...." Her voice peters out to a whisper.

Irena is shaking her head and now fixes her gaze on the photos again. "Mirka and Hanka their parents called them. Mania and Halinka are much better Polish names," she says as if to herself. "I told Krystyna it was too dangerous to take a child when I had one also, but she never listened to me." She speaks as if to herself alone.

"No, no! This is all wrong!" Mania hears the words pouring out of her mouth and cannot stop even though she knows she should. Her world is in danger of toppling. Perhaps she can prop it up with a torrent of words.

"My Mama took me to Wroclaw, to Aunt Antonia's. Then we went to Warsaw so Mama could support us until my *Tato* came home from the Polish army. He was killed at the front and never came back."

Irena and Staszek are staring at her. Witold has put his arm around her shoulders and is holding her tight.

Irena says, "The soldier was not your father."

"What are you saying?"

"Krystyna was not your mother. Now I know why she ran away."

Mania is in a state of shock. She can barely say, "Why?"

"To take you away so that she could keep you. I wanted to keep Halinka too, but her parents took her back," she says sadly, looking at the picture in her lap.

Mania cannot absorb what she is hearing. It is a ridiculous bunch of lies. "My mother ran away with me because our home was destroyed. We had nowhere to live. Besides, she wanted to get us away from the Nazis."

Irena says, "The Nazis were everywhere in Poland. She ran away to keep her secret."

"What secret?"

"That she stole a child that wasn't hers."

Mania's voice is shrill in her own ears. "Stop these lies! I'm telling you, I'm Krystyna's daughter!"

Staszek stands up and confronts Mania. "If you call my mother a liar, you will have to leave."

Irena motions for him to sit down. "My dear, you must face the truth. Krystyna was hiding your father, Marek, in the cellar. She kept you with her like a daughter."

It suddenly strikes Mania. The shadow in the cellar was actually a man. Her father. A hidden Jew. She is dumbstruck. The past that she has reconstructed, trying to fill in the blanks of what Krystyna has not told her, comes shattering down around her.

"All these years I thought I was Krystyna's daughter with the noble soldier and I wasn't? Or is this some kind of cruel joke?" Mania's voice quavers as she says this. She sees anxiety and compassion in Witold's eyes.

Irena is lost in the pictures again. "You and Halinka were such pretty little things."

Flailing around for an acceptable explanation that will keep her vision of herself and her life intact, Mania decides that the old woman is suffering from dementia. Staszek neglected to warn her that his mother no longer has all her faculties. There is no way that all these years her mother could have kept such a huge secret to herself.

As if reading her mind, Staszek says, "My aunt really kept this from you?"

Irena says, "When I told the Brombergs that you and Krystyna died in the fire, they accused me of lying. The nerve! I couldn't bring myself to steal Halinka, so why would I help my sister take Mania? I really believed Krystyna was dead. I can't believe that all those years she was alive." Irena shakes her head.

Staszek says, "Krystyna Koryzma was a good actress."

Mania says, "No, Krystyna Stefanska....." She is giddy with hope. Maybe this has all been a case of mistaken identity.

"Aha!" Staszek says. "Did you hear that, Mama? Aunt Krystyna used the Count's name."

Irena says, "Yes, I remember Krystyna's so-called 'fiancé'. Krzysztof Stefanski . He cut quite a dashing figure in his uniform. He said he'd marry her after the war."

Mania plummets from her momentary high. It would have been far preferable to be the illegitimate daughter of the wastrel son of a noble family than ... than ... no, she will not acknowledge that she might have had Jewish parents until she has much more proof than some demented old woman's word. Staszek may support everything she says, but he was just a child and cannot be relied upon. She is so confused that she doubts she can think straight. She glances at Witold, who grabs her hand and squeezes.

Irena is now examining the picture of Krzysztof Stefanski that Mania has shown her. "Krystyna thought she'd made her fortune snagging that young man. I must admit I was jealous. She was cleverer than me. But it didn't end well, did it? Now that I know she didn't die, I think she did a terrible thing. To kidnap a child is a big sin. I certainly couldn't do it. Where did you live with my sister?"

Mania whispers, "In Warsaw."

Staszek nods. "That makes sense. She took his name and hid in a big city where she could lose herself. And after the 1944 Warsaw Uprising, when most of the city's inhabitants got killed or ran away, the city was almost empty. The people who poured in after the war from all over Poland and helped to rebuild it were just as new as Aunt Krystyna. It would have been hard to find you and Krystyna among all those refugees," he says, directing his remarks to Mania.

Mania asks, "Are you sure I was a Jewish child?"

"Yes, of course," Irena says.

She mulls this over and then she bursts out, "How do I know that you two haven't made up this story because my mother is dead and can't contradict you? You've had all the time since I called to come up with a clever plot."

"What would we gain by lying?" Staszek sounds outraged and Irena opens wide, innocent eyes.

"I don't know.... Maybe for spite ... to get back at my mother. After all, you never really tried to find her...." Mania frantically searches for a rational reason to explain her tremendous rage and hurt. She snatches at another straw. "Maybe you're doing it because you're jealous. You think we're rich because we're from Warsaw ... and ... and ... we're doctors ... and if you give us a sob story we'll help you out financially. Well, I'm not listening any more! Come on, Witold! Let's get out of here."

Mania rises from her chair and stumbles to the door with Witold following close behind.

"You must stay for dinner!" Jadwiga calls after them.

"I'm so sorry," Witold turns at the door. "My wife is very upset. I must go with her."

He catches up with Mania as she rushes blindly down the street. She climbs into the car and sits in the passenger seat shaking. Witold reaches over to put his arm around her.

"Mania, is there anything I can do? Do you want to go to a restaurant for a cup of tea and we can talk?"

"I want to go home."

"It's a long drive, Mania. Let's get something to eat first."

She does not reply and he drives to the first café down the main street. She will not eat anything but after a few sips of hot tea, she seems to melt a little and her hand no longer shakes.

Mania asks, "Witold, do you believe what they said?"

He shrugs. "It sounds plausible."

"But Mama was the embodiment of goodness and truth. It's

inconceivable to me that she could have lied all her life." As she says this, Mania hears Krystyna's deathbed words, "Find them. Make it right." Maybe she was referring to Mania's biological parents and not to her own sisters. The thought shakes her to her roots.

"She was a good woman," Witold says. "Whatever she did, it was out of love for you."

Mania nods. "I know. I never doubted her love. It was steadfast and fierce. But to kidnap a child? Was she capable of that?"

"Love can be a powerful force."

"Think about it, Witold. If what they say is true, I'm not even a Christian. And you know what the church means to me."

Witold leans across the table and takes her hand. "I know religion means a lot to you, so there's no reason to stop being who you are – a good, observant Catholic. If what they say is true, you are only of Jewish descent; only a Jew by blood. Not by conviction, not by upbringing, not in any way that counts."

Mania stares into her teacup and tears come to her eyes.

"Me? A Jew? I can't believe it," she says.

"Mania, you're not bound by an accident of birth," Witold says.

She says, "I don't agree. I can't change what I was born. The Jews are a strange people. It's not just their religion. They have strange customs that they've hung on to for thousands of years. They practice strict dietary laws and don't believe in Christ. People say they're secretive and untrustworthy. Besides, I don't even look like a Jew."

Witold is losing patience with his wife. "Mania, I'm surprised at you. You're an intelligent woman. How can you believe such stupid gossip and superstition? Any Jewish people I know are just like the rest of us. Their religious observance is in a synagogue instead of in a church. We have strange dietary practices too, like only eating fish on Fridays. How would an outsider look at the wafer and the wine that we say is actually the body and blood of Christ? Think about it."

Mania lifts her eyes, which are filled with grief and confusion. "I know. You're right. I just can't get my head around what they said. It would be so much easier to believe that they lied."

"It's possible. But they didn't ask us for anything."

"No, because I rushed out before they had a chance."

Witold ponders this. "The peasantry never trusted the professional classes and the gentry. I can understand the bad blood toward Krystyna when she got involved with the son of the local nobleman. I could sense it from Irena and Staszek. They may also feel resentment toward the Brombergs. They believe all Jews have money and your biological parents were well-to-do before the war. Irena helped them and their baby in their time of trouble. Perhaps Staszek feels that they didn't compensate her enough for the risks she took when they got back on their feet."

Mania ponders this and adds, "And I think Irena has a huge grievance against them for taking back Halinka without a proper goodbye to Irena. I'm sure there's more to that than we heard today."

"If compensation is what he's after, we'll hear from him."

"Oh, Witold! I don't know what to think, what to do! I feel so bad that I over-reacted. *Pani* Glowacka was right. If you start digging, you may find something you don't want to know."

Now that Mania has calmed down a little, Witold suggests that they check into the hotel again, and they can decide what to do in the morning. She agrees and when they get to their room, Mania is so tired that she falls into bed. She sleeps fitfully as her thoughts and emotions roil around inside her. Eventually, the predominant emotion that surfaces is anger – anger at the woman who claimed to be her mother all her life. She had lied and stolen her away from her rightful parents. Mania could have grown up with two parents, even though it was probably Krystyna's hope to marry her fiancé and create a real family for her. Why had she not searched for the Brombergs when she found out that Krzysztof had been killed instead of subjecting Mania to an isolated life with a single parent? She was probably too deep into the deception by then to extricate herself, too attached to Mania to give her up.

Mania now questions everything she previously believed about her mother. The only constant is that Krystyna had loved her. Still, that cannot excuse her from blame for kidnapping a child. As for her biological parents, Róża and Marek Bromberg, Mania is angry at them too. They could not have searched for her very hard. Surely there were agencies – the Red Cross comes immediately to mind – which reunited families and found lost loved ones. It was inexcusable and she could never forgive them. Her pent up rage makes her toss and turn all night.

She is wide awake at six o'clock. Witold is still sleeping peacefully, but she cannot lie still any longer. She steps over to the window and pulls aside the curtain to reveal the grey dawn. On a similar cobblestoned street as the one below, she sees herself holding tight to Mama's hand while hugging her doll, Rutka, with her other arm. Craning her neck back, she catches sight of two faces in the window. She puts herself in their shoes. She sees their child dragging her feet and turning a sad little face for a last look at her parents. She cannot deny the truth of it any longer. It is heartbreaking.

She goes over to the bed and shakes Witold. "Wake up. I want to go back."

"You're up early," he says.

"I couldn't sleep."

"I'm not surprised. You had quite a day yesterday."

"I want to go see Irena again."

"Are you sure?"

"Yes. I want to apologize for my bad behaviour yesterday. And I have more questions for her."

"All right, but let's have breakfast first." He glances at the bedside clock. "It's a little early to pay a visit."

Mania and Witold have breakfast in the main floor dining room. Either they are the only guests or everyone else is still enjoying a couple of hours more of sleep. Mania tells Witold that she struggled all night to come to terms with what she has been told. She describes how the picture of herself with the doll triggered a memory for her that she thinks was the last time she saw the Brombergs.

When they return to their room, Mania picks up the telephone, her stomach churning. They may refuse to see her. Irena may be so insulted that all she wants to do is spit in her eye.

When Staszek answers, Mania says, "Good morning. I want to apologize for running off yesterday."

"You don't have to apologize to me, but my mother was very upset."

"I'm so sorry. It was all such a shock to me."

"It was a shock to my mother, too," Staszek says, "to find out that her beloved sister hadn't died but lived a whole secret life without ever getting in touch with her. What kind of a person would do such a thing?"

"I can't explain my mother's actions to you except to say that she was a good woman and what she did, she did out of love for me. Do you think that your mother would see me today?"

"You're still in town?"

"Yes."

"Wait." He confers, probably with Irena and says, "What more is there to say?"

Mania chooses her words carefully. If she wants further evidence to confirm what he and Irena have told her, she cannot afford to antagonize him

"I would like to know if there's anything else your mother can tell me ... about my ... Jewish ancestors."

"We told you the truth, as God is my witness. But if you would like to come this morning, perhaps Mama will tell you more about them."

"Thank you. We'll be there soon."

Witold and Mania check out of their hotel and head out for the Adamowicz's apartment. When they arrive, Irena once again indicates the seat beside her on the sofa. Witold sits in the armchair and Staszek hovers protectively over his mother's shoulder, while Jadwiga goes to get coffee and sweet rolls.

Irena is holding the photograph of the Brombergs and their daughters in her hand.

Mania asks, "May I have it? I'll make a copy and send it back to you."

Irena looks to Staszek and he nods. "It's okay, Mama. That's her family. She should have it."

"Thank you," Mania says as Irena hands it over reluctantly.

Mania stares for a few seconds at the man and woman in the photo. Surely if they were her "real" parents, something should be stirring inside her. Yet she feels nothing for these strangers except a vague sense of familiarity. She turns it over; inscribed on the back in fading ink is the date June 1941.

"Where did you get this?" she asks.

"When the Brombergs ran into the woods after the fire, Róża forgot the boots I gave her. So I gave them to Andrej. When he outgrew them, they were so worn out, I was going to throw them out. I saw something sticking out from under the insole. When I pulled at it, this picture came out. Róża must have hidden it there. It's the only one I have of my Halinka."

She sounds so sad, that Mania has to believe her.

"Do you know how Mama – Krystyna – got me?"

"No. She didn't want to talk about it. It was before the Jews were put into the ghetto. Before Róża brought me Halinka."

"Can you tell me anything about a garden? Mama talked about a garden before she died."

"There was a garden behind the manor house."

"I think I saw a little girl in it once. And in the river too. Or was it just a creek? I don't know if it's a real memory or just a dream."

"When I brought Halinka over to the garden, it upset Krystyna. She thought it was dangerous. She kept you away from people, even us. Nobody in the village would have believed that you were her child, even though your colouring and your face were just right, because you were already three years old. So she had to come up with a better plan. To be safe, she kept you away from people. You were not taken into the village or to church. You didn't go to school. But even if somehow you were discovered, Krystyna would say that you were a cousin's daughter from Warsaw where things were very dangerous. Then the fire gave her a good excuse to disappear and start a new life."

Mania nods. "I remember running away and the train ride to Wroclaw to Aunt Antonia's." She looks at the picture again and asks Irena what she can tell her about the families of Róża and Marek Bromberg, what kind of people they were, and how they lived. Irena doesn't know much about Marek's family, but she paints a vivid picture of the Bleiweis family: Róża's brothers, who used to tease her and Róża; her cousin Shaindel, who lived with them for a couple of years until she died of a childhood illness; *Pani* Bleiweis, who was kind and generous and always made sure that she and her sister had enough to eat and gave them lots of used clothing that was like new. She talked about the hardware store where she worked for *Pan* Bleiweis, who was very gentle and quiet and gave her lots of responsibility until she left when she married Władek.

Mania asks, "Do you know if Róża and Marek ever tried to find me?"

Irena puts her hand on Mania's. "Oh, my dear, I'm sure they tried. When they came for Halinka, they told me that they had contacted every agency and searched all the lists of survivors. They didn't believe me when I told them that you and Krystyna died in the fire. But they still had your sister, Halinka."

Mania gives a start. She has not yet absorbed this new bit of information. She has a sister. "Did you ever see her after they took her back?"

Irena shakes her head.

Staszek says, "When they left for Canada, they sent us a

forwarding address in case we heard anything about you."

"Did you write to them?"

"Yes, I did," he says, "but they didn't answer. Once I even made a long-distance call. You can imagine it wasn't easy in the fifties. It cost me a lot of money but Mama was so unhappy. I thought that if at least they would let Halinka write to her or send us some pictures. But all Róża wanted to know was if I had any new information about Mania. She just screamed at me about Krystyna stealing you. She said Mama must have helped her and she'd call the authorities that I was trying to blackmail her. Trying to get money. It was terrible."

He stares at his hands clasped between his knees as he recalls the incident.

"Why would she say such a thing?" Irena asks. "We were friends. She trusted me with her baby. Why would she think that I had anything to do with my sister stealing her other child? Especially when I told her my sister was dead, too?"

Mania says, "Staszek, can you give me the address and telephone number you used to contact the Brombergs?"

"Sure, but it was so many years ago that I don't know if you'll find them there."

He leaves the room and comes back with a piece of paper with the information on it that he gives to Mania.

Jadwiga enters from the kitchen carrying an apple cake. "Mama Irena taught me how to bake this. You must taste it."

Mania stares at the cake – one of her own mother's specialties, a cake her mother said she learned to make from her Jewish employer, *Pani* Bleiweis. Her grandmother. Her eyes blur over. She accepts a piece and nibbles at it. She sees that Witold is tucking in appreciatively. Staszek gets up and goes to the sideboard.

"Maybe it's time for a little vodka."

He glances around and Witold nods vigorously. Mania does not feel like celebrating but she will not refuse the glass of vodka that Staszek hands her.

"Na Zdrovie!" he says.

They all repeat the toast and drink. The heat from the liquor takes away some of the chill that Mania feels but she fears if it warms her too much, it will unfreeze the tears. Since she is unwilling to let herself go to that extent, she shakes her head when a refill is offered.

Eventually Staszek intervenes like he did during their first visit. "Mama is really getting tired. I think she has had enough for one day."

As Mania and Witold prepare to leave, Mania takes Irena's hands in hers. "I'm going to try to find Halinka and bring her here to visit you."

"That would make me very happy, my dear," Irena says, a smile lighting up her face.

Mania says to Staszek, "I'm sorry if I overtired your mother. You and Jadwiga have been very kind. Thank you."

Once they are in the car, Mania says to Witold, "I just can't take it all in. They're not even my family."

"You don't have to share the same blood to feel like family. Irena and Krystyna were rescuers. They saved lives. They were very courageous women."

"I know. Still, Krystyna's motives weren't merely altruistic."

"No, you're right. At some point, she crossed a line."

"I still can't believe my parents were Jewish. And I have a sister."

"Give yourself time," Witold says.

How much time? Mania wonders. She has already lived a lifetime based on a false foundation. She cannot imagine how, at this late stage, she can incorporate a heritage, a way of life, and an unknown sister (perhaps even parents if they are still alive) that are so foreign and even diametrically opposite to what she has lived and always believed. She cannot remake herself, of that she is convinced. She could just ignore all of this new information about her origins and continue her life as it was before. Surely, her mother had not intended for her to do anything more than let these people, these Jewish relatives, know that she survived. She feels confused, torn, and miserable. She wishes her mother had just died peacefully without baring her soul. How selfish of her! Her anger surges up again, and she does not know what to do next.

Chapter 16

Rose, Toronto, April 2006

FROM HER ARMCHAIR by the window in her room at Willow Gardens, Rose watches the children play ball in the alley next to the garden of the old folks' home. What a pleasure to see those young bodies move with such exuberance and freedom. Not like the old people on the benches in the garden below. They just sit there like bumps on logs. They do not even talk to each other. Might as well be dead, she says to Mark, but he is not here and she wonders why not. Maybe he is mad at her because she has started to think about Mirka. They had promised each other long ago never to talk about her. It was better that way. As if she had never existed. Still the pain was like cutting out a piece of your heart without anaesthesia. She had never broken that promise except when the nightmares had come. Then, Mark had always been there to comfort her, to calm her down. Now, sometimes Mirka's sweet face appears at unexpected times. What makes her cringe is the sorrow and accusation in the child's eyes. Was it their fault that they had not been able to find her? They had done their best. *Please Mark, don't punish me, and come back. I need you.*

Just then Helen breezes in, full of energy. "Hi, Mom!"

Rose forces a smile on her face. "Hi. I've been waiting for you."

"Ready for art class?" Helen asks.

What a question. Rose loves art class. All else flies out of her mind. "Sure!"

Helen guides her to her walker, but Rose brushes off her help. Since her fall and the stint in the hospital for hip surgery, Rose is supposed to use a walker, but she feels capable of managing by herself, thank you very much!

In the Arts and Crafts Room, Rose's favourite activity is painting. The instructor, Monica, welcomes them warmly.

She points out to Helen a painting on the wall covered with flowers in a riot of colours and says, "Your mother painted that. Isn't it wonderful?"

"It sure is. Mom, you should be proud of yourself. You did such a good job."

Truth be told, Rose cannot recall doing that painting. When she sits down with a brush, her hand seems to move of its own accord. When she first came to Arts and Crafts, she was not too keen on it. She had never painted before and stringing beads was demeaning. The instructor had given her outlines of flowers, kittens and puppies to paint within the lines and Rose had refused. It was what little children did. Underneath her scoffing, though, she had been afraid to embarrass herself. Then one day, as she had sat idle at the table covered with blank newsprint paper while all the other old folks around her were busy with their projects, she picked up a brush and her hand began to perform in free flow. She had dipped it into various paint jars, rinsing it in water in-between colours as the instructor had told her to do.

Besides florals, Rose has also created impressionistic street scenes with rows of higgledy-piggledy houses snug against each other in yellow, orange, and indigo. The sky is a Mediterranean blue and the trees lining the sidewalks have brown trunks and are crowned in varying shades of green. Sometimes, her houses have wrought-iron balconies overflowing with pots of red geraniums. Sometimes they face sandy beaches and deep blue and green seas. Upon closer inspection, little children can be seen on the beaches playing with red and blue and yellow buckets and shovels, making castles and forts and rivers with bridges. Once, she created a street scene of cobblestones, stores, and market stalls with sombre blacks, greys, and browns. She put in stick figures of women wearing *babushkas* and bearded men in long black coats and hats standing stiffly in front of the houses. This picture made her so sad and angry that she defaced it with big brush strokes of black paint before the instructor could stop her.

Now Helen says, "I really like your new painting. Can I take it home, Mom? I'd like to frame it and put it on the wall in my office."

Rose says, "Sure, if you think my dabbling is worth a frame."

Another activity that Rose likes is anything to do with music. At the sing-alongs, she belts out all the old songs even though she claims that, like painting, she never sang in her life before either. While many of the other old folks stare into space or nap or hum along, Rose enjoys herself with gusto, especially the old standards like "You Are My Sunshine," "Five Foot Two, Eyes of Blue," and "On the Sunny Side of the Street." They used to come out of the radio when she and Mark had first come to Canada. Best of all, she loves the Hebrew songs she learned in her youth as a scout or the popular pre-war Polish songs she had once danced to. The words come out of her mouth automatically and suddenly she is back with her scouting troupe in the Carpathian Mountains or in Marek's arms as he twirls her to a waltz or a tango at a wedding or café. Before all their troubles began. But that does not bear thinking about. If she keeps busy, those dark thoughts can be banished.

People are always smiling at Rose in this place. Not just the activity instructors, but also other staff and visitors. People did not used to be this friendly. She has asked Helen about this and Helen has told her that she has changed. That she is more friendly, too. Maybe that is true. Certainly Helen has changed. She is so considerate, so loving. Did they not used to fight? Try as she might, Rose cannot think of what they could have fought about. Helen is the best daughter in the world. Rose loves to introduce her to everyone. No one else's daughter visits as much or spends so much time with their mother.

But one thing Rose will not stand for is people prying into her business. There is a busybody social worker who has come to her room to talk about her "Holocaust experiences." What business is it of hers? Rose sent her packing. She keeps her own secrets, even though most of the time, she forgets what they are. Her memory is not what it used to be. Maybe that is a good thing. If only it was just the bad memories that would disappear. Unfortunately sometimes the good ones go, too.

Rose feels very lucky that she is not miserable like so many of the other residents. She is proud of her willpower that allows her to banish bad thoughts. Like sometimes at night, when she screams and flails around or when Mirka appears to haunt her. Then, when daytime comes, she will not talk to anyone for a long time. Once, they had tried to force her to go to breakfast after a bad night, when she just wanted to be left alone, so she hurled a plant from the windowsill across the room. One of the staff had to come and sweep up the dirt while a nurse tried to force her to take a pill. She had refused and when Helen came and asked her what had upset her, she could only remember that she had not felt good when she woke up but not why. Of course, seeing her daughter banished her bad feelings.

After painting class today, Helen takes her back to her room. She has brought a treat, which Rose appreciates because it is probably something sweet and Rose loves sweets. Also, the food at Willow Gardens is bland. Rose does not complain like so many of the others do. She is glad she does not have to prepare it herself. Besides, the others probably never experienced hunger like she and Marek did. As she reminds Helen, once you have known hunger, you never complain about the taste of food again.

Helen puts a piece of apple cake in front of her on the small coffee table in her room.

"What a lovely cake," Rose says.

"You taught me how to bake this cake," Helen says. "It took me a while to figure out your instructions. I had no idea what you meant by 'mix until it feels right'."

Helen reminds Rose of the frantic call she had made to her for further guidance with the cake, which she was planning to serve as dessert for company one evening many years ago. Rose pretends to remember and they laugh together. She does not understand why she cannot remember these things that Helen brings up all the time when events from her childhood and early years with Marek are perfectly clear.

"Would you like some tea with the apple cake, Mom?"

"That would be nice."

Helen brings back tea from the dining room and puts one cup beside each piece of cake.

"Tell me how you learned to bake," Helen says.

"I had to learn from Krystyna. My mother died when I was fifteen. Before I got married, I knew nothing about being a *balebuste.*"

Rose pauses with a piece of cake halfway to her mouth. Why is Helen looking at her like that?

"Who was Krystyna?" Helen asks.

"Our housekeeper. You remember her. We used to play with her sister, Irena."

Rose frowns. Why does her cousin, Shaindel have such a strange look on her face? What is she saying?

"I don't know any Irena or Krystyna."

Rose stares at her. It is as if she has been somewhere else for a few moments and has just returned and Shaindel has disappeared.

Slowly, she says, "No, of course, you don't remember her. You were just a baby when I brought you to her."

"Who? Irena?"

Bile comes up in her throat. Her head feels jumbled. She puts down her fork. "Who are we talking about?"

"Irena and Krystyna. You said I was just a baby when you brought me to her. It was Irena, right?"

Rose nods.

"How long was I with her?"

Rose picks up her fork even though she does not think she can put a morsel in her mouth.

"I don't know. A short time. I don't want to talk about her or her evil sister, Krystyna."

Rose picks up her cup with a shaking hand. She wonders how Helen has tricked her into talking about things that are supposed to be private. It must have been that cake. It is her own fault for not controlling herself. For saying their names out loud.

Helen is looking at her in a peculiar way again.

Rose asks, "Did you just say something, dear?"

"Yes, I did, but you were a million miles away."

"What did you say?"

"I wanted to know why you're not eating my cake. Isn't it as good as you used to make it?"

"It's delicious," Rose says.

"Krystyna must have been a good baker."

Rose is getting irritated. "Who do you think she learned from? My mother taught her all the traditional Jewish recipes."

"Maybe, somewhere in Poland, Krystyna has a daughter who can bake a delicious apple cake from a Jewish recipe. What do you think?"

"Don't be stupid. I don't want to hear about that woman or her lying sister. I hope they're both dead!"

Rose has put down her fork and cup. Her hand is now shaking too much to hold them. Helen is spoiling their visit.

"I'm sorry. Forget what I said. Just eat the cake. I made it specially for you."

"I don't want any more cake," Rose pushes it away. She needs Mark here. Where is he? She turns in her chair searching for a glimpse of him.

"What are you looking for?"

"Mark, where are you?" She turns to Helen. "Where's your father?"

Helen flinches. She lays a hand gently on Rose's arm. "Mom, Dad passed away almost eleven years ago."

Rose raises her hand to her heart and her face contorts in pain. "I know that."

Rose cannot tell her daughter that Mark is still with her but only she can see him. Perhaps if she lies down, he will come in the daytime. With all this talk about Krystyna and Irena, she needs him here. Right now.

"I'm getting tired. I want to lie down," Rose says.

Helen pushes her chair away from the table. "I'll wrap up the rest of the cake and you can have it after dinner for a snack, okay?"

Helen walks Rose over to the bed, takes off her shoes, and helps her to lie down. She covers her with the afghan and lingers beside the bed for a few minutes until Rose settles down and closes her eyes.

"See you tomorrow, Mom," Helen says and leaves.

As soon as her daughter is gone, Rose whispers, "Mark, are you here? You don't need to hide any more. She's gone."

She can feel him hovering over her before she sees him. Tearing up, she confesses the first stupid mistake she made, letting Helen think that she does not know that he is dead. Then, she tells him about her second stupid mistake – talking about Krystyna and Irena. Helen had tricked her. As Rose confides in Mark, she hears his steady "Sh, sh, sh," and feels his fingers gently stroke her head until all the tension in her body eases away and she drifts off to sleep. When one of the attendants comes to call her for dinner, she is a bit confused but no longer upset.

The next day, Rose smiles when Helen shows up.

"Hi, Mom! It's a beautiful day. Why don't we go into the garden?"

Rose agrees with a sigh. Everything is such an effort. She wishes that they could just sit here, but she does not want to disappoint Helen. Today she will have to use the walker. Helen guides her to the elevator and then outside where they settle near a bench under a tree. The deep fuchsia peonies are in bloom emitting a heady fragrance. Rose closes her eyes and inhales deeply.

Helen says, "Mr. Benedetti had beautiful peonies in his back yard on Major Street."

"The peonies at home were even more beautiful. Magenta and white, bigger than your fist. Shaindel and I used to cut a bouquet for Mama. Their perfume would fill the whole house."

"Tell me about Shaindel, Mom."

"I've told you about her before," Rose says wearily. "She was my cousin who lived with us after her mother died. We slept in the same bed."

"What happened to her?"

"She died when she was nine."

"How awful! What did she die from?"

"Diphtheria." Rose conjures up the image of Shaindel. Such a sweet girl. *Mama thought Shaindel was a good influence on me,* Rose thinks. *I was the wild one.* She chuckles at the thought.

Helen asks, "What's funny?"

"My mother never knew some of the naughty things Shaindel and I got up to. She was a good woman, too busy to supervise us all the time. So we were pretty free to run around like a couple of hooligans."

"What did you do?"

"We stole berries from the neighbour's yard. We tried on Mama's dresses and shoes when she was helping in the store."

Inhaling the fragrance of the flowers, Rose closes her eyes and turns her face to the sun. The warmth feels wonderful on her skin and seeps right through to her old bones. She hates the cold; even a little breeze is too much for her these days. She did not used to be so sensitive. Why, her brother Max would never have taken her skiing if she had been such a prima donna back then.

"You should have some sun screen on," Helen says.

"What for? It's too late for me to worry. I always tanned well. I was a real sun worshipper."

"That's true. That summer Shirley's mother invited us to their cottage for a week, you and her mother lay in the sun every chance you got. You had a hiding spot where you'd lie on your stomachs and undo your halter tops."

Rose opens her eyes wide and turns to her daughter. "You saw us? Was anyone with you?"

"It was just me and Shirley. We never told anyone else. After we got over the shock, we laughed."

Rose shakes her head. "What do you know? We thought we were so private."

As the sun goes behind the building, Helen says, "Let's go back upstairs. I don't want you to catch a cold. I didn't bring you a sweater."

"I'm not cold," Rose says, even though she has begun to feel a bit chilly. "Stop treating me like a child."

Helen sighs and sits back. Every now and then, Rose asserts herself with Helen. She wants to guard whatever little bit of independence she still has or her daughter will take her over completely. She is a great daughter but sometimes she steps in too quickly. It is bad enough that the staff treat her like a child until she reminds them that she is quite capable of still doing many things for herself. Just because she is not as fast or nimble as she used to be does not mean she is an idiot. Her fingers just will not do up shoelaces anymore. So Helen bought her shoes with Velcro fasteners. Buttons are also a problem and zippers are easier to manage. It makes her angry when Helen takes things out of her hands and does not give her a chance to do them herself.

After sitting outside for another few minutes, Rose says, "All right, now I'm ready to go in," and stands up, brushing off

Helen's helping hand with the walker like an irritating mosquito.

Back in her room, they sit for a while saying nothing.

Then Helen says, "Why don't we look at some pictures?"

As Helen pulls out Rose's old black purse from the night table, Rose says, "Why don't we look in the albums instead of in that ratty thing?"

"We always look at Dad's albums. I'd like to see what you have squirrelled away in here, just for a change. Maybe there's a hidden treasure," Helen says with a mischievous gleam in her eye.

Rose does not want Helen going through her purse. She cannot remember what is in it, but a purse is supposed to be private. Helen should not be snooping around in it. She is trying to find words to express her resistance to Helen's intention, but it is too late. Helen has already opened the clasp and the bulging contents begin to spill out on the coffee table. First, an old tube of lipstick rolls out. Rose picks it up to check the colour. The print is too small and she hands it to Helen who informs her that it says "Flamingo Pink." Rose takes off the top and, saying it was her favourite colour, proceeds to put it on her lips.

"Oh, Mom," Helen laughs. "You've got it all over your face. You need a mirror to put on lipstick."

Rose is annoyed when Helen takes a tissue and wipes it off her face. "I used to be able to do this without a mirror."

"Well, you can't any more. And I've never been able to do it," Helen says and leans forward to apply lipstick to Rose's mouth. Rose knocks her hand away.

"Give it to me!" she barks and pops the tube into her night table drawer.

Maybe I will start wearing lipstick again, she thinks, but without Helen's critical eye on her. A necklace of amber beads has spilled out of the bag. She puts that into the drawer too. She forgot she still had that necklace and it will be nice to wear it again. Two lace-edged hankies peek out from amidst a jumble of papers and photographs. No one uses hankies any more. She gives them to Helen, who seems to appreciate them, who knows why.

Taking out a handful of photographs, Helen begins to flip through them and pass them on to Rose. Mostly, they are duplicates of the ones that Mark put in the albums but that she just could not bear to throw out. There is one of Mark's first colour photographs, all faded now, showing her and Helen as a teenager against the fence with the neighbour's peonies in the background. In another picture they are at a picnic on Centre Island. Mark had always set up his tripod and timer so that he could join them. How he had fiddled with the focus on the camera and the timer gadget while she tried to restrain Helen from running off! She and Mark had made it a point to take Helen out of the city on the weekends in the heat of the summer. Toronto Island had been their favourite place but they also found many parks to visit, like Kew Garden in the east end and High Park in the west. Mark had always headed for the flower gardens. They did not have a car in those days but the buses and streetcars took them everywhere.

Another handful from the purse includes Helen's annual school photos. Every year her face changed a little – slimming down, getting more serious, perhaps even a little sad, Rose thinks with a twinge. At about the age of twelve or thirteen, her daughter no longer smiled at the camera.

"Why do you look so unhappy in those pictures, Helen?" she asks.

"Just getting into the troubled teen years, Mom," she says. "Here's one shortly after I cut off my braids."

"That was awful."

"But you have to admit I looked good with short hair."

Running her fingers through it, Helen fluffs out her greying brown hair, still short and curly. Rose will not look at her. That memory does not bear thinking about. Later pictures show Helen in a ponytail and later still, with a bouffant hairdo. Of all of them, the short and curly is the most becoming. There was a period when smooth and bouffant had been in style and they used to struggle with huge rollers to achieve that look. It had been easy for Rose with her straight hair but a nightmare for Helen. Rose lingers over Helen's university graduation photo. The gown, bordered with white rabbit fur, draped over her shoulders. Such a serious look she had on her face. She and Mark had been so proud as they made their way through the crowd of parents and family members outside Convocation Hall to congratulate her.

Rose loves the annual school photos of her grandchildren. Unlike their mother, these children seemed to have no problem smiling large, toothy grins. A strange sensation, something like guilt, comes over Rose. She does not understand it, but then she has a moment of clarity.

"You suffered, Hanka."

Helen's eyes widen. "What did you call me, Mom?"

Rose startles. "What do you mean?"

"You just called me Hanka."

"I didn't, did I?"

"Yes, you did."

"Really?" Rose wonders if Helen is just saying that to trip her up, unless her mouth spoke without her brain realizing it. That troubles her. It is not a good sign. She will have to watch out for that.

Helen stares at her. "You called me that once a few years ago and wouldn't explain why. Was that my childhood nickname?"

Rose nods, not trusting herself to speak.

"How did I suffer?"

With a faraway look, Rose says, "You were such a skinny baby, so sad and ragged."

"What are you seeing?"

"You, as you looked in the ghetto."

"Can you tell me again how you got me out? I never got the whole story."

"I wrapped you up and ran away. I don't want to talk about it anymore. It makes me sad."

Quickly she reaches into the purse again and picks up a couple of passports from 1995. These make her even sadder. They represent her happiest years with Mark.

"I think these are from our last trip," she says.

Helen takes them from her. "Yes, they are. Even though they're just passport photos, you both looked good."

Mark's face, so full of life and energy, stares up at Rose. Even she looks good to herself, so many years ago. Helen hands Rose a tissue to dry her eyes. Rose thinks, *I shouldn't have let her dig through my purse. Thank goodness it's empty now and she'll put it away*. Except that Helen is probing into a side pocket and she is pulling out a yellowed envelope.

"What are these?" Helen asks, taking out pictures from the envelope. They are photos of various sizes in black and white and sepia, some with scalloped edges.

Rose's heart speeds up. A prickle of danger goes up her spine.

"Let me see!" She grabs them from Helen. "These are pictures from before the war. A cousin of your father's in Israel sent them to me a couple of years ago. She escaped before the trouble began." She stares at the photographs as she thinks, *We all felt sorry for Sonja who was going to live such a hard life in Palestine. How were we supposed to know that she would be the lucky one? The only one of the family, except me, to survive.*

"Who is this? Is that you on the right?" Helen asks, pointing to a head and shoulder shot of two lovely young women on ivory postcard paper.

Rose brings it up close to her face and nods.

"How old were you here?"

"Seventeen."

"Who's the other girl?"

"My cousin Elsa."

"What happened to her, Mom?"

"The Nazis took her away to Belzec with the rest of our family."

Waves of sorrow wash over Rose. She wants to ask Helen to stop this bombardment of pain but her daughter is relentless in her curiosity. She is pointing at another photograph with an upright young man in a suit and fedora at a jaunty angle.

"Who's that?"

Rose's voice is now a monotone, overlaid with unshed tears. "My oldest brother, Max. I adored him. He was my mother's favourite. So handsome. Brilliant, too."

Helen is showing her another one. "What's this one?"

Helen holds a photograph with two children – a baby in a woman's arms and a toddler of about two or three with blonde hair in front of another woman. The faces of both women have been defaced. Someone has scratched across them with the angry strokes of a pen, obliterating any possibility of recognition. When Rose looks at it, her heart starts beating so fast that she thinks it will burst out of her chest.

"Give that to me!"

"Who are these people? Who did that to their faces?"

"I did that! They're devils, those two sisters. Krystyna and Irena, may they rot in hell!"

"Why didn't you just throw it out?"

Rose's chin trembles. "It's the only picture I have of the little ones."

"Is that me as a baby?"

Rose nods, making grasping motions with her hands.

"Who is the little girl with the braids?" Helen asks.

"Never mind! Just give it to me!" Rose grabs the photograph out of Helen's hand. She tries to stuff the picture back into the envelope, but her hands are clumsy and she is crumpling it.

Helen takes it away from her. "Let me do it before you tear it."

Rose screams, "Give it back to me! It's mine! You can have it after I'm dead."

Helen gives it back to Rose. "Don't get so excited. I just

wanted to know the little girl's name. Was she one of my cousins who died in the war?"

"Stop pestering me."

Rose gets up shakily, ignoring her walker. She heads straight for the bed. She barely makes it and collapses. Helen helps put up her legs, taking off her shoes and covering her with the afghan. Rose tucks the picture under her pillow and curls up facing the wall.

"I'm sorry if I upset you," Helen says, sitting at the side of the bed.

"Leave me alone," Rose says.

Helen kisses her cheek and leaves. That evening Rose does not feel like getting up for dinner. She lies on the bed not responding to anyone. After a while, she reaches under the pillow and takes out the picture. It is too dark to see, so she leans over and turns on the bedside lamp. Examining it closely by the light, Rose is filled with grief. How pretty Mirka was! She would be a grown woman by now; maybe even almost an old woman. She kisses the picture and tucks it under her pillow again. Calling to her loved ones to come and console her, she falls into a troubled sleep. At some point during the night, a nurse comes in and gives her a pill. She is too tired to resist. Just before her mind goes blank, a thought drifts in: *It is time for me to die and be with my loved ones on the other side.*

Chapter 17

Mania, Warsaw, May – October 2006

WHEN THEY GET BACK to Warsaw, Mania goes to the The Emanuel Ringelblum Jewish Historical Institute. There she examines images of Polish Jewish life in the Warsaw Ghetto, reads some of the multitude of documents on display, especially those about the historian of the Warsaw Ghetto Emmanuel Ringelblum, and sits mesmerized watching the videos about the Holocaust. When she leaves, she is laden down with books from the library.

Mania also searches the Internet for information about the history of the Jews in Poland and the events of the Holocaust. Memoirs and novels are stacked high on her nighttable and contribute to many sleepless nights. How could she have been so oblivious to the major part that Jews had played in Polish life and to the injustice and slaughter that had befallen them? Her head swimming with information overload, she tells Witold that she is ashamed at how ignorant she has been.

He says, "Don't blame yourself. Under the Communists, we weren't taught anything about the Holocaust. We learned about the monumental losses of the Soviet people and its allies in Poland. Add to that that Poland is a Catholic country and Catholics traditionally have had no love for the Jews, it's not unusual that you knew nothing. Neither did most of us."

"At least our people didn't participate in the killing."

"No, that's true, but there were many who didn't behave so well."

"I assume you mean collaborators?"

"Yes, but in other ways too. Like being bystanders. Like stealing their property, inhabiting their homes, betraying those in hiding to the Nazis, and so on. Even the Pope didn't speak out against the Holocaust. After the war, we focused on our own victimhood under the Nazis and didn't acknowledge any responsibility for the murder of the Jews."

"What about people like my mother and her sister?"

"There were brave souls, who endangered their lives to rescue people."

Mania heaves a sigh. "It's hard to reconcile the two sides of my mother – the woman who saved my life and the woman who stole me from my rightful parents."

"In a way, that's what this country is coming to terms with – its multifaceted role in the Holocaust, the range between those who helped rescue and those who helped destroy."

Flashes of Mania's Jewish childhood begin to come back to her at odd times. A tune playing on the radio triggers fragments of a lullaby in an unfamiliar language sung by a shadowy figure sitting at the side of her bed. It could not have been Krystyna because Mama had only sung to her in Polish.

When Anna comes to visit in June, Mania asks her about her earliest memories. Perhaps it will help trigger some of her own.

"Did your Mama sing you lullabies and read you stories?"

Anna mentions a favourite book of her mother's that Mania remembers buying and reading to Marysia. It was the story of the rebellious little goat who refused to do what he was told. It saddens her to realize that she had no such story books when she was growing up. Krystina's only teaching tools until they came to Warsaw were paper, pencil, and the Bible.

Mania takes time off from work to devote herself to giving Anna an enjoyable two-week holiday. She needs a break from her obsession with her Jewish roots. The day that Marysia arrives to drop off Anna, Mania knows that she has to reveal the truth to Marysia about their family history. Witold has gone to his study after dinner and Anna sits on the floor reading a book. The two women linger over cups of tea.

Mania is surprised at her daughter's response to the revelation that Krystina was not her grandmother and that her grandparents were actually Jewish Holocaust survivors.

She says, "Haven't you seen the articles in the papers, Mama? Stories about Poles discovering Jewish roots late in life? There's even a priest who was profiled recently. He found out that his parents were Jews who left him with a Polish couple before being shipped off to their death in Treblinka."

Mania says, "I guess I just never thought it had anything to do with me until *Babcia* died. Doesn't it bother you that she lied to us all her life?"

"Not really. Good people lie all the time to spare each other's feelings. I choose to remember her as a wonderful person. I'm more bothered by how the murder of more than three million Jews affected Poland. A whole lively culture and great intellectual capital were lost."

Overhearing this discussion, Anna tells Mania that they went to the Jewish festival in Krakow and how much she liked the klezmer music.

She asks, "Can I say now that I'm a little bit Jewish?"

"Of course, darling," Marysia says, while Mania thinks, *According to Jewish law, which says that Judaism is passed through the mother, you are Jewish.*

The next day Mania takes Anna strolling through the reconstructed old Jewish quarter of Warsaw. Souvenir sellers display small wooden figures and puppets dressed in long black coats, furry black hats, and long side curls. She has never seen anyone in this attire, but it is possible that in the United States and Israel there are whole communities of them. Is this part of being Jewish? Surely, it cannot just be the music, the food, and the customs? There must also be a spiritual side to Judaism as there is to Catholicism, but the prospect of delving into it is daunting for Mania.

In one store window, Mania sees an eight-branched candle holder. As she stops to examine it, she is transported to another time and place. A man is holding her in one arm while he lights the candles and chants some words. People around a table burst into a festive song.

She steps into the store with Anna and buys a CD of klezmer music. When they return to the apartment, she and Anna listen to it. It is as foreign sounding to her as the chanting and drumming of Africa until a chorus of voices begins to sing a melody that sounds familiar. She checks the CD envelope and finds the name of this piece – "Yiddish Wedding Song" – and suddenly she sees a bride and groom carried aloft on chairs, each holding on to the ends of a white handkerchief, and people dancing around them, singing and clapping in joy.

"*Babcia*, I'm hungry," Anna says, tugging at Mania's sleeve.

Mania is jerked out of her trance and takes Anna into the kitchen to give her a snack. Later, Anna helps her prepare dinner. Mania wraps an apron around the little girl and sets her to peeling potatoes, just as she used to do at her age for her mother when she had come home from school. But Anna has never peeled a potato before and Mania must show her how.

Soon, the fragrant aroma of the dill-infused *rosół* is bubbling on the stove. Closing her eyes and inhaling the familiar aroma of the chicken soup, Mania wonders if it is in Krystina's kitchen or her biological mother's kitchen that she first encountered it. What is a reliable memory? What is a recreation of the mind's desperate desire to remember? What is so deeply interred in the mind that nothing will bring it to the surface?

Taking Anna to church on Sunday, Mania has a sense of dislocation, not knowing if she truly belongs there. Gone is the solace that she always expected and received in prayer and contemplation, in the refuge of a place of worship with others like herself. The duality of her ancestry threatens to tear her apart.

One night after Anna has gone home, she says to Witold,

"After what my real parents went through, they didn't deserve to lose their child. I've tried but I still can't come to terms with what Mama did."

"Perhaps she intended to give you back but as time went by, it became harder and harder until she couldn't bring herself to do it. You were the central focus of her life."

"Still, it's such a contrast. It's hard to reconcile who I thought she was and who I now know she really was. It means I'm not who I thought I was either."

"At your core, you're still you, Mania. As for Krystyna, you have to remember her supreme act of bravery. She saved you from the Nazis. That hasn't changed."

Mania feels tears come to her eyes and she shakes her head. "I know, but when I think about how I'd feel if someone had taken Marysia away from us...."

"I'm not excusing her, but put yourself in her shoes. For four years, she risked everything for you. No one helped her, no one shared the responsibility. There wasn't even anyone she could talk to about what was terrifying her every day. Then she was faced with giving you up, just like that." Mania is stunned into silence. At least she has a family with whom she can share her pain, even if she still feels adrift about her own identity. "It must have been awful," she says.

"Have you come across the literature about hidden Jewish children yet? Some of them have similar stories to yours."

Mania immerses herself in more reading. Her anger at Krystyna abates as her sympathy grows. She is now convinced that as Krystyna's last breath left her body, she wanted Mania to find her birth family or whomever of them is left. She had carried that burden of guilt her whole life.

Mania decides that she has to confront the conflict between her spiritual faith and the faith she was born into. She arranges a visit with Sister Beatrice.

"I haven't seen you at church recently, Mania," the nun says.

"I feel like an imposter. That's why I'm here. I need to talk to you about what I found out from Mama's sister, Irena. She's living in Opole with one of her sons. She had some shocking information for me."

"I'm so glad you found her. What did she tell you?"

"She said that Mama – Krystyna – wasn't my real mother. Did you know that?"

The nun's eyes open wide and she shakes her head. "No, I didn't."

"My parents were Jews who left me with Krystyna for safekeeping until after the war. Irena thought we had both died in a fire and that's what she told my parents, who survived. But Krystyna just ran away with me."

"Oh, my!" Sister Beatrice is speechless with shock.

"On her deathbed what she was trying to tell me was that I should find my biological family."

"You must do it, then."

"I'm trying to deal with it, but I need your help."

"How can I help you, my dear?"

"I don't even know if I'm a Catholic anymore."

"Oh, yes, you are. Your mother brought in your baptismal papers when she registered you in school."

"That's a relief," Mania says, although strangely this does not make her feel as comfortable as she thought it would. "If my parents are still alive, will that make me a Jew?"

"Only by blood. By conviction and faith, you are a good Catholic."

Mania draws a deep breath. "I know what it means to be a good Catholic and I have tried to live as one all my life. I have no idea what it means to be a good Jew. I don't know what they believe, how they pray, or who they pray to."

Sister Beatrice heaves a big sigh. "We all believe in one God, but as you know, the Jews deny the divinity of Christ. They pray in synagogues on Saturday, but I'm sure you know that, too. I'm afraid that I'm not qualified to tell you anything about the Jewish faith. You would have to consult a rabbi for that."

The lines around the old nun's face suddenly seem deeper and her eyes are mournful. Mania reaches for her hand and says, "Please don't worry about my losing my faith. At my age, I have no desire to change my path to salvation."

Sister Beatrice is noticeably relieved. "I am happy to hear you say that."

"Why I want to know more about Judaism is in case I find my biological parents. How will I talk to them? What will be their expectations?"

Sister Beatrice shakes her head. "You can't foresee what they will want. They may be overcome with emotion. It will be traumatic for them. If they are still alive, they will be very old. You will have to be very careful and very kind."

Mania nods. "Apparently, I also have a sister. It's funny, I always wanted a sister but now that I find out I have one, I'm afraid to meet her."

"What holds you back?"

"She's a Jew and a Canadian. She's my sister, but a total stranger, really. Perhaps it's enough that I found Mama's sister."

"Do you think that's what your mother would have wanted?"

"No, of course not. I have to finish what I started."

"Yes, I think you know what you have to do," Sister Beatrice says.

As Sister Beatrice walks Mania out of the convent, she makes the sign of the cross. "Go with the Lord's blessing, my dear."

When she gets home, Mania sits down immediately at her desk to compose a letter to the Brombergs at the address that Staszek gave her. Since his last communication with them was many years ago, she does not know if they still live at that address, but it is her only contact information. For the next couple of weeks she checks the mail every day as soon as she gets home from work but there is no response.

One day Witold comes home with a glint in his eye.

"Guess what, Mania? We can go to Canada for a few days if you want to."

"We can?" This possibility has not occurred to Mania and her heart starts beating quickly.

"There's a conference in Toronto on Post-Traumatic Stress Disorder and I've been asked to present a paper. It's in late October. Are you interested in going?"

Mania's mind teems with the possibilities that such a trip offers. "Of course! There's been no reply to my letter to the Brombergs. Maybe it'll be easier to find them once we're there."

"Let's keep searching the Internet in the meantime. We may be able to get some leads before we go."

Mania feels a surge of energy. "Yes, let's do that. It's hard to get used to my new identity just from books and information on the web. It would be a miracle if either one of the Brombergs is still alive. If not, I hope I can find the daughter at least." She takes a deep breath and adds, "My sister."

"We can try but don't get your hopes up too high," Witold cautions.

In the last few days of summer and into early autumn, they check the Internet daily without success. Then one day, Mania hears a whoop of excitement from Witold's study.

"Come and see what I've found, Mania!" he calls.

Looking over his shoulder, Mania sees a picture of an old woman with iron-grey curls around a smiling face as she wields a brush above a painting of flowers in riotous colours. The caption underneath reads: "Rose Bromberg 95, resident of Willow Gardens, enjoys an art class." In the article beside the picture, Rose's daughter, Helen Teplitzky, is quoted: "My mother loves this class. She never painted before."

"Do you think that's her?" Mania asks, her fingers digging into Witold's shoulders.

"I think it certainly could be. The age is right; the name is the same; and she has a daughter. 'Helen' could be the English equivalent of Halinka."

"This is amazing!" Mania's face flushes with excitement. "You found her! Where is this place?"

"That's the best part," he says. "It's in Toronto."

He gets up from the chair and Mania hugs him. They do a quick jig around his study, bumping into the desk and bookcase.

Disheveled and laughing, Mania says, "Enough!" She starts to pick up books and files that they have knocked over in their excitement.

That evening, Mania composes a letter to Róża. It is the most difficult thing she has ever written. After consulting with Witold, she decides not to reveal her full identity as she did in the first letter that must have gone missing at a former address. Mania does not want to upset the old lady the way she shocked Irena when she showed up alive after she was supposed to be dead.

Mania writes to Rose Bromberg care of the nursing home:

> *September 25, 2006*
> *Dear Mrs. Bromberg,*
> *I am writing to you about a family matter that I would like to discuss with you. I am familiar with your situation during the war and have information that I believe will be of interest to you. I will be coming to Toronto on October 25 and I would very much like to meet you. I hope that you are well. I am looking forward to hearing from you.*
> *Yours truly,*
> *Mania Wiśniewska (Dr.)*

Although she is very disappointed not to receive a reply to this letter either, Mania packs for her trip to Toronto. Flying over the Atlantic Ocean, she hopes that the trip will not be a fool's errand. As soon as they have checked into their downtown Toronto hotel and arrived in their room, Mania searches the telephone book while Witold starts unpacking. There are several listings for the name Teplitzky. She is about to call the first name when Witold stops her.

"Wait until morning. It's after ten and people could be in bed already."

"But I won't be able to sleep all night if I don't talk to her," she says.

"You don't know which one on the list is Helen. You may disturb people who have nothing to do with us."

Reluctantly, she puts down the phone. "I hope I don't lose my nerve by morning."

Witold sits down beside her. "Look, the daughter must know you're coming. You wrote to Róża."

"What if she didn't get the letter?"

Witold acknowledges that possibility and Mania goes to bed tossing and turning until morning. After Witold's departure for the conference, she starts dialing. At the first number, there is no answer.

On her second try, a woman's voice says, "Hello?"

"Good morning. May I ask if I am speaking to Helen Teplitzky, the daughter of Róża Bromberg?" Mania asks.

"Who is this?"

"My name is Mania Wiśniewska. I am here from Warsaw. If you are Helen Teplitzky, I have written to your mother "

"I read your letter to my mother. What is this information that you have for her?"

Detecting a cold reserve in the woman's voice, Mania says, "Has she read my letter?"

"No, she isn't capable of reading much anymore."

"I am sorry to hear it. I would very much like to meet her."

"It's unlikely. I don't want to upset my mother. What is it you want to talk to her about?"

Mania thinks for a moment. Then she says, "Perhaps we could meet and I could tell you? Then you could take me to see your mother?"

"Why can't we talk on the telephone?"

"It is a delicate matter. I would prefer to do this in person."

"What is it you're after? Money?"

"Pardon me? I do not understand."

"Why are you here? Why all this mystery? Is there information you want to sell us?"

Mania sits back stunned. When she speaks again, it is in a clipped tone. "I am not in the business of selling information. My husband is a respected psychiatrist from Warsaw, here for a conference at the University of Toronto. He is presenting a paper on Post-Traumatic Stress Disorder in survivors of war. I have come with him so that I can meet you and your mother."

"My mother doesn't talk about the war. It's too painful for her. And I was too young to remember anything."

"Please. It is very important for me to meet you. Halinka, I know Irena, the woman who was hiding you during the war."

Mania hears a sharp intake of breath.

"Okay. Where are you staying?"

"In the Delta Chelsea Hotel."

"I'll meet you in the lobby at ten o'clock. I'll wear a red jacket so you will recognize me."

Mania hears the click as Helen hangs up. She feels a chill as she catches sight of the sunless skyline outside the window and the choppy slate water of Lake Ontario and selects a brown cashmere sweater and an oatmeal-coloured woollen pantsuit to put on. She slips her feet into brown leather pumps and pulls back her grey-streaked hair into a low ponytail, tying it with a patterned silk scarf. After inspecting herself in the bathroom mirror, she applies a little makeup. When she is ready to go, she sees by her watch that she still has half an hour to kill. She drums her fingers on the bathroom counter; her breathing is shallow and nervous. When it seems as if she cannot sit still in the hotel room for another second, she grabs her purse and heads to the elevator. Being in the lobby early will actually be an advantage. She can check out Helen Teplitzky before the woman sees her.

Mania selects a leather armchair behind a large leafy plant from which she can observe the people swirling by in what looks like an orchestrated dance. She peers at everyone ushered in by the uniformed doorman through the revolving doors. Men and women in business suits carrying expensive briefcases rush by her, while busboys wheel loads of luggage to the elevators, temporarily blocking her view. No Helen in sight yet. She begins to question the wisdom of being in this strange city, arranging to meet someone she knows almost nothing about, all because she has a biological connection to her.

Just as she considers going back up to her room, Mania spots a woman wearing a deep crimson jacket and black skirt. The woman is slimmer and shorter than Mania and is obviously looking for someone. Mania searches her face for family resemblance but sees none. She takes a deep breath and walks over to her.

"Are you Helen Teplitzky?"

The woman gives her an appraising look. "You must be Mania Wiśniewska."

"Yes. I am so happy to meet you." They shake hands. Mania says, "Shall we sit here or go to the coffee shop?"

Helen's eyes on Mania make her feel uncomfortable in this unfamiliar place.

"The coffee shop is good. As long as it doesn't take too long," Helen says.

Not a good sign, Mania thinks. *She wants to get this over with*.

Mania follows Helen through the morning crush of hotel patrons – people who know where they are going, vacationers who do not and are peering at maps, and sleepy couples who are also headed for the coffee shop across the busy lobby. Mania, who in Warsaw is a self-assured person with direction and purpose in life, feels insignificant and foreign here. The red jacket becomes a beacon that she must follow until they arrive at the coffee shop. There, they wait for a few minutes until they are seated on wrought-iron chairs at a glass-topped table. A pert young woman, dressed in a crisp white shirt and black pants, takes their order for coffee. Mania makes small talk nervously about the weather and her first impressions of Toronto, trying to engage Helen in conversation until their coffee arrives. Helen resists, answering her only in monosyllables.

Finally, when they get their cups of steaming coffee, Helen says, "All right, tell me what information you have for my mother."

Mania draws herself up in her chair and thinks, *This is it.*

"Has your mother ever spoken about me?"

"No. Why would she?"

"Because she is my mother, also."

Helen drops her coffee cup heavily onto the saucer, the brown liquid sloshing over the rim. She stares at Mania and says, "What are you talking about?"

Mania leans forward with her arms on the table and directs an unflinching gaze at Helen. "She has never told you about me?"

"Why would she?"

Mania knew she would have to explain why she was still alive, but she never expected that her mother would not have even mentioned her existence.

She says, "Not even a little hint? Not even using the name 'Mirka'?"

Studiously avoiding eye contact with Mania, Helen says, "No, I've never heard my mother mention that name."

Helen's words shake Mania's conviction but her expression seems to contradict them. Różamust have mourned the loss of her older daughter in secret. Any normal mother would.

"As you see, I am surprised. I am your mother's other daughter, the one she thought died during the war."

Helen starts to laugh. "This is ridiculous. I'm an only child. It was a miracle that my parents and I survived. There was no other child. I don't know what game you're playing, but I'm sorry, I don't have time for this."

Helen is about to get up and leave, but Mania puts a hand on her arm. "Please, Helen, just a few minutes. I would like to tell you the story of Irena, who rescued you, and Krystyna, her sister, who saved my life."

Helen listens as Mania tells her how Irena had told the Brombergs after the war that Krystyna and Mania had died in the fire that destroyed the manor house where they had been living.

She says, "But we did not die. Krystyna ran away with me and never told anyone that we were still alive. I grew up believing Krystyna was my mother. Only on her deathbed did Krystyna suggest that I must find my real family."

Helen listens in stunned silence. She shakes her head in disbelief. "That is some story!"

"You don't believe it?"

"No, I don't. It is so far-fetched that I'm surprised you believe it. Did your mother actually tell you that you were Rose Bromberg's daughter?"

"No, she died before she could give me the details. But she did say that I should find my family and make it right."

"And from that you jumped to the conclusion that *my* mother is your real mother?"

"No. First, I found Irena. She told me the whole story. Her son, Staszek, said that he wrote to your parents long ago. He gave me the address and I wrote a letter there but I did not receive a reply. Then my husband found the story on the Internet about your mother in the painting class in the Willow Gardens nursing home. That is how I found you."

Helen still shakes her head. "If there is even a shred of truth in what you say, then it's a case of mistaken identity. Even if your mother's name was Rose Bromberg, you've found the wrong Rose Bromberg. It's a fairly common Jewish name."

"Maybe so, but her family name was Bleiweis, no?"

Helen nods and takes some time to digest this piece of information.

Then, slowly, she says as if processing each fact separately, "Irena knew my mother and her family. That part is true. She would know that my mother's family name is Bleiweis. But as for my parents having another child, that's impossible. If my mother had had another daughter, she wouldn't have kept it a secret."

"But perhaps she did? The woman who said she was my mother kept her secret for many years. And Irena says...."

"I don't care what Irena says! Who knows why she's putting out this improbable story? Maybe she has dementia."

Mania's confidence is once again shaken. She had not expected such a vigorous denial. What if she *is* wrong? She cannot accept that. "Irena's memory is failing, that is true, but I believe that, as a physician, I am capable of distinguishing between fabrication and truthfulness. Besides, Irena's son was there and he confirmed everything she said."

Helen explodes. "That explains it! Irena and Staszek set you up as an imposter to squeeze money out of my mother. When his first effort didn't succeed so many years ago, he must have thought he hit the jackpot when you showed up."

"But I do not understand. Why would he make up such an elaborate story?"

"Anything for money. My mother told me I shouldn't trust Irena and Krystyna. She called them devils."

Mania is so upset that she cannot think straight. When she picks up her cup of coffee to buy time before she answers this vicious insult, her hand shakes so badly that she has to put it back down.

She says, "Irena saved your life. How can you call her a 'devil'?"

Helen drops her eyes. "Maybe she was a good person." Then she looks at Mania again and says, "Actually, Irena didn't act just out of altruism. My parents paid her for looking after me. Until their last penny. My mother warned me that one day she and her sons would try to blackmail me."

"Blackmail? I am sorry. I do not understand this term?"

"It means to threaten people if they don't give you money.

Polish people did that during the war to Jews who were desperate. They would protect them only in return for money or valuables or they would report them to the authorities. After the war, many kept on trying to continue to bilk the few who survived. They think that all Jews are rich and tell them some sob story to make them feel guilty and hand over more cash."

"I am sorry that you believe this about Irena."

Mania wonders if perhaps Irena and Staszek could have made up the story of a long-lost daughter. She had been so eager to find out what her mother had meant by her last words that she was vulnerable to any account that sounded plausible. What they had said about the Brombergs stealing Halinka away without letting her say goodbye could also be a fiction. Mania feels the ground beneath her give way.

Suddenly remembering the tears in Irena's eyes and the outrage on Staszek's face in defence of his mother, Mania says, "No, I cannot believe that Irena and Staszek are bad people. They did not tell me to ask you for money. Perhaps your father can verify what I have told to you."

"My father died eleven years ago." Helen puts some bills on the table and pushes her chair away. "I really must go now."

Afraid that her trip will have been all for nothing, Mania makes one final appeal. She takes out the photograph that Irena gave her and holds it out to Helen.

"Do you know who these people are?"

Staring at the photograph, Helen's face blanches. She opens her mouth as if to say something and then closes it again.

Mania asks, "Is that you with your parents?"

"Yes. What of it?"

"Who is that other child? It is I, your sister."

Helen is silent for what seems like an eternity to Mania. When she does speak, her voice is steady and quiet.

"Not necessarily. My mother has a photograph of me with Irena and another little girl with a woman who apparently is

Krystyna. That other little girl is you, her daughter."

"But why would I be in a picture with you and your parents if I am not part of this family?"

Helen is unmoved. "This isn't a formal family portrait. You may simply have been a child I played with. I don't think it's so strange for a child to want her friend, the daughter of the housekeeper, to be in a picture with her."

"But Krystyna was not their housekeeper at the time this was taken. This was under the Russian occupation when she was already living at the manor house."

"So what? She was visiting."

Mania takes back the picture and says, "You think that I am lying."

"Maybe not you," Helen says in a conciliatory tone. "Maybe not even Irena, who was a good woman. But her son, for whatever reason, is quite capable of lying for his own ends. I think he contacted my parents for money before and now he's found another opportunity."

"And you do not think there is any possibility that I am your sister?"

"Only a DNA test would convince me."

"Will you at least let me see your mother? I would be so grateful. She may be able to clarify who I really am."

Helen gives a bitter laugh. "My mother has dementia. And even if she didn't, do you think she'd recognize you after more than sixty years? There's no point to it."

She gets up and says, "I'm sorry I've dashed your hopes. I know you haven't deliberately set out to mislead me. Goodbye." She turns and leaves.

Mania stays in the coffee shop, her mind full of confusion and sorrow. She had not realized how much she had been hoping that she was on the correct path. Certainly now she can get back to her regular life, but something inside her will never be the same again. There will always be a niggling suspicion, a tiny voice asking, "What if it was true after all?"

She returns to the hotel room and flings herself on the bed to block out all thoughts of Helen, Irena, Staszek, the whole bunch of them. She is fed up and tired. She is ready to go home.

Chapter 18

Mania and Rose, Toronto, October 2006

BEFORE WITOLD GOES to make his presentation at the conference, he tells Mania that they cannot leave Toronto without at least trying once more to persuade Helen to let them see her mother. He says that they will have to develop a strategy when he comes back after the luncheon to which he has been invited. Mania cannot bear to sit around in the hotel room alone to wait for him, so she goes to the Eaton Centre, the massive indoor mall in downtown Toronto, where she threads her way through the throngs of people to find a few small gifts for her family. *What are all these people doing here?* she wonders. *Don't they have to work?* It seems as if everyone is in a manic rush to spend money. She purchases a white silk scarf adorned with red maple leaves for Marysia and a Maple Leafs hockey shirt for Anna, who loves the sport. For Jerzy, she buys a white woollen winter scarf with red, green, yellow and indigo stripes at the ends, which, she is told, is the traditional Hudson Bay Company trademark. Satisfied with her purchases, Mania finds a coffee shop on the lowest level of the mall where she has a sandwich and a coffee, checking her watch frequently to make sure that she will be at the hotel at one o'clock, the time that she and Witold had arranged to meet.

Witold has a big smile on his face when he greets her in the lobby. His presentation went over so well that he had difficulty extricating himself from those who wished to discuss his work further into the afternoon. He promised them that he would spend tomorrow morning with them.

They check Helen's telephone number again to get her address and find a taxi right in front of their hotel to take them there. After about twenty minutes, they pull in front of a three-storey brick house on a tree-lined residential street. They climb out and walk up the cement path to the steps of the porch. As she rings the bell, Mania peers in through the window at the top of the door and sees Helen coming from the kitchen at the back of the house, drying her hands on a dish towel before she opens the door. When Helen sees Mania and Witold standing there, she gasps.

"What are you doing here?" she asks.

"Hello, Helen," Mania says, trying to control the quaver in her voice. "This is my husband, Witold."

"A pleasure to meet you," Witold says, putting out his hand.

Helen reaches out to shake his hand and says a weak "Hello."

"May we come in?" Mania asks.

Helen steps aside to let them into the foyer. "I don't know what you think you'll accomplish by coming here." She folds her arms across her chest.

Mania says, "We will be returning to Warsaw on Sunday. I only wish to speak with you one more time before we will depart."

For a few seconds, the three of them silently regard each other, until Helen says, "All right, come in but I'm not going to change my mind." She checks her watch. "I have only fifteen minutes. I have to go to the nursing home."

Mania and Witold exchange glances as they sit down on the sofa in the living room while Helen perches on the edge of an armchair by the fireplace, still clutching the dishtowel.

"That is good," Mania says, feeling a rising sense of hope. "Perhaps we can accompany you."

"Absolutely not. I told you already I don't want to upset my mother."

Witold gets up to examine the family photographs arranged on the mantel. Picking one up, he says, "This is Róża, yes? With Marek?"

"That's my mother and my father," Helen says, as if deliberately refusing to acknowledge their Polish names.

"A very handsome pair."

He brings the portrait over to show Mania. Mania's heart constricts at the sight of the couple in the photograph, obviously an older version of the young couple in the photo that Irena gave her. As Witold takes another portrait off the mantel, Helen's eyes follow him, hostile and suspicious.

"This is your daughter, yes?" Witold asks, indicating the graduation picture of a young woman with straight blonde hair parted at the side, blue eyes, and high cheek-bones.

Helen nods.

Witold points to Mania and says, "She looks very much like Mania, do you not think so?"

Helen refuses to look at Mania and shrugs as if to ask, *So what?*

Witold picks up another picture and says, "Your son?"

This time, it is a head and shoulders portrait of a young man with twinkling dark eyes, curly brown hair, and an open, wide smile. Helen nods, her mouth tightening with irritation. She is like a cat, ready to spring at any moment. Mania, too, is tense but she is fascinated by what Witold is doing.

"Your son resembles very much our daughter Marysia, does he not, Mania?" Witold continues in a friendly, conversational tone, as if this was a casual visit among friends. "They both have a similar aspect to Marek."

Witold brings both pictures over for Mania to inspect and sits down beside her.

Mania says in wonder, "Yes. There is definitely a family resemblance."

Helen can no longer contain herself. She stands up and says, "Please put them back. I'm sure you didn't come here just to look at my family pictures. Now I really must go, so tell me what you want."

Mania says firmly, "I wish to see Róża. Did you discuss with her that I am here in Toronto and that I would like to speak with her?"

"No, I didn't. When I asked her about Krystyna and Irena recently, she got very agitated and accused them of being liars and thieves. Then she virtually kicked me out of her room. The nurse told me they had to give her a tranquilizer that night. I don't need a repeat performance."

"This is not such a bad sign," Witold says. "It is an indication that her memory of the distant past is good. If the emotions that arise from the memories are troubling, then seeing her other daughter, the one whom she has believed for so long to be dead, should help her achieve resolution and serenity."

Helen turns on Witold. "You know nothing about my mother! Can't you get it through your heads that you've been trapped in a bunch of lies and that Mania is Krystyna's daughter, not my mother's?"

With a great effort at self-restraint, Mania nods. "I am anxious to know the truth. I would be very happy and relieved to know that Krystyna has always been my mother. Only one person can tell me this with certainty – your mother."

"No, my mother has no obligation to tell you anything. As I told you yesterday, if you want definite confirmation of your identity, get a DNA test. I'm not going to raise this issue with my mother and that's final."

"Yes, I can do this when we return to Poland. But we are here now for only a short time. If it happens that I am your mother's lost child, would you not feel sorry that you missed the opportunity to bring me to her?"

Helen is exasperated. "Isn't it enough proof for you that my mother never mentioned you in her whole life? Don't you think she would have mourned the loss of a child?"

Mania says, "Yes, I would think so, too. But I also know

that people can keep secrets for many years. Krystyna did."

Witold says, "People have different ways of dealing with grief. Sometimes, they choose to suppress their painful memories."

"I'm sorry," Helen says. "I can't talk about this anymore. I really must go."

She walks into the kitchen and comes back with a braided bread that she puts into a plastic back.

Mania says, "You have baked this *chałka*?"

"On Fridays I bake a *challah* to take to my mother for the *Shabbes* dinner at the home."

"My mother – Krystyna – also made this bread. For special holidays. When I was a child, she gave me a small piece to make my own little one."

For a moment, Helen stares at Mania and says softly, "My mother did the same thing with me." Then she returns to her brusque manner. "It's not really surprising. My mother told me that she learned to bake from Krystyna."

With an impatient shake of her head, making her curls spring up, Helen slings her purse over her shoulder and takes out her house keys. She almost pushes Mania and Witold out the door. When she realizes that they have no transportation, she explains that they can find a taxi around the corner to take them back to their hotel.

Mania and Witold watch her get into her car and drive away. Without saying a word, they begin to walk in the direction that Helen has indicated. As they have to cross a small park, Mania pulls on her husband's hand to sit down on a bench by the path. She is dispirited and tired.

"So what do we do now?" she asks him.

"Are you ready to give up?" he asks.

"I don't want to, but what else can I do?"

"It's simple. We take a taxi to the nursing home and we meet Róża. I'm not afraid of upsetting her. We are both physicians. Surely we know how to handle a situation like this with delicacy without creating a crisis for the patient."

Mania thinks of Helen's stubborn refusal to consider the possibility that Rose could be Mania's mother and it shakes her confidence. Maybe Staszek has actually created an elaborate hoax for some reason of his own. Irena certainly was not up for such a thing. Now she and Witold are stranded in a park in Toronto. They are far from home and no closer to the truth.

With a sigh, Mania gets up. "Come on, Witold. We might as well go to the nursing home. I need to get to the bottom of this before we go back to Warsaw."

They follow Helen's instructions and find a cab. Mania gives the driver the address of the nursing home. On the way there, she looks out the window but sees nothing. She is rehearsing various scenarios in her head: What if Rose is in an advanced state of dementia and is not capable of having a conversation? What if she is not her biological mother? She will be embarrassed and will have to apologize to Helen for causing such a fuss. What if Rose is so fragile that they induce a physical crisis as Helen fears? All of these possibilities race around in Mania's head until they reach Willow Gardens. Once there, Mania is impressed with the clean lines of the red brick building and its rows of large windows. Under the trees and in the gardens surrounding the property, many old folks are sitting on benches or in wheelchairs enjoying the unexpectedly mild weather for late October.

Mania and Witold enter through the main glass doors into a lobby of gleaming tile and light wood. They head for the receptionist, who gives them the location of Rose Bromberg's room. When they enter the residential units, which are closed off by large metal double doors from the general corridors, Mania cannot help compare the bright, spacious rooms that she glimpses here with the shabby surroundings in which poor Uncle Feliks is spending his final years. They reach Rose's room and Mania stops. She is overcome with indecision, not knowing which outcome she would prefer: that Rose is her mother or that Krystyna has always been her mother. Even at this late date, she could just turn around and go home and pick up her life where she left off, forgetting this whole unfortunate episode. Witold gives her hand a squeeze. She knows that since she has come this far, she cannot turn back now. Through the half-open door she can hear Helen's voice and a lower, older one in response. She knocks and is relieved to hear Helen say, "Come in."

Stepping into the room, Mania sees a plump old woman with gray curls and a face not nearly as wrinkled as Irena's. She relaxes a little. This woman is not frail. On her solid frame she is wearing dark pants, a short-sleeved blue pullover, and a string of pearls. Not even glancing at Helen, Mania walks directly to Rose.

"Wait!" Helen says. "You can't just barge in–"

"We've come to meet you, Mrs. Bromberg," Mania says in a pleasant voice.

Rose says, "Why are you being so rude, Helen? I like meeting people. Please call me Rose."

She smiles and reaches out her hand to Mania and then to Witold as they exchange greetings. Mania sits down on the only other chair in the room, while Witold perches on the bed.

"Are you a friend of Helen's?" Rose asks.

Mania says, "No, not exactly."

Rose leans slightly forward. "Where are you from? You have an accent."

This woman seems quite alert, Mania thinks. "I'm from Poland."

"I thought so! I can always recognize a Polish accent. I'm from Poland, too, but I've been in this country for many years." A frown creases her forehead. "I can't remember how many. Ah, well, my memory is not as good as it used to be. What city are you from?"

"We're from Warsaw."

From the corner of her eye, Mania sees Helen glaring at

her. Rose seems completely unaware of her daughter's hostile attitude to the visitors.

"I'm from Stanisławów," Rose says and names the town of her birth.

"I have not been there, though I do know people who lived there long ago," Mania says. She is about to say more when Helen interrupts.

"Don't you want to go for a walk in the garden, Mom? It's a beautiful day."

Rose brushes her away impatiently. "No, I want to talk to this interesting woman. She may know people from my hometown." Then a thought strikes Rose. "Are you Jewish?"

Mania is speechless. With those pale blue eyes peering right into hers, she does not know how to explain.

After some hesitation, she says, "No, I am not Jewish. But I think I was born Jewish."

"How can that be?" Rose's face reflects her puzzlement. "Did you convert?"

"Please, may I tell you a story?"

"I like stories!" Rose breaks into a big smile.

"You have to forgive my English. It is not so good."

"Your English is great. Better than mine was when I came to this country. I don't think I spoke any English at all, did I Helen?" Her face is blank and baffled.

"No, Mom, you didn't," Helen says.

Rose has regained her composure. "How can I remember such things? It was a hundred years ago!" She throws her head back and laughs. "So start already."

"Mom, we really should go outside. It's a shame to waste such a beautiful day by sitting indoors," Helen says as she turns to her mother and tries to get her up out of her chair. She then looks pointedly at Mania and says, "Please excuse my mother. She doesn't remember her daily routine. This is the usual time for her to get some fresh air."

Rose sets her mouth in a tight, straight line. "You don't

have to apologize for me. I'm not a child. I may not remember what you call my routine but I know what I want. Right now I want to enjoy my conversation with ... what did you say your name was?"

"It is Mania."

A shadow crosses Rose's face. "I used to know a Mania. It's a good Polish name. Have we met before?"

Mania's heart begins to pound. She wants to introduce herself to Rose so badly, but she restrains herself. She does not want to have to deal with an emotional outburst from both daughter and mother.

"No, I do not think that we have met before."

"Hmmm. You aren't one of these social workers coming to interview me, are you? They already sent someone to talk to me about my Holocaust experiences and I said, in no uncertain terms, that I won't do it. They didn't send you, did they?"

"No, I am not one of them." Then Mania takes the plunge. "But I would like very much to hear about the person you knew whose name was also Mania. The one from Poland."

Still standing beside her mother's chair like a guard, Helen breaks in, "My mother doesn't like to talk about her past in Poland."

Once again, Rose stiffens in opposition to her daughter. "You don't have to speak for me, Helen. I can speak for myself."

"But, Mom–"

"No 'buts.' Mania has asked me about something I can answer, though Helen is right. I don't like to talk about the past." Helen looks ready to jump in again when Rose, looking past Mania into a vision of her own, says almost in a whisper, "My Mania was a little Jewish girl."

"Can you tell me about her?" Mania probes gently.

Rose shakes her head and studies her hands. "My husband and I decided a long time ago that it is no use to talk about things that we cannot change. About people who ... have disappeared." She lifts her face and directs an accusing stare at Mania. "The Polish people weren't very good to the Jews during the war."

Mania is taken aback at the old lady's vehemence.

"Yes," she says, "that is very true. But things are better now. There are many Jews from North America who visit Poland. Do you ever wish that you could visit your old home?"

"Are you kidding? I wouldn't step on that blood-soaked land. They took everything away from me and killed my whole family."

Helen is standing by her mother's chair with her fists clenched, watching the interaction between Mania and Rose with fascination and horror. Witold's eyes, alert for trouble, go from one face to the other.

But Mania feels calm. It is as if she is building a frail connection like a fine gold chain, one link at a time, between herself and Rose. She reaches over to lightly touch Rose's hand. At first Rose makes as if to snatch it away but then she leaves it in her lap. Her eyes stare off past Mania's shoulder, seeing a vista only visible to her.

Mania says, "Was it not the Nazis who did those terrible things?"

Rose nods mechanically. "That's true. But there were Polish people who helped the Nazis. They betrayed us."

"Yes, I believe that."

"We thought they were our friends. Our neighbours. What they did was unforgivable."

Mania nods, and they sit together quietly. Finally Mania says, "I said I would tell you a story. Do you still want to hear it?"

Rose's attention is immediately diverted. "Oh, yes, I do."

"I'll start by telling you about the Jewish children, who were left by their parents with Polish people during the war. Some of them were found after the war by one or both of their parents or by relatives who survived and were taken to America or Israel or Canada. Others, whose parents were murdered by the Nazis, remained in Poland. They were raised as Catholics.

They are all grown up now. Some of them are finding out on the deathbed of their Polish parents that they were born to Jewish parents."

Rose's eyes have locked on Mania's while she has been speaking.

"Do you know any people like this?" she asks.

Mania takes a deep breath. "That is the main part of my story. There were two little sisters whose parents left them with two Polish women, who were also sisters. One of these girls was returned to her parents after the war. The other one remained with her Polish caregiver who became her mother. Just before this Polish mother died, she told the girl, who was now a grown up woman, that she had to make things right. The daughter didn't know what she meant. It was a secret. So she made up her mind to find out what the secret was and to make this right, just like her mother asked her to do."

Rose is hanging on every word of the story. She asks, "What was the secret?"

"First let me tell you what clues she followed to find it out. She knew that her mother had a sister whom she had not seen for many years. Maybe this sister would know the secret."

"Did she?" Rose asks in breathless anticipation.

"She was not easy to find. But yes, when the daughter found her, this sister of her mother's knew the secret. The secret was that the daughter was Jewish."

"Oh, my! How could that be?" Rose asks, confusion clouding her eyes.

"Her Polish mother did not give her back to her rightful Jewish parents after the war. She kept her."

Rose clasps her hands so tightly that her knuckles turn white. She closes her eyes and screws up her face in concentration. "This story sounds familiar."

"Does it remind you of the Mania you used to know?"

Rose nods and there is fear in her eyes as she asks Mania, "Do you know her?"

Mania holds Rose's clenched hands in hers and says, "Yes, I do. I was the little girl. I am that Mania, all grown up now. And Krystyna was the Polish woman who kept me away from you."

Rose's face goes ashen and she pulls her hands away from Mania. She stares into her lap and starts rocking back and forth in her chair.

Helen puts her arms around her mother protectively and turns on Mania. "You've upset my mother just like I knew you would. You must stop now!"

Rose lifts her face to Mania. "Who are you? Are you visiting me from the other side like all my loved ones?"

Now Mania no longer has any doubts. The connection she feels between herself and Rose is stronger than mere pity at the woman's pain. Rose is no longer a stranger to her. She gave birth to her. She gave her up for safekeeping. No amount of time can erase that fact.

"I am visiting from Poland with my husband, who is sitting on your bed. Please tell me about the little girl, Mania."

"Mom, you don't have to do this," Helen says, kneeling at her mother's side. She turns to Witold. "Please, tell your wife to stop."

Witold says to Mania, "How is her pulse?"

Mania takes Rose's wrist. "It is not too fast. I think she will be fine. She needs to talk about this." She speaks directly to Rose. "You have suppressed this secret inside you for so many years, have you not, Róża? You will feel better when you let it out. Then you will lie down and rest." Mania looks at Helen. "I am a doctor. Please do not worry. I will not let her go into distress."

Tears have begun to run down Rose's face. In a voice barely above a whisper, she says, "Are you really my Mirka or the spirit of my Mirka?"

"Look at me, Róża. How can I be a spirit? Can you not feel my hand on your arm? Spirits are insubstantial. When you see them, they are the same age as the last time you saw them. I am not a child. I am almost an old woman myself."

"But you died in the fire."

"No, Krystyna took me away. She knew it was too dangerous to stay. Besides, we had no place to live after the fire destroyed the house. First we went to Wroclaw to Antonia, and a few weeks later, we went to Warsaw."

At the mention of Antonia's name, Rose revives a little. "That *klafta!* She said the same thing as Irena – that you died in the fire. I knew they were liars!"

Mania sighs. "Irena believed that Krystyna and I were dead because she saw the fire and she did not see anyone escape. But Antonia? I do not know why she lied. Maybe it was because she hated Jews. I am sorry. She caused you a lot of pain because of her lies."

Rose, who had momentarily stopped crying, breaks into fresh sobs.

"So I am your daughter, yes?" Mania cannot believe the words as they come out of her mouth.

"You have to prove it," Rose chokes out through her tears.

"How can I prove it?" Mania asks.

Helen gives her a tissue. "Mom, please let me send them away. This is too much for you."

Rose wipes the tissue over eyes and blows her nose. "No. I want to know. My Mirka had a birthmark. Just under her bellybutton. Show me."

Without hesitation, Mania pulls down the waistband of her pants. There is a round brown mole just where Rose has said it would be. Nothing and no one can hold Rose back any more. She lunges for Mania and sobs in her arms. Helen covers her face with her hands.

Mania strokes Rose's back until she calms down. She, too, is crying silently. After a while, she puts Rose gently back in her chair and dries her face. Finally, she asks the question that has been troubling her since she found out from Irena that her parents were Jews.

Holding both of Rose's hands, she asks, "Why did you stop looking for me?"

Rose's eyes open wide in horror. "We didn't stop! Even when we came to Canada, we kept checking with the Red Cross for years. We thought they were all liars – Irena and her sons, and Antonia, too. We asked for help from the survivor unification agencies. We put notices in the newspapers. We offered a reward. I always knew in my heart that you were still alive!"

At that moment, one of the staff comes into the room. She stops after only a few steps and takes in the scene of Rose and her visitors.

"Is everything all right here?" she asks.

Witold speaks up while the women ignore the intruder. "Yes, everything is fine. Rose has heard some surprising news, but she is fine."

"Dinner is in half an hour. Will she be coming to the dining room?"

"I do not think Rose will feel up to it. Perhaps she can lie down for a while and then someone can bring some food for her on a tray before bedtime?"

"Yes, I'll see to it." Seeing Rose's ravaged face, she adds, "Do you want me to send in the nurse now to take her vital signs?"

"No, that will not be necessary. My wife and I are physicians and we are caring for her. Perhaps the nurse can come in when we leave shortly. She may need a mild sedative if she is agitated and cannot sleep."

"I'll tell the nurse."

Now, Rose has her own questions for Mania. "Why didn't you find me sooner? When Mark was still alive? He would have been so happy."

"I did not know until my mother – Krystyna – died. She kept her secret until her deathbed and even then, she only had enough breath to hint that I had to find someone and make it right. I did not know what she meant for a long time."

"When did she die?"

"Almost a year ago. It has taken me that long to trace you to Canada. Irena and Staszek helped."

"They did? I always thought that they helped Krystyna steal you away from me."

"No, they really believed that Krystyna and I were dead."

"So I was right! Krystyna was evil! How could I know she would turn against us after being our friend and helper? I hope God is punishing her for causing so much grief to Mark and me."

Mania recoils as if she herself has been dealt a blow. Krystyna, who was her beloved mother for so many years, does not deserve this. She hears herself using the same words that Witold and Sister Beatrice spoke to her: "Do not be too hard on her memory, dear Rose. She loved me so much that she could not bear to give me up. It does not excuse what she did, but in the end, she saved my life."

This seems to be too much for Rose to comprehend. She is swaying with fatigue and overstimulation.

Mania says, "I think maybe you should lie down now for a rest."

Clinging to Mania's and Helen's hands, Rose lets them lead her to her bed.

"I don't believe this is happening," she keeps repeating.

"You need to rest now, but I will be back tomorrow," Mania says.

Helen and Mania remove Rose's shoes but she will not lie down.

"I'm afraid of falling asleep," she says. "What if I wake up and find out that this was all a dream?"

Mania rummages through her purse and takes out an envelope, from which she removes the picture of Róża, Marek, and their two young children.

When she shows it to Rose, the old lady gasps. "Where did you get this?"

"From Irena. She found it in the boot where you hid it when you were in hiding."

"Oh, my God! Can I have it?" Mania nods and Rose clutches the photo to her breast. Her watery eyes fill with gratitude.

"Put it on the pillow beside you," Mania says. "When you wake up and see it, you will know that this was not a dream."

When Rose lies down, Helen says that she will stay until Rose's bedtime. The staff will keep an eye on her during the night. If there are any problems, Helen promises to call Mania at the hotel. Otherwise, Mania should come to her house by ten o'clock in the morning and they will drive to the nursing home together.

"We have a lot to talk about," she says.

"Yes, we do," Mania agrees. "I will stay as long as you and your – our – mother want me to."

She kisses Rose's cheek, hugs Helen, and together with Witold, she leaves to return to the hotel. In their room, Mania collapses on the bed in exhaustion. She urges her husband to go to the reception scheduled for his conference that evening. She has so much to think about that she will welcome a few hours alone.

Now that all the ambiguity about her origins has dissipated, she is euphoric. She still cannot believe that in such a short time her whole identity has changed so dramatically. She does not know yet how this will affect her life, but she is not worried. She has lots of time to learn about her Jewish heritage and to figure out how much of it she will incorporate into her life. She is eager for a meaningful connection to this newly-found Jewish family. She hopes that Rose can accept that she is a Catholic and that it is too late for her to change that aspect of herself. But it is not too late to learn about Judaism and her Jewish family, which she intends to do.

She will extend her visit in Toronto and will continue the contact with regular visits, telephone calls, and letter writing even after she leaves. With Irena's obvious pain at the loss of

Halinka, Mania also hopes that she can persuade Helen to visit her rescuer before it is too late.

But first things first, as her mother Krystyna used to say. Tomorrow, she wants to journey into the past by asking Rose how it all started: how she ended up with Krystyna while Helen was turned over to Irena. She wants to know if it was a mistake or the only possible decision that her parents could make to save her life. She does not know how much Rose will be capable of telling her, but she will treasure whatever her first mother will reveal to her. She drifts off to sleep in the knowledge that she has had two loving mothers.

Chapter 19

Róża, Stanisławów, October 1941

OUTSIDE IN THE STREET, gunshots rang out. Inside the apartment, Róża flinched as if each bullet lodged in her body. She paced the floor with an unsteady gait, rocking her sick infant who would not stop crying. Putting her lips to the child's forehead, she confirmed the fever that she could see in the flushed face and the glassy eyes. The poor little thing kicked out her skinny legs and arched her back and shrieked in a pitiful way as Róża walked back and forth in a frantic attempt to calm her. Marek stood by, watching helplessly.

Róża said, "Get me a cold, wet washcloth so I can try to take this fever down."

"Did you give her some aspirin?" he asked.

"Of course. I put the powder in her cereal, but she kept spitting it out. I don't know how much I actually got into her. I'll try some more in an hour if the fever doesn't go down."

Marek hurried to the sink and got the washcloth. He held the compress to Hanka's tiny forehead but she twisted and turned her face away from him. Róża was hanging on to her self-control by a thread. If the baby did not stop screaming soon and if the Gestapo heard her, they would come and drag them all away. Today there was a general roundup of all Jews and it was only a matter of time before the pounding on their door would come. In exasperation, Róża handed the baby to Marek and slumped into one of their two remaining chairs, her head sinking into her hands.

"It's all that noise outside that keeps her from settling down," Marek said, as he shushed and rocked Hanka.

Róża did not agree. She got up from her chair to check the baby's forehead again. She was still burning up.

"She needs a doctor." Róża reached for the baby, but Marek pressed her closer to his chest.

"Where do you think you'll take her? It's suicide for a Jew out there. Especially a woman carrying an infant."

She realized that he was right. She took the washcloth and wrung it out in cold water again. She prayed fervently that the aspirin and the cold washcloth would start to work. Every few minutes, she checked Hanka's forehead with her lips until eventually she detected a cooling off of the skin. As the fever receded, the baby fell into an exhausted sleep. *Perhaps*, Róża thought, *she feels more secure and comfortable in her father's arms. He's not as tense as I am.* Róża could not hide her fear as well as he could. She could not control her nervous movements and sporadic tears. Marek managed to maintain a steady and calm exterior no matter what turbulence was going on inside him.

Our apartment is our prison, she thought. Suddenly, she noticed an eerie silence from outside. After the commotion on the stairs and in the hallway as their Jewish neighbours had been dragged out, and after the shooting in the street, the silence was unnerving. When Róża put her ear against the door, she could not hear a sound. How had the jackboots missed their apartment? Róża and Marek exchanged glances and he must have read her mind because he shrugged and said only one word. "Luck."

They had lived in this apartment for four years, ever since they were married. Róża had been so proud of the little nest that they had created to welcome their children. But now everything was gone. The walls were bare. There were white rectangles and nail holes where their prized possessions had hung: pictures, mirrors, a piece of needlepoint made by Róża's mother. Most of the furniture was gone, too, except the armoire with the butterfly design inlaid with three kinds of wood. They had not really been able to afford it, but they had both had good prospects for a comfortable future and decided to splurge on one good piece of furniture. They could sell it for enough money to buy food to sustain them for a while, but they were keeping it to use as a front for the hiding place in the wall that Marek had created.

They had sold Marek's mother's mahogany dining room set and their bedroom set for a pittance. The only things left were the kitchen table, two chairs, the mattress from their bed and the cot for the baby. Three-year-old Mirka slept beside her baby sister on a comforter laid on the floor. Bartering their personal and household items for food had become a way of life – dangerous but necessary. They were without work, money, or friends among their Polish neighbours and former colleagues. Only Krystyna, the oldest daughter of the housekeeper, Marta, who had worked for Róża's family, could be counted on for help. Just keeping themselves and their children alive had become their main preoccupation. Even so, there was never enough to eat and they had all become thin and hollow cheeked. Mirka's cheeks, once chubby and pink, were now thin and pale, and her blue eyes had lost their sparkle.

Róża turned to her husband. "Marek, what are we going to do? They'll be back."

"You're right," he whispered so as not to wake the baby, who lay completely limp in his arms. "The Nazis missed us this time. We'll have to trust in our hiding place."

"It's only good for emergencies. What are we going to do about going somewhere where we can be safe? One of the Polish neighbours is sure to betray us."

Although she was still a young woman, Róża felt that the last few months had aged her. The burden of responsibility for the safety of her children weighed her down. She felt herself weakening. Only the thought of what would happen to her children if she collapsed kept her going.

"We have to make plans to leave," she said.

"You're right but not yet," Marek said. "It's too dangerous. They'll sweep us up off the street. Where can we go?"

"How about to Ewa, your *mamka*?"

"No, I can't do that to her. She's not a young woman any longer and she lives alone. Besides, she's right near the police station. They'll be sure to check on the homes around there first."

Róża went back to her mental list of possible people who could hide them. When she and Marek discussed them, it turned out that there was no one whom they could trust or whom they wanted to endanger. Most of their Polish friends had already deserted them, crossing the street or looking the other way when they encountered them on their rounds to scrounge for food. As for their Jewish friends, no one wanted to hide with people who had one baby, let alone two, because they were too unpredictably noisy.

In frustration, Róża said, "Maybe we should give ourselves up. They say that it's for relocation. Even if we have to do manual labour, it would be more bearable than this."

"I don't believe them," Marek said. "I think that they're taking people to their death."

"So many people? How could that be? Wouldn't we know about it?"

"We will soon enough. Mark my words."

They examined the dangers of staying and of running away from every angle. Róża was relieved that they had at least made one decision already and that was about Mirka.

When the knock on the door came, Róża and Marek exchanged terrified looks and dashed for the armoire. At the sound of the second knock, Róża stopped. It was gentle, without any banging and shouting, "*Juden raus!*"

Marek motioned for her to take Mirka and the baby into their bedroom.

"Who's there?" he asked.

"It's me, Krystyna."

As soon as Róża heard who it was, she emerged from the bedroom with the children. Marek had opened the door and was pulling Krystyna inside. The expression on Krystyna's face reflected a mixture of compassion and fear. She had known Róża since childhood. *How different I must look to Krystyna*, Róża thought, from the self-confident, attractive young woman she had been before the war to the haggard and wild-eyed mother of two that she was now. Handing the baby to Marek, Róża fell into Krystyna's embrace and began to cry.

"You must help us," she said, pulling away and drying her eyes on her sleeve.

Krystyna said, "I will do whatever I can." She approached Marek and reached out for the baby.

"Can I hold her?" she asked.

As Marek laid Hanka in Krystyna's arms, the baby began to whimper, but Krystyna's crooning and rocking soon quieted her.

"How thin the poor little darling is," Krystyna said, her eyes filled with pity.

Róża slumped back into her chair said, "I have no milk for her. And now she is sick and won't eat even the little bit of cereal I made for her. Krystyna, what will become of us?" She burst into a fresh bout of weeping.

Mirka, who had stood by all this time watching the adults with curiosity and puzzlement, became distressed at her mother's show of emotion. She crawled into Róża's lap and said, "Mama, don't cry."

Róża buried her face in her child's hair, avoiding the child's frightened eyes. How could she, the parent responsible for her daughter's safety, let the poor thing see how powerless she was to protect her? The thin body trembled in her arms – her shoulder blades were like chicken wings, her knees like knobs on twigs. Every bone dug into her mother's body. Marek, aware of the conflict raging within Róża, laid a hand on his wife's shoulder.

"It'll be all right, Róża. It won't last. We'll all be reunited in no time."

His words reminded her of what they had to do. How to broach it with Krystyna? First she had to calm down Mirka, to put a good face on so the child would not panic.

"Mama's fine, *kochana*, see?" She wiped her face with her hands and forced a smile on her lips. She kissed the child and tried loosening the grip she had on her, but Mirka burrowed deeper into her mother.

Marek asked, "What's happening out there, Krystyna?"

Róża and Marek had not been out of the apartment in a few days, afraid of all the German soldiers in the street. When they peered out through a crack in the curtains, they could see the Nazis goose stepping in formation and driving by in their Jeeps as if they owned the street, which they did now. Their harsh voices came right up to their third-floor apartment. When soldiers were not around, the street was deserted.

"Don't go out," Krystyna said. "They're rounding up the Jews wherever they find them. On the street. In stores. Pulling them out of their homes."

"We heard them here earlier, but somehow they missed us, thank God. Do you know where they take them?" Marek asked.

"First to the town square and then…."

Róża said, "A few weeks ago, there was an announcement for Jewish professionals to come to the square and they'd give us jobs somewhere else. I wanted to go but Marek wouldn't let me. I thought they could always use a teacher and a pharmacist."

"And where are your brother Benjamin and his wife now?" Marek said. "If they'd really given them jobs, don't you think they'd have written us by now?"

Róża nodded miserably. "You're right. So where are they taking them today, Krystyna?"

Krystyna couldn't meet Róża's eyes. "They say that there was a lot of digging at the Jewish cemetery last week."

"Oh, my God! Why?" Róża's face went pale with horror.

"For a huge pit as a mass grave."

Marek burst out, "They are animals! We must run away."

Krystyna said, "There are police everywhere. I don't know if you will succeed."

Róża said with resignation, "We might as well stay here."

"I'm afraid you won't be able to stay here for long either. They are building a fence around the Jewish quarter and all the Jews living in the rest of town and in the surrounding area will be moved into what they call a *ghetto*."

For a few minutes, they sat in silence. Róża thought, *It is too late for Marek and me, but I have to save the children.*

Krystyna said, "I've brought you some food."

She handed the sleeping baby back to Marek and started unpacking bundles from the basket she had brought. Róża felt the gnawing in her stomach as she devoured with her eyes the bread, potatoes, beets, and eggs laid out on the table. Krystyna had even brought milk for the baby.

"Krystyna, you're an angel!" Róża said.

"Do you have anything else for me to barter?" she asked.

They had already given her many of their things. Now Róża went to the bedroom to get her the pillowcase stuffed with more linens from her trousseau. For a moment, she wondered whether Krystyna kept any of these things for herself, but she quickly dismissed this ungenerous thought. Krystyna was the only one who was helping them. They had to trust her. She was taking a huge risk coming to their apartment. Now they were going to ask even more of her.

Putting the pillowcase next to Krystyna's chair, Róża took Mirka's hand and stood in front of the woman who was once again cuddling her baby.

"Krystyna, we need your help." For a moment she could not say anything more and kept her eyes on Mirka's golden hair.

Krystyna gazed up at Róża, her fair brows knitting together, her blue eyes troubled and wary. Róża could see that her friend was frightened and her stomach clenched as she prepared to make another request.

"What is it?" Krystyna asked.

Róża knew only too well that this woman could be shot if she was seen helping Jews. She was about to put her in even greater danger. Krystyna had been like an older sister to Róża, who had had four older brothers. She had first come to their home with her mother, Marta, their housekeeper, but when Marta died, she stayed on to help in the kitchen. Krystyna used to bring along her little sister, Irena, who became Róża's playmate. Róża had been putting their friendship to the test for the past few months, since the Nazis invaded, but now she had something to ask her which she would never have contemplated in her worst nightmares.

She said, "Krystyna, can you please take Mirka with you? I'm afraid for her."

Sensing a heightened tension in her mother's body, Mirka pushed her face up against her mother's leg and wrapped an arm around it. Róża patted her head, while Krystyna stared at her in stunned silence.

Finally, Krystyna said, "I don't know if I can do it, Róża. I won't be able to get her out of town. Whose child will I say she is if I'm questioned?"

"You can say she's the child of your sister in Wroclaw."

"Even if I manage to get to the village, nobody will believe me. The neighbours will betray me to the Gestapo. They know that Antonia has no children."

"So, say that a cousin sent her from Warsaw to get her out of a dangerous city into a peaceful village."

Krystyna shook her head. "No one will believe that I have cousins in Warsaw."

In desperation, Róża turned Mirka around to face Krystyna.

"Look at her, Krystyna. She has straight blonde hair and blue eyes just like you. Her nose is like a ski jump. Who would know she's a Jewish child? It will be just for a few weeks."

"A few weeks?" Krystyna scoffed.

Marek said, "The Russian army is strong. They've had a temporary setback, but they'll return in a couple of months and throw these bastards out."

"I pray to God you're right," Krystyna said.

Gently, Róża pushed Mirka toward Krystyna and held out her arms for the baby. She had to harden her heart as she watched her daughter gazing back and forth from her to Krystyna in complete confusion. *Poor little thing*, Róża thought, *she doesn't understand what's happening, that her parents are sending her away for her own good*. Then the child crumpled to the floor in a flood of weeping.

Krystyna's face turned white. "Please don't ask me to do this."

Róża and Marek stared at each other over the children's heads, bolstering each other's resolve.

"We'll pay," Marek said.

Róża cringed. She knew that Krystyna would need money to look after Mirka but the offer had to be made unobtrusively and diplomatically. She hoped that Krystyna was not offended that Marek had reduced their need for assistance to a financial transaction. Róża took the baby from Krystyna and passed her to Marek. Then, she clutched Krystyna's hands, hands Róża knew were strong enough for all manner of physical labour yet gentle enough to curl around an infant.

"I beg you, please take Mirka. I'm sure she won't endanger you. I have a forged baptismal document for her," she said, pulling it out of the pocket of her dress. "If anyone questions her identity, you can use that as proof that she's a good Catholic girl. Teach her the catechism. She learns fast. Take her to church with you."

Krystyna was breathing rapidly as she stared at the floor, deep in thought, while Róża prayed. When Krystyna's eyes alighted on the slumped body of the little girl on the floor between them, sobbing her heart out, her face softened. She took the document from Róża and inserted it inside the front of her dress. Then she bent over, stood the child up and pulled her close with a smile. Mirka put her hands behind her back, stiffened her body and continued to cry. She turned her red-rimmed eyes to her mother.

"I don't want to go!"

Róża knelt down in front of her. "You have to go, *moja kochana.* When this madness is all over, we'll come to get you. I promise."

Róża, did not know if the child could understand what she had said. She was only three years old and yet she had already experienced more misery in her short life than most adults. Wiping away her own tears, Róża took Mirka into the room she shared with Hanka. She picked up the little girl's favourite doll and put her arms around it. Mirka pressed it to her thin chest and her sobs subsided a little. Róża took a bundle of her things that she had prepared and led her back into the other room. As she handed the bundle to Krystyna, the two women did not need to exchange words. Marek bent over to kiss and hug his daughter. He slipped one of their gold coins into Krystyna's hand. Now they only had one left for an emergency.

Mirka cried in big, hiccupping sobs. Róża wondered if the child would ever forgive her for sending her away. Her only consolation was that this was the best way she knew how to save her life. She crouched and hugged her darling daughter tightly again and planted kisses on her wet face.

"Be a brave girl," Róża said. She turned to Krystyna. "Now it's time for you to go."

Krystyna took Mirka's hand. "Do you like kittens?"

The child stopped crying momentarily, looking up at this familiar woman who had always been nice to her. She nodded.

"You can have one of your very own then," Krystyna said. "Do you like the name Miñu-miñu?"

Mirka nodded again.

"Miñu-miñu is a black kitten with a pretty white face. She has a pink nose with a black spot right beside it. Her paws are white too. If you're really nice to her, she'll even sleep on your bed with you."

"Can I bring her home?" Mirka asked.

"We'll ask her when we see her," Krystyna said.

This seemed to pacify the child while Krystyna turned back for one last time, saying, "I think I'll call her Mania. It's a good Polish name."

As the door closed with a finality that ripped into Róża's heart, she collapsed against Marek.

"Come," he said, leading her to the window, the baby sleeping on his shoulder. "Let's watch."

Róża pulled the dark curtain aside a crack to see Krystyna cross the street with Mirka, hanging on to her doll with one hand and to Krystyna with the other. The child dragged her feet as she kept glancing back at the apartment window. Róża could not bear to see that desolate little face but she remained frozen in place until the woman and the child disappeared around the corner. Then she let the curtain drop. Fear and guilt flooded over her. Had they done the right thing? Marek assured her that it was the only thing that they could do. He placed the baby in Róża's lap and went to get her a glass of water.

The baby's solidity helped to connect Róża to the reality of their situation. Marek was right. What they had done was the best chance to save Mirka's life. She wondered what would happen if she and Marek did not survive – what kind of a life would their daughter have? Would she end up as a poor Polish peasant, uneducated, marrying young, and scratching out a meager existence with her husband from a small patch of land, growing old and worn out before her time? No, that wasn't likely. Krystyna had pulled herself out of that life. She had met Krzysztof, the son of the local landowner, and after the war she said that they would marry and probably live in town or in the manor house. If she and Marek did not survive, Róża was sure that Krystyna would raise Mirka as her daughter. Just then, a mewl of protest came from Hanka in her arms and she was reminded that very soon, she would have to devise a plan to save the baby as well. She had to hang on to any shred of hope left within her.

Glossary

agrest (a'-grest) – gooseberries
Babcia (Bab'-cha) – Grandma
barszcz (barshch) – beet soup
Bozhe miy (Baw'-zhe meey) – "oh, my God" in Ukrainian
brzushek boli' – my tummy hurts
chałka (hal'-kah) – plaited sweet white bread; see *challah*
challah – Jewish egg bread
chutzpah (khuts'-pah) – gall, brazen nerve
ćorka (tsoor'-ka) – daughter
Dom Spokojnej Starosci (dawm spaw-koy'-ney star-os'-chee) – old folks' home
dzięki Bogu (jen'-kee Bow-goo) – thank God
dziękuję (jen'-koo-yeh) – thank you
dziewcyznka (jef-chin'-ka) – little girl
Es toig nish – Yiddish for "it won't do" or "it's unacceptable."
goyish – Yiddish adjective for something that is not Jewish
grosik (gro'-shik) – penny
greenes – Yiddish pejorative term used by North American Jews for newcomers who came after the Holocaust
Juden raus! – German for "Jews out!"
Judenrein (Yoo'-den-rein) – German for "cleansed of Jews"
kartoflanik (kar-to-flan'-ik) – Polish for Jewish potato kugel or pudding
klafta – Yiddish for bitch
klotz – Yiddish for clumsy person

kochana (ko-kha'-na) – dear
koleżanka (kol-ezh-an'-ka) – female friend
krupnik (kroop'-neek) – honeyed vodka
kto ten dziad (ktaw ten jud) – who's the old man?
kugel (koo'-gul) – Yiddish for potato pudding; see *kartoflanik*
mamka (mum'-kah) – wet nurse
Meine teire tochter, die bist allein vi a shtein – My daughter, you are alone like a stone
mója (mo'-ya) – my
na zdrowie (nuh zdraw'-vieh) – to your health
nie (nyeh) – no
Pan (pahn) – Mr.
Pani (pahnyi) – Mrs.
partyzanci (par-ty-zan'-chee) – partisans
paskudnici (pas-kood-nee'-chee) – ne'er-do-wells
Pesach (Peh'-sakh) – Hebrew for Passover
piernik (pyer'-nik) – honeycake
pierogi (pye-ro'-gy) – dumplings
porzeczki (po-zhets'-kee) – currants
Prababka (Pra-bab'-ka) – great-grandmother
rosól (raw'-soow) – chicken soup
rynek (ry'-nek) – marketplace
Seder – Jewish family ritual and meal for the first two nights of Passover
Shabbes – Yiddish for Sabbath
shtupping – Yiddish for pushing
sioszycka (shyos-chits'-kah) – little sister
shul (shool) – Yiddish for synagogue
szmatka (shmat'- ka) – little rag
Tato (Tah'-taw) – Dad
Wigilia (Vee-gee'-lyah) – Christmas Eve
yarmulke (yar'-mool-keh) – Yiddish for skull cap
zloty (zlo'-ty) – Polish currency

Proper Names

In Polish, women's surnames end in "a," men's names end in "i,", e.g. Stefanska and Stefanski. Using a person's given name is often quite formal and often that person can have two or three nicknames or diminutives. For example, Mania can be the nickname for Amalia but it can also have the diminutive, Manka. I have tried to minimize the number of names for each character.

The following is a pronunciation guide:
Adamowicz – *Adam-aw'-veech*
Andrej – *An'-jay*
Baba Jaga – *Bah'-bah Yah'-gah* – witch in East European folklore
Barczak – *Bar'-chak*
Bazylika Mariacka – *Ba-zy'-ly-ka Ma-ree-ats'-ka* – St. Mary's Basilica
Bełżec – *Bel' zhotс* – site of first of Nazi German extermination camps created for purpose of implementing the secretive Operation Reinhard, which entailed the murder of some six million Jews during the Holocaust. The camp was situated in German-occupied Poland about 0.5 kilometres south of the local railroad station of Bełżec, in the *Distrikt Lublin*, operated from 17 March 1942 to the end of December 1942. The burning of exhumed corpses on five open-air grids and bone crushing continued until March 1943. Between 430,000 and 500,000 Jews are believed to have been murdered by

the Nazis at Bełżec.
Bojarski – *Bo-yar'-sky*
Galicia – *Ga-lee'-tsia* – formerly southwest province of Poland; now part of Ukraine
Glowacka – *Glo-vats'-ka*
Halinka – *Ha-leen'-ka* – dimunitive for Halina
Hanka – *Hun'-ka* – Yiddish diminutive for Hannah
Jadwiga – *Yad-vee'-gah*
Jakubowska – *Yah-koo-bov'-skah*
Janusz – *Yan'-oosh*
Jerzy – *Yer'-zhee*
Mania – *Man'-ya*
Marysia – *Ma-rish'-ya*
Mirka – *Meer'-ka* – diminutive for Miriam
Opole – *Aw-paw'-leh.* City in southern Poland
Pużniki – *Pooj-nee'-kee* – village in Stanisławów Oblast (region or province)
Reizele – *Ray'-zeh-leh* – Yiddish diminutive for Rose
Róża – *Roo'-zha ("zh" like the "g" in genre)*
Stanisławów – *Sta-nees-wa'-voof* – formerly historic city in southeastern Poland; now in western Ukraine as Ivano-Frankivsk. Population in 1941 approximately 75,000, 40 percent Polish, 40 percent Jewish, 15 percent Ukrainian and five percent other minorities.
Staszek – *Sta'-shek* – diminutive for Stanisław
Tadeusz – *Ta'-day-oosh*
Vładek – *Vwa'-dek* – diminutive for Władisław
Wiedergutmachung – program of reparations that the German government paid to the direct survivors of the Holocaust and to those who were made to work as forced labour or who otherwise became victims of the Nazis.
Wiśniewska, Wiśniewski – *Vish-nyehv'-skah, Vish-nyehv'-skee*
Witold – *Vee'-told*
Zosia – *Zaw'-shiah*

Acknowledgements

I owe a great debt of gratitude to my parents, Charlotte and William Tannenzapf, who, unlike the characters in my book, did not withhold the past from me. My father was a great raconteur and eventually wrote his memoir of the Holocaust at the age of eighty-nine. My children, Rob Krakauer, Lianne Krakauer and Shulamit (Susan) Krakauer, were always an attentive audience and are a repository of the family lore for the future. Sadly, most of my extended family perished at the hands of the Nazis.

I want to thank my Polish cousin, Sylwia Wroblewska, for introducing me to my family in Warsaw, and her daughter, Joanna Wroblewska-Nell, who made the reunion possible and who with her husband, Werner Nell, led me to the city of my birth, Ivano-Frankivsk, Ukraine, formerly Stanisławów, Poland.

I am grateful to my friends, Helen Drazek Wajs and Shifra Ivri, for sharing their childhood memories with me.

I want to acknowledge all of the wonderful writing teachers from whom I learned so much: Joe Kertes, Barbara Kyle, Helen Humphreys, Cynthia Holz, Lesley Kruger, and Jane Bow. My early readers were also very helpful, especially Susan Vander Voet, Helen Senor and Lianne Krakauer.

A big thank you to those at Inanna Publications who helped to get this book out: Editor-in-Chief, Luciana Ricciutelli and Renée Knapp, Publicist and Marketing Manager.

As ever, love and appreciation to my husband, Hank Lobbenberg, who is always there when I need him.

A very early version of Chapter 2 was published under the title "Escape from the Ghetto" in *Marking Humanity: Stories, Poems, and Essays by Holocaust Survivors*, edited by Shlomit Kriger, in 2010.

Photo: Jonni Super

Renate Krakauer's career included senior roles in education, and municipal and provincial governments. She has published award-winning short fiction in a number of literary journals, among them *Parchment*, *The Storyteller*, and *Foliate Oak*; essays in the *The Globe and Mail*, journals and two anthologies; a memoir *But I Had a Happy Childhood*; and two plays. *Only by Blood* is her first novel. Renate lives in Toronto with her husband. She has three adult children, two stepsons, and six grandchildren.